Is it possible that aliens
Universe observe what happen
have no knowledge of this?

It would seem so.

During the last few months of a U.S. Presidential race, right out of the blue a series of extraordinary events affect America.

Activists with a revolutionary streak, who appear willing to stop at nothing, emerge from nowhere and begin to create mayhem.

What is going on? What are they after? Do they have any hope of success?

So many more questions than answers.

Not only that, but one key politician, William Donaldson, finds himself unknowingly in a love triangle with a girl who is also sleeping with one of the activists. An incredibly dangerous position to be in, particularly with a *femme fatale* such as her.

As the future of America hangs in the balance, like a ride on an out-of-control roller coaster, there is no telling how things might work out ...

And yet, all the time, almost invisibly, two extraterrestrials, Zyron and Axma, look on with great fascination.

Edward Anthony Rayne was born in London, England and educated at Oxford University. He has lived and worked in the United States and knows New York City and Hollywood particularly well. His paternal grandmother was American.

IDEAS IN THE AIR

EDWARD ANTHONY RAYNE

By the same author

Hollywood, the Holy Grail, the Great Pyramid and the Mystic Dawn

Copyright © Edward Anthony Rayne, 2011

The moral right of the author has been asserted

All rights reserved

Without limiting the rights under copyright reserved above, no part of this publication may be reproduced, stored in or introduced into a retrieval system, or transmitted, in any form or by any means (electronic, mechanical, photocopying, recording or otherwise), without the prior written permission of the copyright owner of this book

ISBN-13: 978-1469907239
ISBN-10: 1469907232

PREFACE

Quite when the events that follow took place is hard to say. They seem to have happened in *our* world, but not really. In truth it is more the case that they unfolded in a parallel world like ours but not ours – almost in a parallel Universe you might say.

The New York you see is like the New York of modern times, and the America you see is the same way too. But they are not the same – the twin towers of the World Trade Center still stand, and no one much has heard of Osama bin Laden or Al Qaeda, and 9/11 is just another day in the calendar. And, on top of that, many, many other things are different also.

And yet, at the same time, so much feels so familiar. So very, very, very familiar that it's almost impossible to describe.

PROLOGUE

Not such a long time after relations between the United States and Russia had seemed to enter a new era of harmony everything had turned sour. It was a crisis of daunting dimensions.

The countries which had until recently been known as the Eastern Bloc had borrowed more and more hard currency, which in the end, perhaps placing pragmatism before prudence, the West had been only too glad to lend. But, far from the Russian economy improving, it had only continued to stagnate. Quite soon debts had grown and interest rates risen beyond the point where repayment was a serious possibility. Worse still, international stock markets had suffered another of their increasingly frequent and dramatic crashes – and this time there was no sign of any recovery.

Rampant global inflation had made money hardly worth the paper it was printed on. Normal commercial transactions had become impossible. A system of barter between countries had taken over.

But barter on this scale was like going back to the Dark Ages. Weak nations with little to trade quickly found themselves deprived of even such basics as oil or grain – billions not millions were in danger of starvation. Stronger nations coped for a time but soon began to squabble as shortages became intolerable. Capitalists blamed 'ex-Communists' for incompetence, 'ex-Communists' blamed Capitalists for greed. But attributing blame was pointless.

All kinds of remedies and compromises were tried but it was as if the foundations of modern civilization had crumbled beyond repair. As the pressure on key leaders grew greater the trust between them grew less. Increasingly whatever products the countries with greatest military might, namely the United States and Russia, could not procure by legitimate means they would simply take. But with a cake now much too small to share out something had to give – and it did.

Given the desperate nature of the situation probably anything could have precipitated disaster. However, a harvest failure after a lousy summer in both East and West came close to the final straw. When the coldest winter of the century then followed, the camel's back was truly broken.

Faced with famine the United States and Russia came openly to blows. What they hoped to solve is hard to say – but all the enmity of old rose like a Phoenix from the ashes. Incident followed incident, retaliation followed retaliation, armies were mobilized, life became cheap. And as the conflict escalated neither side showed the slightest wish to climb down. It was as though a fever of the mind had gripped those in charge, moderation was but a voice in the wilderness – if it was even as much as that.

Then out of the mire came a moment of sanity. A truce was called, secret negotiations were set up, the World's two major nuclear powers, the two combatants still as capable as ever of mutual annihilation, agreed to meet and talk. But the position which confronted them was next to impossible. The harsh reality was that the only hope of a lasting solution was to cut the World's population by half. If this was not to be done by war then it would have to be done by other means. Many would have to be left to die in order that others be allowed to live. Whole cities would have to be earmarked 'to wither on the vine'. Rigid timetables would have to be set and then stuck to.

It seems inconceivable that the two most powerful nations on Earth could have reached agreement on such a plan. But they did – for it was merely the acceptance of the lesser of two tragedies. And of course they both also knew there would be great problems in implementing it – first and foremost nobody must be told, careful deception would be essential, it was obvious that only if the masses were kept in the dark would what had been decided stand a chance.

How much of a chance was never put to the test. For before the ink had even dried a female interpreter, who had been working with the United States' team at the talks, leaked every detail of the plan to the public – every detail of which population centers would be allowed to live and which would be left to die.

When arrested and questioned the female interpreter said her conscience had forced her to spill the beans, she said she could not be party to what amounted to premeditated mass murder, she said that any solution had to be better than this solution.

Even so, one has to wonder whether the female interpreter had really thought the consequences of her action through. And although, when she was tried in a day and sent to the electric chair the next her last words were of regret, the damage had been done. Her revelations had caused world-wide hysteria. Any plan was now dead. Fresh fighting was only round the corner. Within days the point of no return was vanishing rapidly behind in the distance.

~

Somewhere out in some distant galaxy, millions of light years from Earth, a spaceship cruised. The vessel was slick, elegant, stream-lined and graceful. It had large windows and its interior was more akin to a luxury yacht than a vehicle capable of withstanding anything. Indeed, the ship's design was an example of a technology way beyond our comprehension. It could land on the hottest of suns or densest of black holes, or speed through the most violent of asteroid storms, all without so much as a scratch. Velocity and Time were meaningless concepts – any chosen destination could be arrived at "instantly".

Up on the spaceship's flight deck sat its sole occupants, Zyron and Axma. Around them were banks of controls, keypads and video screens. In front of them, between a pair of windows looking out into space, they had one especially big screen which they were keeping a very close eye on as they manipulated their controls.

Whatever they were doing Zyron and Axma were clearly very busy. They were not flying the ship, that was unnecessary, such tasks were automatic. But they were busy all the same, and evidently rather enjoying themselves.

Zyron and Axma might have been brothers, they certainly looked fairly alike and behaved towards each other like the best of friends. In some ways their appearance was human. They had heads, bodies, arms and legs. They were dressed in colorful jackets and striped knickerbockers and wore brightly colored hats which covered what hair they had. In fact the overall color scheme of their attire from head to toe could only be described as gaudy. But what was most striking about them was the strong angularity of their features. Their chins and cheek-bones ended in points, as did their noses and ears and their wide mouths and large luminescent eyes. It was the same with their long pointed fingers and sets of spiky teeth which glistened every time they smiled. They had a sort of geometric, cubic quality about them.

And yet there was nothing in Zyron and Axma's appearance which was particularly hostile or intimidating. On the contrary, their mischievous giggling and laughter gave one every reason to consider them rather endearing. They seemed like two cheeky goblins and right now something on their big screen was making them laugh a lot. They reached to adjust their controls at ever shorter and shorter intervals. Whatever it was they were looking at on their big video screen, they were finding it highly entertaining.

'Aha, I like it!' chuckled Axma. 'Your position's now hopeless! I can see I've got you!'

'There's still a chance!' replied Zyron smiling as he battled with his controls.

'I don't think so!' Axma laughed. 'I've got a clear advantage and it's match point!'

'Somebody's still got to fire the missiles!' exclaimed Zyron.

'What do you mean!' retorted Axma with a big, big grin, 'Of course the missiles will be fired! Of that I've made very sure! I can see you're clutching at straws!'

'Not necessarily!' came back Zyron's defiant reply.

'Then Zyron, you must live in cloud-cuckoo-land! When that female interpreter let the cat out of the bag that half the planet were going to be left to starve to death it was all over! If I'd been you I would have conceded defeat there and then!'

'Well, maybe I've just got too much fighting spirit!' chirped Zyron.

'You must have, Zyron!' said Axma. 'And in this underground bunker you're going to need it! And making me play my next shot from this bunker ain't going to help you – this game isn't golf you know!'

'Very funny!' responded Zyron. He knew he would be goading Axma equally as much if the tables were turned. 'Just you wait and see!'

'I will!' exclaimed Axma, 'But try anything you like – it isn't going to work! I've got it sown up.'

'Well, play your shot in the bunker and see what happens!' said Zyron eager to get on with it. And as Zyron and Axma re-focused their attention back on the spaceship's big video screen the picture on it did indeed show an underground military bunker somewhere on Earth.

~

Deep in a dimly lit bunker dug at least three hundred feet below the surface U.S. Air Force personnel waited anxiously. Nerves were frayed, people were hollow-eyed, they had been on maximum alert for weeks. Everyone present had been vetted, trained and psychologically tested to the hilt, but it was now becoming an endurance test.

The bunker formed part of the command chain between the President, the Early Warning Systems and the long range missile silos. Colonel Lloyd was the officer in charge, he stood in the middle of the room keeping an eye on his men. A large, tough, bruising man, the countenance on the Colonel's face left no doubt as to his sense of duty, his will of steel, his implacable professionalism, all of which had been all the more reinforced by over twenty five years in the armed forces.

Near to where the Colonel stood, seated at computer terminals, were Lieutenants Weiss and Sparrowcroft. Other men manned backup and support equipment but it was these two Lieutenants who were at the sharp end. It was they who had to relay any fire order to the missile sites.

The reason there were two Lieutenants was a procedural failsafe – it was organized so that no one could issue a launch instruction on their own. The same principle existed in the missile silos where actual firing required two keys to be turned simultaneously, the keyholes being too far set apart for any one person to reach both at once.

On the wall of the bunker was a massive illuminated map surrounded by various digital displays. Twenty-four hour clocks kept track of time.

It was mid-afternoon and about half-way through this shift. Lieutenant Sparrowcroft reached to take a sip of his black coffee, his hand was just a shade unsteady, he had a light film of sweat on his brow which he wiped away.

For everyone in the bunker it was a strange routine. It consisted of waiting and waiting in constant readiness, while all the time hoping and praying nothing would transpire. They all knew what the signal would be if it came – a loud klaxon would sound, digital displays would lock on to secret codes, targets would be highlighted on the map, computer screens would await the entry of final instructions. No job could be more demanding – for those in the bunker, once the klaxon sounded, years of preparation would culminate in just twenty seconds of frenzied activity.

Lieutenant Sparrowcroft had lived through the launch sequence a thousand times, both in his own imagination and during countless practice simulations. He hoped as much as anyone that it would never really come about. Yet as he sat there that afternoon he knew it might. In fact, since the American female interpreter had made her fateful revelations about the exact content of the secret United States/Russian talks, the position had deteriorated so much worldwide it seemed almost as if there were no way out. Sparrowcroft thought of his wife and children, of his parents and friends, of the man he once heard say on TV 'if the button is pushed the living will envy the dead'. He sighed and tried to think of something else, he took another sip of coffee. As the coffee passed his lips the klaxon sounded! The coffee cup fell right out of his hand.

'Launch signal!' shouted Colonel Lloyd with unflinching authority as his eyes scanned the whole scene. Immediately flashing indicator lights on the bunker's massive illuminated wall map started to trace the incoming trajectories of Russian missiles. The list of targets on Sparrowcroft's screen left no doubt this was going to be an all-out exchange.

Lieutenant Weiss went immediately to work, however Sparrowcroft seemed paralysed. Weiss could not help but notice.

'For Chrissakes snap out of it!' he urged in a very pressing undertone. 'You're holding things up!'

Sparrowcroft did not respond, out of character though it was, particularly for someone with all his training, he was beginning to tremble.

'Lieutenant Sparrowcroft! Get a hold of yourself!' glared Colonel Lloyd walking right up to him.

Sparrowcroft only trembled all the more, he was cracking up, he swiveled his chair to face the Colonel. 'This is going to mean the end of the World!' he spluttered. 'I can't!'

The Colonel reacted quickly, he had no choice. 'Someone else step in! Take this man away!' he yelled across the room.

Two personnel rushed over and hauled Sparrowcroft from his seat. Another servicemen took his place. Sparrowcroft was led away. He offered no resistance, but he was sobbing loudly.

'Ready!' announced Sparrowcroft's replacement.

'Fire command initiated!' responded Lieutenant Weiss.

~

No more than maybe two seconds later in the control room beside a missile silo in the middle of the New Mexico desert the two launch crew had their keys at the ready. They turned them.

Out in the desert missiles rose from the ground amidst massive clouds of consumed propellant and accelerated upward and upwards, at a seemingly eerily slow pace, into the bright blue sky. Soon the smoke cleared and the engine noise faded. Silence reigned again.

Up in the atmosphere missiles from both sides crossed paths heading in opposite directions. As they drew to the end of their few minute journeys, their warheads were released for re-entry.

~

In the spaceship in the distant galaxy Axma, even more cocky than before, was now beside himself with glee. 'Hee, hee, hee! I've done it! What did I tell you! Missiles everywhere!' he laughed as he looked up at the large video screen. This is a real firework display! Moscow, bang! St Petersburg, bang! Washington, bang! London, bang! New York's next, let's see it!'

A picture of New York was summoned up on to Zyron and Axma's big screen. For a moment or two the City appeared as it would on any clear day, then suddenly in one huge blinding flash nuclear explosions ripped it apart.

'Hee, hee, another one bites the dust!' giggled Axma glancing over to Zyron. 'This is what I call destruction! Do you want to see any more?'

Zyron grinned at his friend looking faintly resigned. 'I suppose not,' he replied, 'but let's zoom out, just to be sure.'

'Okay,' chirped Axma, and he leant forward to adjust the settings on part of his control console. Straightaway the whole Earth appeared on the big screen as if photographed from the Moon. It was being blistered with explosions. Slowly but surely the blue surface of the planet began to blacken. In a while the only source of color was the occasional plume of red or orange which burst out around its edges as new missiles fell.

'Ha! Ha! Ha! What a calamity! Okay, Axma, you win,' said Zyron finally conceding defeat with good humor.

'Thanks,' chuckled Axma looking altogether very pleased with himself. 'You blew it some way back in the game.'

'Did I, where did I go wrong?'

'That's for you to work out – Don't expect any free coaching sessions from me my friend! All the same my congratulations on messing up that Lieutenant Sparrowcroft in the bunker – that was nice play!'

'Yes, thanks for the compliment. Must say I really screwed him up pretty good! It was neat!'

'Very neat!' confirmed Axma. 'But it was too late by then, and anyhow I had you covered whatever you did!'

'You had me covered whatever I did?' Zyron responded in half disbelief.

'You bet, believe me you'd painted yourself right into a corner!'

'Really?'

'Yes, really!'

'Oh well, I guess one can't win them all,' shrugged Zyron with a philosophical smile. 'But at any rate, just for the record, we might as well see what happened afterwards.'

'Sure,' said Axma, 'always interesting! For openers we'll jump on a hundred years – but if you're feeling hopeful you're going to see any signs of Life, don't hold your breath!' Axma leant forward turning a dial on the controls. A new picture came up, but all it looked like was a huge circular lump of rock, which was completely in keeping with what Axma had expected. 'There you go,' he said, 'Earth one hundred years on! Exactly as I told you! Nothing! Just a lifeless globe!'

'Expand it, do a close-up on New York City,' asked Zyron fascinated to get some more details.

Axma obliged flicking a switch, another picture filled the screen, it only showed just about the bleakest landscape possibly imaginable. 'There you go, Zyron ... Not a pretty sight is it!'

'That dark desolate landscape was once New York City?' Zyron remarked in astonishment.

'Afraid so,' replied Axma. 'Wouldn't recognize it would you?'

'Ha! No, you wouldn't. Things really don't look too good down on Planet Earth do they! Try further ahead still'

Axma happily turned his dial again, but now no matter how much he did so the picture did not alter at all. 'This is a thousand years on, now ten thousand years, now one hundred thousand years! But you can see, there's no change! You know very well what that means!'

'The planet's completely dead,' nodded Zyron.

'That's right, Zyron, it is! And who killed it off? You did! You well and truly did make a mess of it!'

'I suppose I did,' admitted Zyron, momentarily looking a little downcast. 'But you know what?' he added suddenly breaking into a mischievous grin. 'If I really did make such a hash of it this time around, then there's only one thing for it! We'll have to start again!'

'You mean you want another game?' Axma grinned back excitedly.

'Absolutely!'

'Double or quits then! Same rules'

'Yes, same rules, same time period!' said Zyron.

'Great! Let's reset it!' exclaimed Axma rubbing his hands. And with great gusto Zyron and Axma reached down to their controls. Their long pointed fingers were here, there and everywhere pushing buttons, zeroing dials, punching in data. The results of their efforts came thick and fast. On the big screen the blank landscape that had been New York de-exploded into its former glory. As Time continued to run backwards new buildings vanished as older ones appeared. The picture moved faster and faster soon merging into a kaleidoscopic blur. Then it stopped. All that was now on the screen was a mass of shifting molten lava. This was the Earth as it had been at its very dawn.

'No point in going back any further, is there?' queried Zyron.

'No, none at all. Just a matter of re-assembling the pieces!' replied Axma manipulating the controls with a maestro touch. 'Here we go.'

Time ran forward on the screen again. Oceans appeared from nowhere, continents drifted into place, ice ages came and went. Finally, as Axma skilfully brought things to a halt, present day New York stared them in the face.

'That's it. That's exactly where we were before', announced Axma. 'I won last time so I'll take first go!'

'Okay, Axma, you "serve", but in that case I'll take the *girl*!'

'You want to take the *girl*, Zyron?'

'Yes, I do,' said Zyron

'But you realize, Zyron, that that means you have to give me 10 points "start"?'

'Yes, of course. But I'm still taking the *girl*.'

'Okay, Zyron, you take the *girl*!' exclaimed Axma beaming from cheek to cheek. 'But under the rules I'm entitled to know what sort of *girl* she's going to be! So what is she?'

'Well, definitely not a "female interpreter"!' quipped Zyron recalling such a female's unfortunate role in the previous game.

'Understandably not,' smiled Axma.

'No, she's going to be something completely different.'

'Which is?' pressed Axma dying to know what Zyron had in mind.

'I'm going to make her a journalist,' said Zyron. 'Yes, a sensational looking female journalist! You just wait till you see her!'

'Nothing like a pretty girl to liven things up,' replied Axma licking his lips.

'Precisely!' enthused Zyron. 'The last game was good but this one's going to be even better! Fasten your seat-belt, and may the best man win!'

'May the best man win!' echoed Axma limbering up his long fingers over the bank of controls. 'And,' he added, 'when I see a sensational looking female journalist you can be sure I'm going to be real careful!'

'You'd better be!' joked Zyron. 'And since, Axma, you're making the opening move, where's the opening move going to be?'

'Well, if we're dealing with pretty girls, a bedroom seems as a good place as any!'

'Aha! A bedroom! Yes, that's a very good place indeed!' chuckled Zyron.

And so, with Zyron and Axma's eyes firmly fixed once again on their large screen, the next game got under way.

'That's a pretty swish bedroom we're looking at!' quipped Zyron.

'Yes, a really classy place to sleep in, and do other things in too!' smiled Axma.

'Absolutely,' concurred Zyron.

And, as they both momentarily paused to consider their strategies, one thing could be said for sure: the bedroom in New York up on their screen was beyond question pretty fancy.

Moreover, at this moment in time, it was far from unoccupied ...

CHAPTER 1

In the very luxurious bedroom of an expensively appointed New York apartment it was the middle of the night. A single light emitted a dim glow as William Donaldson held Rosanne close and kissed her one more time. It was a long passionate kiss. William then drew his body away and climbed out of the bed. As he did so she still stared into his eyes and let her hand flop down off his shoulder as he reached for his shirt.

'I must be going,' he said as he slung the shirt across his back.

'William, you're always saying that,' she replied in a tone which was as resigned as it was full of displeasure. She sat up drawing the sheet over her breasts.

William Donaldson lingered looking at her beautiful face. He could tell from her expression she was not happy. It was particularly evident in the way her spectacularly blue eyes seemed to be not focusing on him but at some imaginary distant horizon, also in the way she ran her delicate hand through her long blonde hair twisting and turning and tugging it with undisguised irritation.

But William Donaldson was Mayor of New York, and he was married with children. That on its own might not have mattered had he not had far greater political aspirations. At the age of forty he already had great wealth and influence but if he wanted to reach the top he knew his best chance was to keep his image purer than pure. He truly loved Rosanne and he had always tried hard to show it. To humor her he had showered her with gifts including this smart apartment in which he now stood. But he saw no other possible role for her than that of a mistress, and whether she liked it or not, he was now returning home to the Mayor's residence at Gracie Mansion. He wanted the best of both worlds and he was used to getting precisely that.

Even so, by the way Rosanne seemed to be about to react, William could sense trouble, and he seriously hoped to avoid it. 'Rosanne, don't look so glum,' he said gently. 'You know you mean more to me than anything',

Rosanne pouted then tried to put on a half-hearted smile. 'Then why don't you do something about it?'

'I will, but give me time,' he pleaded, obviously not revealing the whole truth of how little chance he saw of their relationship ever becoming full-time.

'Shit, William,' she said with a hint of anger, 'Time, you're always asking for more time. Can't you see this isn't the way I want it! I love you, but this is no way to live!'

'I know it isn't.'

'Then do something!' Her voice was adamant.

'We've been through all this before, God knows how many ...'

'I know we have,' she interrupted sarcastically.

William looked exasperated, he knew he was walking on eggshells, he drew a deep breath before continuing. 'Rosanne, you know the risks I'm taking as it is and you don't have a family to think of.'

This annoyed Rosanne all the more. 'Terrific,' she shouted, 'all you're really saying is that I have to fit in with you! You turn up when you feel like it and then disappear off in the middle of the night and whatever I feel doesn't matter a damn!'

William said nothing in response, he was already nearly dressed.

'And as for your family!' Rosanne continued with venom. 'If they're so terribly important to you what are you doing here! I think this has gone on long enough – if you're serious I want some sort of commitment right now!'

'Maybe after this Presidential Election. Then things'll be quieter,' William said refusing to be provoked.

'I don't care about the Election! I care about me!'

'And I care about you too,' replied William keeping his calm as he walked out the door.

Rosanne did not think the conversation was over. Her silence as he disappeared into the living room was tactical. She felt he would not leave things quite so much in the air, that his sudden exit was only for effect, that he would stroll back in and at least want to make the peace.

For a few moments her heart was pounding. She was ready either to make up or to continue to fight. But when she heard the front door open and then click shut she realized she was not going to get the chance to do neither. Slowly, deliberately, she lay down again, pulled the sheet over her head and, in a sudden spontaneous uncontrollable rush of emotion all the adrenalin in her body collapsed into tears.

She wept fretfully for some time, pausing now and then to churn everything over in her mind only to set off fresh floods once more. She knew she loved William. Yet she also knew another part of her hated him. She struggled hard to make sense of her feelings but had got nowhere before she eventually cried herself to sleep. In any case, she knew herself well enough to admit that usually as far as she was concerned her contradictions were a problem for other people to deal with and not her, and if it turned out they couldn't, then too bad for them.

All the same, much as she tried, Rosanne only managed to sleep on and off for a couple of hours. Finally she could sleep no more and though it was barely daybreak decided to get up. She went to pull back the curtains and saw it was going to be a bright sunny day. This lifted her spirits. She thought of William and the night before, but now things did not seem quite so bad. Anyway she had an appointment that morning down in Greenwich Village which she was rather looking forward to.

As the doorman hailed her a cab outside her apartment building on 89th and Madison Rosanne checked her watch. It was ten o'clock, she would arrive in good time at the address she had written down close to Washington Square.

In the cab on the way she opened up the slim brief case she had with her. It contained a file of notes and a small digital voice recorder. She freshened her memory by re-reading the notes and by the time she had finished the archway that formed the centerpiece of the Square loomed up ahead.

She paid the driver and walked up to the entrance of a loft building. She rang the door bell. This building was both the home and the studio of Robert Cook, currently the most celebrated modern painter in America. Rosanne's assignment that morning was to interview him.

Rosanne Lindblade was a journalist, a very pretty professional journalist.

As the door bell rang Robert was at work in his studio which was spacious and airy. He was spraying paint on to one of the large abstract canvasses which lined the walls. 'Can you get it?' he called out to Dawn in the kitchen next door.

'Sure,' she replied heading out towards the entryphone in the studio's lobby. 'Who is it?' Dawn asked as she spoke into the microphone unit.

'Rosanne Lindblade, Prestige Publications.'

'Come along up,' she said releasing the lock.

Rosanne entered the building and climbed the flight of stairs leading up to the loft. Dawn stood at the top holding open the lobby door. 'Nice to meet you,' she said greeting Rosanne.

'And you,' Rosanne replied smiling.

'I'm Dawn, Robert's girlfriend. Robert's expecting you, I'll show you through.'

'Thanks.' And as she was led into the main studio Rosanne noted to herself how pretty Dawn was.

'Hi,' said Robert warmly, putting down his spray can. 'Please forgive the slight mess in here.'

'Oh, don't worry about that,' Rosanne smiled. 'I'm just pleased to be here. People say getting an interview with you is harder than getting an audience with the Pope!'

Robert laughed. 'I only talk when I've got something worth saying. I mean why talk for the sake of it?'

'I agree,' replied Rosanne still smiling. 'I wish everybody was like that!'

'So do I!' quipped Robert. 'Come on, feel free to make yourself at home.'

'Can I get either of you some coffee?' Dawn asked.

'That'd be great, just milk no sugar please,' answered Rosanne becoming relaxed.

Dawn went back to the kitchen, she knew Robert always took his coffee black.

Rosanne looked Robert over. She had seen photographs of him but in the flesh he was far better looking than she had imagined. He had dark brown hair and even darker eyes. His face was perfectly shaped with high cheek-bones and a chiseled jaw which set off the dimple in his chin to good effect. If intelligence shows in faces it showed in his. His lean frame boasted broad shoulders and he stood about six feet tall. His hands were remarkable too, they were masculine but very refined, the hands of a true artist Rosanne thought. As for his age, she already had that on file. He was thirty-eight. All in all Dawn was a lucky girl Rosanne reflected.

Robert had sensed the way Rosanne had looked at him and he had also studied her. She really was the apotheosis of physical beauty. However, his mind quickly reverted to the interview. 'Shall we go and sit down?' he said strolling towards some armchairs at the far end of the studio.

'Thanks,' replied Rosanne turning her attention to the paintings on the wall as she passed them by. 'All these must be part of your "new" series incorporating the theme of light and darkness?'

'That's right. They're supposed to symbolize all the opposing forces within us and around us,' he explained, pleased to be talking to someone who appeared to have done their research. 'But I can come back to that later. Where do want you want to begin?'

'Hard to say,' said Rosanne as she sat down and took out her small digital voice recorder. 'By the way you don't mind this machine, do you?'

'Not at all,' he asserted in a breezy tone. 'I really do want this interview to be "on the record"!'

'Okay then, here we go,' began Rosanne now fully at ease and picking up her notes. 'I think you'd be the first to admit you're a rather controversial artist. So maybe we should start by examining your influences?'

'Influences!' reacted Robert with a wry smile. 'Trust you to zero in on those!'

At that point Dawn returned with the coffee.

~

Elsewhere, but not at all that far from Greenwich Village, it was mid-morning and an armored security truck moved down a street in the borough of Queens, heading towards Manhattan. It contained an especially valuable cargo. In the cab of the truck were Jim and Kenny, both experienced security guards and both ex-policemen. Kenny drove and Jim acted as observer.

Because the load was so valuable, they also had an unmarked car driving in front of them. The men in this carried pump-action shot guns and their role was to stick to the truck like glue. Nobody could guarantee anything, but this two vehicle convoy was no easy target.

But vigilance was of the essence and as they stopped at some red traffic lights Jim had noticed something in his side mirror. 'We have a black Buick behind us, it's had plenty of chances to overtake.'

'Then report it,' replied Kenny from his position behind the wheel.

Jim lifted his radio phone. 'This is HK89 to Control. We have a potentially suspect vehicle on our tail. We're at the intersection of ...'

While Jim was talking on the radio the traffic lights changed to green. The security truck moved on, and so did the black Buick. Sitting up in their cab Jim and Kenny knew full well they were probably just being extra cautious. But it was their job to report everything and they were in no doubt that their safety depended on it.

No more than six blocks away, on the same route as the security convoy, a garbage truck crawled along a side street which ran off to the right of the main road. Members of its crew went to and fro between doorways carrying out their normal business. At first glance there was absolutely nothing to suggest anything out of the ordinary.

Even so it was most unlikely that these men were worrying themselves too much about the cleanliness of this neighborhood. Their interest was in other things. Eliot Streitch sat in the cab of the garbage truck. Beside him was Matts, and next to Matts was Warren who was at the steering wheel. Matts wore headphones with a pilot style mike extending down to his mouth.

The three men viewed the steady stream of traffic crossing the busy junction in front of them. They also watched another garbage truck slowly approaching down the street directly opposite on the far side of the main road. This second vehicle was closely followed in its tracks by a giant mobile crane. Eliot Streitch's expression indicated that he was only seeing exactly what he expected to see.

'The security truck's three blocks away,' announced Matts.

'Warn the others,' Eliot instructed, Matts obeyed.

In the cab of the security truck Jim put down his radio phone and turned to Kenny. 'They're sending two more escort cars as extra back-up, the local cops have also been alerted.'

'Good. We take no chances,' Kenny replied.

'I'll let the guys up front know too', said Jim picking up his radio phone again. 'This is Jim in HK89 to Casper ...'

'Yes, Jim, receiving you?' responded Casper on the radio from the escort car's front passenger seat.

'Have requested extra support heading into Manhattan, just precautionary'

'Understood,' Casper acknowledged.

In the cab of his garbage truck Eliot and Warren slipped black hoods over their heads. 'They're now within fifty yards!' said Matts co-ordinating everything by radio.

'Okay, give it to them!' shouted Eliot.

Matts nodded. 'We go!' was all he said into his mike. Warren put his foot flat down on the accelerator. And hearing Matts' message, the driver of the other garbage truck on the far side of the intersection was seen to do the same.

After weeks of rehearsal the plan was set in motion and it was designed to be fast. The black Buick swerved blocking the traffic behind. The garbage trucks shot out towards the convoy from right and left. One went for the front ramming the escort car clean off the road, the other skidded to a halt at the van's rear – the security van was sandwiched. Eliot jumped out with a machine gun. In one long burst the occupants of the escort car were dead. Stage one was complete.

'Jesus, we're being fucking hit, assistance, urgent!' screamed Jim into his radio phone from inside his cab.

It was known that the super-toughened glass used in the security van's windscreen was one hundred per cent bullet proof. But this problem had been allowed for. Two hooded men who had been hiding in the back of Eliot's garbage truck climbed out carrying a rocket launcher. They fired it straight at the van's cab. The round was armor piercing and penetrated the windscreen with ease. The cab exploded in a ball of fire. With impressive efficiency other hooded men stepped forward with extinguishers to put out the flames. The giant mobile crane rumbled out into the main road right on cue and stopped beside the smouldering van. Four more hooded men emerged from the rear of Eliot's garbage truck bringing with them packs of explosive charges.

'Fit the plastic and winch it up!' shouted Eliot.

The four men attached the explosives to the rear doors of the security van and at the same time steel cable was lashed around what remained of its cab. Like clockwork a huge earth transporting vehicle, which had been kept out of view, arrived on the scene.

The mobile crane hoisted the security truck some twenty feet off the street, its rear end dangling downwards. The crane then swung the van directly over the earth transporter's massive trough.

A split second later the plastic explosives detonated and the van's two inch thick steel doors were blasted open. Bulky heavy packages fell out dropping down into the transporter with a noisy clank. With them also fell the bodies of two security guards who had been riding inside.

The mobile crane swung the mangled shell of the van away again and dumped it back down where it had picked it up. Two hooded men climbed up into the transporter's trough and slung the senseless bodies of the two guards down on to the street. The earth transporter sped off.

By now a long tail-back of traffic had built up in both directions. People near the front looked on in horror, drivers further back honked their horns impatiently not realising what was going on. police vehicles were threading their way through the jam towards the incident.

The police sirens could be heard approaching where the garbage trucks blocked the road, but only the getaway remained.

'Into the cars!' ordered Eliot. But as he spoke the first police car arrived.

'Police!' shouted Warren.

'Let loose on them!' Eliot shouted back.

The two men with the rocket launcher knew what to do. They aimed and fired, the police car became a blazing inferno.

A moment later a police helicopter zoomed in.

'Drop your weapons! We repeat, drop your weapons!' came the voice from the helicopter via a loud-hailer.

'Take out the chopper!' barked Eliot again.

The rocket launcher team had reloaded and were ready. The chopper was hit and crashed to the ground falling in flames on top of some of the held up traffic.

'Move it! Everybody get out of here!' Eliot emphasized with urgency.

Soon all the men had dumped their hoods and outer overalls and piled into the waiting cars. Eliot was last to depart. He got into a car alongside Matts. 'Blow the trucks!' he told him as the car was being violently reversed away.

Matts pushed a button on a radio device. Both garbage trucks disintegrated in spectacular explosions.

Eliot and Matts' driver then swung the car round hard and within a few minutes they had driven to a large warehouse less than a mile away.

Eliot and Matts got out and went inside.

No time had been wasted. In the middle of the warehouse stood the huge earth transporter and it was being unloaded. Gil, who had not been at the robbery, walked over. 'It's all there,' he said.

'Five tons of gold?' Eliot asked seeking confirmation.

'Yes, about,' answered Gil.

'We did it,' said Matts with a quiet grin.

'We did,' Eliot Streitch replied without a hint of emotion.

~

In the studio down in Greenwich Village time had flown by for Rosanne, seldom had she enjoyed interviewing someone so much, she hung on to every word Robert said.

'My Art is simply a reflection of how I see the World and how I think it's going – that's if it's going anywhere,' he continued. 'In all honesty I think that's fairly typical of most artists.'

'So you're a pessimist?' she inquired wide-eyed.

'Sometimes, not always.'

'And when you feel pessimistic, Mr Cook, can you identify why?' she asked pensively.

'Society,' came back an immediate clipped response. 'And, by the way, my name's Robert.'

'Okay, Robert. Tell me about the times you're more hopeful?'

'When there's a chance there might be a change,' he smiled.

'What sort of change?'

'Big change!' his voice becoming bolder. 'The society we've let evolve is beginning to run out of control, and if we don't alter course soon we're going to hit the goddam rocks!'

Rosanne could sense the passion in this last remark. 'You think it's that bad?' she ventured.

'No, I think it's a whole lot worse!'

'So then who's to blame?' she asked just a little bemused.

'Well, don't blame the people, most of them don't have any say. If you've got to point a finger at someone then you've got to point it at the politicians. It's them who preside over this uncaring, ungiving, "live-for-today-forget-about-tomorrow" mentality.'

'But this is a democracy,' she pointed out.

'That's what it's supposed to be!' he exclaimed with irony. 'But I'd say the present choices put on offer to the people are pretty pitiful! Worse, whenever there is some sort of good idea put forward, which is pretty rare, it usually just gets grid-locked out!'

Rosanne gazed at him, she was fascinated.

~

Over in Queens, debris and wreckage lay around the burnt out security truck and blankets covered the bodies of the dead. Police and their vehicles were everywhere. Televisions News teams had set up and crowds lined the sidewalk aghast at the destruction.

Police hauled back a section of barrier letting a large black limousine through. The limousine drove right up to the middle of the devastation and stopped. William Donaldson got out escorted by Steve Strauss, one of his principal aides, who looked younger than his twenty-nine years. Overwhelmed by what lay in front of them both men gazed around in disbelief.

Some yards away a TV reporter spoke into his camera. 'This is the scene of carnage in Queens, New York City today as Mayor William Donaldson comes to look for himself. Bullion with an estimated value in excess of $200 million was taken in a robbery which police have described as only matched in its efficiency by its viciousness. Twelve police officers and security guards plus eight members of the public were killed, another twenty-seven individuals are in hospital with injuries.'

William Donaldson began a tour flanked by Police Commissioner McMichael and other officers. He was lost for words. 'Jesus Christ!' he muttered under his breath as he looked down on the row of covered corpses.

'None of them stood a chance. Not a chance,' observed the Police Commissioner grimly.

Donaldson only numbly shook his head.

Steve Strauss, who had moments earlier been temporarily way-laid by Media representatives, hurried up to his boss again, 'Mayor Donaldson, the TV Networks want to know if you'll speak with them?'

'No, tell them I am too shocked and disgusted – I will issue a statement later.'

'Okay, sir,' Steve replied.

In Robert's studio Rosanne switched off her small voice recorder and collected up her notes.

'Is that it?' Robert inquired.

'Yes, that's it, no more questions,' she smiled.

The phone rang, Robert picked it up. 'Hello?' he said to the other party. 'It's for you,' he then announced to Rosanne.

'Thanks,' said Rosanne taking the receiver. 'Yes, Rosanne Lindblade speaking ...'

'This is Mayor Donaldson's office,' said the voice only audible to Rosanne. 'I've been asked to tell you that the appointment you have with him for an interview will have to be postponed.'

'I see,' Rosanne replied.

'He will contact you to re-schedule it,' the voice went on.

'Okay. Thanks for letting me know,' she said hanging up. 'That was Mayor William Donaldson's office, just a change of arrangements for an interview,' she informed Robert.

'Him?' remarked Robert raising his eyebrows.

'Yes. I realize you certainly wouldn't approve of his politics!' she grinned emphasizing the word "his" with double force.

'No, I wouldn't,' answered Robert dryly.

'Well, us journalists get to meet all sorts!' she quipped with an almost imperceptible trace of nerves.

'I guess you do,' said Robert with a smile. 'So when will this story on me appear?'

'Next month', she replied. 'The copy date's next week. I can send you the proof if you like?'

'Yes, I'd like to see it. But I tell you what, why don't you bring it round, or I could meet you somewhere?'

Rosanne's face lit up. 'All right, I'd love to. I'll give you a call.'

'Do that,' he said as they both rose to their feet and headed towards the lobby.

'Shall I say goodbye to Dawn?' asked Rosanne peering in the direction of kitchen.

'No, she's gone out,' he told her. 'I'll say goodbye for you, and thanks for being such a good listener.'

'My thanks are to you,' she smiled. 'Bye bye for now.'

'Bye bye,' said Robert closing lobby door behind her.

As Rosanne descended the stairs to the street she felt great. She could not know for sure whether Robert was interested in her or just interested in his article. But she sensed a mutual attraction and that was enough to send the blood rushing through her veins. And as for William? Well, she was still in love with him, but she felt calmer and stronger and altogether less willing to be pushed around.

Turning her thoughts to how she was going to write up the article Rosanne reached Robert's downstairs front door, unlatched it and emerged on to the sidewalk. However, as the door was about to swing shut, a man of about thirty or so dressed in a scruffy denim outfit reached out and grabbed hold of it. 'It's okay,' he said to her in a relaxed voice narrowly avoiding brushing into her, 'I'm going in.'

Rosanne merely glanced at this man without paying him any particular attention. She walked over to the curb to find a cab.

Meanwhile the man carried on up Robert's stairs. The man was Eliot Streitch.

CHAPTER 2

When Robert heard a knock on his lobby door so soon after Rosanne had gone he thought she might have left something behind. On the other hand, if this were not so, he had a good idea who it would be. He re-entered his lobby and was not long in suspense.

'It's me!' he heard Eliot call. Immediately Robert opened the door. Eliot strode in. 'We pulled it off, no hitches.'

'Good,' replied Robert barely disguising his elation and taking in Eliot's usual blank expression which registered little. 'And the gold is off-loaded?' Robert went on.

'Yeah. A guy from some Third World government paid us $140 million in cash. Don't ask me which because I don't know.'

'It doesn't matter, does it,' commented Robert.

'No, it doesn't. Doesn't matter at all. What does is what we now do with it,' stated Eliot dryly.

'That's right', agreed Robert drifting into the studio, Eliot following him. 'And Dawn has everything?'

'Yes,' nodded Eliot. 'She'll now be well on her way,'

~

One of the things about transactions conducted outside of the law was that if they could be made to happen at all then they could usually be made to happen fast. This instance was no exception – the gold had been converted into money with no questions asked virtually immediately, and formal proof that the agreed payment had been deposited in secret offshore bank accounts established minutes later. So, with everything on track, Dawn had only had to make one stop on the way to collect what she needed before heading directly to Kennedy to catch a flight.

By the time her plane landed at Nassau on New Providence Island in the Bahamas it was dusk. In the airport building beyond Customs and Immigration a black local waited holding up a card which read 'INTER ISLAND AIR TAXIS'. Dawn walked over to him, she was only carrying one piece of hand baggage. 'I think you're for me,' she said showing him a booking coupon.

'Yes,' the man replied checking the details on the paper slip. 'You ready to go right away?'

'Sure.'

'Okay, mam.'

The local led her through a side exit to a jeep parked outside. 'It's just a short ride,' he said as he got into the driving seat and Dawn sat alongside. He drove her over to a small sea-plane waiting in the far corner of the runway. The propellers on the sea-plane were already turning and the noise was quite deafening. Dawn hurried aboard.

The sun had sunk out of sight and the pilot flew on in darkness for nearly an hour. Dawn simply had to trust in his navigational abilities. Suddenly an unknown voice came over the plane's radio, 'I can hear your engines.' A moment later a powerful flare was shot into the sky illuminating everything.

Dawn could see below her a medium-sized container ship anchored in an otherwise deserted bay lined by sandy beaches and tall palm trees.

'That's your ship,' the pilot indicated.

Dawn did not reply. The sea-plane went in to land.

A second flare shot up as a dinghy was launched and sped towards to the plane as it drew to a halt.

In the dinghy was Stefan, a wiry little man who wore a short beard on his chin. He spoke in a thick accent which might have been Spanish or Portuguese. 'You all right?' he asked somewhat distantly as he nudged the dinghy up to the plane's doorway.

'I'm fine,' she replied clambering in and finding somewhere to sit.
'I assume you have the money?'
'Yes.'

'Good,' he said throttling up and waving the pilot farewell. He banked the dinghy round and steered towards the ship. As the plane took off again Dawn glanced back at it and her heart sunk just a little. She wondered anxiously to herself what was in store. But this was only a fleeting thought, she realized it was too late to have reservations.

The dinghy did a half-circle of the ship in order to the reach the spot on the waterline where cables hung down to winch it up. As they passed the stern Dawn noticed the ship's name, "Belle Epoque", and underneath it "Liberia". Dawn knew what Liberian registration meant, it was simply a flag of convenience, it said next to nothing definite of a ship's true ownership or origins.

The cables were attached and the dinghy began to be winched upward. Whereas from the air the ship appeared medium-sized from this angle it seemed vast. She asked Stefan what was "Belle Epoque's" exact tonnage. Nineteen thousand tons he replied.

Reaching the top Dawn was pleased to get her feet on the deck. It was now so dark she could scarcely pick out the faces of the half dozen crewmen who were standing around. All she noticed was that some of them were orientals. 'Okay, come this way,' said Stefan firmly who was obviously the Captain. Dawn obeyed as she was taken into the ship's aft superstructure.

They arrived in Stefan's private cabin. 'Now let me see the papers,' he demanded in a tone which was clearly not intended to win any points for charm. Unperturbed Dawn opened her bag and handed over a thin wad of documents and one other piece of paper. The thin wad consisted of bearer bonds worth $3 million and negotiable anywhere in the World. These represented payment to Stefan and his crew for the charter of the ship. The other piece of paper provided confirmation that the cargo on board was paid for. 'You'll find everything satisfactory,' she volunteered.

Stefan was not the sort of person who trusted anyone and took his time examining what she had given him. He then looked up at her. 'Yes, the money arrangements are in order. We can proceed.'

'Good,' replied Dawn already having taken an instant dislike to him. She had also noticed that he carried a gun in a shoulder holster under his jacket. He really was a shifty character she thought.

'I will show you to your quarters,' he said.

~

In the family living room at Gracie Mansion it was mid-evening. Mary Donaldson sat in a chair opposite her husband. They were alone together. She remained a handsome woman though perhaps her looks were not quite what they once were. Her personality differed greatly from William's. Unlike him she was always mild-mannered and soft spoken and much preferred the background to the limelight. Indeed, her main interest was their two children, Gwen and Simon, who were still very young as for the first few years of their marriage she had had difficulty conceiving.

William was taking another of what had been a stream of phone calls in connection with his mayoral duties. 'Yes,' he said harassed and strained, 'Of course I will be at the police funerals!' He paused impatiently listening to the other party. 'Look for Chrissakes what do you expect! Is that now understood loud and clear? Good!' He slammed down the phone. 'Jesus you can't believe how stupid some people are!' he uttered in exasperation as he reached for a sip of scotch.

Mary just looked at William, she was all too aware that he could have a short fuse and seeing him get rather heated was something she was used to. At any rate, today with the robbery in Queens had been no ordinary day and she felt any suggestion from her that he should try to relax would not have been well received.

A nanny walked in with Simon and Gwen who were dressed ready for bed.

'Good night, Daddy, good night. Mummy,' said Gwen with a charming smile.

'Good night,' waved Simon.

Mary got up immediately and went over to them. 'Goodnight Gwen, goodnight Simon, both of you have sweet dreams,' she said kissing them each in turn.

But William did not move from his chair. 'Goodnight, sleep well,' was the best he could manage in a plainly uninterested voice. The nanny sensed the Mayor's mood and dutifully led the children out again.

Mary was hurt by William's apparent indifference. 'William, can't you give Gwen and Simon a little more attention than that? It's as if you don't love them.'

William sighed and drew a deep breath. He raised his eyes to the ceiling, pausing in an effort to prevent himself saying something he might regret. 'I love them a lot!' he then told her firmly.

'Then try to show it,' she pleaded.

'Honey, I'm tired and under pressure! Try to understand!' he responded irritably not even bothering to look in her direction.

Mary instantly thought better of attempting to pursue the subject and William was glad to see she had the good sense to do so. He knew she was a fine woman and a good mother but she had a tendency to nag which he could not stand. The last thing he wanted to do now was to get into yet another pointless debate on how he could be a better father, which was an issue she endlessly raised and seemed to thrive on. Anyway these days he found all exchanges of views with her intolerably tedious regardless of what they related to. Yes, he was pleased for Mary's sake that she let the subject drop – otherwise, probably sooner rather than later, their discussion would only have ended in her tears.

Then as he sat there in silence Rosanne inevitably flashed across his mind. He had hoped to see her that evening but the events in Queens had precluded it. This was just one more source of irritation on top of several others. He took another sip of his scotch and looked over to Mary who had meekly sat back down in her chair. He racked his brain to think of something harmless to talk to her about. But the silence seemed unbreakable.

~

Earlier that evening Matts, the technical expert who had co-ordinated communications at the heist, had joined Eliot Streitch and Robert in Robert's studio in Greenwich Village. Their conversation had become heated at times and now had gone on for some hours, nevertheless it was transparently a conversation between friends.

'It isn't really a matter of technical considerations!' Matts emphasized wiping his strong spectacles with a handkerchief, 'technically we can pull off most things.'

'But we have to think of priorities,' Robert chipped in. 'If we're to get anywhere we have to be sure that we do things in the right order.'

'Yes, it has to be a natural progression,' Matts concurred.

'That's obvious,' pointed out Eliot bluntly.

'So we have to decide,' came back Robert.

'What does the Professor think?' Eliot inquired – it was odd to hear Eliot refer to a Professor, on the face of it it seemed rather incongruous.

'The Professor's advice was simple', replied Robert. 'Two words – maximum momentum.'

'Well then, doesn't that say it all?' retorted Eliot. 'If the Professor said that we know what's next!'

'Okay,' confirmed Matts with a knowing look.

'Okay,' nodded Robert. 'That's the way we go.'

CHAPTER 3

The funeral of the policemen killed in Queens took place at a cemetery on Long Island exactly one week later. Police pallbearers slowly carried eight coffins – for some of the security guards were included too – down a driveway fringed by plush green lawn. A police band played the Funeral March and New York policemen, shoulder to shoulder, stood to attention along the length of the route.

Behind the coffins in the funeral cortege walked William and Mary Donaldson, Police Commissioner McMichael and many other dignitaries. TV News crews discreetly covered proceedings from pre-arranged camera positions.

A chapel lay at the end of the driveway and the procession entered it.

The service was long and full of emotion. The moment came when William was to make a short address. From his seat at the front of the packed congregation he stepped forward towards the lectern. His face portrayed the full sense of gravity due to such an occasion.

He began by praising the courage of the New York police, he spoke of the importance of law and order, he underlined the horror of man's inhumanity to man. He said what he thought was right about Society and he expounded on what he thought was wrong. He pulled no punches where he felt there was a need for new initiatives to be taken.

Finally he reverted to the theme of the personal tragedy involved. 'Our hearts go out to the families of these brave men, cut down in the course of their duty, cut down by an act of brutal savagery.'

As a parting gesture William turned directly towards the mourners and saluted them with a small brief bow of his head. He then descended back to his pew. It had been a magnificent performance.

'Now let us pray,' said the voice of the priest.

~

Later William bid his farewells and headed back to Manhattan. He had lined up a meeting in his private office at the Mayor's residence at Gracie Mansion with Police Commissioner McMichael. The purpose of the meeting was to review the progress of the investigation.

However, no soon as the meeting had got underway, it was not long before tempers became somewhat frayed. 'So you're saying we have nothing!' William said incredulously to Commissioner McMichael who sat opposite him in the private office.

'Nothing,' replied McMichael, still dressed in the full uniform he had worn at the cemetery.

William did not like what he heard at all. He felt his reputation was on the line as much as anybody's and this made him uptight. 'This robbery has got headlines all around the world! If you're saying we don't have a clue I think we look pretty stupid!'

'These people killed five patrolmen and seven security guards!' replied the Commissioner indignantly. 'And don't forget that three of those security guards were ex-cops. Make no mistake there is no lack of priority on this!'

William could see the Commissioner was as frustrated as he was, he backed off. 'Okay,' he said raising his hands and lowering his voice. 'But remember I didn't like burying those policemen any more than you did!'

'I know you didn't,' conceded the Commissioner who also saw no purpose in confrontation. 'But you asked me a question and I gave you an answer. At the moment we have nothing.'

'Well, let's both hope it changes real quick.'

'I'll keep you informed,' said McMichael heavily as he rose to his feet.

'Thank you,' replied William.

The Commissioner left and William stopped to think. He fidgeted around with his hands tapping his fingers on the desk, he swept back his full head of hair which had slid over his forehead, he tried to straighten his tie which actually did not need straightening. His mind was drifting and it was only drifting one way – towards Rosanne. He had spoken to her only once in the last week and she had been perfectly friendly. However, his schedule had been so full and the blare of publicity so great in the aftermath of the robbery, there had been no opportunity to see her. He resolved to call her. He lifted his phone, 'Get me Rosanne Lindblade at Prestige Publications, will you?'

Rosanne was at her desk as she answered her phone. 'Hello? Rosanne Lindblade ...'

'I have Mayor Donaldson for you,' the switchboard said.

Rosanne immediately smiled, she was well drilled in the rather bizarre style of conversation which went on between William and her any time he called her office. 'Good afternoon, Mayor Donaldson,' she said trying to sound as professional as possible.

'Good afternoon,' replied William, his manner distinctly guarded. 'I feel badly about switching our interview around so much.'

'That's okay, I fully understand,' she responded tactfully.

'Well, the reason I'm calling is that I have a hole in my diary later today – Is there any chance of us meeting then?'

While she spoke Rosanne saw Jack Grant her Senior Editor approaching, in consequence her voice became even more businesslike. 'I don't see why not,' she replied, 'that would be fine.'

'The same sort of time we set before?' suggested William somewhat cryptically.

'Yes – the same sort of time we set before,' echoed Rosanne fully understanding what he meant. 'Until then then, bye bye for now.'

She replaced the receiver and looked up towards Jack Grant who was now standing in front of her. 'Hi, Jack. That was Mayor Donaldson, you know I'm supposed to do a piece on him?'

'Yes, you told me,' answered Jack with a smile.

'The trouble is he's had to cancel out a couple of times.'

'Well, you be sure you eventually get to see him! That guy really is news!'

'Don't worry, I will,' she replied very poker-faced – in fact doubly so since Jack and her had once been lovers.

'Good. But at any rate, Rosanne,' he announced shuffling through some typed sheets he had in his hand, 'I have your feature here on Robert Cook.'

'You like it?' she smiled.

'Well, yes and no. I think the sections dealing with his Art are fine, but when it comes to his political views!'

'But Jack?' she protested.

'Rosanne, we're in the publishing business!' He could not have sounded more adamant. 'We have an up-market readership to consider and the big corporations that advertise with us! All of whom we're not about to risk offending! It is not this magazine's function to offer a platform to people who just seem to want to criticize everything in sight! Rosanne, it really is as simple as that.'

'Oh, come on! Isn't this being a bit absurd?' she objected. 'He's only an artist for God's sake.'

'No, I'm sorry!' he answered. 'Parts of the piece are too strong, too outspoken – I've marked the passages.' He handed her the typed sheets.

'You really mean this?' she frowned as she flicked through them.

'Rosanne, just tone it down a bit, I can't run it as it is.'

Rosanne stared down at the sheets shaking her head.

'I think most of it is excellent,' added Jack feeling some flattery would not go amiss. 'Unless you'd perhaps prefer that I got someone else to do the work?' he further added after a calculated pause, knowing this was almost certain to bring her round.

He then waited for her reply.

But Rosanne was evidently finding it difficult, she seemed to be taking the whole thing very much to heart. The interlude soon became rather lengthy. As he waited Jack began to wonder quite why this article should be such a big deal. Nevertheless, he resisted the temptation to offer any more persuasion. Just as he had started to ask himself whether she had lost her voice he found his patience was rewarded.

'Okay, I'll do as you say', she finally said. 'It won't be as good, but okay ...'

'Thank you,' said Jack privately congratulating himself as he walked off. After all he knew who he was dealing and had learnt from experience that the best way to handle Rosanne was to be very definite – it did not always work but this time it had. He counted it as a minor triumph.

Naturally Rosanne did not see it in the same light. As Jack disappeared back to his office she could have killed him. She thought of all the effort she had put in to make the article a mirror image of everything Robert had said. Now the carpet had been pulled from under her feet. Out of sheer annoyance she picked up a sharpened pencil and stabbed it hard into her desk, momentarily she wished the desk had been Jack.

But Rosanne also had a good nose for no win situations and she recognized this as one of them – she was not the boss, Jack was, and she was no longer sleeping with him. Moreover, she only had two days left before her copy-date deadline and a substantial re-write was now going to be required. She had better get on with it she thought. This article was important to her. She decided to make a start there and then. She pulled her chair up to her computer keyboard.

Later on she was still typing intently when a voice interrupted her. 'Excuse me, Miss Lindblade,' said Pedro, who was the office cleaner, 'please can I reach under your desk and empty out your trash-can?'

Rosanne, jolted out of her concentration, first looked up at Pedro, and then looked down at her watch. It was gone six o'clock. Astonished she quickly glanced around her and saw that the rest of the office was empty. Her face froze. 'Gosh Pedro, is it really after six?' she asked in a fluster.

'Nearer to seven', confirmed Pedro with a benign grin.

'Jesus,' she exclaimed. 'My God I had no idea, I gotta get going!'

Pedro just shrugged and kept grinning as Rosanne quickly backed up a copy of her revised article on to a memory stick, shoved it and her various papers into her briefcase and rushed out of the empty office. Clearly she had let herself lose all track of time.

Even though she luckily quickly found a cab on the street below, Rosanne on the way home to 89th Street felt in a state of panic. She had only ever once before been late for a clandestine rendezvous with William, and on that occasion only by less than ten minutes, yet he had been livid and had made her promise it would never happen again. Now it had, and not just by a mere ten minutes but a full half hour! Wishing every traffic light en route would immediately turn green, which of course it refused to do, she trawled her mind for a good excuse. But feeling ever more anxious by the minute her mind seemed a blank.

Arriving at 89th and Madison Rosanne got out of her cab and hurried into her apartment building more or less ignoring the doorman and hall porter both of whom she normally greeted with a smile.

'Every all right, Miss Lindblade?' Larry, the doorman, called after her noticing her somewhat agitated demeanor.

'Yes, yes, fine thank you, Larry,' she called back not wishing to delay a second longer than necessary and pressing the elevator button at the same time.

'Good to hear it, Miss Lindblade, okay, Miss Lindblade,' she heard Larry respond as she stepped into the elevator and the doors closed. She hurriedly glanced into the mirror on the elevator's wall to check her appearance. She looked great. Then, as she pondered momentarily, somehow the intonation of Larry's friendly "okay" resurfaced and resonated and lingered like an echo in her head. It was as if the word 'Okay' was written up in huge neon lights on a giant billboard in her mind's eye. Yes, she thought, everything is okay, why should I be so nervous? After all, she reflected, she really hadn't done anything wrong. Far from it. Yes, Larry was right, everything really is okay.

And so as the elevator headed up towards the sixteenth floor, seemingly solely triggered by this non-descript aside from one of the doormen, Rosanne's attitude changed completely. All the feelings of guilt she had had about being late ceased to exist. She impressed upon herself that she was not being late deliberately, it was purely that she had been working. Moreover, it was William and not her who had suggested this particular time and he had suggested it entirely to suit himself. Most of all she did not need to be reminded that when they last met he had left her to go home in the middle of the night and they had not parted on the happiest of terms. Indeed, her resolve stiffening all the time, she now if anything actually now felt cross with herself for worrying about keeping William waiting in the first place – perhaps a startlingly swift shift in position by most people's standards, but that was not how Rosanne saw it.

Thus, when she emerged from the elevator doors on the sixteenth floor and she saw William's angry face standing outside the door to her apartment, far from pouring out profuse apologies she just stood here.

'Where have you been?' asked William barely controlling his fury.

'I was delayed at the office,' was all Rosanne said, feigning not to notice William's quivering lips.

'How insensitive can you be!' he half-shouted, hardly able to contain his anger but forcing himself to keep his voice down. 'I've been standing here over half an hour!'

Rosanne merely affected a small, disdainful, indifferent, grimace. In fact her mood had now altered so much that she was in two minds whether or not to go straight back to the elevator again. Instead she decided simply to ignore William's protestations and brushed by him towards her door. She reached for her keys which she kept in a flap in her brief case.

She entered the apartment still refusing to be drawn. He followed. The atmosphere could have been cut with a knife. 'We agreed on the phone,' he began again in a tone no less angry and urgent, 'that we would meet at "the same sort of time as we met before". That expression you know very well means six o'clock!'

'You and your stupid coded expressions!' she caustically replied quite indifferent to the glaring countenance on his face.

'Shit, Rosanne!' he exploded. 'Don't try and give me that! You know as well as I do we can't speak openly on the phone! Worse still, can you imagine how embarrassing it is standing in that corridor for half an hour! What do other residents think seeing me loitering outside your front door like some dog on a chain!'

'William,' she said clinically, narrowing her eyes at him, 'number one I suggest you calm down, and number two stop being so paranoid! For God's sake in the time we've known each other people must seen you coming and going here plenty of times!'

'Jesus Christ!' he protested loudly. 'They may have seen me, but that's all they will have done! They don't know why I'm here and if they did you know how badly it could reflect on me! What I'm saying Rosanne is that every time I come here I'm running one hell of a risk and I'm running it because I love you! So it's not fair to expect me to push my luck any more than I have to!'

Rosanne raised her eyes to the ceiling. 'Fairness!' she yelled back. 'We're now talking about fairness are we? That sounds great coming from you!'

William drew in air, he would have hit back even harder but the glare on her face made him think twice.

Rosanne had not finished anyway. 'I'm late, okay I'm sorry! But end of story, I don't want to hear any more about it! Okay!' She looked straight at William with double intensity. 'Okay!' she repeated once more with added vehemence.

William, realising she was prepared to give as good as she got and conscious that he did not want things to get out of hand, forced himself to cool down. He always prided himself on knowing what was in his best interests – After all he had actually come to make love not war and therefore did not want to ruin his chances. 'Okay, let's forget it,' he said, suddenly sounding like a different man. 'I'm sorry too.'

Rosanne slipped off her jacket and decided she would have a drink. She had gone quiet but this was not unusual for her after voices had been raised. She had an icebox by her bar and removed a half empty bottle of white wine from it. She poured a glass and topped it up with ice cubes. All the time William did not take his eyes off her.

'Oh sorry, if you want a drink, you know where it is,' she said sounding pre-occupied as she turned back towards him.

'That's okay,' he smiled. 'Rosanne, you look gorgeous.'

This compliment brought just a flicker of a smile to her face, but there was no way anyone could tell exactly what she was thinking.

William could see she was still moody but he knew this could be deceptive. Often after a sharp exchange he found she was especially ready to be caressed. He was certainly ready himself, he was feeling very aroused, he moved towards her to kiss her.

But as he advanced she stepped aside. 'No, William, not so fast. I want to talk,' she said in a sullen tone.

'Oh, come on Rosanne, we can talk afterwards.'

He reached out to touch her, but again she retreated. 'No, I want to talk now – we have all evening.'

William knew that they did not have all evening, and so he moved to try and kiss her one more time. 'No, William, you're not listening to me. I said I want to talk now!' A distinct trace of aggression was coming back into her voice.

William reluctantly dropped his outstretched arms and leant awkwardly on the edge of the settee. 'All right, let's talk then, but I suppose I'd better tell you something first which I know isn't going to be popular. Time is precious, I can't stay long this evening.'

He hesitated for her reaction, he knew he was on shaky ground. He did not have long to wait.

'What? What did you say?' Rosanne came back frowning heavily.

'Rosanne, I have a fund-raising dinner tonight at the Waldorf with Oakley Cunningham, it's important. Oakley Cunningham may well be the next President of the United States. I have to be there!'

All the time as he spoke Rosanne's rage was gathering into a storm. An instant later she erupted. 'You have a nerve!' she hissed through her lips.

'Rosanne ...' he interjected, disturbed by the look on her face.

'How dare you!' she shouted at him.

'Rosanne ...' he implored her.

'Just get out!'

'Rosanne, try and see it from my point of view.'

'So you come here thinking you're just going to get a quick fuck! I said get out!'

William went over to her to try to calm her. 'Don't even touch me!' she screamed.

'Rosanne, be reasonable!'

'Everything else in your life comes first! Except me!' she yelled. 'Even that wife who you say you're so bored with! Well, I can tell you I'm not some kind of cheap screw who's going to play second string! I've eaten enough shit from you! I said get out! I hate you, I really hate you! So go!'

William was shell-shocked, he just stood there in silence for a moment or two. He knew Rosanne was highly-strung but this level of vehemence had taken him by surprise. He tried to think fast, to think of something which might save the day, but of all the options open to him he quickly realized that only one was viable. 'Okay,' he said quietly, 'I will go.' And stony-faced and perplexed he walked out the door.

Rosanne watched him leave without any remorse. She was defiant, she did not regret a word, William had got no less than he deserved. She briefly gathered her thoughts and gave herself time to let her anger subside. She then kicked off her high heels, sat down on her settee, and opened up her brief case to get the memory stick containing Robert's article from inside.

~

At the other end of town a very different discussion was going on. In the studio in Greenwich Village Eliot and Matts had reassembled with Robert. Warren and Gil were there too. As was Zak, another associate of about the same age group as the others.

All sorts of maps and diagrams had been laid out on the floor and these were now being folded up again.

'The weather's going to be dark and cloudy,' said Matts.

'Okay then, this is the real beginning!' said Robert to all the others. 'Be sure to let me know.'

'I will,' replied Eliot getting up from his chair.

Everyone except Robert headed out into the dusk.

CHAPTER 4

Oakley Cunningham was physically a big man, he was no more than five feet ten but weighed over two-fifty pounds. But this was not the only way in which he was larger than life. He had a forceful personality mixed with much charm and considerable presence. He was one of those few men in politics who were blessed with genuine star quality.

Cunningham was from Philadelphia and came from one of the oldest and most prestigious families in the United States. He was one of the Senators for his home state of Pennsylvania and had created an image for himself as the hard-hitting champion of traditional American values. He was now running for President for the first time and was firm favorite to win. His critics saw him as too right wing, his supporters saw him as a savior. His strongest supporter of all was none other than William Donaldson.

Outside the Waldorf Astoria on Park Avenue the police had cordoned off the main entrance. The hotel had long experience of hosting major functions but that evening's fund-raising dinner to honor Oakley Cunningham ranked alongside any of them. First of all, the nine hundred guests who were to dine in the Grand Ball Room had paid a minimum of $1000 a head. Secondly, wherever the Senator for Pennsylvania went there was always a buzz.

The police cars escorting Cunningham had radioed ahead to warn the patrolmen outside the hotel that his arrival was imminent. The waiting onlookers on the sidewalk sensed the heightened atmosphere. In no time the sound of sirens filled the Avenue and a motorcade of twenty vehicles complete with motorcycle outriders rolled up. Oakley Cunningham got out of his limousine and was immediately surrounded by secret service bodyguards who formed a loose circle around him.

For a man of his size he was agile and had a spring in his step. He walked the short distance across a red carpet towards the hotel's entrance waving to well-wishers on all sides. When he entered the lobby a hush fell over it. All eyes were trained on this imposing figure. Then a fat Bell Captain called out. 'Good evening, "Mr President"!'

Oakley beamed back at the fat Bell Captain with a look of delight, the tension was broken and the hush subsided.

'Senator Cunningham, Mayor Donaldson's already arrived, he's waiting for you upstairs,' informed an aide who came up.

'Good,' replied Oakley as he and his entourage filed into an elevator.

~

Rosanne had moved over to her home computer had and copied over to it from the memory stick all her revised work on Robert Cook's article. She aimed to finish it there and then. She was an expert typist and had no need to look at the key pad as she speeded through page after another. Eventually she reached the end and with an expression of relief printed a hard copy of the finished piece. The intensity of her activity suggesting that quite apart from any other deadlines she was working to she was also working to one of her own. When she picked up the phone and dialed her motive became apparent.

In Greenwich Village Robert was busy on one of his canvasses as the phone rang. He was expecting an important call later that evening, but he knew it was now still theoretically far too early. The phone ringing at this unexpectedly early hour therefore worried him. 'Yes ...?' he replied edgily.

'Robert Cook?' asked the voice.

'Speaking.'

'This is Rosanne Lindblade, you remember me?'

'Of course I remember you,' he smiled, his face suddenly relaxing.

Rosanne looked pleased. 'Well, I'm calling because your article's more or less ready and you said you'd like to see it.'

'I would. How is your schedule?'

'I don't know,' she hesitated. 'This may seem a silly suggestion, or it may be inconvenient, but how about this evening – I could bring it round?'

This slightly threw Robert off balance, he paused and glanced at his watch. Then he made his mind up. 'Sure,' he told her warmly. 'No time like the present.'

'I'll be there as soon as I can,' she enthused.

~

Oakley Cunningham and William Donaldson sat wearing their black ties and tuxedos in the suite set aside for their use in the Waldorf prior to the dinner. Oakley overflowed with confidence as he brought William up to date on developments in his campaign and ran through his latest thinking on a variety of political issues. Such policy pledges as the death penalty for drugs dealing, the creation of U.S. trade barriers against Chinese imports and a sweeping reassessment of the Welfare system in tandem with massive cuts in Government spending were all high on his agenda as sure-fire vote winners.

As he spoke William listened courteously agreeing with everything he said. However, William was subdued and it was obvious.

'You know something, William?' commented Oakley his voice booming less than it normally did. 'You're not the fun guy I usually look forward to seeing this evening. Is something worrying you?'

William knew exactly what was gnawing at him, but the thought of discussing it made him feel uneasy, he settled on a diversion. 'No, nothing Oakley. It's just been a tough couple of days in this town.'

'Sure it has,' replied Oakley much too perceptive to be deceived. 'But I've known you from a long way back – You're not fooling me – What is it?'

William made no initial reply, he clenched his hands tightly together, he was very uncomfortable. But then he decided to get it off his chest. 'Okay, Oakley,' he began in a grave voice. 'I suppose you do know me too well. Yes, there is something eating at me – my marriage isn't what it should be.'

Oakley pulled himself up in his chair as if this change in posture would assist him to digest more clearly what he was being told. Yet there was nothing in his body language which hinted at disapproval. On the contrary, he was a lot older than William and really his manner only suggested that he wanted to be helpful. 'Is there someone else?' he asked in a relaxed tone.

William seemed slightly to blush. 'Hell, Oakley, I don't want to burden you with my personal problems!' he responded all the more uncomfortable.

'I asked you is there someone else?' Oakley pressed. 'I asked you as a friend.'

'Yes. Yes, there is,' William admitted ruefully.

'And it's serious?'

'Yes.'

'What are you going to do about it?' Oakley's tone was direct but nonetheless unmistakably sympathetic.

'What can I do?' replied William with a hint of desperation. I have my reputation to consider – both political and personal.'

'No, you don't,' assured Oakley in a fatherly sort of way. 'We have this Election won. Nobody's voting for you anyway! I'm the guy they'll be voting for! Just you remember that! No, old pal, if you want my advice make your own decision on what you feel is for the best, then proceed accordingly.'

William looked up. 'You mean that?' he murmured in semi-disbelief.

'Yes. Of course I mean it,' answered Oakley. 'In my opinion it's the only thing to do. Now William I want you to cheer up!'

William smiled.

'Okay,' continued Oakley getting up from his seat and feeling he had done his good deed for the day. 'We had better start to head downstairs.'

'Yes,' said William looking a lot happier. 'What's your speech going to be on tonight?'

'Welfare, combined with the Debt that goes with it!' was Oakley's clipped reply.

'It's a good choice of subject, particularly here in New York City, we're handing out a bloody fortune in welfare payments!'

'I bet you are! And it's the same across the whole country!' exclaimed Oakley. 'Why should 80% of the population subsidize the other 20% who are losers! It's got to stop!'

'Yes, I know – It's a disgrace.'

'That's putting it mildly!' Oakley nodded emphatically.

William opened the door of the suite and they entered the hotel corridor where secret servicemen stood silent guard.

'And by the way, William, thanks for the money, it will be put to good use in these last few weeks before polling day!'

'Don't mention it, Oakley, it's the least I can do. And thanks for your advice.'

'You don't have to thank me, William. The main thing is that everything is going our way. Even this robbery in Queens just goes to show that the present Administration does not have law and order under control!'

A few paces later they arrived at the elevator a secret service agent had summoned for them.

~

'Hi,' said Robert into the entryphone in his studio lobby after Rosanne had rang the bell on the sidewalk below. He then opened the upstairs door and waited listening to her footsteps as she climbed the stairs.

'Good evening!' she smiled reaching the top and planting a kiss on his cheek. 'I feel I know you well enough by now to give you a kiss!'

'Well, why not,' Robert smiled back. 'Come on through. I'm cooking some pasta if you're interested?'

'Really,' said Rosanne just being polite, 'I didn't mean to put you to any trouble'

'It's no trouble,' he replied, 'no trouble at all – Sit yourself down. Can I get you a drink?'

'I'd love a glass of white wine, lots of ice in it,' she stipulated with a grin.

'Okay, lots of ice, easily done,' said Robert heading out to fetch it.

Rosanne sat down and looked around. A thought occurred to her. 'Where's, where's Dawn?'

'She's away at the moment, out of town, her job involves a quite a lot of travel,' he answered re-entering with two of glasses of white wine.

'Oh,' said Rosanne intrigued. 'What does she do?'

'She's a make-up artist, works on TV commercials and so on.'

'I see,' said Rosanne trying to appear natural, though the thought that Dawn was absent and that she and Robert were alone sent a tingle down her spine.

'Hang on a moment, I'll be right with you,' stated Robert going into the kitchen, 'just want to check the pasta.'

'So tell me,' he shouted casually from beside the stove next door, 'am I going to be pleased with this piece you've written or not?'

'Well, that's really putting me on the spot!' laughed Rosanne as he strode back in. 'I think maybe the best thing is just for you to read it through first.'

She took out the freshly printed sheets from her brief case and handed them to him.

~

With the lights of Manhattan in the background three jet black rubber dinghies were pushed out from the bottom of a disused pier on the East River. The men who pushed them out were dressed in black clothing and their faces plastered in thick camouflage paint.

Inside the three dinghies were several unlabeled containers and Eliot jumped aboard one of them as Warren and Zak already seated inside it reached for a pair of paddles. Eliot heard his walkie-talkie crackle and held it up close to his ear to receive a message.

'The others are in position?' asked Warren in an undertone.

'Yes, we go,' replied Eliot lowering the walkie-talkie.

The dinghies crept off into mid-stream.

~

Robert and Rosanne sat around and the empty pasta plates lay on the floor beside them. Robert kept going backwards and forwards through the pages of the article. He was silent and he was frowning and his face had gone pale.

'You've read it three times, you don't look too happy with it,' she observed.

'No, I'm not,' he answered dismayed raising his eyes towards her. 'If I had known I was going to end up with this wishy-washy muck I wouldn't have agreed to talk to you in the first place!'

Rosanne did not take offense, instead she just paused a moment. 'I know what's bothering you,' she sighed. 'It's because it's all about your Art and covers nothing else. I mean it says nothing about your general views. Isn't that it?'

'If it says nothing about my general views then it can't say anything about my Art – the two go hand in glove! One is completely meaningless without the other!' he protested upset, and being upset was not something he usually showed. 'For example,' he went on. You write here: "*Robert Cook is an artist with a social conscience, although his paintings sell for in excess of six figures he professes not to be interested in money. It's not that Cook is anti-material, it is just that he believes that the accumulation of personal wealth is unlikely to satisfy the soul ..."'*

Robert looked at her aghast. 'You make me sound like some idealistic dreamer who has no contact with reality! You obviously just don't understand!'

In a way Rosanne found this outburst rather appealing, but in another she was afraid she might drop in his esteem. She hesitated again, this time not out of indecision but simply to gain maximum effect. 'Actually,' she then replied, removing more papers from her case. 'You're being unfair. I did understand. This is the article I originally wrote.' She gave it to him.

Robert gazed at her confused. 'Read it, you'll see the difference,' she coaxed him with a small smile.

He had only glanced at the article for a minute before the color returned to his cheeks. He began to quote: '"*Cook's Art is inspired by a horror of where society is heading – He maintains we have placed ourselves in a pressure cooker that must lead to dire consequences ...*"

'Now that's got a cutting edge!' he instantly commented.

'You like it?' she asked seeing full well she had no need to ask the question.

'Yes, very much!' he exclaimed enthusiastically beginning to quote again: '"*Cook simply scoffs at any accusations of him ever having had any pro-Communist or anti-Capitalist sympathies, he would also hotly deny any suggestion that he sees himself as a revolutionary, or an anarchist, or whatever other disagreeable label might come to mind – all that he does passionately insist upon is that he has a deep concern for humanity ...*"

'That's right! As for Communism I always hated that with a vengeance – it was far worse than anything we've ever had here!'

Rosanne had to laugh, she found the sudden transformation in his mood amusing.

'"*Cook asserts,*"' he read on, '"w*e are witnessing in front of our very eyes a gradual disintegration of the many of the things that make life worth living ...*"

'Yes, you did understand!' he applauded.

'Thank you,' resounded Rosanne taking pleasure in his pleasure.

Robert continued, '"Cook says '*This is the richest nation on Earth, if we cannot do something more about poverty we should die of shame ..."* And, *"'Somehow humanity has to curb its selfishness, otherwise they'll be nothing left to be greedy about.'"*

'Those were exact quotes, word for word!' pointed out Rosanne.

'I know they were! The whole flow of this is really first class!' he congratulated with a real glow in his voice.

Finally Robert spotted one last phrase which, judging from his inflection, might almost have been his favorite: *'"When Cook was asked did he therefore feel that anything was going to happen to put things right, his cryptic reply was only that: 'The one thing I am sure of is that things won't stay the same.'"'*

'Bravo!' he exclaimed tossing the article on the floor and clapping loudly. 'Just tremendous! That really is more like it! Why on Earth didn't you show me this in the first place?'

'Well, I could have done,' announced Rosanne somewhat apologetically. 'But the problem is that my Editor won't print it that way.'

'Why's that?' he frowned

'Come on Robert, don't be naive. He thinks it's too much to put in a magazine like ours.'

'And what do you think?' he quizzed looking at her straight in the eyes.

'You know very well, I'm on your side. But the fact is it isn't my decision.'

'Well, in that case we have to work out a compromise.'

'Compromise?' she repeated looking puzzled. 'I don't see a lot of room for that.'

'There's plenty of room for it! We keep the meaning but soften it up a bit, then they'll buy it.'

'I doubt that very much,' she demurred.

'It's worth a try,' he insisted as he found a pen. 'You have one of the biggest circulations in the country, if at all possible I would like to see this article out containing at least a degree of accuracy!'

Rosanne stared at him again, she still had her doubts. But whether this was a futile exercise or not she was willing to go along with it. Men like Robert were much too few and far between and she felt more and more drawn towards him. 'All right,' she said. 'Show me what you want to do.'

~

At the Waldorf the guests were finishing their lemon meringue pie and beginning to sip their coffees at the dozens of circular tables dotted around the middle of the Grand Ball Room. Looking down on them at one end on a raised platform was the long top table where Oakley and William sat occupying the best positions of all. It was beyond question an evening of sparkling excess. The jewelry on display alone must have amounted to several king's ransoms.

Everything had gone well and even William was enjoying himself – in between polite conversation with the people around him he had already formed a very clear idea of what he was going to do about Rosanne. However, it was now time for the main speech and he turned to Oakley. 'I'll make the introduction for you.'

'Okay,' nodded Oakley.

William immediately stood up and spoke into the microphone placed on the table in front of them. 'Ladies and Gentleman,' he said, he waited for quiet. 'Ladies and Gentlemen, I am very pleased you have all been able to join us here this evening, and I am privileged and delighted that we are honored by the presence of Oakley Cunningham, our candidate for the Presidency of the United States of America!'

William sat down and Oakley himself then rose to the microphone getting a tumultuous reception. 'Thank you, thank you, William – those must have been the two most expensive sentences you've ever uttered!' This quip provoked nervous laughter among the guests, which was exactly as Oakley intended. 'The reason I say that,' he went on lifting his voice to its limit before pausing just long enough to build up the suspense. 'The reason I say that, is that your Mayor, William Donaldson, has personally pledged a further two million dollars to our campaign funds!' The audience broke into spontaneous rapturous applause which lasted what seemed like at least a minute. 'No,' he continued with a smile, 'kidding aside, I thank you William from the bottom of my heart, you're not only a strong supporter but a very dear friend.'

William smiled back, he was touched by this accolade from the man he saw as very much his hero. Amidst more applause Oakley briefly adjusted the printed speech cards he held as he prepared to carry on.

~

Underneath the Queensboro Bridge at East 59th Street, one of the main arteries on to Manhattan, there was much activity. From a rope attached high up among the steel girders the dark figure of a frogman in diving suit slid down towards Eliot's dinghy. Virtually simultaneously another frogman surfaced from beneath the river only yards away.

'Everything all right?' Eliot asked them.

'Yup,' replied the frogman who had just been underwater.

'It's under control up top too,' said the other one who on removing his diving mask turned out to be Zak.

'We head downtown,' instructed Eliot as he helped them back aboard.

Zak and Warren took up their paddles again.

~

Guided by Robert, Rosanne had written out a revised article by hand. 'That should do it,' he said as he checked it through. 'It's still got the right ingredients but now it's more relaxed.'

'Okay,' she replied clearly thinking about something else at the same time.

Robert got up from his seat. 'So you'll submit this new version to your Editor?'

'Yes, I will ...' she said quietly. 'I'll try and see him in the morning.' Her voice trailed off almost into nothing.

Rosanne gathered up the pages of the article and slowly and meticulously placed them in her case. As she stood up her expression was blank except for her eyes which darted listlessly one way then the next as if she did not know where to look. Her every movement seemed to be at half speed, and when she finally got round to snapping shut the catch on her brief case it was as if this small and simple task had required a major effort for her to accomplish. 'Robert ...?' she suddenly said, her pupils dilating.

'Yes?' he replied seeing her move almost involuntarily towards him.

But by now she was only inches away from him and her only action was to lean forward offering her mouth in a kiss. She closed her eyes in expectation, only to open them again prematurely.

'No, Rosanne, no ...' he said gently, in fact more than gently for there was tenderness in his voice too.

'I'm sorry,' she whispered as she drew back from him.

Robert looked at her, some kind of pain lay somewhere just below the surface of his face. 'No, don't say you're sorry,' he told her. 'You're much too beautiful ever to have to say that to anyone.'

And by the way he spoke Rosanne could see that he meant it and it only made her feel all the more in love with him. She tried to compose herself, she found it very confusing, she could only assume that Dawn had greater importance to him than she had chosen to believe. But that was not a situation her feelings permitted her to accept, as she stood there absolutely everything in her wanted him, she only wished and wished he might change his mind and take her in his arms.

But all Robert did was keep looking at her, his dark eyes never blinking. He made no move. And, in what seemed an eternity, he said no more.

'I suppose I'd better be going,' announced Rosanne a little awkwardly.

'Yes, I hope we stay in touch,' he replied.

'Yes, me too,' she said conjuring up the semblance of a smile.

Robert took her to the door and showed her out. Not a single further word was exchanged between them.

On the street below she quickly found a yellow cab. '89th and Madison,' she said not betraying how wretched she felt. The driver was not the type who would have been interested anyway. Indifferent to everything except earning his next buck he set his clock running and headed away from Washington Square.

Robert had watched her get into the cab from his upstairs window, he felt badly that he might have hurt her, but it was an impossible situation. Especially on that evening of all evenings. He sighed now regretting he had even let her come by. He decided to do the thing he usually did when he wanted to get his mind off something, he decided to paint. But as he mixed a palate he heard the phone. He had the receiver in his hand even before he first ring was over.

'It's nearly "Post Time" at Aqueduct,' informed the voice.

'Good,' was Robert's monosyllabic reply as the other party instantly rang off.

~

As Rosanne's cab headed north she was thinking hard, she was clearly toying with some idea, suddenly she spoke through the cab's protective grill. 'Driver, I've changed my mind, I'd like to go to 33rd and Park.'

'Okay,' he replied blankly, the street sign on the approaching corner showing that they were already about to cross 29th.

Three minutes later Rosanne entered the address on 33rd. It was the apartment house where Jack Grant, her editor, lived. The porters in the lobby had seen her many times and showed her straight to the elevator. She wondered what Jack would make of her unexpected visit but she was not too bothered. Rosanne was a creature of impulse, she had spent her whole life giving people surprises – sometimes even herself.

She rung his door buzzer. 'It's Rosanne,' she called out as she heard his footsteps on the floor tiles getting nearer.

'Rosanne!' he exclaimed as he opened door. 'What are you doing here?'

'I'm not disturbing you, am I?' she asked with a smile strolling in without waiting for a reply.

'No, I was just having a quiet evening,' answered Jack. 'But Rosanne, it's always nice to see you, but what are you doing here at this time of night?'

'I was passing, that's all.'

'Well, you look pretty dressed up to me, you been out to dinner or something?'

'No, I don't count this as all that dressy,' she replied referring to her outfit, which was actually quite a skimpy knitted woollen one piece. 'I've been having supper with some girlfriends.'

'So do you always wear that much make-up when you see your girlfriends?' he teased.

'Oh, never mind about that, Jack,' she said smiling realising her story was perhaps not entirely plausible. 'I'm here because I want to ask you something.'

'Okay, about what? Not about "old wounds" I hope – what happened between us on a personal level is long over.'

'Of course it is,' replied Rosanne. Good-looking though Jack was, even discussing their romance, let alone, Heaven forbid, renewing it, was the very last thing on her mind. 'No Jack,' she said, 'I'm calling strictly as a friend, I want your opinion.'

'All right you want my opinion, but about what? And why now?' he asked somewhat perplexed. 'I know you – there's got to be some scheme going on somewhere!' Indeed, Jack knew all too well how cunning Rosanne could be and he remembered all too vividly that their affair had ended on a sour note. And this knowledge made him doubly anxious not to fall for some ploy. If she was up to something, and she clearly was, he knew from experience it was better to be cautious. His somewhat impatient look conveyed to her that she had better hurry up and say whatever she had to say.

Rosanne got the message. 'I've been worrying all day about this Robert Cook article,' she began totally straight-faced. 'I've re-written it, I had to do it by hand because there's something wrong with my computer at home, I want to show it to you.'

This really made Jack think. 'Jesus, sometimes you really are a mystery,' he said flabbergasted. 'Why this couldn't wait until the morning I don't know! But okay, show it to me then.'

Quite unmoved by Jack's incredulity Rosanne calmly sat down and opened her case. 'I've made it a more light-hearted profile – Although he's still critical it no longer makes him sound threatening. Though I hate admitting it, I have to say it's a big improvement.'

Of course in reality she did not think it was a big improvement at all, it was merely part of her sales pitch. She reckoned she knew by now that the best way to soften Jack up on something was to make him feel he had been right all along. It was a sucker punch for which he invariably fell.

'You always had nice handwriting,' he complimented her as he started to go through it.

~

A truck stood innocently parked on a quiet Manhattan street. There was nothing distinctive about it except that had it been daylight one might have noticed that it had not one but four radio aerials.

Inside the truck were Matts and a technical assistant, the walls of its interior were stacked high with electronic equipment. Matts was wearing headphones and microphone again. 'Everyone else is ready, you all sorted out?' he queried into his headset.

'Yes,' replied Eliot into his walkie-talkie speaking from his dinghy floating near the twin towers of the World Trade Center.

'Okay then, three minutes, I'll issue the standby,' came back Matts.

'Do that,' said Eliot dryly.

~

At the Waldorf, Oakley was coming to the end of his speech. He was a superb speaker, in full flow his voice had an almost musical quality to it. There was no trick of oratory he had not mastered. He had the audience eating out of his hand. 'This country,' he boomed out across the Ball Room, 'this country was built on the merits of hard work, free enterprise and the acceptance that if you want to spend a dollar you first have to earn a dollar!

'But,' he paused, 'but now,' he went on, 'we have slipped into a different, more dangerous climate, one that favors the weak, not the strong ... One that encourages passengers and parasites and does all too little for those with energy and initiative ... One that says if you can't make an effort to provide an honest living for yourself and your family then, that's okay, we'll bail you out! And, even worse, to do so we'll run up greater and greater deficits until we are all crushed under a mountain of debt! A mountain of debt that will unfairly act as a deadweight on generation after generation to come!

'Honored guests, I state categorically that the current Administration's present approach to welfare payments is not preventing poverty, it is promoting it! The welfare program and the public debt that goes with it is something not doing good, it is doing harm! It is crying out for drastic reduction! And, when I assume high office, drastic reduction is what it will receive!'

The whole Ball Room jumped to their feet and clapped. The applause was no longer tumultuous or even rapturous, it was adoring and ecstatic.

When the commotion had been given time to die down Oakley moved aside from his seat. 'Let's go in among the guests,' he said to William. 'Squeeze the flesh as the saying goes.'

The two men descended into the main area of the Ball Room and quickly got down to business. Oakley knew better than anyone how much the odd shrewdly directed warm handshake or word of praise was worth in terms of influencing the size of additional campaign contributions many of those present would make.

~

Inside the truck parked on the quiet Manhattan side street Matts and his assistant watched all their instruments. 'We're getting a clear radio "answer back" from all equipment at all locations,' informed the assistant who also had a headset.

'Good,' Matts replied. 'And all our people are clear?'

'Yes,' confirmed the assistant.

'Maintaining countdown then – Ninety seconds.'

~

Rosanne had steered Jack through her revised article blow by blow. 'As you can see it's now got a much more mellow flavor to it,' she pointed out as he came to the end of the article's final page.

'Yes,' he replied fully agreeing. 'You've taken the sting out of it, that was all that was needed. It's okay, absolutely okay.'

'You sure?'

'Sure I'm sure. It's fine. I mean there's still the occasional risky comment, but we can live with that. I mean if anything his predictions of doom and gloom now just sound faintly preposterous. Nobody's going to mind that. No, Rosanne, I have to hand it you, you've done a good job.'

'So it will go out as planned?'

'Well, that was the object of exercise, wasn't it? What more do you want me to say!'

Rosanne's delight was transparent. 'Thanks Jack,' she said flashing the smile which had won the day for her so many times before.

~

Inside Matt's truck, still positioned where it had been all along on the Manhattan side street, the moment he had been counting down towards was about to arrive. 'Six, five, four, three, two, one,' he announced into his microphone in slow, steady, carefully considered, methodical precise steps. The deliberate, measured, gaps between the numbers making the six seconds seem like quite a lot longer.

Then came 'Zero.'

And then if anyone had happened to have been looking from the top of the Empire State Building they would probably have thought war had broken out. Starting at the Queensboro at 59th Street, in a series of massive explosions, less than a second between each, all eight bridges on to Manhattan were blown sky high.

It was most spectacular of all downtown where the Brooklyn, Manhattan and Williamsburg bridges were situated so close together. The effect of the consecutive blasts one after the other here was to send up a tower of flame which momentarily reached to the clouds.

~

In Jack's apartment the noise of the explosions halted the conversation. 'What was that?' Rosanne asked anxiously.

'I don't know,' answered Jack nervously going over to the window. 'It's gone quiet again.'

'It was loud, and more than once, like thunder, can't you see anything?'

'No, there's nothing to see,' he replied as he scanned the skyline for some clue.

'How strange.' Rosanne got up to look for herself. 'No, I agree, I can't see anything either,' she said relaxing as she moved back from the window.

'I don't know,' he shrugged. 'Might have been a plane crash or a gas leak? There's nothing we can do anyway.'

'I guess not,' she replied. 'At any rate, I must head along anyhow. Thanks for your time, Jack.' She picked up her brief case and drifted towards the door.

Jack went with her and kissed her affectionately on the cheek. 'Good night, Rosanne. And good luck with whatever's behind this extraordinary enthusiasm for this article!'

Rosanne just smiled and left. Whatever sound they had heard outside a short while before they had now both forgotten about.

~

At the Queensboro at 59th Street the scene of chaos had to be seen to be believed. The mangled spans of the bridge drooped down into the East River amid searing flames. Burning vehicles were strewn around all over the place, some of them hanging precariously towards the water from the few sections of the bridge that somehow had escaped total destruction.

'Get back! Get back! The bridge has collapsed! Get back!' yelled a solitary policeman attempting the hopeless task of re-directing the traffic approaching the vicinity.

Robert was painting again in his studio, but when his phone rang this time his response was a lot more relaxed than it had been at the start of the evening. He had heard the explosions, he predicted what the message would be. 'Hello?' he said as he answered.

'We won. Paid eight dollars flat! It breezed it!' said the voice on the phone.

'Thanks for letting me know,' he replied hanging up. He raised his eyes to the heavens, he was pleased.

He walked straight back to his canvas, feeling ever more elated as he went. He chuckled to himself about the horse racing code they had chosen to use that evening. It occurred to him that horse racing was a rather frivolous thing to mix up with something as important as what they were aiming to do. But then, on the other hand, they had to use something – to have spoken openly on the phone would have been an unnecessary risk. The words "eight dollars flat" began to reverberate around his head, they had taken on a magical ring, they were the words which meant the operation had been a complete and unqualified success. This really was the beginning!

~

At the Waldorf there was no sign of activity abating, in fact on one side of the Ball Room a dance band was in the process of warming up. Oakley continued to distribute liberal doses of personal magnetism in all directions and, moving from table to table, everywhere he went William went with him. It might have been said to some extent that William was basking in reflected glory but, in all fairness to him, it was true to say that he possessed more than ample amounts of charisma all of his own.

Nevertheless, unexpectedly, as the two politicians carried on with their tour of the tables, William's aide, Steve Strauss, entered the Ball Room from a side door some distance away from them. He had not been at the dinner and was still wearing his day suit. His face showed something wrong and he hurriedly pushed his way through the crowds.

'We have the "snow-belt" in the bag! California and the South, that's where we've got to concentrate!' boomed Oakley loudly to the current table of guests he was standing beside.

'But we're going to get there!' enthused William smiling broadly.

'That's right William, we sure will!' concurred Oakley, 'And you know something else ...'

But then, as Oakley carried on speaking, William felt a tap on his shoulder, he looked round. 'Steve?' he smiled in complete surprise.

Steve wasting no time spoke excitedly into the Mayor's ear. As William listened the smile evaporated from his face, immediately he turned uneasily to grab Oakley's attention. 'Oakley,' he said trying to keep his voice down. But initially Oakley was too engrossed in holding forth to his eager listeners to hear.

'Oakley!' William repeated, in a louder and more urgent tone. This time Oakley looked round at him with a hint of disapproval as much as to suggest how dare anyone interrupt him. But William was undeterred. 'Something has happened,' he whispered loudly into Oakley's ear. 'We must go!'

Oakley looked at him perplexed. 'What?'

'I mean it! It's very serious!' replied William in an undertone so urgent that it left nothing to doubt. 'This is no routine matter!'

Less than fully convinced Oakley all the same afforded William the benefit of the doubt. 'Excuse me, will you,' he suddenly said to the group of guests he had been talking to. 'I have to go and take a phone call. I'll try and be back as soon as I can.' Then, without delay, he strode off with Steve and William towards the Ball Room's side door. 'So what is this all about?' he asked slightly irritably after they had moved sufficiently far away from the main throng.

William collected himself before looking Oakley straight in the eye. 'Every bridge into Manhattan, all eight of them, has been destroyed by explosive!'

'What?' frowned Oakley in astonishment.

'You heard me,' William re-iterated.

'And where did you get that information from?' retorted Oakley semi-dismissively. 'You sure this isn't just some kind of wild rumor?'

'No sir, it's a fact,' Steve assured.

Oakley blinked, for one brief moment it was one of the few times in his life he found himself lost for words.

Not lingering a second longer the three men hurried the rest of the way out of the Ball Room.

CHAPTER 5

Matts and his assistant had had the advantage of foresight. With the bridges destroyed they had immediately made a dash through the Lincoln tunnel on to the mainland. For one thing, had their truck been left on Manhattan and subsequently been found, it might have provided some highly incriminating clues. For another, the value of the equipment on board was too high just to throw away.

Matts and his assistant passed under the river with ease. However, half an hour later, it would have been a different story. With no bridges the tunnels became hopelessly clogged. Thousands upon thousands of vehicles found themselves with nowhere to go. In no time at all there was a traffic jam in the streets of Manhattan the like of which had never before been seen. In the center of town the cacophony of car horns became one solid wall of sound.

'This is unbelievable!' said Rosanne in the back seat of a cab stuck on Park Avenue and having to raise her voice to make herself heard. 'What's going on?'

'Somebody said something happened with the bridges,' came back the driver's rather vague reply.

'We've gone less than half a block in forty minutes!'

'What am I supposed to do about it,' he replied throwing up his arms. 'You want to know what I think? If you want to get up to 89th Street before daylight I suggest you walk!'

Rosanne found this remark singularly unhelpful. She scowled under her breath and turned her head to take another look through the rear window. She was clearly considering all her options. 'The traffic is moving a little faster going the other way,' she observed. 'Can you turn around?'

'What good that going to do? That ain't going to get you to 89th.'

'Obviously not!' she responded with irritation, by now finding the cab driver was rather getting on her nerves. 'But I've got another idea. Just hang a "U", can you?'

'Okay. It's you who's paying,' he conceded as he slowly edged the cab around.

~

In his apartment on 33rd Street Jack had settled down again to watch a movie on TV. He was only half concentrating when the head and shoulders of a newscaster replaced what should have been a commercial break. 'We interrupt this program to bring you a newsflash,' announced the newscaster. The TV picture changed to a shot of a collapsed burning bridge, the newscaster's voice gained pace. 'This was the George Washington bridge and the scene is the same at all the other bridges into Manhattan!' Jack leapt to feet to get closer to the screen. 'At precisely 10.30 p.m. this evening a series of giant man-made explosions ripped into them without warning. Many people in cars who were using the bridges at the time are feared dead. So far the New York Police Department have been unable to come up with any explanation as to who was responsible. We now go over live to our reporter Barbara Mandel who is at the scene on East 59th ...'

Jack looked stunned.

~

William Donaldson and Oakley Cunningham had returned to their suite in the Waldorf along with Steve Strauss. Commissioner McMichael had joined them plus some of the secret servicemen. 'Okay, if the traffic isn't moving an inch we had better stay here for the time being,' said William tensely pacing back and forth round room. 'What fresh details do we have?'

'All the bridges went at exactly the same time,' replied the Commissioner. 'We think detonation was probably done by radio control. We still don't have casualty figures yet, but they've got to run into at least a couple of hundred.'

'Several hundred?' gasped William. 'Jesus! But who? Who would want to do such a thing?'

'Somebody's got to be crazy,' interjected Oakley, 'it doesn't make sense.'

'No, it doesn't,' agreed the Commissioner flatly.

'No sense at all! What possible point is there in doing this?' added William getting angry. 'Can't somebody tell me what is the point!'

The sheer force of the Mayor's semi-rhetorical question, its tone so enraged and exasperated, for a moment seemed to silence the room. Then suddenly a voice spoke up. 'It's clearly a terrorist act,' announced Scott Taylor, a man anonymously dressed in plain grey suit standing near the door.

William looked at him indignantly almost as if he should not have spoken. 'Well, that much is surely kinda goddam obvious!' he said sarcastically. 'And, anyway, who are you?'

'Scott Taylor, Central Intelligence Agency, I'm here working helping advise Mr Cunningham's secret service protection squad.'

'I see, sorry I didn't mean to bite your head off,' said William apologising for his abruptness. 'But given it's terrorists, who are they, where are they from, and *what* are they hoping to gain by doing this?

But before anyone could reply the phone rang, Steve Strauss was nearest and picked it up. His expression instantly indicated that this was no ordinary call. 'Mayor Donaldson, it's the President for you.' William immediately took the receiver.

~

Not only had it been Matts and his assistant's priority to get away quickly from Manhattan that evening. The same applied to Eliot and his collaborators in the dinghies. Consequently Robert knew he would be on his own until the next day when everything would be discussed and therefore, though it was getting late, he occupied himself working on in his studio. After all painting was his chosen career and, as with most outstanding artists, any accusation of obsession would probably have been taken by him entirely as a compliment.

However, a wandering mind was also an important part of an artist's make-up, and Robert was no exception. His thoughts drifted from one thing to another but, try as he might, there was no escape from Rosanne featuring greatly. He cast his mind back through the whole evening. Having first asked her there, then firmly regretted having done so, he now kicked himself for having let her leave. After all she would not have known what the messages about the horse at Aqueduct meant, it would have just seemed like he had had an innocent bet.

Of course there was Dawn to consider, who he loved dearly, and was now stuck out in some strange ship on some ocean. And again, there were a multitude of other problems which could not be simply dismissed. But whether Rosanne's entry into his life was something he welcomed or not, it was not something he could easily resist. The more he dwelt on it the more he wished he had not forced himself to have been so careful.

Then the door bell rang, it was close to midnight. Robert nearly decided not to answer but on reflection thought better of it. He slowly went to the lobby entryphone. 'Yes?' he said gingerly.

'It's Rosanne. I can't get home.'

Robert's heart nearly stopped. 'What?' he frowned.

'Robert, I can't got home,' she repeated.

'You'd better come up then,' he replied, disguising the turmoil he felt. He released the door and waited for her.

'Hi,' she said entering and catching her breath. 'Something has thrown the City into chaos tonight, nothing's moving.'

'Really?' he answered without so much as a flicker of an eyelid.

'The traffic is ... Well, I don't know how to describe it, there is no word – the traffic has just totally stopped!'

'Stopped? Why's that?'

'I don't know for sure, all I've been doing for the last hour is sitting in a cab!'

'Jesus,' frowned Robert completely dead-pan, his acting ability was competent to say the least.

'But anyway I've already got your article cleared,' she smiled looking at him closely.

'That was quick.'

'My editor lives on the way home, I stopped by.'

'Aha,' replied Robert now understanding how she came to get caught in the traffic. He gazed at her, she looked even more radiant than before.

'Seeing this piece is so important to you, I wanted you to know as soon as possible.'

'Well, thanks,' he replied studying everything about her in ever increasing detail.

'But Robert,' she said stepping closer, her voice cracking with emotion. 'That's not the only reason I'm here again. I had to come back. I couldn't stop thinking about you.' She wrapped her arms around him and buried her head on his shoulder. 'I couldn't help myself, I really couldn't.'

He pulled her closer to him and held her tight. He could feel her erect nipples pressing into his chest from under her dress. He rang his hand slowly up her back and passed his fingers through her silky blonde hair. The warmth of her body felt wonderful as she clung to him as if her very life depended on it. 'I'm very happy you did come back,' he told her softly.

'I'm so glad,' she whispered. 'I love you. I love you more than you will ever know.' She drew her head back just enough to see his face. As she brought her lips to his he could see there were tears in her eyes. But these were now tears of joy.

'I love you too,' he said when their first kiss was over. It had not been the sort of kiss anyone would ever be likely to forget.

'Let's not waste any more time,' she murmured smoulderingly as she removed her shoes.

'Let's not,' he replied. He led her through to the bedroom. In one swift motion she pulled her dress over her head and lay down spread-eagle on the bed. She was not bashful by nature, nor did she need to be. The body she exposed was true perfection in every way. Her torso was hour-glass and her long slender limbs seemed to stretch on forever. She leant forward and pushed her panties down over her ankles letting them fall from her toes on to the floor. She was now completely naked. She lay back again and watched Robert undressing. She was breathing deeply and massaging herself unashamedly. She was in an heightened state, half out of control, and that was the way she liked it. When he finally climbed over her she was not disappointed and nor was he.

~

TV coverage of the bridge fiasco went on throughout the night. From scores of different cameras there were shots of the damage from every conceivable angle. There were opinions offered and rumors suggested of every variety imaginable. There were interviews with firefighters, with medical personnel, with survivors, with Mayor Donaldson and with Commissioner McMichael.

But only when the morning came was the true extent of the devastation fully visible.

A helicopter with a TV camera and reporter aboard flew over the southern tip of the island. Below it were the Brooklyn, Manhattan and Williamsburg bridges, all reduced to heaps of collapsed twisted metal barely rising above the water. Pictures from the chopper were being relayed live as the reporter spoke. 'This is the state of all the bridges into Manhattan today. Damaged beyond repair is how most experts are describing them. And quite apart from the tragic loss of life, the disruptive effect on the whole Metropolitan area is considered virtually inestimable. Police have closed the Lincoln and Midtown tunnels to all but emergency vehicles. The City is paralysed. Nothing, simply nothing, like this has ever happened before.'

Robert and Rosanne watched this broadcast from their bed. 'I'm numb, really numb,' she said pulling herself closer to him, her voice quiet and subdued. 'It's horrible, just so horrible. Think of all those people killed.'

'Yes, it doesn't sink in all that easily,' he replied gently. He reached for the remote control and switched off the TV. He could tell she was genuinely upset and he found himself having to comfort her more than he had bargained for.

'What have they done to deserve it? What purpose can there be in an act such as this?' she pleaded.

'I don't know. It's just senseless,' he responded dead-pan.

'Senseless, it's worse than senseless,' she said shaking her head.

'Yes, I know it is, Rosanne. But don't let it get to you. There's nothing we can do, really there isn't. There's really nothing more one can say about it.'

'I know there isn't. But how can people do such a thing?'

'I don't know,' he said kissing her lightly on the lips, 'I don't know.'

For a moment she then stared at him, and with much relief he could sense that her initial shock was beginning to subside. It was not a conversation he had found easy and he hoped it was now over.

'I just hate to think of all the suffering,' she sighed. 'So much pain and misery, I just hate to think about it ...'

'Yes,' he answered slowly. 'So do we all.' And when she had no further reply he got up and walked towards his bathroom.

~

That same morning the "Belle Epoque", the ship Dawn had clandestinely met up with after flying to Nassau, was out on the high seas. A gale was freshening and in all directions the horizon was only the meeting place of grey skies and stormy waters. On the ship's bridge a crew member manned the wheel and Stefan and Dawn stood nearby.

It was over a week since they had left the Bahamas and in that time Dawn had never felt so isolated. Stefan had no interest in talking to her beyond brief exchanges relating only to business. And the dozen or so crew turned out to be a mixed bag of Koreans, Algerians and Portuguese who spoke no more than a smattering of English. Before long she was reduced to spending most of the day in her cabin alone. She had prepared herself mentally for this voyage but even so she was finding it something of a trial.

Stefan took a glance at the ship's radar and then moved away again. 'When are we going to know where we are going?' he asked Dawn impatiently.

'Soon,' she replied blankly. It was a question over the last week she had already grown tired of answering.

'But this is unreasonable – we cannot keep on endlessly changing course!' he declared abrasively.

Dawn forced herself to appear calmer than she felt. 'Until we're contacted you are going to have to be patient.'

'Patient!' he shouted excitedly. 'What are you talking about! I thought this was going to be quick! So did the crew! And it's not so simple! What about the Coastguards! What about the satellites in the sky! Vessels seeming to go nowhere sooner or later start to attract attention!'

'I realize that every bit as much as you do,' she answered still trying to keep things as defused as possible.

'So when will we be contacted?' he glared.

'I don't know yet,' she replied gritting her teeth. 'I really don't know. But soon. That's all I can say.'

'It had better be soon.' He turned and headed off the bridge leaving her standing there. Once his footsteps faded she glumly returned to her cabin. She consoled herself that if the truth be known the person on board most eager to receive a radio communication was not Stefan but herself.

~

Mayor Donaldson had spent the entire morning visiting the sites of the bridges and the Queensboro was his last stop on the circuit. He stood by the East River bleakly watching teams of U.S. Navy divers and Army engineers examining the wrecked structure. Steve Strauss came up to him. 'I've got the total on all the bridges, sir, 191 dead and 470 injured. It's only because it's August and the water's warm that the fatalities aren't higher still.'

William slowly shook his head. 'Incredible,' he sighed staring into thin air. He had already heard so many grim facts in the last twelve hours that he was too drained to find a stronger reaction.

An Army officer walked over to them dressed in his denim fatigues. 'Good morning, Mayor, Colonel Graham, U.S. Army Corps of Engineers.'

'Good morning, Colonel,' he responded. 'Is there anything more you can tell me that I should know?'

'I don't think so, sir. I know you've been round the other bridges. All I can say is that the team who placed these charges were expert – blowing bridges of this size is no piece of cake. They knew exactly what they were doing, inside and out.'

'And like elsewhere no clues at all?'

'No sir. Standard detonators, standard radio triggers, regular high explosive. Whoever did this left no calling cards. They've covered their tracks perfectly.'

William heaved another frustrated sigh. 'Thank you, Colonel. I think we're due to meet again at my offices later.'

'That's right, sir.'

'I'll see you then,' he said as he and Steve moved on.

~

Rosanne had left Robert's studio after breakfast. They had agreed to meet again that evening. Robert had then waited for his visitors among whom would be Professor Paul Stewart. The Professor arrived at eleven o'clock sharp. He was always punctual and had come to Manhattan the night before to avoid any complications connected with the bridges. He was a spritely man well over seventy and always carried a cane and wore a bow-tie, both of which had become his trademarks to generations of Economics students at Princeton University. His mind was as alert and as fast as anyone one could ever hope to come across, and his bright blue eyes sparkled and twinkled in such a way that all who met him were drawn to him. He also possessed an infectious sense of humor which accompanied him everywhere he went.

The Professor drank quite a lot but it never seemed to affect him. Bourbon on the rocks was his favorite and today was no exception. Robert poured him one immediately he entered the studio and they toasted the success of their joint undertaking.

Shortly later when Eliot, Gil and Warren turned up the Professor asked for his glass to be refilled and they all drank a second toast. Even Eliot managed a flicker of a smile.

But this was not a celebration and none of them regarded it as such. They were there to hear Professor Stewart's views and after a couple of minutes he rose from his seat and began to pace the room. The others waited for him to speak. There could be a theatricality about him on some occasions, as if he felt suspense added impact, and today appeared to be one of them. He crossed the room once, his cane striking the floor loudly with every stride, then he crossed again, it was only after he turned for the third time that he suddenly came out with it. 'The starting figure is 300 billion dollars!'

'That much?' questioned Robert without showing any special surprise. He knew that the Professor would have it all worked out, as did the other three.

'Yes,' he replied scanning their faces with his twinkling eyes. 'But that is only for the first year and what we propose to do will take at least five! In year two 600 billion dollars will be needed, in year three 900 billion, in year four 1,200 billion and in year five ...'

'1,500,' Eliot interjected.

'Correct,' smiled the Professor. 'And the reason it's phased that way is that the system will take time to adjust. Only so much cash can be absorbed at once.' He paused a moment and grinned. 'Of course I realize we're talking about a great deal of money here, but I have run and re-run the projections on the computers at Princeton and anything less would do no more than scratch the surface!

'Okay,' said Robert picking up the phone. 'I'll call Matts to issue our demand. He has the wording, all he needs are the numbers.'

~

William Donaldson chaired a meeting he had called in a conference room at New York City Hall to try to unravel the mess created by the destruction of the bridges. About a dozen people seated round the table formed the core of those present. These included Steve Strauss, Commissioner McMichael, the City Treasurer and other municipal officers. Oakley Cunningham and Scott Taylor from the CIA also sat in. In fact it was because Oakley had become sufficiently impressed by what he saw as Scott's methodical mind that he had suggested to William that the CIA man again be present.

William had an agenda in front of him designed to tackle each particular facet of the problems they faced one by one. As the meeting progressed specialists and advisers were trooped in and out. A construction contractor and Colonel Graham of the Army engineers were currently giving their views on the massive task of getting the bridges operational again. 'At least a year! Don't be ridiculous! The President has given unlimited Federal Aid on this!' William protested.

'It's not a matter of money, it's a matter of time,' answered the contractor politely. 'These bridges are going to have to be re-built virtually from scratch. Piles are going to have to driven, stress factors re-calculated, all in all it's a huge task.'

'So these "damaged beyond repair" reports aren't media exaggeration?' the Mayor said.

'I'm afraid not, sir,' the Colonel replied.

'If you really want the truth I'd say we're talking eighteen months, and that's working round the clock,' added the contractor.

'Shit!' exclaimed the Mayor, slowly but reluctantly coming to terms with the scale of what the City faced. 'Okay then,' he ventured after a brief pause, 'I guess we're just going to have to live with it. Meanwhile the Army goes ahead with the plan to assemble temporary pontoon bridges.'

'Very well, sir,' said the Colonel getting up. He and the contractor left the room.

'Okay, next we have the guy who's going to organize the emergency river ferries,' the Mayor said checking his list. 'You sure you want to sit through all this, Oakley?' he then added in a quick aside wishing to ensure he was not taking up too much of the Senator's time.

'No, William, I'm fine, I'm here to be of help in any way I can,' was his instant response.

'Thanks Oakley, I appreciate it,' said William proceeding to get straight on with business. 'Okay, let's bring the ferry guy in can we!'

A secretary went to the door to fetch the representative of the ferry company, but at that very same moment a City official entered with an urgent air and walked straight over to Mayor Donaldson. 'The TV Networks are on to us, they're getting a message through – it's from people claiming they did this!'

William frowned, as did Oakley and all the others round the table. 'A message? What is this message?'

'They're putting it on a fax to us now, Mayor. We'll have it any second.'

'All right put the ferry guy on hold!' William instructed the secretary.

~

Robert had turned the TV in his studio on but left the sound down as they all knew it would not be long before another newsflash was put out. Professor Stewart was on to his fourth bourbon on the rocks but Eliot, Warren and Gil drank no more.

Warren and Gil were both recently turned thirty, just a couple of years younger than Eliot. Along with Zak they were the backbone of a team of only roughly twenty men. All four of them had met in the Military but had long since been out of uniform. Their faces showed a hard edge but strangely enough no real presence of malice. 'You know we hurt a lot of innocent people last night,' commented Warren in a measured tone.

'We did,' replied Robert.

'And it pains us all,' added the Professor with genuine sincerity. 'But we are like generals planning a battle, to ensure victory there will always be casualties on both sides.'

'Exactly,' said Eliot dryly. 'The fact of the matter is that the way we're doing it is the only way to do it.'

'Regrettably so,' nodded the Professor. 'Gentle persuasion is not an alternative.'

'Wouldn't even get us past square one!' Eliot stated categorically. 'When you're dealing with assholes, you have to deal with them accordingly!'

'Very true,' replied the Professor. He put his glass of Bourbon down and started to walk around again. 'All in all the position could not be clearer – To get what we want we have to hit them where it hurts!'

'And right now the ball's in their court!' Robert declared.

'It is indeed!' the Professor exclaimed with another twinkle in his eye. 'And one thing is for certain – it's going to cause a stir!'

~

The fax of their message had duly arrived at City Hall and it was received with astonishment. They had gone through it line by line, their wide mouths open. Twice Steve Strauss had been sent to speak with the TV Networks on the phone to try to trace its source. Even so by the time he returned to the room for the second time the mood of most of those round the table was becoming lighter.

'Okay, I've learnt exactly how the message got to them,' Steve informed as he sat down again. 'It was found in a series of unlocked cars on parking lots near each of the Networks' offices. They received phone calls giving them the parking lot location, car make and number plate. And there's more to it than that, when they went to look for the message they discovered it had actually been transmitted into these cars using portable fax machines fitted under their front seats! The fax machines were fitted with disposable SIM cards, so much less chance of any digital trace than the Internet, and of course the vehicles were stolen too. Frankly, all in all, this delivery system was pretty much as foolproof as you could get!'

'That is quite something,' acknowledged Commissioner McMichael. 'I've never heard of people going to as much trouble as that.'

'Maybe not, but this must still be the work of cranks!' William responded looking at the piece of paper again, his expression now really only one of amazement. 'What the fuck do they hope achieve!'

'Well, that's the big question,' smiled Oakley clearly seeing humor somewhere. 'Show it to me one more time.'

William duly passed the paper over and Oakley put on his reading glasses. 'You know this really is about the most over-the-top thing I've ever heard!' Oakley quipped mockingly as he studied it. 'I know it's inappropriate to laugh but frankly I'm beginning to find it very hard not to.' The Senator began to quote from it out loud: '"*We are anonymous but we are in your midst. We executed the gold robbery in Queens and we removed the bridges from Manhattan to give you a flavor of our power! We demand unequivocally that BOTH United States political parties prior to the forthcoming Presidential Election guarantee that, when either is elected, the welfare budget and associated programs be increased by 300 billion dollars a year for each of the next five years.*"'

'You know how much that is!' Steve took the opportunity to jest. 'It means 300 billion in the first, 600 billion in the second and so on, taken cumulatively that's nearly 5 trillion dollars!'

'It's insane – you can't even begin to take it seriously!' William exclaimed.

Oakley had to smile again. To him the document was becoming more and more of an absurdity as every minute passed. 'Listen to this,' he said moving on: '"*We do not care where the money comes from but you know as well as we do there is money to spare! IF THIS DEMAND IS MET WE WILL AT LEAST BE PARTIALLY SATISFIED. BUT, IF IT IS NOT, YOU WILL HEAR FROM US AGAIN, AND IT WILL BE SOON!*"'

Oakley shaking his head but still smiling handed the fax back to William. 'Yes, I've got to agree with you – Cranks! There really are some sick people around! If this isn't a hoax I don't know what is!'

'Not necessarily,' suddenly announced Scott Taylor. He had deliberately said nothing at all up until then. And unlike the others his face had not even once shown so much as a glimmer of a smile.

Oakley was startled by Scott's comment. 'You think this is for real?'

'In my opinion, yes,' he answered, aware now that he had become the sole focus of attention in the room.

Oakley sounded even more staggered. You're telling me the people who sent this are genuinely who they claim to be?' There was no smile on his face any longer, nor anyone else's.

Scott hesitated, he wanted to choose his words carefully. However, once decided, he was never a person frightened to say what he thought. 'It's much too elaborate to be a hoax,' he explained, his voice carrying the authority of firm conviction. 'More importantly we can be sure that whoever did this must have had advance warning of the bridges going up. A few hours wouldn't have been anything like enough time to put this together. Stealing cars, fitting faxes in them, parking them in the right place – that adds up to days of preparation.

'Then there's another point, which is just as valid: What stands out most of all about the gold robbery and the bridge destruction? Ruthlessness no question, but even ahead of that I'd put complete thoroughness. And what do we encounter again here in the way this demand has been sent to us? Complete thoroughness.

'It's definitely the same people!'

As he stopped speaking Scott saw Oakley and William nod. It was clear they had listened and were unable to disagree. 'All right,' said Oakley after he had reflected a moment. 'But does it really make any difference anyway? Nobody's going to take any notice of this lunatic proposal on Welfare in a million years!'

'Absolutely!' agreed William. 'If anything these people are even more nuts than we thought! They haven't got a hope!'

'Of course they haven't got a hope,' Scott responded. 'And they may well be nuts. But on what we've seen so far, I think underestimating them would not be wise. Whoever they are, they are very, very dangerous. I would say they are capable of anything. Who knows what they might try next. They must be found!'

William nodded gravely. 'Yes, they must be!'

'And fast,' said Oakley staring across the table. 'Meanwhile I'm going to tell them exactly what I think of their demand!'

'The President has done the same,' informed Steve.

'Issued a rejection?' checked Oakley.

'Yes, and the Networks tell me it's very strong.'

'Well, mine will be even stronger!' declared Oakley. 'But I'm glad to hear the President can at least do something right, if only very occasionally!'

Oakley's political jibe re-introduced just a touch of humor to the meeting. There was no love lost between Oakley and President Charles Guthrie and their frequent acidic remarks about each other had become something people had grown to relish.

~

The wait in Robert's studio for TV coverage of their message was not in vain. First there was a newsflash. Then a fuller report in a scheduled bulletin followed shortly later: 'And to return to today's headline,' read the newscaster. 'Unnamed terrorists have claimed responsibility for the demolition of Manhattan's bridges and the bullion heist in Queens. Their expressed aim is a near five trillion dollar hike in Welfare programs. Both the President and Presidential challenger Oakley Cunningham have issued statements unreservedly dismissing this demand ...'

Robert flicked off the TV. 'Predictable,' he said in a clipped tone.

'Very predictable,' said the Professor.

'The fools think they can ignore us,' stated Eliot.

'Yes, but we never thought it would be that easy,' said the Professor with a smile. 'The main thing is the news is out. We now go and see Matts in Connecticut. Matts is such a technical genius.'

'And we tighten the screw immediately?' asked Eliot.

'There is no virtue in delay,' answered the Professor picking up his cane, the twinkle in his eyes as strong as ever. 'No virtue at all.'

'So tonight then?' queried Eliot.

'If we can,' the Professor replied.

CHAPTER 6

After Rosanne had left Robert's studio she had gone home to 89th Street. The journey had taken longer than usual but at least the traffic was moving. She had changed her clothes and then set out for her office. With the copy date now imminent it was necessary to get Robert's article typed up and into the printers as soon as possible.

It was mid-morning by the time she walked into the reception area of Prestige Publications. Not that this mattered as her job did not really involve strictly fixed hours. In any case it turned out that most of the staff who did not live on Manhattan had been unable to get into work anyway.

Rosanne saw Jack and they chatted for several minutes, the only topic of conversation understandably being the bridges. She then went to her desk and settled down.

Just before one Jack came over again and told her he was going out to his lunch appointment. Like many executives in the more glamorous end of the publishing business Jack was big on long lunches. Rosanne told him that she intended to call it a day once she had finished and would most probably not be there when he returned. Jack had no objection to this.

For her own lunch she called in a tuna fish salad from one of the local delis and kept pressing on with the piece. By 3.30 it was done and she headed down to the street to find a cab. Both the upheaval and the passion of the previous night were beginning to catch up with her and she was looking forward to taking a couple of hours rest.

Like yesterday Larry was once again the doorman on duty at 89th Street. 'Good afternoon, Miss Lindblade,' he said opening the cab door for her.

'Hi Larry,' she smiled. Larry was always cheerful and she liked him.

'We've taken delivery of a flower arrangement for you Miss Lindblade. Only came a few minutes ago. I tell you it's huge, we have it in the lobby.'

'Oh? From whom?' she asked with a hint of excitement.

'I don't know,' he replied. 'There's an envelope with it I believe. Anyhow you'll need a hand up with it.' He opened the lobby door for her and they headed in.

'Gosh!' said Rosanne thrilled as soon as she saw the arrangement sitting in the corner. 'It's wonderful!'

'I knew you'd like it,' replied Larry as he stooped to pick it up. And as they walked towards the elevator he could see her staring at the attached envelope dying to open it. But she refrained.

Not that Larry wanted to be in on the secret. He knew Rosanne had an army of admirers and it could be any of them. Moreover, his salary was only modest and he counted heavily on tips to get by – it was not in his interests to be indiscreet. The elevator bell sounded and they entered.

'Terrible thing last evening,' commented Larry as they rode up.

'Truly awful,' she replied, though at this point in time her mind was really rather more concentrating on the envelope.

'I just don't understand it,' added Larry.

'Nor me,' she concurred somewhat distantly.

The elevator doors opened and they emerged on to the sixteenth floor. Rosanne had her keys at the ready and they went straight in. Larry had to go slowly as the arrangement was almost too wide for the door. However, with a certain amount of delicate manoeuvring he was able to squeeze it through. 'Where would you like me to put it, Miss Lindblade?'

'Let's see,' she said looking around, 'over there by the window I think would be best.'

'Sure.' He carried it over to a table beside the curtains.

'Thanks again, Larry,' she smiled pushing a $10 bill into his hand.

'Always my pleasure, Miss Lindblade,' he replied as he left.

Rosanne had the envelope in her hands even before Larry had closed the door behind him. Her heart was beating fast. She already knew from the handwriting on it that this was something that had been done via a florists. But this just added to the mystery. She had instantly made a mental list of all the various possibilities, at the top of which she had understandably placed Robert at number one. Yet since her list had actually extended down as far as the low teens it would have been true to say that the sender's identity in her estimation was by no means a foregone conclusion.

At any rate now, as she withdrew the card from the envelope, it was at last time for her to put the accuracy of her guesswork to the test.

However, when she came to read the card, the combination of message and sender was not something that had crossed her mind at all. It simply read: *'MY LOVE, I AM DIVORCING. WILLIAM.'* And that was all it said.

And, after a moment, Rosanne's first reaction was to smile.

~

A large secluded country house in Connecticut set in three hundred acres was where the group of political activists had their headquarters. Robert had bought it about two years previously with his own money. Nevertheless, the purchase had been made through nominees so that its ownership was not in his name.

One of the features of the house were its extensive cellars and Matts had spent over a year secretly installing something approaching ten million dollars worth of equipment in them. Once again this undertaking had been financed by Robert. Even so, though Robert's painting career had made him very wealthy, there was a limit to his resources. It had been to make sure that they had virtually unlimited funds that Eliot had proposed the bullion robbery.

Professor Stewart, Eliot, Warren and Gil arrived at the house by helicopter at shortly after four o'clock in the afternoon. Robert had decided to remain in Manhattan.

Eliot, Warren and Gil were all trained helicopter pilots and, as with everything else, nothing had been left to chance – for months they had flown once or twice a week between the house and the East 34th Street heliport so that their comings and goings would appear sufficiently commonplace to any onlookers as not to attract any undue attention. Though naturally, by the same token, it was not a trip they wished to be seen undertaking too often either; but today, with the Professor, it was important.

Matts was at work at one of the several computers in the basement as the Professor and Eliot entered. 'So far so good, eh?' said the Professor waving his cane.

'So far so good,' concurred Matts.

'And the next stage is problem free?'

'Of course. When have I ever let you down?'

'Never Matts, but maximum momentum has to be maintained.'

'It will be,' he said turning his head away from his computer screen. 'But even I was amazed by the figures you put in the demand! I mean I knew it had to be a lot, but nearly 5 trillion – I was astounded!'

'Well, everybody was!' smiled the Professor. 'But if there's going to be any lasting effect it's really very simple. If you split $300 billion a year between what is at the very least 40 million poor people that only gives them less than $150 a week each, which doesn't exactly go very far ... Then we've also got to build housing, build hospitals, build schools, educate and rehabilitate those who need it, and so on and so forth. It's never-ending!'

'Yes, I suppose when you look at it that way it isn't so much after all,' conceded Matts, briefly taking off his strong glasses to give them a wipe with a handkerchief. 'Then so be it!' he declared returning his spectacles to the bridge of his nose. 'And as far as tonight goes, everything is in place. We will have ten units in the field and that will be enough.'

'Good,' said Professor Stewart looking delighted. He gazed down at this thick set, bald headed, short-sighted little man with something akin to reverence – In technical matters the Professor knew that Matts ruled supreme. 'And how exactly will we do it?' he ventured to ask, more from curiosity than from any need of assurance.

'Timed charges of course,' Matts replied. 'Otherwise we'd need at least twenty times more men than we have. But the result will be the same. We'll bring down a few dozen power lines, disable around fifty crucial circuit breakers and then create one "short"! As one power back-up device cuts in it will blow another – In no time at all the effect will be to build up a chain reaction! It's going to create havoc, real havoc! The whole Inter-State Electricity interconnection system will be up shit creek!'

The Professor nodded approvingly patting Matts on the back.

'I'll go and re-check that none of our men have any last minute hitches,' announced Eliot.

'Okay,' replied Matts. '3.00 a.m. Eastern time!'

'To the second,' concurred Eliot heading off.

~

William had adjourned his meeting at City Hall after it became clear that every one needed a break. After all he and Oakley had only had two hours sleep and Commissioner McMichael none. It had got to the stage that fatigue had made clear thought more or less impossible.

William had then been driven back to Gracie Mansion alone, and called from his car on the way to arrange for the flowers to be sent to Rosanne. Remaining obsessively secretive about his private life he had even gone so far as to tell his driver to pull over and stand outside the limousine while he made the call.

Then, on arrival back at the Mansion, he went immediately to Mary and told her he wanted to have a serious talk. Cold-blooded as it seemed he now wanted to clear the air. He suggested they use his private office because there they would not be disturbed. Mary agreed, she could tell from his manner what it was likely to be about.

When he began the discussion there was inevitably a certain amount of beating about the bush but once he had made himself plain she took it remarkably well. In her heart of hearts she had long ago come to accept that their relationship had disintegrated.

'It's no good, Mary,' he said purposefully. 'You know that, and I know that. We are better off if we go our separate ways.' He had leant over backwards to keep the conversation low key and was succeeding. 'I propose you move to our apartment on Fifth Avenue and obviously take Simon and Gwen with you. We will still see each other from time to time because of the children, but really I think this is something we have to face up to.'

'This is a sad ending to twelve years,' she replied quite composed and, in a way, strangely unbitter. Indeed, if anything her relative apathy just served to act as another damning indictment of the failure of their marriage.

'I know it's a sad ending, Mary,' he continued, 'but staying together is not an alternative. And, contrary to what you think, I love Simon and Gwen very much. But I'm sure they stand a better chance of re-adjusting at this early age than if we tried to hang on until they are older.' William had an uncanny knack of justifying everything to himself in such a way that he was always able to feel he was in the right.

Mary just nodded, she was an intelligent woman. Argument would have achieved nothing. And anyway William's trite generalization about what age was best for children to see their parents break up was of no interest to her. All she cared about were her own children and it was clear she cared a great deal more than he did.

'Financially,' William went on, 'you do not need me to tell you that you will never want for anything. I sincerely wish our parting to be as amiable as it possibly can be.'

'Yes,' she agreed quietly. 'Neither of us have any desire to make things any more difficult than they already are.'

'Thank you, Mary. Thank you for being so understanding. And Mary?'

'Yes?'

William hesitated just a second, things having gone so well, he did not want to appear indelicate. 'I was wondering what sort of timetable you had in mind?'

'Don't worry, William,' she replied briskly, but still without any apparent bitterness. 'I've already decided, I will go today,'

'You absolutely sure?' He said not wishing to appear too hasty.

'Yes, I'm quite sure,' she said. 'I'll call the apartment now and tell them to expect us.' Their Fifth Avenue apartment was always kept fully staffed and ready to move into.

'I'm sorry it's turned out this way,' he added slightly unconvincingly.

'It's too late for apologies William, much too late.' She got up and left. It was only in these parting words that she let any emotion show, and it was not bitterness, it was contempt.

~

As usual Robert painted throughout the day. He and the Professor might be the intellectual architects of the plan they had put together, but in its early stages their role was strictly behind the scenes. It was not that he was in any way frightened to get his hands dirty, it was just that when it came to the operational side he accepted that there were other people better qualified.

He knew that at 3 a.m. that night a far greater trauma than the bridges would hit the nation, but he felt the end more than justified the means. Any moral doubts had long since vanished. It was not even something he gave thought to any more.

If he was having to do any thinking it was about Rosanne. He saw no conflict between having her around and his other activities, but he knew in some ways he might be tempting fate. In addition, pangs of conscience about Dawn were real, if only intermittent. What would happen when she returned from the "Belle Epoque" he was for the time being prepared to conveniently ignore.

However, as far as overall deception went, he did not see Rosanne as a problem. Now the Welfare demand was public he saw no reason not to admit he had some sympathy with it – after all his political views she had by now committed to paper in triplicate. But that would be as far as it would go. Under no circumstances would he dream of taking her into his confidence.

Robert checked the time. It was six o'clock. Nine hours to zero hour, two hours to when Rosanne arrived. If he were asked which event he was looking forward to more it was questionable if he would have been able to reply. He was only human.

~

Rosanne had had her nap. As a person she needed plenty of rest and did not function well when she was worn out.

She had gone to sleep thinking about William and had woken up thinking about Robert. Now, as she applied some light touches of make-up in her dressing room mirror, she was thinking about both. Then, before she had reached any conclusions, her door bell rang.

Still wearing a kimono she had bought on a trip to Japan she went to her front door and looked through its spy-hole. 'William!' she called out in surprise as she released the lock.

William entered smiling, he kissed her affectionately on the lips. 'I see you got the flowers,' he said gesturing towards them.

'Yes, thank you, they're fantastic,' she enthused.

'But what about the note that came with them?' he grinned.

'Is it really true?' she smiled.

'I finally decided I had no choice!'

Rosanne threw her arms around him. 'I'm very pleased!'

'I talked it over with Oakley Cunningham, then I had the crisis with the bridges, then I thought about it some more, then I told Mary.'

'Did you?' said Rosanne as she unwrapped her arms. 'Come and sit down. What did she say?'

William and Rosanne went to the sofa. 'In the end it wasn't that difficult,' he replied, unsure of whether it looked better to underplay or overplay it. 'She knew our marriage was long over.'

'It's great news,' she said getting up and going over to her bar. 'Let's drink to it.'

William had already noticed there was nothing underneath her kimono and having a drink was not what he had in mind. He stood up and went over to the bar too. He looked straight into her eyes. 'Rosanne, you're not going to bawl me out are you?'

She stared back at him. 'What? Why should I bawl you out?' she asked.

'With Oakley in town and all the problems we have, I have to head off again ...'

'That doesn't stop us having a drink, does it?'

But now she was only being playful and he could see that what he was thinking she was thinking too. 'I don't want a drink,' he said gently taking hold of her. She smiled. He slipped his hands on to her shoulders inside her kimono. He invited a kiss. She readily consented.

Soon his hands moved to her breasts and she let the kimono slide down to the floor. Again she was naked and again they kissed, longer and harder. She undid his shirt and ran her hand down the full length of his front. She let it rest there until she felt the pleasure might be too much. She pulled him closer and closer. Slowly she lifted her legs off the floor and wrapped them around him. Again the sound of her breathing was filling the room again she was losing herself in her own private world. 'Take me,' she whispered curling her tongue round his ear. 'Take me now, I can't wait ...'

~

Matts had spent months studying the electricity supply industry in the United States. There were hundreds of utilities producing large amounts of power and just a handful with really massive output such as the Tennessee Valley Authority. But he knew the achilles heel was not the generating capacity itself but the system of distribution to the customers.

Power was transmitted into people's homes and work places through a complicated grid. Whereas there was no single unified national network servicing the entire country, there were many arrangements which existed between different States and regions. These arrangements formed a patchwork which largely overlapped.

The advantage of this sort of networking was well known. If power failed in one area then capacity could be switched from surrounding districts to make up the shortfall. Indeed, most of the time this would happen within a fraction of a second without the consumer even being aware of it. However, this approach also had its dangers in that, if things went wrong, not a small but a huge area would be blacked out.

Of course, ever since 1965 when New York City and most of the North East had been without power for thirteen hours, the precautions taken by the authorities were much improved. Peaks in demand were now monitored by sophisticated computers. Faults could be located far faster. Back-up supplies put on line virtually immediately. Additional 500,000 volt overhead transmission lines provided operators with greater flexibility. Even the circuit breakers, the giant fuses which protected so many key parts of the system against overload, had a response time previously thought unachievable.

Yet all these measures were designed to deal with what were basically standard contingencies. Types of events which occurred from time to time but which were essentially random or freakish. And whereas it was partly this unpredictability that made them such a nuisance, it was also the fact that problems tended to be scattered around which made them containable. Even if several power stations went off stream simultaneously or there were a series of transformer burn-outs or lightning knocked out dozens of pylons, disruption would normally be kept to a minimum.

The trouble with what Matts had in store was there was nothing random about it. And no number of contingency plans would have been of much use. The odds of faults arising in the pattern and sequence he had concocted were billions to one against. But he had the odds fixed so this was not his concern.

Matts, Eliot and Warren left the house in Connecticut at dusk. Professor Stewart had been driven back to Princeton hours earlier.

Eliot had spent the last couple of hours of the afternoon checking and re-checking everything. He was entirely satisfied that all units were in place and ready to go. They had men in Nevada and Colorado, and in Texas and Tennessee. They had men in Washington State to cut off the vast transmission line that linked utilities on the West Coast with the Peace River project in British Columbia. They also had men in Illinois, in the Dakotas and in Wyoming, in fact everywhere that Matts' plan dictated. It was going to be an evening of intensive activity.

As for Eliot, Matts and Warren, they would be concentrating on Up-State New York. They would use the helicopter since they had much ground to cover and one location at least needed to be approached from height. They carried with them to the chopper several containers of equipment. Once loaded up Eliot started the rotor blades turning and they were on their way.

~

It was nearly ten o'clock at night before a cab drew up outside Robert's studio. It was Rosanne – two hours late.

'What kept you?' Robert asked as she entered his lobby. He was not particularly annoyed, just slightly irritated.

'Oh, the traffic's still bad,' she replied all smiles and quite unflustered. 'On top of that I got caught up on the phone, business you know, unavoidable. I'm sorry.'

'Oh well, no big deal,' he said giving her a belated kiss. 'It's good to see you.'

'And you,' she said. She was wearing another short, provocative outfit. Her long immaculately shaped legs slightly glistened from being freshly bathed in some exotic lotion which not only made them look even more fabulous than they already were, but also gave off the most delicious intoxicating fragrance.

Robert showed her into the studio where he had not so far bothered to clear up the bourbon glasses after that morning's meeting with the Professor.

'So what sort of day have you had?' he asked casually, his eyes taking in her beauty.

'Not bad, considering,' she said in a light-hearted throwaway sort of tone. 'Seems you've been having a bit of a party!' she quipped on noticing the glasses strewn around.

'Oh, just some friends that dropped by,' he grinned.

'I see. Heavy drinkers, huh?' she added seeing that there were not one but two empty bottles of bourbon on the table. Though, in truth, the first of them had started the day with no more than an inch in it.

'My friends, not me,' Robert smiled hardly able to avert his eyes from her legs. 'But anyway, I've still got some food in the oven. You hungry?'

'Maybe later,' she replied putting her arms around him, 'I feel hungry, but not for food. Let's make love.'

'Yes,' he said under his breath as he kissed her.

~

Zak and a colleague dressed in workmen's overalls walked up to a manhole on Sixth Avenue. The window lights of Macy's department store shone in the background. It was the dead of night.

They carried with them a canvas hold-all.

'It's under here,' said Zak as he stood by the curb. 'We need the crow-bar.'

His colleague took a crow-bar from the hold-all and together they prized open the manhole cover. Beneath it was a steel ladder fixed to the walls of the cavity leading down below the street. Zak glanced around and with the sidewalk deserted they descended into the gloom.

Some fifty feet below street level they reached a chamber which contained a large electrical transformer. This equipment stepped down the high voltage transmission current to the 110 volts used by consumers.

Switching on torches they examined the equipment. 'Standard twin circuit breakers,' said Zak looking over the complex wiring.

'Yeah,' his colleague replied, 'One breaker's supposed to protect the other.'

'Not tonight it won't,' Zak quipped. He took out explosive charges fitted with timers and placed them by the circuit breakers. 'Okay, that's it.'

'Three done, two more to go,' said the other man.

The two men climbed back up and headed off to their next destination.

~

At a different location out in open country, not far from Pittsburgh, Pennsylvania, Gil and a colleague stalked up to a tall transmission pylon. They had a satchel bag with them.

'Hundreds of thousands of volts running along those cables,' said Gil gazing up in the darkness towards the top of the structure. 'Going to be quite a sight when it comes down.'

'I think when it goes "up" is what you mean,' his colleague replied. 'There's enough explosive in this bag to put even the Eiffel Tower into orbit!'

'Yeah, and maybe even further than that!' agreed Gil as he began to strap packages of explosive to the base of each of the pylon's legs.

~

In Up-State New York, a couple of hundred miles to the North of where Gil and his colleague were, Eliot, Matts and Warren flew their helicopter towards a big sub-station, another vital link in the electricity distribution network. Overhead transmission lines stretched away from this installation in all directions.

They had timed their approach to be as near to 3.00 a.m. as they dared. Initially Eliot kept high so that the rotor blades would be well clear of the spider's web of cables below them. But when they got within a hundred yards of the sub-station he adjusted the controls to lose altitude.

'That's where we have to drop it to set up the short,' announced Matts pointing downwards into the center of the complex as they hovered above.

'Okay, taking it down some more,' replied Eliot dropping the helicopter to less than a hundred feet. 'You ready to release it, Warren?'

'Yup,' he answered opening up the chopper's side door. On the seat beside him he had a sizeable package attached to a length of rope. 'Is this as low as we can get?'

'Yes,' replied Eliot concentrating hard at the helicopter's controls.

'Okay, here we go!' Warren responded. 'It's 2.58 a.m. so let's be sure we don't hang around!'

'We won't,' Eliot assured him in a staccato tone.

Warren began to carefully push the package off the seat and out of the door. He then used the rope to ease it down to the exact spot which Matts had indicated. Even with the seconds ticking away his movements were slow and precise. He was far too professional to hurry. Hurrying could lead to errors and errors were not the name of the game. Finally he let go of the rope. 'All right! It's done!' he shouted sliding the side door closed again.

Eliot took the chopper rapidly upwards and banked away at full speed. He could not have cut it much finer. A moment later the device detonated. The ground shook and the air vibrated. A manmade lightning storm was unleashed. Brilliant streams of electrical energy shot far and wide. Secondary shorts leap-frogged along cables way out across the landscape. Then, at the heart of the substation, the clouds of sparks were soon replaced by raging fires.

And it was exactly the same story elsewhere. At every site the plan went perfectly, and its effects were instantaneous.

Everywhere lights went out, phones went dead, TV screens went blank. Everywhere elevators stopped, production lines seized up, ice boxes began to warm. It was perhaps a blessing that most people were asleep and would not know what had hit them until the break of day.

~

Panic was only just below the surface in the electricity control room which serviced most of the Tri-State area of New York, New Jersey and Connecticut.

'For God's sake, we're getting reports of failures everywhere!' shouted Max Kramer, the chief supervisor on duty.

'I know we are!' replied a technician. 'Most of the country is off line!'

'Shit! There's no way this can happen!' uttered Kramer on the verge of tearing his hair out.

'Well, it has! The entire goddam system is in disarray! Every time we try to switch in reserve supplies we're getting huge overloads. Lots of electrical fires too! And it's same wherever you look – Chicago, Denver, Houston, San Francisco, you name it!'

Indeed, even as they spoke, the Fire Service in Manhattan were struggling to save the whole of a city block next to Macy's department store.

'But how? How is this possible?' Kramer asked after he had paused to gather his thoughts.

'Max, you know and I know, there's only one possible explanation. First there's a set pattern to these faults and, more importantly, accidents like this just don't happen! This can only be one thing! This is sabotage!'

'Sabotage?'

'Yes. This is deliberate. These faults have been set up to make every part of the network collapse just like one long line of tumbling dominoes! And I'll you something else, our only course of action is to shut down all generating capacity! This is going to take days to straighten out! Maybe as much as a week! What effect that's going to have I don't even want to begin to think about!'

Max Kramer did not reply, he just stood there in silence.

CHAPTER 7

There was not a cloud in the sky when the sun rose from the East over Manhattan. Brilliant sunbeams played on the rooftops of every landmark, it looked like just another hot August day. But here, and elsewhere, all was not as it seemed. As countless electric alarm clocks failed to go off millions would soon be in for a rude awakening.

In Greenwich Village Robert and Rosanne had made love the night before and then eaten and then made love again.

Over dinner they had talked about many things and Robert had learnt a lot about her. Her parents were now elderly and her upbringing had been fairly humble. Not terribly humble but humble enough.

She had managed to get into Wellesley College and had supported herself there by modelling during the vacations.

After college she had continued her modelling career for a couple of years with dazzling and lucrative success. But some time ago she had given it up. This was not because she had peaked, for even now she was only twenty-nine, it was because she had decided she wanted to do something more intellectually demanding. The endless photographic sessions and fashion shows had simply become a bore.

Yet, even as she "retired", she had found herself inundated with offers. Offers of exclusive cosmetic contracts worth millions of dollars a year, offers by industrial giants to front their advertising campaigns for anything from diet cola to shoe polish, offers of major parts in TV series and Hollywood movies. But everyone was turned down. She had a mind of her own and she wanted to use it and what appealed to her was journalism.

In contrast Robert had said little about himself. He had preferred to listen. One of the few hard facts he did reveal was that he had been to college too. When she inquired which college the answer was hardly a surprise – Princeton.

When the early morning light stirred them they had made love a third time. In the right mood and with the right man Rosanne could be nearly insatiable.

And now they lay quietly side by side in bed.

'Being with you makes me feel so happy,' she said softly to him.

'Yah,' he replied gently pulling her closer.

'I knew it from the instant we met,' she went on. 'One of those magical things you can't explain.'

'Yes, I sensed it too,' he said reflectively. 'But ...'

'But what?' she asked looking at him, she had seen a small frown come and go on his face.

'Oh nothing, nothing really, nothing at all ...' But his tone for once was not convincing.

'Is it Dawn you're worried about?'

'No. Not especially ...'

'That's not a very good answer.'

'Okay,' he sighed, 'maybe it's better to be honest.' Though if this was honesty it was of a very edited variety. 'Yes, I am just a little worried. Four years with someone is a long time. But it's not a problem, really it's not.'

'No, of course it's not,' she said soothingly. She rolled herself on top of him and held his face in her hands. 'Love has no conscience. This is the way it was meant to be.'

'I know,' he smiled. He kissed her and tried to forget his dilemma.

'To hell with the rest of the world! That's what I say!' she said boldly as she sat up. She glanced around the room. Bright rays of light were squeezing through the gaps in the blinds. 'It looks like it's going to be another beautiful day.'

'Yeah, that was the forecast,' he replied.

She leant over to switch on a bedside lamp. It did not come on. 'You know something?' she said.

'What's that?' he responded.

'Your bulb's gone. Try your side.'

'Okay,' he said completely dead-pan and flicked the switch on his lamp to and fro a couple of times without success. 'I don't know. Might be the fuse,' he muttered in a laid-back drawl.

'I'll try the TV,' she suggested as she pressed the remote control unit beside the bed. The TV remained lifeless. 'Nothing,' she said mildly irritated. 'Must be the fuse, where do you keep your fuses?' But before Robert could reply she noticed a transistor radio in the corner and went over to fetch it. 'Let's see what happens here,' she said bringing it back to bed.

Robert watched her, privately finding it faintly amusing, this side of things he was well prepared for.

Rosanne turned on the radio and rotated its tuning dial until she hit a station. When she did it practically fell out of her hands.

'This is a special broadcast,' the radio voice began. 'Power supplies have been blacked out in most areas of the country. The "Manhattan Bridge" Terrorists have claimed responsibility. A brief communiqué issued by them states: "If anyone thought we were kidding they now know better. Where is the promise of welfare money! You will hear from us again!"'

By now Rosanne was looking aghast at Robert. Robert remained expressionless. The radio began to fade and crackle. 'The public are urged,' the voice continued, 'not to panic and to stay at home unless any journey is really necessary. We now switch over to the White House from where the President is about to address the Nation ...'

The radio kept fading, by the time the President came on he was almost inaudible: 'Fellow Americans, today, as you know ...' And then the signal disappeared.

'What's wrong with it?' exclaimed Rosanne swivelling the aerial.

'I should think the batteries,' Robert replied totally unmoved. 'They were probably flat in the first place.'

'Don't you have any spares?'

'No. Hardly ever use the thing.'

Robert's calmness was beginning to disorient Rosanne. 'Didn't you hear what they're saying?' she asked him tensely. 'There's no power! How can you be so nonchalant!'

Robert looked at her a moment, she was on her feet starting to get dressed. 'I told you something like this would happen,' he replied. 'I told you in the interview and I told you so again last night.'

It was true that the previous evening the issue of the welfare demand had come up. But Robert had stuck exactly to his plan. He had underlined his sympathy for the cause and then changed the subject.

However, now, in the light of this latest development, Rosanne was less disposed to let matters rest. 'Come on,' she said reaching for her tights. 'You and your ideas, it's all very well saying that society has got to change, but now somebody is ...'

'Doing it!' he interjected.

'Yes, but think of the consequences.'

'What consequences?' he responded, his voice less laid-back. 'This is something that needs doing and it can't be done any other way. Let's just hope it leads somewhere! You've got millions of people out there who are being trampled over every day of their lives, and its mostly through no fault of their own!'

'But Robert ...'

'No, Rosanne,' he interrupted dropping his voice back to a gentler volume. 'If you're going to tell me there is some other way, that somehow things might change of their own accord, you're wrong.'

Rosanne was finding his whole attitude more and more difficult to cope with. 'I don't know what to say to you,' she sighed. 'What's happening is really extreme. Gee, how you can be so cool about it all!'

'Because it's what's needed,' he emphasized.

'Jesus, welfare is one thing, I can go along with that, but the rest of this ...'

'Well, you think about it some more,' he smiled. 'Just look on it as strong medicine for a very sick patient.'

'Yeah, sure,' she replied no less confused. 'Next you'll start telling me the operation was a success but the patient died!'

'No, I won't,' he laughed. He stretched out his hand and drew her into a kiss. She was now fully dressed. 'Rosanne, I love you so much. Try and understand.'

'I'm trying,' she replied quietly, 'I just find your attitude so weird.'

'Well, don't,' he assured her.

They disengaged their embrace and she went over to pick up her purse. Her thoughts had drifted towards the day ahead, obviously her normal daily routine was now pretty much out of the question. 'Now I don't know what to do,' she announced. 'There's no sense in going into the office – forgetting everything else we're on the forty-fourth floor and I ain't climbing the stairs! On the other hand I haven't got much to do at home either. I feel sort of at a loose end.'

'You're welcome to stay here if you want. Though I have to go out myself.'

'I see,' she responded, taking her time to chew over her options.

'Really the best thing may well be for you to hang on here, I'll be back by late this afternoon.'

She shook her head. 'No, not if you're not going to be here in, no point.'

'Well, up to you,' he said, getting out of bed. 'But anyhow,' he added, 'you told me where you live, but I don't have your phone number — I looked and but you're not listed. I know it won't be much use while the power's out, but what is it?'

This question made Rosanne freeze. The posture of her body visibly stiffened. With William now bound to be coming around more often she did not want to risk any awkward phone calls. It was a quandary which seemed to paralyse her. 'Obviously not today,' she started to answer, her tone unmistakably defensive and somewhat forced, 'in fact obviously not until the power's back on, but if you really need to you can usually get me at the office.'

Robert frowned. 'What's that supposed to mean?'

She looked less and less relaxed as she searched for a plausible answer. She was feeling under pressure, which was the one thing she hated.

'There's someone else?' he asked, his tone distinctly less easy-going than usual.

'No,' she replied not looking him in the eye.

'Then why won't you give me your number?'

'Look!' she declared edgily. 'I have *your* number, I don't see why you need mine!'

'So it's don't-call-me-I'll-call-you!' he said standing up and slinging on a dressing gown. 'You want it to be a one way traffic sort of thing! You know I don't think that's entirely fair!'

'I said you can call me at the office,' she replied chillily. And underneath this chilliness she was beginning to get angry.

'You still haven't said why I can't have your number!'

'What do you want me to say?' she retorted loudly. 'Why are you pushing me like this?'

'I ask for your number, you won't give it to me, it doesn't make sense. What is it you're hiding?' There was no doubt he had no intention of letting go. 'Rosanne, I would like to have an answer!'

At this she snapped, she was furious. 'Well, you're not going to get one!'

'Why?'

'Shit man!' she glared. 'I really don't like inquisitions!' She picked up her earrings from a side table and shoved them into her purse, she moved towards the lobby, she was fuming. 'All right!' she shouted turning to him, 'I had a lot of nuisance calls! My landline is fixed not to take incoming! Does that satisfy you?'

'Most people who have nuisance calls change their number, why didn't you?' he countered. 'And anyway you must have a cell phone?'

'Oh for Chrissakes!' she yelled out, all the more angry. 'I've had enough of this! If you're one of those guys who wants everything explained you'd better start looking for someone else! I'm going!' She was already halfway out of the bedroom door.

'Rosanne!' he called after her perplexed.

'Just go and fuck yourself!' she shouted back crossing the lobby and unlocking the door to the studio's exit. Robert caught up with her.

'Jesus, what's going on!' he exclaimed exasperated. 'You really don't seem the same person you were five minutes ago ... Come on now, don't be so ridiculous, we can talk this over. Stay and have some breakfast.'

'Great idea!' she replied with venom. 'There isn't even any hot water to make a cup of coffee with! And if there were I'd throw it in your face! Go fuck yourself!'

'Rosanne! Rosanne, what's wrong?'

But she was well on her way down the stairs and the only reply he got was the sound of the door slamming below. He was more than a little shaken, he was quite startled. It was a side to Rosanne he had not expected existed.

He sat down a while and tried to fathom what the problem could be. But even after he had shaved and showered he was none the wiser.

~

A short while later that morning Robert headed down on to the street and took a cab to the end of West 39th Street near the Lincoln Tunnel. This had been announced the previous day as a temporary river ferry pick-up point and he had arranged with Eliot to meet him on the far side.

As he walked from his cab towards the large sign on the waterfront reading "Emergency Ferry Station" he could see ferries plying their way to and fro. Their decks were crowded with commuters standing shoulder to shoulder and the line of people in front of him waiting for the next boat stretched out over a block.

From the nearby mouth of the Lincoln Tunnel he noticed a convoy of half a dozen or so military trucks emerging. He could tell from their markings that they were National Guard.

Just before he reached the back of the queue for the ferry a middle-aged police patrolman began to walk towards him. He was one of several police standing around. As he saw the officer approach Robert felt a twinge of nerves, he knew no matter how much care he took he was always running a risk that somehow someone or something might expose him.

'Excuse me, sir,' said the patrolman in a direct and matter-of-fact tone.

'Yes?' replied Robert fighting to disguise any trace of tension.

'I take it that your trip is necessary?' The patrolman's gaze if anything becoming sterner and more penetrating.

'Yes, it is,' said Robert, all the time wondering why it seemed he was being singled out.

'So you got work to do or business to conduct over on the New Jersey side?'

'Yes,' Robert replied, his heart pounding, desperately searching for a believable story if he needed one.

'That's okay,' said the patrolman waving him on, 'we're asking everybody that – we're just trying to ease the traffic.'

The relief Robert felt was huge. 'I understand, officer.'

He strolled on to take his place in the line for the ferry. After a couple of minutes it became apparent how painfully slowly it was moving. He could see people's long faces as they shuffled along braving temperatures which had already hit the high eighties. Everyone was quiet and orderly but everyone seemed dazed. He felt sorry for them, he really did.

Eventually his turn came and he paid his $2 to make the crossing. Out in mid-stream he took in the view up and down the river, the wreckage of the George Washington bridge in the distance to one side, the drab khaki sections of a half-built army pontoon to the other. The scene and everything connected with it struck him as all in all rather depressing. Though he would have been the first to admit that his state of mind might well have amplified his impressions. For, in the aftershock of Rosanne's outburst, he certainly felt downcast. Maybe the whole incident-cum-altercation had been his fault anyway, he somewhat illogically contemplated. But then he reminded himself that he had been around quite long enough to know the tricks that love can play. Moreover, he also knew he had to focus his thoughts on matters of wider importance. By the time he disembarked and walked over to where Eliot's car was waiting he was fully ready for the day ahead.

'Hi, how you doing?' asked Eliot through his open car window.

'Okay, thanks,' replied Robert climbing into the passenger seat. 'And you?'

'Nothing to complain about,' he said dryly as he steered the car away. Their destination was the house in Connecticut which would take them forty-five minutes or so.

'Looks like things are really starting to move after last night,' commented Robert once they had turned on to the main road.

'Yeah, it's beginning to sink in – They've introduced emergency measures, called in the National Guard ...'

'Yah, I saw a lot of military vehicles coming into Manhattan.'

'I'm sure you did,' replied Eliot with one of his rare grins. 'They're coming in in force, while the lights are out they're worried about looting! Well, I suppose that kind of figures – Got to be a heavy temptation!'

'A very heavy temptation,' nodded Robert using his slow drawl. His eyes scanned the road signs of the intersection coming up ahead and he stared at the surrounding scenery, unexciting though it was. It crossed his mind that, out in this open space, things seemed so relatively normal compared to Manhattan. Though of course he realized this was only an illusion which the unlit darkness of night would soon destroy.

'You heard the President spoke to the Nation?' said Eliot swinging the car north on to the freeway.

'I sort of half heard,' Robert answered, 'but I don't know what he said.'

'Oh, quite a few things actually. But Matts has it all recorded, so you'll be able to listen to it and digest it for yourself.'

'Good,' he replied as they drove on.

~

William Donaldson had hastily convened another meeting at New York City Hall. Commissioner McMichael was there, as was Oakley Cunningham and Scott Taylor plus other military and civil personnel connected with the emergency.

The atmosphere in the conference room was fraught to say the least.

'Look!' said William stridently who was in a lecturing mood. 'These people have hit us three times in a row – the robbery, the bridges and the power! And now all we do is sit around and talk as if our main problem is finding ways to contain the damage they've done! I don't think that's our main problem, though it's problem enough, our main problem has got to be tracking them down!'

'And it's a national problem now,' commented Commissioner McMichael rather disingenuously.

'Yes, obviously it is!' William barked. 'But naturally whereas I'm concerned about the whole country, my first responsibility still has to be for New York City. And since New York City is where, is where, this, this mushroom cloud, first took hold, it rather leads me to believe that it's here we have the best chance of identifying these people!'

'Yes,' replied the Commissioner. 'But at present we still have nothing to go on. We need a breakthrough.'

'A breakthrough!' exclaimed William aghast. 'I just don't understand this! Anybody would think we were looking for the invisible man! These people are right in our midst, they admit it, that's what their message said! And you keep telling me we have nothing to go on! What's the matter with you people! Even Steve here managed to find out about the faxes within ten minutes! Has that been followed up?'

Commissioner McMichael was understandably not enjoying what seemed like an assault on his and his Department's capabilities. 'Mayor,' he answered on the brink of raising his voice, 'any clues attached to the faxes have been followed up as exhaustively by us as they would be by any Police Department in the world! The fact of the matter is that the fax machines were of Taiwanese manufacture and were part of a consignment stolen over a year ago. Between that theft and their use to communicate the message to the TV Networks they may have passed through dozens of different hands. I hope you now realize that that is the sort of trail that inevitably only finishes up in a dead-end. As for the SIM cards connected to the portable faxes, you've got the same problem of untraceability. I can only repeat that this has hit right out of the blue, it's just as much a nightmare to me as it is to everybody else round this table.'

'That's beautiful!' replied William sarcastically. 'So it's a nightmare! So what do we do about it! Just stick our heads in the sand!'

'Mayor, I don't think this is very constructive!' answered the Commissioner beginning to show his indignation. 'We have every available man on this, and we're going at it twenty-four hours a day!'

'But it's not getting us anywhere!' William protested.

'Mayor, I really don't think this kind of criticism is called for!' reacted McMichael strongly. 'If you think ...!'

'Gentleman, please! Let's cool it down!' Oakley interrupted. If things were going to disintegrate into a full-scale row he wanted no part of it. His presence, however, was such that his intervention was effective. He turned to Scott Taylor, 'So what views do the CIA have?'

'Not a great deal either I'm afraid,' he replied gravely. 'And it's the same with the Bureau and the other Agencies too. These people are organized — Boy are they organized! They have sprung from nowhere, and they have considerable and varied knowledge and expertise! Worse still, we have no reason to assume they are even criminals in the "criminal" sense.'

'What do you mean not "criminals"?' questioned William Donaldson disbelievingly.

Scott pondered a moment. If he had one characteristic which stuck out above all others it was how extraordinarily seriously he took himself. He was a career CIA man and thrived on the analysis of complex situations. Furthermore, he saw this crisis as an opportunity to make his name and was already clearly liking his newfound prominence. Having collected his thoughts he answered: 'The normal criminal is out for personal profit, right? But apparently not in this case. What I'm saying is that though their actions are criminal their motives are not — And that makes it about a hundred times harder to get a handle on who we're up against!'

'Yes, that is the problem,' agreed the Commissioner. 'We're faced with a needle in a haystack. We could round up every known criminal and lunatic from Portland Maine to San Diego California but I doubt it would help. And although we strongly suspect a military link somewhere down the line, do you know how many ex-servicemen there are in the United States? Millions! Even when we narrow it down to men with explosives experience we're talking tens of thousands. It's one hell of a task.'

William nodded. 'Okay, I take the point.' His voice was now a little more restrained. 'But Jesus, it's as if we're having circles run around us! It's crazy!'

'Mayor, it's barely thirty-six hours since the bridges,' Scott took it upon himself to point out. 'I know it's cold comfort, but it is early days.'

'Yes, it is,' accepted Oakley heavily. 'Maybe for the time being we've taken this as far as we can. What's next William?'

William took note of Oakley's lead and glanced at his agenda. 'No more from the White House?' he asked turning to Steve Strauss who had been given the job of monitoring Washington's every move.

'No sir, nothing since this morning's emergency radio broadcast.'

'Okay then, we move on to the implementation of the emergency measures. General Brooks, can you fill us in?'

General Brooks was the officer co-ordinating the National Guard in the Metropolitan area.

~

Robert, Eliot and Warren sat with Matts in a corner of the large cellar of the house in Connecticut. They were listening to the recording of that morning's address by the President.

'So bear with me,' said the voice of President Guthrie, 'I will speak with you again very soon.'

'That's it,' said Eliot as Matts flicked off the recording machine. 'Shows you how easy it is to bring a nation to a halt.'

'Yes, it does,' replied Robert. 'I'd like to hear the key passages we marked again, can you play them back, Matts?'

'Sure,' answered Matts, he resetting the recording to its beginning.

When he reached the right place he restarted the machine and the President's voice resumed: 'Hospitals, military installations and major government buildings have their own independent sources of electricity generation so, until these few hours are up and we all have power back on, you can rest assured that the vital elements in our system are being maintained ...'

'Okay, hold it there,' said Robert breaking in. Matts stopped the machine. 'That was lie number one – we know electricity won't be restored for days!'

'Absolutely,' concurred Matts.

'But he's got to lie hasn't he?' chipped in Warren. 'You don't tell the truth when the truth is unacceptable!'

'Sure,' echoed Eliot, 'it's a bit like when you get on a plane and there's a delay – they just keep telling you every half hour it's going to be another half hour, else you'd try and change your ticket and that would be bad for the airline's stockholders!'

'That's right,' smiled Robert. 'Okay, run it on Matts.'

Matts set the recording of the President's address running again: 'These people are our enemies and most surely will be tracked down and brought to justice ...'

'He's got a long way to go!' quipped Eliot in a quick aside.

The President's voice carried on: 'However, as the one thing which terrorists seek most of all is publicity, I hope you will accept that I have requested the Media to impose a discretionary news blackout on the reporting of their activities ...'

'Hold it again,' requested Robert. Matts did so. 'Restricting the Media, now that's a smart move.'

'Not one we didn't expect,' said Eliot.

'Yes, but it comes quicker than we thought,' he replied.

'It's overcomable,' said Matts. 'We've got the facilities.'

'You sure?' checked Robert.

Matts grinned at him. He had become so used to his colleagues always questioning the feasibility of his claims that he now regarded it as quite humorous. 'Yes, I'm sure,' he replied. 'When we make our next move we can still get it over.'

'Good,' smiled Robert, 'and I've got a visual idea for it which I'm going to work on.'

'What are you thinking of?' asked Eliot.

'Well, if we're going to break in on broadcasting I think the presentation needs to be pretty unusual, something really quite distinctive. I mean we can't exactly show our faces!'

'So what's the idea?' Eliot wanted to know.

'I'm thinking of something "animated", sort of like a cartoon ...'

'A cartoon?' queried Matts somewhat intrigued.

'Yes,' smiled Robert again. 'You wait. It'll be good. It'll take me a short while, but we can't do anything in that department until power is back on.

'Anyhow, let's hear some more of the recording.'

Matts obliged and the voice of President Guthrie returned: 'To protect neighbourhoods and businesses I have called on the National Guard. A curfew will be imposed tonight from dusk to dawn and I do not hesitate to say that such activities as looting or robbery will not be tolerated.'

'Okay, Matts, switch it off,' stated Robert. 'He's just rambling on really, just trying to put on a brave face. We've heard all we need to hear. Right now I think we ought to be thinking about the ship.'

'You going to make contact?' asked Matts as he stopped the recording.

'Yes, let's go,' Robert replied standing up.

'Okay,' said Eliot standing up too.

The four men then went over to the cellar's staircase leading up to the house's cavernous front hall, the walls of which were decorated with the heads of moose, elk and stag. Their footsteps reverberated on the hall's marble floor as they crossed towards the front door.

They emerged on to the gravel driveway in front of the house which was in fact, with its neo-gothic turrets and spires, almost more like a castle. It had been built by an eccentric English millionaire in 1903 and he had used it as a hunting lodge. Some years later he had blown his brains out when he had discovered his wife was having an affair with his best friend. Subsequently the place had had many owners. In the end Robert, or rather his nominees, had bought it relatively cheaply from a movie producer who had been so foolish as to singlehandedly finance his own film only to find that his judgment of public taste had been awry.

Robert, Matts, Eliot and Warren proceeded to walk the short distance under an avenue of mature oak trees towards the garage area which had once upon a time been horse stables. Matts unlocked one of the garage doors. Inside was the communications truck used during the bridge operation. Alert as ever to factoring out every possible unnecessary risk they would drive to an isolated location before employing the equipment on board to radio the "Belle Epoque".

'You want to drive or shall I?' Robert asked Eliot.

'I don't mind.'

'I will then,' smiled Robert getting into the driving seat.

'Be my guest,' replied Eliot as he climbed into the cab alongside and Matts and Warren got into the rear section of the vehicle.

In bright sunshine they headed off down the driveway.

An hour later the truck halted on a sloping wooded track beside a small clearing. They were two thousand feet up in the Catskills and miles from anywhere.

They all got out.

'This is the place you selected?' Robert checked with Matts.

'Yes, it is. You can smell the mountain air.'

'You can indeed,' smiled Robert taking in the breathtaking view.

Matts leant into the rear of the truck. 'Someone give me a hand with this.'

'Sure,' Warren replied, and he and Matts lifted out a portable satellite dish which they carried into the center of the clearing.

'Run out the cable,' Matts shouted back to the other two.

Robert and Eliot responded taking a long coil of cable from the truck and unspooled it across the grass towards the dish.

Once the cable had reached him Matts quickly connected it up and returned to the transmitter inside the truck. Warren remained out in the clearing order to assist in aiming the dish.

Inside the truck Matts busied himself making final adjustments. 'This won't take more than a couple of minutes,' he told the others.

~

Dawn stood alone on the deck of the "Belle Epoque" staring out across the vast desolate expanse of water. It was another grey stormy day and the colour of the ocean seemed to match exactly the colour of her blue-green eyes. It was not particularly cold but she wore some oilskins borrowed from the crew. She kept their hood down as she found the sensation of the spray beating on her face strangely soothing. It somehow served to nullify some of the emptiness she felt. The wild windswept way that her long damp auburn hair half-clung to her pale skin rather suited her. She looked extremely pretty.

She took solace from these strolls on deck. If nothing else they went some way towards breaking the monotony. For with the exception of frequent visits to the bridge to check the ship's position she had very little to do.

Even so, loathsome as she was finding every minute on board to be, her commitment to the undertaking did not falter. She knew full well, as did Robert and the others, that she was by no means the ideal person to send on a mission such as this. But there had been good reason why it had needed to be her.

Her relationship with Stefan had deteriorated so much that they were now scarcely even on speaking terms. He was one of those few people who seemed almost to go out of their way to be disliked. While he had not shown any physical violence towards her, she could feel violence was something he breathed. Certainly verbally he took pleasure in bullying, belittling and intimidating her at every opportunity.

Of the few things she had discovered about him only two were of any passing interest. One was that he was half-Brazilian, half-Hungarian. The other that he was homosexual.

His origins were for practical purposes fairly meaningless since he claimed to have spent no more than a few months of his adult life in any one place at any one time. Though the nomadic pattern of his career did help to explain the ease with which he supervised the multi-national crew – there seemed to be no language in which he was not fluent.

As for his homosexuality, it was blatant. Indeed, two of the younger deckhands appeared only to be retained to service his every pleasure. Not that she cared about this in the slightest. In fact she welcomed it. He was obnoxious enough as it was without the added complication of unwanted sexual advances. It was just a pity from her point of view that his particular preferences happened to coincide with such an unconcealed hatred of women.

Of course Dawn had been warned about Stefan before she had set out. She knew he had a reputation for being difficult and that, as a professional smuggler, money was his sole concern. However, although the terrorists had all had reservations about involving an outsider such as Stefan in their plans, the arguments in favour were clear-cut.

For a start Eliot and his men were too few in number to be everywhere at the same time anyway. But, quite apart from that, other considerations were just as important. They needed a large ship and Stefan and his contacts had the capability to procure one without problem. Secondly their shopping list of cargo required several different ports of call in several different countries and Stefan had the advantage of being intimately familiar with every major port in the world.

Last but not least, in the shady circles in which he operated, Stefan had a record which was something of a rarity – his success rate was one hundred per cent. This was what made him so expensive, his total payment was to be $6 million, the second half falling due on completion.

And it was Stefan's combination of exhorbitant fee and impossible temperament which had made Dawn the only sensible choice of courier.

In real life she was no more a make-up artist than Robert was a gambler at the race track. Until recently she had held a responsible job on Wall Street and her financial background had been of great value to the terrorists. It was she who had arranged nominees for Robert to buy the house in Connecticut. It was she who had devised means to camouflage Matts' substantial equipment purchases. Most of all, it was she who had organized the bearer bonds for Stefan.

Consequently if Stefan had found some problem, real or imaginary, with the bonds it was only she who had the knowledge to straighten it out. The alternative of risking a misunderstanding was unthinkable. It would probably have led to no ship and no cargo. That would have been a disaster. Dawn had had to go because it was too important for her not to.

~

'Just swing it over a little further,' Matts shouted from the truck over to Warren beside the dish in the clearing. 'And a little more. And a little more still. Okay, stop! That's perfect – we're locked on!'

Stefan was up on the bridge of the "Belle Epoque" when he received notification via the ship's intercom that a message was coming through by satellite. He had already noticed Dawn meandering round the deck and rushed down to fetch her.

She was leaning on the railings not far from the bow of the "Belle Epoque" as he emerged from the superstructure. 'You!' he shouted.

Dawn turned to see him coming towards her.

'Your device is bleeping!' he called out.

'Sorry?' she called back. The sound of the sea had drowned out his voice. The device he was referring to was a telephone scrambler that she had taken with her to ensure communications remained private. Before her departure Matts had shown her how to install it in the ship's radio room. This is where it had sat silent for the past ten days.

'Your device is bleeping!' he repeated with greater urgency as he got nearer.

This time Dawn heard. Her expression brightened instantly. She immediately started to run in his direction and onwards towards the superstructure. But as she passed by him on the deck she felt herself being hauled back by a vice-like grip. Stefan had grabbed the back of her oilskin's hood, in fact he had aimed to tug at her hair but his hand had narrowly missed. 'Not so fast!' he stated bruisingly. 'We walk briskly but we do not run!'

'Ahhh!' she cried quite startled and a little afraid. 'Let go of me! Don't you want the message?'

'Let them wait a few seconds!' he barked still holding on to the oilskin. 'I am not running, and you are not speaking with them without me present!'

Dawn knew she had no choice but to obey. He finally released his grip on her. They walked on at his speed.

In truth Stefan would have liked to have had words with them in her absence. But the scrambler did not work without a four digit code being punched into it and she was only person who knew it.

They headed into the superstructure and went to the radio room. Dawn picked up a headset and entered the necessary code into the device.

'Be sure to tell your friends that we are sick of waiting out here!' Stefan said tersely.

'I will,' she nodded bending the headset's mike over her mouth.

'We have her,' announced Matts as he sat in the rear of the truck with the other three all wearing headphones squeezed in alongside him.

'Hello, Dawn,' said Robert concentrating hard into his headset microphone. 'We're calling to up-date you. What is your position? Over ...'

'Three hundred miles South West of Iceland. Over.' As a result of her frequent trips to the bridge this information she had right on the tip of her tongue.

'I see,' responded Robert in a deliberate tone. 'Everything is to plan at this end. But for you it will be a few more days. Over.'

'I understand, but the crew are becoming restless. Over.' Dawn could feel the heat from Stefan's nostrils literally breathing down her neck.

Hearing this made Robert frown. He hesitated. 'Well, tell them it won't be long,' he said 'We'll be back to you shortly. Over.'

'Okay,' she came back with an air of resignation. 'And Robert?' she added, strain in her voice becoming increasingly apparent.

'Yes?'

'Remember half the reason I'm doing this is because I love you.'

This put a lump in Robert's throat. 'And I love you too,' he replied. 'And I'm thinking of you. Take care of yourself. Over and out.'

Robert removed his headphones. As did the others. He pondered the situation for a moment. He felt not only inwardly personally torn about Dawn but had also a niggling doubt in his mind about her present well-being.

'She didn't sound very happy, did she?' commented Warren breaking the silence.

'No, she didn't,' Robert sighed. 'She didn't sound right at all. And she's not a complainer by nature either.'

'Maybe they're giving her a really hard time?' Warren conjectured.

'I don't know,' said Robert.

'Well, you don't have to be a fucking genius to tell things aren't as they should be!' said Eliot with a hint of anger. 'As if the fucking crew on board that ship weren't earning enough out of this! I tell you I don't like it! And one thing is for sure, we don't want to risk anything going wrong!'

'No, we don't,' said Robert looking tensely at him. 'What do you suggest?'

Eliot drew in a deep breath then responded decisively, 'Warren and I will take a boat and go out to the ship. We'll go rightaway. It can't be left as it is.'

'Yah, you're right,' Robert nodded slowly.

'Okay,' instructed Eliot, 'get her back on the radio, Matts. We'll set up a rendezvous off Newfoundland.'

Matts did as requested. With all the equipment tuned in making the second contact was a formality. The rendezvous was agreed. Dawn was delighted. Even Stefan to some extent seemed placated.

The four men packed up the dish and drove back to the house in Connecticut. As the sun began to slowly sink in the sky their return journey was uneventful.

'You returning to Manhattan?' Eliot asked Robert as they arrived back and got out of the truck in the house's driveway.

'Yes,' he replied.

'I'll get one of the guys to drive you to the ferry station then. Warren and I have to step on it to get out to sea before dark.'

'Okay, thanks,' replied Robert. 'I guess the curfew has its inconveniences even for us!'

'Yeah, you could say so,' said Eliot dryly. 'Be seeing you ...'

'Have a good trip.'

'We'll try,' said Eliot, and he and Warren headed into the house.

Robert paused a moment, he was thinking. He then turned casually to Matts who was about to remove some heavy duty batteries from the truck for recharging. 'Matts there's just one other thing?'

'Sure, tell me?' he replied as he loosened some bolts which held the batteries in place with a wrench.

'When you get the chance can you tap into the unlisted numbers directory of New York Telephone?'

'When the power's back on – no problem.'

'That's okay, no great rush. I want the number of a Rosanne Lindblade, she lives on 89th at Madison.'

'Will do,' said Matts.

'Thanks,' Robert replied.

CHAPTER 8

William's tense and difficult meeting at City Hall went on until dusk that evening. When it was over Oakley suggested he give him a lift home which, even though he had his own limo waiting outside, he accepted. Oakley made this offer quite often as it gave them a chance to have a private chat. And anyway the thrill of riding in a motorcade was something which William secretly never tired of.

City Hall was way downtown near the Financial District so the distance to Gracie Mansion in Carl Schurz Park overlooking the river at East 88th Street represented nearly half the length of Manhattan. Not that this inconvenienced Oakley as he always took up residence in the Carlyle Hotel on 76th Street whenever he was in town.

On the journey uptown the two men sat alone in the back of Oakley's limousine. The front seat beside the driver was occupied by a secret serviceman. In the fading light the streets seemed spookily dim and deserted making the flashing lights of the escort cars appear all the more prominent. Groups of National Guardsmen patrolled the sidewalks, their khaki trucks parked here and there at frequent intervals.

The conversation had briefly lulled as William leant forward to push the button raising the glass partition between the front and rear seats. Oakley glanced at him inquisitively wondering what had prompted this action.

'Speaking personally for a moment, Oakley,' said William in a confidential tone, 'I've reached a conclusion about my marriage. I've decided to end it. Mary accepts it's for the best. I wanted you to be first to know.'

Oakley gave William's statement a moment's thought before replying. 'I much appreciate that courtesy, William. I realize it's not something you have done lightly.'

William reached into his breast pocket and took out a sheet of paper which he handed over. 'I shouldn't think it will get more than a passing mention until some kind of normalcy returns, but this is the press announcement. I think it's better to place these things out in the open.'

Oakley glanced briefly at the announcement. 'Yes, William, very appropriate,' he commented approvingly. 'I mean what the hell, divorce is never nice, but it happens every day!'

'Yes. I suppose so,' the Mayor sighed philosophically.

The motorcade swept on across the deserted intersection of 57th Street and Fifth and swung up Madison towards the Upper East Side. With virtually no traffic to contend with its progress was quick.

The glass partition in the limousine remained up.

'Actually,' said William drawing in a deep breath, 'I'll get out after the next block.' The motorcade was about to cross 87th Street at Madison.

'You're not going back to Gracie Mansion?' asked Oakley mildly surprised.

'No,' he answered a little uncomfortably, for even with the Senator he could not help being overly conscious of his public image. 'This is where my new lady friend lives.'

Oakley's eyes opened wide. 'Oh, I see,' he responded with a friendly wink and a smile which put William immediately at ease again. He reached forward lowering the partition. 'Driver,' he instructed in his booming voice, 'alert the escort cars we're about to make a stop to drop off Mayor Donaldson!'

'The next corner, sir?' checked the driver.

'Yes, far right-hand side,' interjected William.

'Okay, sir.' The driver picked up his radio telephone and spoke, 'pulling over a moment, far right-hand corner 89th.'

'Okay, understood,' came back a radio voice.

The twenty car motorcade duly halted.

'Thanks Oakley,' smiled William tapping him on the shoulder as he got out.

'See you tomorrow,' nodded Oakley returning the smile. The motorcade continued on its way.

William strolled along the sidewalk and into entrance of the apartment building.

Although it was still just about twilight outside the lobby of the building was dim. Only a few small sparsely placed temporary lights provided illumination.

'Good evening, Mayor Donaldson,' greeted Larry the doorman instantly recognizing him.

'Good evening,' said William both formal and cordial. 'What a day this has been.'

'Sure has, sir,' said Larry who was quite used to the Mayor's comings and goings. 'Without the elevators you can imagine what it's been like for people. Then how do people cook, how do people take a hot shower, how do people keep cool with no air conditioning, how do people do anything …!'

'Yes, I know,' agreed William seeking to cut the conversation short. He knew that discreet as Larry was he could also have an irritating tendency to be overly chatty.

They moved towards the staircase door at the rear of the lobby.

'There is some light on the stairs,' Larry volunteered, 'but it's pretty dark elsewhere. If you like I'll walk up with you?'

'That's very nice of you, but I'll be okay.' Even if Larry probably did suspect who he was visiting William was not about to serve up confirmation.

'Let me lend you a flash light anyway,' said Larry taking one out of his pocket. 'It'll make it easier for you.'

'Thanks, much appreciated,' the Mayor replied accepting it. 'I'll make sure you get it back.'

'Don't worry about that, sir, always a pleasure,' said Larry. But by now William had disappeared through the doorway and begun his ascent.

Despite the plushness of the building, which would have put any luxury hotel to shame, the staircase, normally unseen by the residents, was drab and bare. William climbed flight after flight, his footsteps echoing in the silence and the unsteady beam of his flash light casting strange shadows. Larry's description of "some light" was something of an exaggeration, it was really dark. In fact not just dark but disagreeably stuffy and claustrophobic too.

William considered himself fit but climbing sixteen floors was not exactly an everyday occurrence for him and he had to stop twice to get his breath back. On one occasion the light of his flash lamp caught a large cockroach. It made him jump as it scurried for its bolt-hole in a vent just inches from his face. 'Jeez!' he muttered ducking his head out of its way. He carried on.

Finally he saw "16" written on a door and with great relief pushed it open, his lungs were beginning to ache.

Orienting himself he pointed his lamp in the general direction of Rosanne's front door and made his way through the gloom over to it. He instinctively tried to ring the door bell but got no response. He then remembered – no electricity. He knocked instead.

'It's William,' he called out still recovering his breath.

Almost immediately the door opened and Rosanne stretched out her arm to him. 'Come along in,' she said softly.

Candles burnt in the room, they embraced.

~

Robert had returned to Manhattan from the house in Connecticut equipped with a flash light too. As he climbed the dark flight of stairs up to his studio he had only narrowly missed being stranded by the curfew, but had induced a cab driver at the 39th Street temporary ferry station to chance one more fare for the day with the promise of an extra $20 over the clock.

With the flash lamp he entered the pitch blackness of his studio lobby and futilely flicked a light switch on and off as if to confirm the lack of power.

He then shone the torch up to a trap door in the ceiling alongside which was a pull-down ladder. He reached for a pole propped up against the wall with a fish-hook attachment at one end. He used this to lower the ladder and started to climb.

From the rooftop in the very last remnants of daylight the city looked quiet and dark. He crossed over to one corner of the flat roof where there was a wooden cabinet with a door. He opened it to reveal a motor.

He pulled the motor's rope starter cord and it began to turn quite noisily. He quickly re-closed the cabinet door shutting in the noise and descended back into his studio.

The windows in his main studio were fitted with heavy blinds. He drew these down and then proceeded to try another light switch. Powered by the generator on the roof the room was suddenly bathed in bright light.

He walked over to his working desk and took out a thick wad of blank white drawing paper. Looking relaxed he mounted one sheet on an easel and began to draw.

What he was drawing was initially not particularly clear but the first few strokes seemed to suggest the shape of a head.

~

All the same, while Robert was drawing, and while William and Rosanne made love, a party was going on in an altogether less salubrious part of Manhattan. In a rundown tenement building a couple of blocks from 125th Street in the middle of Harlem perhaps sixty or seventy people were doing their best to enjoy themselves. The room where the party was being held was on the third floor and long and narrow. At one end large windows overlooked the street below. Gas lamps and candles threw out a glow of orange light which diffused through the thick hanging tobacco smoke. Empty bottles and beer cans littered the tops of tables. In one corner a small ensemble played acoustic guitars and bongos which some people danced to sweat dripping off their bodies in the sweltering heat. And in another corner near the windows sat Cornwall, Tom, Jam and Ray who, like everyone else present, were black. The four of them were talking about the present situation ...

'Half the time I don't have no money for electrics anyway – so it ain't so bad,' said Tom with a shrug.

'Yeah, but right now nobody got no electrics,' commented Jam, who was a huge man. 'I mean nobody – you get what I'm getting at? Can't you see my angle?'

'See you angle?' answered Tom fairly low key. 'Well, not especially.'

'But, man,' interjected Cornwall in a rasping whisper, 'you have to think about it, man – this whole city, this whole country is DARK, the thought kind of freaks me – just consider the opportunities!'

'Yeah, that's exactly it, man, just think of all the easy pickings,' agreed Jam tantalisingly, 'makes you feel kind of itchy, makes you wanna scratch your skin.' He wriggled his fingers over his face.

'Yeah, pickings maybe, but I wouldn't call them easy,' said Tom shaking his head and glancing out the window seeing a military truck go by, 'you've got all those dudes out there, National Guard, hundreds of them, I mean you can't do nuthin'!'

'We could just blow them way, no problem at all,' said Cornwall in his rasp – he had once been knifed through his vocal chords in a fight.

'Just blow them away! Sure, like hell you could,' sneered Tom. 'Don't give me that bullshit!'

'It ain't bullshit!' said Cornwall aggressively.

'It's bullshit, man!' Tom re-emphasised.

'No, it fuckin' ain't!' said Jam. 'Stop being so fuckin' stupid, Cornwall's right, we got a fuckin' chance, we should fuckin' take it!'

'Well, it's easy for big guys like you to talk like you're King Kong!' said Tom. Indeed, not only Jam but Cornwall too really did both have the builds of basket ball players. 'Fact is they've got us under their thumb!'

'Fuck that, you think what you wanna think!' responded Jam.

'Yeah, just you think what you wanna think!' echoed Cornwall disparagingly.

'Yeah, man, I sure as hell will,' said Tom. 'You wanna try take 'em on it's your fuckin funeral! I wanna die peacefully in my own bed!'

'Yeah, yeah, yeah, you be a wimp if you wanna be,' scoffed Jam.

'Me? I' ain't no fuckin' wimp, no way man,' retorted Tom scarcely rising to the taunt. 'But on this we're just goin' to have to agree to disagree! Okay!'

Cornwall and Jam merely chose to smile the slightly smirking smile of the entirely unpersuaded.

'But anyway,' continued Tom suddenly deciding to change the subject and turning his attention to Ray who had said nothing, 'where's your sister Millie? Why ain't your sister here with us, Ray?'

'I dunno, said she was coming,' Ray replied.

'Maybe she just got intimidated by those assholes in uniform out there!' suggested Jam sourly.

'Yeah, that's what's fuckin' happened!' said Cornwall. 'She probably started out on her way and some jerk in authority told her she gotta turn back. I say, Tom, you oughta go fetch her, she only 'cross the street! Unless you're too much of a wimp even to do that!'

Tom flashed his eyes unappreciatively at Cornwall's latest remark, but looked hesitant all the same, not that in fact he was timid in any way at all, in truth he had spent more years in penal institutions than the other three men put together. The bottom line in Tom's mind was simply that he had learnt to be leery of getting into trouble.

'Come on, man,' prodded Jam, 'where's your spunk! You goin' with her ain't you, you want her to be here! I say go get her!'

Tom still pondered.

'Yeah, man, they're right,' Ray decided to urge. 'She wouldn't want to be missing out. So come on let's go fetch her, I'll go with you, won't take us two minutes.'

Tom glanced out through the window across the street. It was deserted. Finally, having thought it thoroughly over, he rose to his feet. 'Yeah, okay, we'll go get her.'

'That's right, man, you do that, that's more like it,' smiled Jam rolling a joint of marijuana.

'See you in a minute,' said Ray, and he and Tom headed towards the door and down on to the sidewalk.

As they emerged on to the street it was still deserted. All they could see around them were the grey silhouettes of delapidated buildings. They began to cross. However, as they did so a police patrol car rounded the corner. Officer Finch was at the wheel and beside him was Officer Simmons.

'What those guys doing?' commented Finch seeing Ray and Tom in the car's headlights.

'We'll find out,' said Simmons picking up his radio. 'Officer Simmons here, about to check out two guys at 123th and Morningside Avenue.'

The squad car pulled over beside Ray and Tom, they had made no attempt to run. The officers got out with their guns drawn.

'Okay, freeze! Hold it right there!' Simmons ordered. Ray and Tom obeyed. 'Where do you think you're going?'

'Minding my own business?' Ray replied.

'Minding your own business, huh?' responded Simmons with sarcasm.

'We're just goin' to collect someone, we've got a party,' said Tom.

'Yeah? And what about the curfew?' said Finch officiously, lengthening the syllables in "curfew" as if to add effect.

'We don't mean no harm,' Tom replied aiming to be reasonable.

'You don't mean no harm, that's what you all say!' sneered Simmons becoming tough. 'Get your hands up and face the wall, real slow!'

'Look, man ...' Ray tried to say.

'You heard me! Do it!' shouted Simmons.

Ray and Tom resentfully raised their hands and turned to the wall.

Cornwall and Jam were watching all this from their window above the street, they were angry. Other men at the party had also drifted over to look too.

'Look at those motherfuckers,' said Cornwall, referring to the two police officers. 'They're just kinda asking for it!'

'Yeah,' answered Jam, 'when are they goin' to learn to keep their noses out of other people's business!'

'Not until someone shows them!' said Cornwall with growing menace, 'who's got a fuckin' CB?'

Someone held up a walkie talkie.

'Call around!' shouted Cornwall, his eyes aflame.

Officers Finch and Simmons were thoroughly frisking Ray and Tom.

'I told you we don't mean no harm, man!' uttered Tom who was starting to lose patience.

'All we was doin' was fuckin' crossin' the street! Man, give us a fuckin' break will you!' protested Ray.

'You just fucking shut up, both of you!' said Finch.

'Yeah, speak only when you're spoken too!' added Simmons.

'So what are goin' to do? Arrest us?' asked Ray.

'Yeah, you bet we are, we're taking you in,' said Finch.

'No, you're not!' said Cornwall suddenly coming out of the shadows. Behind him was Jam, both of them had shot guns.

Finch swung round with his gun to face them, but Cornwall was already pulling his trigger. The blast into the officer's stomach lifted him six feet into the air. Jam simultaneously fired at Simmons the impact catapulting him across the front of his squad car.

Then in the wake of the gunshots came the sound of police sirens and at the same time a patrolling National Guard truck turned into the street.

'Move it!' said Cornwall taking no more than the quickest of glances at the dead bodies of the two policemen.

'Sure will!' said Jam stuffing an oily rag into the patrol car's gas tank and then setting fire to it. 'Look out and watch your arse!' he shouted back as he dived into the shelter of a doorway.

An instant later the police vehicle's gas tank exploded in a huge ball of flames. The National Guard truck, closing fast, slammed on its brakes and skidded to a halt. It came to rest no more than twenty or so yards from the blaze. The guardsmen inside wasted no time in jumping down on to the street. 'Okay guys, take it steady,' said a sergeant signalling to his men to fan out towards the burning wreckage.

But it was an order they had no time to obey. Suddenly, with no warning and certainly with no mercy, from many windows up above, gasoline bombs began to rain down. Not just a dozen or so, but a torrent, unleashed from all directions, and aimed with lethal accuracy and nothing less than lethal intent.

Scarcely knowing what had hit them the guardsmen scattered in disarray. Within seconds the whole street was a sheet of flames. Still more gasoline bombs kept pelting down.

A guardsman making it back to the front of the truck reached in and grabbed its radio. 'Get us some support, and now!' he shouted. 'We've got big trouble on 123rd!' And in the background, even as he spoke, the sound of small arms fire from surrounding streets had already started up. There could be no doubt about it – Mayhem was spreading with the speed of the wind.

On Lenox Avenue groups of youths were soon on the rampage, buildings were being torched, cars overturned.

In no time, support unable to get through, the guardsmen from the truck on 123rd were in full disorderly retreat, every man for himself, their stranded vehicle left behind to be engulfed by the inferno. In surreal contrast Cornwall, Jam, Tom, and Ray and many others ran along the sidewalk of 123rd unopposed and oblivious to danger. Everywhere fires were burning.

'We're goin' to break out man!' shouted Cornwall with an air of triumph which most people would not have understood. 'You can see it's happenin'!'

'Yeah, man, this is it! Tonight's the night!' shouted Jam.

'That's right, man! Ain't nuthin's goin' to stop us now!' yelped some other voice. And as the group ran through the streets their number grew and grew.

There was a National Guard Command Post at Douglas Circle at the North Western limit of Central Park thirteen blocks away from 123rd. It was not long before the reaction of those manning it reflected the scale of what was erupting. 'It's getting out of control! Repeat, out of control!' screamed a frightened guardsman into his walkie talkie, his colleagues around him already returning fire with their rifles.

Rioting spread quickly Eastwards across the City, a row of shops at 109th and Lexington became the target of a stampeding mob. A dozen or so men prized off a store window's steel security grill, others picked up bricks and hurled them shattering its glass.

'Stop or I'll shooted!' shouted a National Guardsman running on to the scene. 'I said ...' but then he crumbled to the ground hit in the chest by a bullet. Rioters simply trod over his body as they grabbed merchandise from the shop window. Once stripped of everything readily to hand another fire bomb was thrown in.

At the Command Post at Douglas circle it was only midnight but it was no longer dark, flames from many buildings were lighting up the sky, clouds of acrid smoke stung the eyes, the sound of gunfire was all around.

'Block them off at Cathedral Parkway!' yelled a young National Guard officer to a squad of men desperately trying to contain the situation. 'We've got to hold them there!'

'Jesus Christ! How can we hold them there!' shouted a guardsman. 'They're beyond that point already!'

'Well, try and help the fire fighting people through anyway!' responded the officer unnerved and panicky.

'Okay!' replied the guardsman rushing off. From their point of view all they could see in every direction was pandemonium.

~

Robert was still drawing in his studio as he sensed the heightened atmosphere outside. He switched off his lights and lifted a blind to peer out the window. Military and police vehicles, sirens wailing, were clearly all being ordered uptown. He did not know exactly what was going on but he could imagine.

He calmly re-lowered the blind, put his lights back on and returned to his easel.

~

In the bedroom in Rosanne's apartment William had lit a candle and stood naked. He too had been looking out the window. 'I'd better go,' he said to her as she lay in bed.

'Why? she asked sitting up sounding less than pleased.

'Can't you hear!' he exclaimed irritably. 'There's trouble out here!'

'William, it's the middle of the night!' she replied. Her tone was insistent. 'What do you think you could do!'

'I may be needed! No one knows where I am!' he said tensely.

But this explanation appeared to be lost on Rosanne. 'Needed for what?' she asked. 'Well, I need you too! I can hear there's trouble, and I'm scared! I don't want to be left alone!'

'Rosanne, you're quite safe here,' he assured.

'Am I?' she frowned, 'it doesn't sound far away to me!'

And in reality it was not – 109th Street was only a mile away.

'That's all the more reason why I have to go!' stated William. 'It's my responsibility! I ought to be around! It's as simple as that!'

Simple it might be, but Rosanne remained unimpressed, and William could see she was. 'It's the middle of the night!' she repeated more loudly. 'What use could you be!'

'Rosanne! I'm Mayor of this town!'

'And big deal if you are!' she replied sourly.

'Rosanne, there's no sense in arguing I really have to go!'

'I'm not arguing with you,' she shouted, 'I'm telling you!'

'Telling me what?' he questioned.

'Telling you that you're not going!'

'Look Rosanne!'

'No, William, none of this "look" stuff! I'm telling you – and you'd better believe me – that if you go now you'll never see me again!'

'Rosanne, I've done everything for you, I'm getting a divorce, what more do you want? Don't be absurd!'

'I'm not being absurd!' she shouted loudly. 'If you're going to go, go! And bye bye! And as for this stinking apartment you can keep it, I can buy one of my own! So go! You make me feel sick!'

William was shaken, he stopped to think, he shifted around nervously in front of the window, the silence in the room was only punctuated by the crack of gunshots and wail of sirens outside. 'Okay,' he said.

'Okay what?' she asked.

'I said okay,' he replied moving back towards the bed. 'I'll stay.'

Her mood transformed, nothing pleased her more than controlling her men, she smiled and outstretched her arms to him. Feeling extremely guilty about his decision he welcomed the comfort of her attentions.

~

The next morning Manhattan did not look itself. The familiar skyline was intact but towards its northern end many palls of smoke were drifting up into the still air.

It had only been dawn which had saved the National Guard from a total rout, they had been forced to surrender one block after another. In the end they had managed to hold a fragile line running the width of the island at 96th Street. Had this line fallen, with every available man already committed, the rape of the rest of the City would have been inevitable.

As it was reinforcements were rushed in in the early hours and by breakfast time the authorities had regained the upper hand.

North of 96th, as the sun climbed higher, the scene in street after street was near identical – burnt-out buildings, burnt-out shops, National Guardsmen with dogs patrolling bayonets fixed.

By the time working hours commenced William had made it down to City Hall. He met there with his usual cabinet. The mood was very subdued. 'It's catastrophic,' he said shaking his head studying a rapidly prepared list. 'This damage is unbelievable. In Manhattan alone ...'

'It spread wider later,' said Commissioner McMichael in a businesslike tone. 'We tried to get you in the night but we couldn't find you.'

'Yes, I'm sorry about,' replied William rather sheepishly. 'As you may have heard I've just split up with my wife, I needed some time to myself.'

'Well, as it turned out your assistant Steve here covered for you,' said McMichael, 'but Mayor let it be said your absence didn't exactly help. Quite a few precious minutes were wasted trying to locate you.'

At this William privately wished he could have dug a hole and buried himself. 'All right, Commissioner, all right. I've given you my apology – I cannot do more than that.' He stared McMichael straight in the eye. 'And it's not as if I'm to blame for what happened last night.' He then turned to his aide hoping to make this the end of the subject. 'But thank you Steve for covering for me'

'That's all right, sir,' said Steve who was unfailingly deferential towards his boss.

'Even so,' said McMichael not quite finished, 'in future ...'

'Commissioner, let's let matters rest,' interrupted William with a hint of forcefulness, he was becoming a little red in the face. 'I repeat I'm sincerely sorry. It was an error of judgment. I was wrong. But let's not dwell on it, it's of no benefit to anyone!'

McMichael could see he had made his point, he decided to let it go.

~

Out in the Atlantic it was midday and sunny as Eliot and Warren sat aloft the steel platform of a fifty foot deep sea fishing boat. They had set out on schedule the evening before from New Haven, Connecticut and were nearly a third of the way into what they calculated would be a three day journey. With them were four other members of their group who were acting as crewmen.

As Eliot and Warren gazed out to sea they listened to a transistor radio they had with them.

'Manhattan, Brooklyn, the Bronx and Newark, New Jersey,' said the radio reporter, 'are today reeling as they recover from the worst night of violence in their history. The latest toll is 408 dead, over a thousand injured, over three thousand arrests and damage estimated at tens of billions of dollars. Though all is quiet this morning President Charles Guthrie has sanctioned a "shoot-on-sight" directive against all curfew breakers ...'

Eliot switched off the radio. 'Phew! Didn't take long did it?'

'No, sure didn't,' agreed Warren.

'Couldn't be better,' Eliot stated dryly. 'The fucking politicians are really going to have to start fucking thinking!

'Yes,' Warren replied measuring his words rather pensively. 'We've certainly come a long way since we started ...'

'A very long way,' nodded Eliot, looking out across the ocean again. He fell silent, Warren's remark had triggered off a flow of thoughts in him, he cast his mind back and briefly reflected on how it had all began.

The beginnings of the whole scheme were in fact quite simple. If anyone had represented the common link at the outset it had been Professor Stewart. It was he who had introduced Eliot to Robert, and later Robert to Matts. From then on things had moved swiftly as they so often do between people of like beliefs.

Eliot was actually thirty-four and his history might well have made him most psychologist's dream of a classic case study. He had never known his father and had been brought up by his mother in impoverished surroundings in a small town close to Chicago, Illinois.

He had loved his mother and she had loved him, but not only was she an alcoholic but she had also suffered a succession of nervous breakdowns during his formative years.

In his early teens he had been enrolled as an Army cadet because his maternal grandfather had been a military man and it was sort of a family tradition. Shortly thereafter his mother was diagnosed as having cancer of the uterus and within a year she was dead. At the time his elder sister, with whom he had now long since lost contact, told him that if they had had more money their mother might well have lived. He had never forgotten this.

He went on to become a good soldier. Some might say too good. For the Marine Corps turned him into a killing machine and later on he was seconded to other even more elite units. In both hemispheres and in many specialist, mostly covert, operations he was to see a great deal of combat. The American public could never be told what he had done for them, but had they known they might have been grateful.

Then, at the age of twenty-eight after ten years' service and several commendations, he discharged himself.

And it was now that any psychologist's vision of a maladjusted stereotype would have been proved wrong. For, whereas he made no attempt to exploit his military connections to get a well paid job, nor did he either slide into the confused, alienated lifestyle often associated with a misfit. Instead he returned to his native Chicago and worked as a firearms instructor in a swanky up-market gun club by day, and signed on for night school in the evenings. He had been deprived of a proper education and he sought to catch up.

More significantly still, it was during these studies that he came across a book written by a certain Economist at Princeton.

"The Causes Of Poverty In A Capitalist Society" by Professor Paul Stewart had a deceptively unenticing title. Long though it was, and highly technical as its appendices were, the main body of the work was very readable. It had been published many years earlier but had all but vanished without a trace because its contents ran so contrary to accepted mainstream thinking. Eliot, however, found himself unable to put it down.

The book could only be described as Left-wing in the loosest of terms. It was not anti-wealth, it was not even anti-millionaires, but it was firmly in favor of a constant redistribution of wealth between rich and poor. In this sense it was strongly interventionist in a way which was poison to all those holding the "free market laissez-faire" tenets it so forcefully attacked.

The extent of the interventionism it prescribed could be gauged by the opening paragraph of its introduction: "*All markets are unstable, all markets are imperfect and all markets are prone to distortions which may be as irrational as they are undesirable. The fundamental issue confronting a central government must therefore be whether to intervene or stand aside. Regrettably attitudes to this question have become wildly polarized. However, the fact is that whereas ill-judged intervention is worse than no intervention at all, intelligent intervention will certainly increase the overall happiness of an entire society. I would therefore say it follows that intelligent intervention is what Politicians are elected for – in short GOVERNMENT means intervention, otherwise why have any government anyway?*"

The Professor argued that was there a natural tendency for money to flow from the poor to the rich in one direction only. He maintained that if this tendency were left uncorrected the effect was inexorably to slowly but surely decrease the level of wealth in general. He claimed for an economic system to remain healthy money had to be kept circulating in much the same way as the blood in a human being's body. The consequence of too much money getting into too few hands and being allowed to stay there he likened to gangrene. He went on to cite many historical instances to support his case and listed the painful results of on numerous occasions too little being done too late.

In his closing chapters he highlighted the many changes in social and taxation policy he regarded as essential to the restoration of what he termed "dynamism" to the system. Furthermore, concerned in particular about the poor though he was, he went to great pains to stress that such changes were of crucial importance to all income groups and not just the under-privileged. In fact, returning to his medical analogy, he saw poverty as merely a disease which a body after an initial course of medication would rid itself of its own accord.

Finally, in a down-beat epilogue, he despaired of the chances of his recommendations ever being taken up. It seemed an impossibility. Existing prevailing wisdoms were far too deep-seated and a host of vested interests merely served as a strangulating second line of defense. And yet, he concluded without apology, if nothing were done, the future could only range between the at best pessimistic and the at worst apocalyptic.

Eliot read and re-read the work, not only was he impressed, he was persuaded. The only thing he disagreed with was that nothing could be done. He had seen dictators topple, he had seen governments fall, he had seen repressive regimes rendered impotent. And none of these events had happened by accident, they had been orchestrated. So it could be done! He ought to know. He had done it himself.

Whether the same principles could be applied in the United States he was not sure, but he could see no reason why not. To get the sort of intervention the Professor wanted a different kind of intervention would have to come first, but so be it. In the guise of an admiring reader he decided to write to him. What he said in the first place was cautious, but he did go so far as provide some clues as to his background.

To his surprise within a week the Professor wrote back asking him if he would care to make a trip down to Princeton. Needless to say Eliot accepted. More to the point, when they did meet, they got on immediately. And, once the initial ice was broken, it was here that the introductions to Robert and Matts were made.

In effect Professor Stewart and Robert had never lost touch since his days as a student. Matts, on the other hand, had arrived on the scene by a more roundabout route.

Matts Frederiksson was only a first generation American. He had been born in the States but his parents were from Sweden. He was in his mid-forties and had studied at MIT. He had then spent several years at NASA before being tempted away by IBM to work on various advanced systems architectures. Subsequently he had become tired of this type of research and had taken a post at Princeton to assist in the development of economic models. It had been the Professor who had appointed him. Not only did the two men quickly become firm friends but they soon found out that they shared the same ideas.

And while at one time Matts had lived on a hippie-style commune, this had in no way influenced his assessment of the Professor's work, he had simply become so familiar with it that he had no doubts about its merit. No matter how many different ways they programmed their computers the result was the same – society was better off when wealth was "actively re-cycled" than when it was not. That was enough for Matts.

So, whereas the Professor was the link, it was Eliot who formed the final catalyst. They now had everything they needed – the money, the know-how and the muscle – and they intended to do something.

Extra recruits were not a problem, Eliot knew where to look. The ranks of the Armed Forces were far less populated with numbskulls and dickheads than the average civilian probably imagined. Moreover, if you had spent months in the field with men there was little you did not get to know about them. The suitability of those he selected was not something open to dispute.

And if one asked, looking at the entire group from the Professor downwards, why a handful of men were prepared to embark on such a hazardous exercise, the bland answer would have been the correct one – because they wanted to, because something in them told them it was right. It was like asking people why they took up Holy Orders, or why they disapproved of killing animals for food, or why they chose to climb a mountain, or why they fell in love. At the end of the day, once superficial explanations were dispensed with, they probably could not tell you – they just did.

As the boat swayed in the swell a voice jolted Eliot out of his reverie, 'You two going to have a bite to eat?' called out one of the other men from the deck below.

'Sure, what's cooking?' Eliot asked.

'Burgers and beans,' came the reply.

'Sounds okay to me,' he answered, and he and Warren climbed down from the fishing platform.

Old axioms still appeared to hold true, no matter what sort of soldier you were, armies still marched on their stomachs!

~

William Donaldson was having a drink in his private office at Gracie Mansion with Oakley Cunningham. It was early evening. The sound of a mobile generator whirred from outside in the Mansion's garden.

The day had been extraordinarily hectic as massive plans were drawn up to try to prevent any repetition of the violence of the night before. In parallel the investigation to find the terrorists had carried on relentlessly. Commissioner McMichael had provided detailed up-dates of police efforts; and Scott Taylor, by now acting as a sort of unofficial general intelligence coordinator for Oakley's side, had filled everyone in on the work of the various Agencies. Already thousands of people had been interviewed, countless phone taps authorized, and hundreds of just very marginally possible suspects put under round the clock surveillance. But on all fronts all there was to report remained completely unchanged – a continuing, frustrating, fruitless blank.

It might well have been thought that since Eliot and his men were ex-military they would have been among the first to warrant the attention of investigators. But there was a snag here which the authorities were likely to have some difficulty in overcoming. Not only had Eliot and the others assumed new identities but they were all officially "dead". Matts had arranged this over a period of time by getting into the relevant computer files and implanting false data. For example, Warren had suffered a premature cardiac arrest, Zak had died in a plane crash, Gil had been killed in action in Iraq, Eliot had gone so far as to jump under a subway train, and Matts himself had just settled for a simple drug overdose. All in all it seemed like a pretty sorry tale, but, more to the point, the long deceased did not usually commit crimes from beyond the grave.

At Gracie Mansion as they had their drink that evening Oakley's energy level was holding up, but William's was not. Feeling tired and worried he took another gulp of his scotch. 'But Oakley, we know that power's still at least forty-eight hours away.'

'Yes, but that's quicker than first expected. Presidential half-truths aside!' he replied, adding the quip to try to bolster his friend's morale.

'But it still gives us say three more nights of potential hell,' answered William, his voice flat and dejected.

'No, no, I doubt it,' said Oakley. 'I think it'll be okay now.'

'Yes? You sure of that?'

'William, how can any of us be sure? But I think the situation is covered. Try and look on the brighter side! Bad as things are they could have been a whole lot worse!'

'Could they?' said the Mayor, his tone sounding increasingly drained. It seemed for once that not even Oakley's ebullience was quite working its usual magic.

~

With the generator on his roof pumping out electricity at full steam Robert kept on working in front of his easel. By now he had done a whole pile of drawings. He had connected his radio up to a power point and listened to it as he worked: 'And to recap on the events of this cataclysmic night and day,' said the voice of a radio announcer, 'everything remains calm across the Nation this evening ... Speaking from the White House President Guthrie has denied widespread accusations that he initially deliberately misrepresented the amount of time it would take to reinstate power supplies ... And lastly, as a footnote, Mayor William Donaldson of New York, the man in the midst of this crisis, has made it public that he is seeking a divorce.

'For those of you able to be with us, we now resume Rock music ...'

As the opening bars of Led Zeppelin's "Stairway To Heaven" wafted round the studio Robert decided again to switch off his lights and look out the window. In the dusk he saw two Armored Personnel Carriers crawl by and he noticed they were not State Militia. Eliot had taught him how to recognize military insignia and he could tell that these men were full-time paratroopers. Moreover, they were more than just paratroopers, they belonged to the United States Rapid Deployment Force – a spearhead unit, theoretically the "crème de la crème".

The sight of this made Robert smile a little. It indirectly reminded him of what John F. Kennedy said at the time of his famous visit to Berlin, "*We have never had to put a wall up to keep our people in*". And whereas he did not feel what he saw now was anything like as bad as that, he could not help but think that it served to confirm his views: If a society was forced to resort to using crack troops against its own civilians something had to be wrong.

He re-drew the blind and went back to his drawing.

~

William returned to 89th Street and spent the night with Rosanne. Maybe after the criticism he had received over his unavailability the night before this was foolhardy, but he needed her.

The sunlight of another hot August day stirred them early. It had been, for William anyway, a night of death-like sleep. 'I slept well, I needed to,' he yawned as he reached towards her.

'I slept like a log too,' she replied, 'I didn't hear a thing. No sirens, no disturbances.'

'Yeah, nor did I,' sighed William contentedly slipping his arm firmly around her. 'But I guess it's hardly surprising, there are twenty-five thousand Military out there. The main thing is that their presence worked. Thank God ...'

She leant over to kiss him affectionately. 'So you think that's the end of it?' she asked.

'You're talking about the chapter or the book?' he replied, the problems of the previous day were clearly one by one filtering back into his head.

'I don't know, you tell me,' she said.

'I don't know either,' he replied again, his anxiety transparent as he stared towards her. 'Frankly until we have these people behind bars I wouldn't want to commit myself.'

'It's that much of a ...'

'Yes, it is,' he frowned forcefully. 'We don't know who they are, but when we do they deserve to be skinned alive.'

His steel blue eyes left no doubt that he meant what he said. And it was exactly when she saw this burning intensity in his handsome features that she found him the most irresistible.

In fact totally irresistible. She shifted her body to make love, and make love they did.

CHAPTER 9

That same morning, as some semblance of civil order seemed to have returned to the island of Manhattan, Robert packed his drawings into an artists' portfolio bag and headed out to Connecticut. To get a cartoon done within a period of a week or so he knew he needed the help of computers and, in that department, Matts was obviously the man.

He took the same route as before using the emergency ferry to get across the river and then being met by a car on the other side.

'Hi Matts,' he said as he entered the cellar of the house which was its usual hive of technical activity.

'Hi,' Matts replied from in front of his computer terminal.

'You heard anything from Eliot?' Robert enquired.

'I know they got off on the boat okay, that's all,' said Matts.

'Good,' said Robert noticing him staring down at his portfolio bag.

'So this is it, is it?' asked Matts with his eyes still fixed on the bag.

'That's right,' smiled Robert holding his work with the same covetous affection as might a mother with a newborn child. 'Or at least it's a start, when I go back to the Village later there's still some work to do.'

'Well, let's see,' said Matts dying to have a look.

Robert began to untie the ribbons which held the bag's flaps together. 'I warn you it's a little rough, we're going to need the computer graphics here to tidy it up.'

'What you call rough is what most people call perfect!' grinned Matts knowing that Robert only worked to the highest standards.

Robert placed the portfolio bag on the table in front of them and unfolded its flaps, the top drawing was revealed. 'Okay, there you are! Those are my two characters!'

'Gee!' exclaimed Matts when he saw them. 'They look rather cute!'

'You like them?' smiled Robert.

'Yes, very much,' said Matts. 'They're like a couple of cheeky goblins, and you've made them so colorful, right down to their knickerbockers!'

'Well, I thought a few splashes of fun here and there wouldn't do any harm! Have a look at the next one.' Robert slid aside the top drawing to reveal the second in the pile. 'This is them smiling.'

'Jesus,' joked Matts, 'what sort of diet do these guys eat with pointed teeth like that!'

'I don't know,' laughed Robert, 'maybe they eat people like Oakley Cunningham!'

'Ha!' laughed Matts his sense of humor much tickled.

'At any rate,' said Robert quickly flicking through to show Matts a few of the other drawings, 'I think they'll make suitable ambassadors for our next move!'

'They definitely will,' concurred Matts. 'Ha! Look at those long pointed fingers, I wouldn't let them scratch my back! And their eyes, they're so mischievous looking and yet so intelligent'

'I can see you've fallen for them, Matts!'

'I certainly have, I think they're great! They're like a cross between extraterrestrials and something out of a Brothers' Grimm fairy tale! Yeah, they're too much! Have you given them names?'

'Yes,' smiled Robert, 'Zyron and Axma. Zyron's wearing the green hat, Axma the purple one. They were the first two names that came to mind that seemed to fit.'

'Zyron and Axma, yeah, suits them. So, tell me, Robert? How do you want to put this together?'

'Well, I'm rather in your hands,' he replied as he continued to flick through. 'As you can see after the first half dozen or so they're just outlines without color, I mean to color them all would take ...'

'That's all right,' Matts interrupted, 'we can handle that. Now I have the basic color scheme I can set the computer palate to color in the rest of the outlines for you.'

'The wonders of technology,' smiled Robert relieved.

'Yes, the wonders of technology,' echoed Matts. 'Similarly once I have their silhouettes digitally scanned in I'll be able to morph their movements pixel by pixel. That'll greatly reduce the number of drawings required.'

'Really?' said Robert slightly amazed and making no pretence that he fully understood exactly what Matts was talking about.

'Yes, shouldn't be any problem,' confirmed Matts as they reached the bottom of the pile, 'I can see what you're aiming at. Let's go and do some test graphics.'

'Okay,' Robert replied.

And, as the two of them began to gather up the drawings, Matts had to laugh again. 'Ha! I've really got to hand it to you! These cartoon characters are fantastic, I give you ten out of ten!'

'Thanks,' he smiled as the two of them headed over towards the graphics equipment.

~

The "Belle Epoque" ploughed on through stormy waters towards the agreed rendezvous off Newfoundland.

Stefan had summoned Dawn to the cabin which doubled up as his office. This was not something he did very often but when such "invitations" did arise she always knew she was in for some kind of verbal battering. Brave girl she went to the meeting as usual ready to take whatever abuse came her way on the chin.

As Dawn sat there Stefan pored over his navigational charts. 'You listened to the radio?' he said briefly glancing up. 'Your country's in a mess! Not surprising when your Government sends pieces of trash like you to do their dirty work!'

'I'm saying nothing,' she replied in a flat tone.

An agent of the United States Government she most certainly was not, but she knew that the impression that she was had to be preserved. This was because Stefan only "worked" for governments, that was the real basis behind his success rate and that was how Eliot had originally come across him. Twice in the past he had done jobs for the United States and both times Eliot had been his hirer – secret arms for Afghanistan, secret arms for South American political factions, those types of thing. Of course any nation backing such undertakings always hoped to remain anonymous but as a rule guessing its identity required no special feat of imagination. And so too on this assignment Eliot had led Stefan to believe that his employers were once again the same. Had he not been persuaded of this it was very unlikely that he would have agreed to do it.

'What do you mean you've got nothing to say!' growled Stefan running a pair of dividers over his map. 'You must be dumber than I thought! You've got no electricity! You've got your army out on the streets! And all you can tell me is that you've got nothing to say! Well, I can tell you if I were in your shoes I wouldn't be too happy! I wouldn't be happy at all!'

'I'm really not in a position to comment,' she said defensively.

'That's just because like most Americans you don't have a brain in your head! You know what I really think of the United States? I think it's the pits!'

Dawn refused to be provoked.

'Anyway,' said Stefan folding up his chart, 'we'll reach your people tomorrow some time after sunrise, they'd better have something constructive to say!'

'Okay,' she said getting up to go.

'Sit down!' he shouted. 'I didn't give you permission to leave!' His manner was not even one normal people would use to address a dog.

Dawn sat down again, narrowing her eyes at him just a little.

'Okay, now you can go!' he told her. She duly left. Clearly, on top of everything else, he also had some form of perverse power complex.

~

Rosanne spent most of the day at home, where she found her mind wandering all over the place. She had always been a person of rapidly changing feelings and mercurial moods but over these last few days she felt almost as if she was on a rollercoaster.

As the afternoon wore on boredom and a sense of claustrophobia got the better of her, she had the urge to go out. The only problem was where. Then she decided – she would go and see Robert. Naturally she remembered storming out of his studio a couple of days earlier but this memory represented no obstacle to her. For a start she was much too used to men forgiving her for just about everything. Secondly, on matters of conscience, she had what amounted to the most wonderfully convenient variety of instant amnesia.

She grabbed a cab and headed for Washington Square. Knowing the buzzer would not work she went to his door and thumped it hard calling out his name.

Her initial efforts produced no result. However, having travelled all this way, she was not about to give up easily. She persevered.

'Robert! Robeerrt! Aren't you there?' she shouted up to his windows for about the fourth time in less than five minutes.

But yet again there was no reply.

'Robeeerrrt!' she shouted louder still. Certainly persistence was not a quality she lacked when she felt like it.

But even though the evening light was beginning to fade there was no sign of him. He was actually still on his way back from Connecticut.

'Robeeerrrt!' went out the cry again. It was becoming mildly ridiculous.

Then, as she stood there, two paratroopers rounded the corner on foot. They were armed to the teeth with high velocity rifles fitted to powerful infra-red telescopic night-sights.

After witnessing one more call of "Robeeerrrt!" go out at ear-shattering volume and seeing how pretty she was they could not resist going over to her.

'You locked yourself out or something?' asked one of the paratroopers with a smile.

'No,' she smiled back putting on a hint of a flirt, 'I'm just trying to visit a friend, but it seems he's not in.'

'Well, I wouldn't hang around here too long,' replied the same paratrooper, 'remember the curfew.'

'Yes, I realize,' she said, 'I guess I'd better be thinking about heading on.'

She smiled at them again with just a twinge of nerves as she moved on. Friendly as they were towards her, she could see that these were really hard men, definitely not the type you would want to get on the wrong side of or run into in a dark alley.

~

William Donaldson, after another exacting day of meetings and conferences, was dropped off by his own stretched Cadillac on the corner of 89th Street. He walked the last few yards over to Rosanne's apartment building and entered its dim lobby.

'Good evening, Mayor Donaldson,' said the familiar face of Larry dressed in his usual doorman's cap and coat.

'Good evening,' he replied heading straight for the door leading to the staircase.

'Let me lend you a flashlight again.'

'Thanks,' he said taking it.

William began another ascent.

~

Meanwhile, at about the same time, Robert arrived back at his studio. As before he had only just beaten the curfew, though in fact he had found out that if you were in a cab and knew where you were going the authorities allowed you a few minutes grace. This was common sense in so far as the alternative of leaving people stuck out on the streets would have made matters worse not better.

As soon as he had unlocked his front door he went up to his roof, set the generator in motion, and returned to his studio to resume sketching.

~

Three hundred stairs later William emerged out of puff on to the sixteenth floor. He walked over to Rosanne's door. Giving it a firm knock he announced his arrival, 'Rosanne, it's me!'

But no one came to the door.

He waited patiently for a short while before knocking a second time. 'Rosanne!' he called again, his expression was beginning to become rather vexed.

He listened carefully, but not a sound came from inside the apartment.

'Rosanne!' he shouted giving it one more try. 'Jesus!' he exclaimed under his breath giving the door a real thump. 'Rosanne!'

But after a several more seconds there was still no response. Looking and feeling disgusted William turned back towards the stairwell.

~

At the same time, Robert continued to draw in splendid solitude inside his studio. At this very moment he was doing some intricate work on Zyron and Axma's smiles. Something in him made him want to make their teeth look sharper and shinier still. Between strokes with his crayon he looked at their cheeky angular faces, their large intelligent large eyes, their spiky fingers, their dazzling multicolored outfits, their mischievous grins, their eccentric hats. Somehow the sum of all these elements combined to give these two extraordinary figures an impact and a presence which even surprised him. Yes, even he had to admit to himself that he was more pleased than usual by these fantastic products of his own imagination.

~

However, one person not in solitude, splendid or otherwise, was Jack Grant. In his apartment on 33rd and Park Rosanne sat beside him with her legs curled up on the settee.

Candles burnt and she was sipping a glass of red Napa Valley – in the unrefrigerated heat the thought of unchilled white wine did not appeal to her.

'Well, it's obviously out of the window now,' Jack said cordially, 'there's no way I could run your piece on Robert Cook. I've had it pulled from the publication. I mean to run it in the light of the events of the last few days would be in the worst possible taste!'

'Yes,' she reflected pensively, 'I suppose some of the things he says now appear a bit close to the wind.'

'Very close to the wind!' quipped Jack.

'Yes, you're right,' she nodded. 'People would see it as rubbing salt into the wound.'

'And a lot of salt at that!' he quipped again, pleased that she was accepting his decision without a fight.

'Oh well, too bad,' she sighed. 'Quite a lot of wasted time and effort ...'

~

William waited listlessly with Larry in the doorway of Rosanne's apartment house. He was doing his best to hide the anger he felt. By now the sun was well down and the few minutes grace before the full curfew was enforced had long elapsed. He had to find a way to get back to Gracie Mansion and he was not about to attempt the journey on foot – No one knew better than he did that the shoot-on-sight directive against curfew breakers was for real.

'Okay, here comes a police car!' he said to Larry seeing the vehicle's flashing lights approaching. 'Try and get its attention.'

Larry gingerly advanced one pace into the dark street and put his fingers in his mouth to make a shrill whistle.

The whistle produced the desired effect. The squad car slowed down and halted outside the building.

'Good evening, officers,' William edgily called over from just inside the doorway. 'It's Mayor Donaldson. I need a lift back to my residence.'

The officer in the passenger seat was initially not totally convinced by the claim of this figure whom he could see only in shadowy silhouette. He lifted up a strong flash lamp and shone it at William's face. His tone immediately altered in surprise, 'Mayor Donaldson! Gee I'm sorry, sir. Come right on over.'

'Thanks,' said William striding forward. 'And thanks to you too,' he said to Larry handing him a $20 bill.

William climbed into the back seat and the police car drove off.

~

Once the discussion concerning Robert's article had ended Rosanne had gone fairly quiet. Jack knew her well enough to know that this could mean anything, she had this strange habit of drifting off as if she were visiting some distant corner of the Universe.

Suddenly she half-frowned as if she had something she badly wanted to say. But then she seemed to change her mind and instead just took another sip of her wine. 'Well, I can't get home now,' she calmly announced.

'Yes, I suppose you can't,' he replied in a tone more or less relaxed. 'But remember the past is the past.' Beautiful as she was he had no wish to get re-entrapped.

'No, Jack,' she said turning to him suddenly watery-eyed, 'I'm not after anything from you.' Her voice was full of emotion, clearly his remark had somehow opened the floodgates on what she had been about to say a moment before. 'I've got much too much confusion in my head as it is!'

Her distress was patently obvious. 'What's the matter?' he asked gently.

'Oh God,' she said only just fighting back tears, 'I don't know if I want to talk about it.'

Jack chose not to reply. He watched her hesitating collecting her thoughts.

After a few moments she decided to speak. 'Okay, Jack, because we were once together I feel I can be open with you.' Her voice was very strained. 'I've got myself into a situation I don't think I can handle – I'm in love with two guys at the same time.'

'Go on ...' he said trying to appear sympathetic.

'I can't name names, I really can't. But you would have heard of them both!' She paused again to gather herself. 'Okay, perhaps I haven't always been the most faithful of people, but it's never been like this ...'

Jack was tempted to press her for the names of the two men, but thought better of it. In any case he knew, perhaps thankfully, that she was always very secretive about her conquests. He settled for a more limited question. 'So do these guys know each other?'

'No, they've never met, and obviously have no idea! But they're both crazy about me, and I'm, well I'm just so confused.' Rosanne had to run her fingers over her eyes to stem the tears. 'I tell you it's making me demented! One minute I want one, the next I want the other, I feel as if I'm losing my mind.'

Jack decided that he had to pause for a moment's thought himself. It was true that he had never seen her quite as upset as this, but he could not help but feel cynical. Moreover, they had broken up because she had left him abruptly for another man. Consequently, although he did not dislike her, he felt he owed her nothing. Indeed, if she were looking for genuine sympathy, he was the wrong person to turn to, all she was likely to get from him were a few things she did not want to hear. 'Okay then,' he said keeping his voice low key, 'answer me this – Is this really so unusual?'

'What do you mean unusual?' she said not picking up his thread.

'Don't take it badly, Rosanne, but sometimes on the subject of love I don't think you'd even know it if you found it!'

'What?' she frowned indignantly.

He could see her expression changing to anger but he was undeterred. 'As far as I can see you look at love in terms of pure physical attraction and beyond that you can't see beyond the end of your nose!'

'Hold on a minute!' she tried to interrupt.

'No, I'm going to finish,' he insisted. 'You asked my opinion, so let me give it to you. If you want the truth I'd say that all that's worrying you about these two guys is that sooner or later things will come to a head and you'll end up the biggest loser!'

'Shit! Well, thanks a lot!' she shouted quite incensed. 'I come here at my wits' end and all you can do is make criticisms! You don't understand a thing! In fact you haven't even got a clue what you're talking about! When I'm in love it's deep, really deep! But what do you care, you haven't got any sensitivity! I always knew you were a pig!'

She waited for his response her eyes aflame. But he did not react. He had no regrets about what he had said. If she was going to make a scene, too bad.

One thing was for sure – the silence did not last long.

'You know something, Jack? You must be a real penis!' By now her tone was stinging. 'A real one hundred per cent "A-1" asshole! In fact a complete and utter nobody! How I ever got involved with a jerk like you I don't know, I must have had a screw loose or something! But never mind! I'm going!' She swept her dainty feet off the settee and rammed them into her shoes.

Jack just sat there, he refused to be rattled. Her insults meant nothing. When she was like this he just wondered who she really thought she was.

Nonetheless, some hitherto unexpressed resentments connected with the end of their affair still bubbled inside him. And these, plus something that seemed to have slipped her memory, added up to an opportunity too good to miss. 'So you're going are you?' he said permitting himself a trace of sarcasm. 'Well, that's always been your tactic, I've heard it so many times before that I've almost lost count. Whenever you come under any form of attack you tell people "you're going" – It's a sort of cheap safety valve for you!'

'Nobody talks to me like that!' she screamed at him as she stood up.

'Don't they? Well, I didn't invite you here, you just turned up.'

'Well, fuck you!' she yelled at him with unabated fury. 'I'm going!'

'I'm not stopping you,' he said casually. 'But haven't you forgotten something? You can't. The curfew!'

'I don't care!' she shouted hysterically. 'I'm not staying here!'

'Well, if you want to risk getting shot on sight, that's your affair,' he told her calmly. 'You could be shot on sight you know, the authorities aren't bluffing. They're not bluffing at all! I tell you baby, rather you than me!'

This statement stopped her dead in her tracks. The mental picture of the two paratroopers in the Village with their belts of live ammunition came straight back to her. For a second or two she tried to keep glaring at him in hopeless defiance. But then something had to give, and it did. She crumbled back on to the settee sobbing uncontrollably.

'Oh Jack, if you knew how I felt,' she cried choking back the tears. 'I feel like I was being torn apart inside, torn apart by sort of, sort of undercurrents pulling at me which I don't understand, almost like I was a "puppet" on the end of someone else's string!'

'No, no, Rosanne,' he said now not unkindly. 'Don't be like this, try and calm down. I'm sure that it's just that you've got this whole thing blown way out of all proportion.'

'No, I haven't,' she sobbed.

'Well, anyway I suggest you sleep on it. We can talk about it some more in the morning. You can have the bed, I'll take the settee.'

~

A glorious sub-Arctic sunrise crept over the Atlantic Ocean off Newfoundland. The "Belle Epoque" had reached the rendezvous point and was holding position. For over half an hour Dawn and Stefan had stood out on deck watching Eliot's deep sea fishing boat grow larger as it neared.

Finally it came alongside and Eliot and Warren, with back-packs slung over their shoulders, began the ascent of a rope ladder.

Leaning over the railings as they climbed Dawn felt so overjoyed that she just wanted to stretch out to hug them. But then she reminded herself that this was probably not a time for shows of affection.

In any case when they arrived on deck Eliot only afforded Dawn the briefest of glances before turning to Stefan. His tone was direct. 'Hello, Stefan, if that's your name, I hear you've been restless.'

'Yes, I have,' replied Stefan with thinly veiled hostility. It was clear that whatever their relationship had been in the past friendship had not been part of it.

'Well, now things are moving,' said Eliot leaving no doubt that he considered himself in charge. 'You can tell your Navigator to steer South.'

'And then where?' Stefan asked.

'We're going to Boston, full speed! Go tell them on the bridge.'

'Okay, I will,' he said his manner as surly as ever. He headed off.

'And Dawn?' said Eliot.

'Yes, Eliot?'

'You can go back on the fishing boat, you've done enough. The boat can take you into St John's, Newfoundland, you can then take a plane – You'll be back in New York a lot quicker.'

'You sure?' she asked praying there was no chance that he might change his mind.

'Yes, I'm sure. And you deserve it. I know Robert'll be pleased.'

'Thanks,' she said just touching his arm in a gesture of boundless gratitude. 'I'll go and get my things.'

Eliot nodded and with a new spring in her step she hurried off towards the superstructure.

'And Dawn?' he called after her.

She turned to glance back at him.

'Well done, very well done.'

'It was nothing,' she answered in the true spirit of martyrdom before continuing on her way.

CHAPTER 10

Later on the same day that Eliot and Warren had reached the "Belle Epoque", dusk fell again over Manhattan. Once more, little by little, the unlit skyscrapers began to fade into sad grey unappealing unlit monoliths.

Then, suddenly, across the whole City, the lights came on!

Rosanne was alone in her apartment at the time. The first thing she heard was the sound of her air-conditioning units pumping out cool air. She sprang up excitedly from her seat and rushed over to turn on the lights. They worked! Not content with this alone she tested her TV. It worked too! She was ecstatic. As was everyone. After days of deprivation power was restored.

Then, a moment later, her landline phone rang.

She paused and considered whether to pick it up – she knew it might be William, who for security reasons was so cagey about cell phones that he had always avoided calling her on one. Yet whoever it was had certainly not wasted any time. In fact no time at all. And this she found putting off. So, impulsive as ever, she decided to leave it to her answering machine. Her voice on the machine's "outgoing" message cut in: 'I'm not in right now, but if you wish to, please speak after the tone.'

She waited expectantly for the "beep" to signal the start of the caller's message, assuming there was one.

What seemed like interminable seconds later the "beep" came, and there was a message: 'Rosanne, it's William speaking. Whatever happened to you yesterday, why weren't you there when I came round? Whatever the reason we can work it out – Give me a call.' After that he rang off.

For a few moments she stood motionless reflecting. She then went to her phone and dialed.

Her call was answered fairly promptly. She drew in a deep breath, 'Hello, Robert, it's me.'

'Oh, it's you is it?' he smiled sounding his usual laid-back self as he stood by the phone in his studio.

'You see the power's back on!' she said slightly self-consciously.

'Yes, I've noticed,' he replied dryly.

Just a hint of an awkward silence followed.

'Look, Robert,' she resumed, 'I really think I owe you an apology about the other morning.'

'Is that so?' he replied dryer still. Whatever she was trying to say he was going to make her say it.

'Yes, I really do,' she went on convincingly. 'I think the power failure and everything surrounding it just sort of freaked me out – I just felt so weird and was acting so strangely, but really now I feel so much better – but I know I must have seemed crazed – I'm sorry, I'm really sorry.'

'So you're telling me you're reformed character?' he smiled.

'I guess so, but don't hold me to that!' she said back.

'Well, I'll tell you one thing!' he jested, 'I'm not going ask you for your phone number again!'

'Ha!' she laughed. 'But anyway,' she paused, 'I was wondering whether you would like to get together?'

Robert's expression showed that he would. 'Okay. When were you thinking of?' he asked. 'You know the curfew is over as well now?'

'Do I take that as a hint?' she smiled.

'Yeah, you bet you can take it as a hint! Why don't you come straight on over?'

'Great,' she said.

~

The deep-sea fishing boat with Dawn on board chugged into the harbor at St John's Newfoundland towards the end of the day. She then had to get to the airport at Gander and find a flight.

It turned out the next plane for New York was at 9.15 p.m. and she got her ticket with only minutes to spare.

As she waited for the flight to be called the airport was abuzz with the news that United States electricity supplies were back to normal. As she rode out on an airport bus towards the aircraft the fact that she would not be returning to darkness made her feel all the more excited.

Her plane took off right on time.

~

In Greenwich Village Rosanne and Robert sat side by side in his studio finishing a meal he had cooked.

'I must say, for a man, you're a pretty good chef,' she complimented him.

'Well, thanks,' he replied.

'But I still don't understand your whole approach to this,' she ventured about to take one last mouthful.

'My whole approach to what?' he asked.

'Oh, what we've been talking on and off about all evening. Basically speaking your attitude towards the people who have caused this crisis. Okay, you keep telling me you've got sympathy with them, but let's be realistic!'

'What do you mean realistic?' he questioned.

'I mean I can't see them getting anywhere. Actually, if you want the blunt truth, I'd say it's inconceivable – the most powerful nation on Earth isn't going to back down in the face of threats! No way.'

'I wouldn't be so sure,' grinned Robert. 'I really wouldn't be so sure.'

'Oh, come on! They can't possibly have a prayer.'

'Not necessarily,' he said breezily, yet his light-hearted tone also had a disagree-with-me-if-you-dare quality about it.

Rosanne simply shrugged her shoulders and smiled. 'You know something?' she said. 'I don't like to admit it, but sometimes you *really* make me wonder!'

'Why's that,' he asked with another grin.

'I don't know, just some of the things you say. But I love you all the same!'

She leaned over to give him a kiss.

~

Dawn's flight landed on schedule at Kennedy and she made her way through Customs and Immigration without hindrance.

Outside the terminal building she found a cab. 'Any chance of getting over to Manhattan?' she asked the driver as she climbed in.

'Sure,' he replied in a blank tone. 'As long as you've got time on your side – The traffic still ain't moving too good.'

'I understand. You mean because of the bridges and so on?'

'Yeah, it don't exactly help, that much I can tell you. Okay, which part of Manhattan you want?'

'Washington Square, Greenwich Village,' she told him.

'Okay, here we go.'

He put his cab into gear and drove off.

~

'Aahh! Aahh! More! More! Harder! Oh my angel!' screamed Rosanne rhythmically in a delirium of pleasure as Robert thrust into her on the bed. 'More! Harder! Please! Aahh! Harder still!'

'Rosanne, I love you,' he panted.

'More! Please more!' she screamed, some people made love louder than others but she was certainly about as loud as you could get.

Robert went at her harder and harder.

'Aahh! Aahh, harder still!' she shouted as she lay under him. 'Aahh! More! Harder!'

Robert had known her long enough to know she liked her sex quite rough, but the energy she put into it was almost frightening. The more he thrusted the wilder she became, she twisted and turned and arched her body underneath him as if his own body weighed nothing. She seemed to have the strength of three men.

'Oh! Oh!' she pleaded frantically. 'Yes! Oh yes! Go on! I love you! Oh God I love you! Go on! More!'

Her head and shoulders had worked their way half off the bed, but somehow she then curved her body in a snake-like motion forcing them, and him with her, back on to the sheets. At the same time she rolled around so that she was now on top of him. Beads of sweat dripped off her forehead. Forcing her tongue into his mouth to kiss him she rolled herself back beneath him again. No, she did not have the strength of three men, it was more like ten.

And all the while her passion just grew and grew, and all the while the sounds of her pants and gasps and cries became more and more. It seemed nothing, absolutely nothing, could ever be enough for her.

~

Dawn's cab rattled along the uneven steel surface of an Army pontoon bridge which sprawled across the river towards East 34th Street.

Where the pontoon finished and dry land began a hastily constructed temporary ramp fed traffic on to First Avenue. From here Dawn's cab made its way over to Fifth and turned South for the last mile and a half of the journey to Washington Square.

~

'Oh Rosanne, Rosanne!' he murmured.

'Oh yes! Yes! Now! Please now! Aaahhh!' she cried as her climax came, and his too. Hers seemed to repeat and repeat. She flung her arms and legs out sideways as straight as bolts, her feet braced rigidly, her toes spread out like the talons of some bird of prey. She let out one more long cry and closed her eyes in ecstasy. Her breasts heaved beneath him as she gasped for air. But still her orgasm was not quite yet spent.

Then suddenly she fell silent and her body went limp. They lay still a few moments until, slowly but surely, she started to entwine her limbs around him. He remained inside her as they kissed and caressed again. Her craving for love and affection was by no means over, her lust had no limits.

But as she hoped to coax him and inspire him into making love to her yet again, the door buzzer rang.

'Who's that?' she frowned as she continued to fondle him.

'I don't know,' he replied, 'anyway I'm going to leave it.'

Their lips joined in another kiss.

But a moment later the door buzzer rang a second time in a longer more insistent burst. This made Robert's eyes flicker just a little nervously, he knew it was always possible that it might just be something important.

'I'd better see,' he said disengaging himself.

'Must you?' she said.

The buzzer went a third time. 'Yes, I think I ought to,' he said putting on his gown. 'But don't worry, I'll be back.'

He headed out towards the door-phone in the lobby. 'Hello?' he said into it.

'It's me, I'm back!' shouted Dawn excitedly from down on the sidewalk.

Robert went pale, there was a rare hint of panic in his face. 'All right,' he responded as calmly as he could. He released the doorstairs door and he dashed back into the bedroom.

'Get your clothes on!' he told Rosanne urgently.

'What?' she said blinking.

Still looking pale he had to suck in air before he replied, 'It's Dawn I wasn't expecting her!'

Rosanne looked aghast.

'Come on, hurry!' he said dropping his voice for fear of being overheard.

She hesitated a moment. Robert gazed at her despairingly, he prayed she was not about to make a bad situation even worse. Slowly she then sat up. 'Okay,' she said sulkily. She began to get out of bed.

'Robert, you haven't opened the lobby door!' came Dawn's voice from the top of the stairs.

'One second!' he shouted back rapidly putting his clothes on too. 'Shit I'm sorry, Rosanne,' he said switching back to an undertone.

Rosanne just glared at him stonily, having come in one of skimpy one piece outfits she was already nearly dressed.

'Go on through to the studio!' he urged her.

'Why don't you just tell her!' she replied in an angry emotional whisper.

'I will!' he pleaded. 'But not right now!'

'Shit, it's after midnight! I don't see how you're going to explain this!'

Robert thought rapidly, an excuse came to him: 'We were going over your article, clearing it with your Editor on the phone, who "happens" to be out in California!'

Rosanne drew in a deep breath, she was far from happy. Even so she co-operated and walked through into the studio carrying her shoes with her so as not make any noise.

'Robert!' came another call from Dawn on the staircase.

'I'm coming!' he shouted as he hurried over to the door and finally unlatched it.

Dawn stood there smiling. 'I was beginning to wonder what was going on!'

'I'm sorry,' he said reflexively.

She strolled in. 'I hear when we put the lights out we caused ...'

Robert raised his hand to his mouth in a desperate gesture to shut her up. However, round the corner in the studio, Rosanne had not failed to hear. She looked extremely intrigued.

'What? What's the matter?' frowned Dawn.

'Nothing,' answered Robert tensely, 'but so you don't get the wrong impression I ought to tell you that Rosanne Lindblade is here.'

'The journalist?' she said alarmed by her own indiscretion, and at the same time a little confused.

'Yes, we've been going through the article,' Robert began to explain. 'The power failure stopped everything, so this is the first chance we've had, we were in the middle of a conference call to her Editor, who's in L.A.'

'Oh?' said Dawn in a muted tone drifting further into the lobby.

'Well, come and say hello,' he said.

They went on through into the studio.

'Hi!' said Rosanne forcing a smile.

'Hi, how are you?' said Dawn smiling too.

'I'm fine, we were just working late.'

'So I understand,' said Dawn trying to appear relaxed.

'But we've finished now,' added Rosanne biting well into her lip, 'and it's getting pretty late, so I must be thinking about going.'

'I don't mean to turn you out!' said Dawn.

'No, don't worry, you're not.' The undercurrent of chilliness in her voice fortunately passed undetected by Dawn. 'No really, it's time for me to go. And anyway, I'm sure you two must have a lot to talk about.' She moved towards the door. 'Good night, nice seeing you.'

'Nice seeing you too,' said Dawn.

'Good night, Rosanne,' said Robert playing it for all it was worth, 'thanks again for putting in so much time.'

'Don't mention it,' she said, just allowing herself one piercing glance into his eyes. 'It's okay, I can find my own way out.'

'You sure?' he replied.

'I'm sure.' And with a final frosty smile she left the room.

Robert and Dawn waited until they heard the lobby door close before they spoke again.

'You don't think she heard me, do you?' Dawn asked anxiously.

'I don't know,' he replied looking at her. 'Thankfully you didn't say very much.'

'God, how I was to know there was somebody here?'

'You weren't,' he said trying to reassure her. 'Don't worry about it.'

'I still feel a fool ...'

'Well don't, it really wasn't your fault,' he insisted. 'Just try and relax.' He went right up to her. 'But anyway,' he said looking into her eyes, 'I haven't even welcomed you home properly yet!'

'I guess you haven't,' she smiled.

Robert embraced her and they kissed. And, in fairness to him, he was sincere.

They disengaged and Dawn stared lovingly into his face. But then, her lips quivering in hesitation, she felt compelled to ask a question, 'And Robert?'

'Yes?'

'All this stuff about the article and the conference call, it is the truth?'

'Of course,' he said softly, 'I know it seems strange, but there you go.'

Believing him unquestioningly she instantly hated herself for even letting the thought enter her head, 'I'm sorry, I shouldn't have asked ...'

'No,' he smiled, 'it's better that you did.'

She smiled back watery-eyed. 'Oh, it's so good to see you, just so good.'

'And you,' he said hugging her again. 'You're a wonderful girl. And a plucky one too. It must have been miserable for you.'

'The worst days of my life,' she said tears suddenly running down her cheeks. 'I just thank God that Eliot came.' She held him tighter still. 'Anyway, it's over now.'

~

By the next morning the "Belle Epoque" was only a couple of hours away from Boston. Eliot and Warren took a walk around the deck with Stefan. In places the deck was laden two or three high with yellow containers. The purpose of their tour was to establish what types of cargo were where.

'And those?' asked Eliot pointing to a row of containers.

'Nothing much,' replied Stefan. 'More decoys – just various types of farming equipment again.'

'Okay, and those?' he said indicating towards another row.

'Same thing.'

'Okay. And you're completely certain none of our stuff is below the "weather deck"?' Eliot asked seeking assurance.

'No, nothing. Below the sealed hatches all we have are empty containers. Every item of your shopping list was loaded exactly as requested! Nineteen containers in total.'

'Good,' said Eliot. Indeed, the expression "shopping list" could not have been more appropriate: years of experience had taught both Stefan and Eliot that, at a price, anything was obtainable.

They moved on to another part of the deck which had been left clear. It had been at that this very spot that Stefan had grabbed Dawn by her oilskins.

'And this is the space where the "fake" cargo you told me about will be loaded,' announced Stefan. 'I trust that is organized!'

'It's organized,' replied Eliot staccato. He had no intention of putting up with any nonsense from the unpleasant little man.

'Okay,' said Warren pointing to double-check everything for himself, 'so it's that row of six, and that row of six which go off. Twelve containers.'

'Correct,' confirmed Eliot.

'But what about your other seven?' questioned Stefan a little perplexed.

'We're not going to need them,' said Eliot.

'What?' frowned Stefan.

'I said we're not going to need them! Understand?'

'Okay,' said Stefan looking confused but acquiescing. 'So what about Customs?'

'What about them? I don't see any particular problem.'

'But Customs can be tough!' Stefan protested.

'I know they can be tough! But we've done our homework. Okay!'

'I'm still concerned!' said Stefan getting agitated.

'Well don't be!' said Eliot. 'All you have to do is do as you're told!'

'I'm not so sure that I ...'

'Look!' interrupted Eliot. 'Just fucking shut up and do as you're told. Got it!'

Stefan did not look happy, but that was the end of the conversation.

~

While the "Belle Epoque" sailed towards Boston William Donaldson sat alone in his office at City Hall. He was in between commitments and had a few minutes to himself. Looking preoccupied he picked up his phone and dialed an internal number, 'Steve, I need to see you for a minute.' He replaced the receiver and waited for his aide to appear.

Steve Strauss was unquestionably a very competent young man. He had been to Harvard and ever since he could remember he had had a keen interest in Politics. For a couple of years he had worked for the Executive Branch at the Office of Management and Budget and therefore had a comprehensive knowledge of the Washington scene. He had been brought to William's attention by Oakley Cunningham who had first met him through his son who had been Steve's College contemporary. When the Mayor offered him the chance to be his principal aide he jumped at it. William's universal reputation as a politician going places made it not only a plum job but also an excellent stepping stone. Moreover, the appointment had proved to be a most satisfactory one with Steve and the Mayor developing an excellent working relationship right from the beginning, this rapport no doubt boosted by the fact that William could see that his protégé was in awe of him.

Moments later there was a knock and Steve entered William's office.

'Ah Steve,' said the Mayor, 'sorry to bother you, but come and sit down.'

'Sure,' said his aide. He pulled up a chair on the opposite side of the desk and waited to hear what it was William wanted. All the same, by the way he was looking at him, he could immediately sense that the Mayor was less than fully at ease.

William paused and cleared his throat. 'Steve,' he began somewhat awkwardly, 'there's something I want you to do.'

'Yes?' Steve replied, still observing his boss's discomfort.

William picked up a piece of paper and handed it to him. 'I want you to go to this address on 89th and Madison and gain entry into this apartment, you'll need to take a locksmith with you.'

Steve looked very surprised. 'Sorry,' he blinked, 'but may I ask what this is about, sir?'

'Don't worry,' the Mayor assured, 'it's all above board. In fact, technically speaking, though it isn't public knowledge, I am the owner of this apartment.' Indeed, in so far as he had paid for it, this was true.

However, hearing this only made Steve look all the more puzzled. 'But Mayor, excuse me, you'll have to forgive me for being, er, just a little, but I feel I ought to …?'

'No, no, not at all,' William quickly interposed, 'I can quite understand your wanting an explanation.

'Actually it's a personal matter, a lady lives there called Rosanne Lindblade, she's a close personal friend, hopefully my future wife. I've tried to reach her repeatedly in the last twenty-four hours but without success – It's beginning to worry me.'

'Oh,' said Steve hesitantly now feeling slightly embarrassed, 'please forgive me, I really wasn't meaning to pry.'

'No, it's perfectly okay,' he responded. 'You're fully entitled to know. But anyway, I realize it's asking a favor, but will you go?'

'Yes, sure,' answered Steve. 'How about getting into the building itself? Will that be any problem?'

'No. I've spoken with the doorman who knows me quite well. I told him I accidentally left some important papers there. Just show him your Mayor's Office ID and that'll be enough.'

'Okay, sir,' he replied standing up, 'I'll set about getting hold of a locksmith rightaway.'

'Thanks a lot, Steve, I'm much obliged.'

~

The "Belle Epoque" sailed into Boston Harbor. Eliot, Warren and Stefan stood on the bridge with a Navigational Pilot who had come aboard. The large cranes of a container depot loomed up ahead.

'That's the pier, take her in,' said Eliot.

'Okay,' replied Stefan.

Warren lifted a pair of binoculars and studied the waterfront. He could see Zak and Gil standing on the quay talking with two customs officers. Beside them was row of yellow containers identical to the ones they had on deck.

'Zak and Gil down there?' asked Eliot.

'Yup,' said Warren.

'Good,' nodded Eliot.

Two tugs came alongside and minutes later they were docked.

On the quay Zak and Gil continued their discussion with the Customs Officials. A freight supervisor had joined them.

'So what is it you're putting on here?' inquired one of the customs officers holding a clip-board.

'Farming equipment – Combine harvesters and tractors,' answered the freight supervisor checking a clip-board of his own.

'Yes, thirty-five containers, all bound for Nigeria, West Africa,' interjected Gil who seemed to have taken on the role of the equipment manufacturer's representative.

'Okay,' said the other customs officer in a relaxed tone. 'Let's have a look.'

'Sure,' Gil replied.

The group of men moved towards the row of containers.

'Okay, that one,' instructed the customs officer with clip-board.

'Jess, Hank, give me a hand,' shouted the freight supervisor to a couple of dock workers across the way.

The workers came over and helped unseal the container.

'Tractor wheels,' said the officer with clip-board as he peered inside. 'Okay, fine.'

'Okay, let's see this one then,' pointed the other customs officer.

'Come on, give us a break won't you!' said Gil light-heartedly. 'This shipment has a deadline, you're not going to put us through the mill are you?'

'I said open it up,' answered the officer civil but firm.

Once again the two dock workers broke the seals on the container requested. Its contents turned out to be tractor engines.

'Satisfied?' asked Gil.

'Yup, you can carry on,' said the same officer.

'Thanks,' said Gil.

The freight supervisor picked up his walkie-talkie and spoke to the crane operator, 'Okay Bob, take 'em away.' Within moments the clamps of a container crane locked on to the first container and hoisted it up towards the "Belle Epoque".

From up on the bridge Eliot, Warren and Stefan had observed everything. 'Okay, we go down,' said Eliot as the first container was safely lowered on board.

The three men left the bridge and emerged from the superstructure on to the deck. They took up a position by the ship's railings and for the time being simply continued to watch the loading operation.

However, after twenty or so yellow containers had been neatly deposited on board they strolled over to take a closer look at them. It was apparent that not only did the "new" containers look identical to the ones that they had sailed into port with but that they bore serial numbers that were the same as well.

'Okay, Stefan, get your on-board crane to start shifting things around,' instructed Eliot.

Stefan obeyed and headed back into the superstructure. Shortly later the arm of the small crane attached to the deck of the ship swung into motion. One by one it began to jumble up some of the recently loaded containers with others which had been there all along.

Stefan returned carrying a wad of papers.

'You ready?' Eliot asked.

'Yes,' replied Stefan.

'Okay, go. In a moment Warren will signal.'

Once again Stefan disappeared off. If he seemed strangely accommodating it was only because he sensed that the end, and therefore another $3 million, was now more or less in sight.

Zak and Gil were still on the quayside with the customs officers and freight supervisor.

'Hey, why's that crew member waving?' remarked Gil noticing Warren flapping his arms around up on deck. The customs officers turned to look.

Simultaneously Stefan hurried down the ship's gangway holding up his wad of papers. 'There's an error with this consignment,' he announced urgently.

'What do you mean?' frowned Gil.

'My instructions were to take on board container numbers "023" to "045" – one hundred tractors and fifteen combine harvesters. But we have also received numbers "046" to "057", that's wrong.'

'That wasn't what I was told,' said Gil dead-pan.

'Well, here I have my duplicate order forms,' responded Stefan handing over his wad of papers. Gil and Zak proceeded to study them carefully. Both sides were playing their "parts" to perfection.

'Yeah, there does seem to be something of a mix-up here,' commented Zak.

'Well, let them sort it out at the other end,' said Gil.

'No, that's no good!' said Stefan quite adamantly. 'The Nigerian Authorities will not accept anything that is not on these order forms!'

'You sure?' asked Gil.

'Definitely I'm sure!' said Stefan. 'They are very strict, there has to be an import license for everything which they will then match up with the order forms – They find one item without a license, well they could impound the whole cargo!'

'Jeez!' sighed Gil.

'Let me have a look at those documents,' said the customs officer with clip-board. Gil passed them to him and he glanced through. 'Yes,' he said, 'there's a mistake. This guy's right.'

'I know I am!' said Stefan. 'There is absolutely no point in having this unlisted cargo on my ship! In fact if you want the truth you're just inviting trouble, have you any idea what Nigerian officials can be like!'

'Okay, okay, point taken,' said Zak. 'I guess we have no choice but to unload the unwanted containers and take them back to the plant.'

'Yes,' agreed Gil. 'As long as that's all right with you Customs guys?'

'Sure, go right ahead,' nodded the customs officer with clip-board.

'Thanks,' said Gil. 'I'll go call our trucking company and get them down here.'

'You do that,' said the freight supervisor. 'And Captain?' he added turning to Stefan.

'Yes?' Stefan answered.

'It'd be a help if you get one of your crewmen to point out to us which ones have to be lifted off again.'

'I will,' he replied heading back on board. For sure he would show them with pleasure which containers to unload, but they would not be the same ones as had been on the quayside an hour earlier. He was already counting his money.

All remaining loading and unloading did not take long. Once it was complete Eliot, Warren and Stefan walked back to the bridge.

'So that's that,' said Eliot. 'We can put out to sea again.'

'You're not leaving now?' replied Stefan sounding less than pleased.

'No, a small boat will meet us and take Warren and me off later.'

Stefan gave Eliot a chilly look. 'Okay, I am tired of taking orders, but okay.'

And so, with the sun still high in the sky, the "Belle Epoque" weighed anchor and departed.

As the ship faded into the distance a fleet of twelve trucks began to arrive at the container depot. With all the terrorists' usual efficiency a yellow container was loaded on to each and hauled away.

The only twist to the Boston operation had been that the two customs officers were actually on the terrorists' side anyway. For, although they were genuine Customs employees, they were also men Eliot had known from his army days. The container mix-up had purely been for double indemnity. The two officers had simply advised that the more real you made it look the smaller the risk of mishap would be. And that was the sort of thinking Eliot liked to hear.

CHAPTER 11

In the cellar of the large house in Connecticut, Robert, Matts, Professor Stewart and Dawn stood in front of a TV monitor. The

Professor looked as dapper as ever in his grey suit and bow-tie, his cane in one hand, his glass of bourbon in the other.

On the TV monitor a "freeze frame" showed Robert's cartoon characters, Zyron and Axma, standing side by side. Zyron's green hat, which looked a bit like Robin Hood's, had had a large red feather added to its side. Axma's purple hat, in the style of a Moroccan fez straight out of "Casablanca", had a bright yellow tassle.

Zyron wore a violet tail-coat, white shirt and floppy red bow-tie with black polka dots. His red and black striped knickerbockers matched his bow-tie and his black patent shoes were rimmed with red buckles.

Axma also had a tail-coat, but his was electric blue. His shirt was pink and his bow-tie, even bigger than his friend's, yellow and white. His knickerbockers were green and purple, and the bow on his black shoes yellow.

In addition they both sported multi-colored low-cut brocade waistcoats with glittering jewelled buttons and the cuffs of their shirts were adorned with expansive frills. Last but not least, seen full length, Robert had given them both slightly plump bodies.

All in all the two of them really were an extraordinary sight. Partly they belonged in another century, but which century one would have had to ask, certainly no single century. Partly perhaps they could well have been figures out of some weird and fantastic dream, but it would have had to have been some dream. Partly too, as Matts had already observed, they might really have been from out of this world.

'Just roll it on a bit,' said Robert to Matts.

'Sure,' he replied pushing a button.

On the TV monitor Zyron and Axma's legs and arms began to move, as did their lips – though as yet without words. Their big blue luminescent eyes sparkled cheerily, their huge blinking eyelids gave them an infectious charm. First Zyron mouthed something, then Axma then Zyron, then Axma again. As one spoke the other one would sometimes smile. Their interplay was hypnotic. The pace of their performance lightning fast. They had star quality, no other act could have lived with them, on stage they would have been an instant sell-out. And, of course, the whole dimension of sound still remained to be added.

The cartoon clip kept rolling on.

Zyron uttered another unheard sentence and plucked the red feather from his green hat. The feather turned out to be a quill. With a big smile he tested it splashing the beige floor with a few drops of white ink. He flicked his long fingers at Axma who responded by removing his purple fez cap and reaching into it. Like a conjurer Axma withdrew a miniature blackboard from the cap and placed it on the floor between them. With a wave of his hand the blackboard magically expanded in size until it had filled half of the back of the screen. Axma took a bow in expectation of applause. Zyron walked up to the board and prepared to write on it with his red quill.

At this point the picture halted. Everyone was laughing, the Professor most of all.

'That's the end of that section,' smiled Matts, 'we haven't told Zyron what to write yet!'

'Ha! Brilliant Robert! Just brilliant!' chuckled the Professor leaning on his cane so much that it looked as if it might snap.

'I'm pleased you like it,' Robert smiled back.

'You should have been a professional animator!' congratulated Dawn.

'No, not me,' Robert grinned, 'I think I'm a little too serious-minded to do this kind of thing full-time!'

'That I appreciate,' laughed the Professor with a twinkle in his eye, 'but Dawn's right, it's pretty darn good! Even right down to the bow-ties!'

'Yes, but notice no cane!' quipped Robert. 'That might have made it a bit too obvious!'

'I doubt it!' joked the Professor. 'Engaging as they are I hope I don't look like them!'

'No, of course you don't!' Robert laughed.

'I was only kidding!' smiled the Professor. 'But Robert, there's one thing I can't resist asking, where on Earth did you get this idea?'

'I really don't know,' he grinned, 'the truth is these two colorful characters have been floating around my head for weeks! I suppose they just sort of walked in there uninvited! Where they came from your guess is as good as mine! You know how it is, ideas are in the air!'

'And lucky people like you just reach out and pluck them from the ether!' exclaimed the Professor. 'All part of the mysterious process of creation!'

'Seems so,' smiled Robert with a modest shrug. 'What more can I say?' Though, had not Dawn been there, he might have added that, whereas he could not explain how he got the idea, he most certainly vividly remembered the exact and precise moment when. It was not a moment he was likely to forget – it was the very same moment that he had first set eyes on Rosanne.

'Still, we ready to press on with the final couple of sections?' said Matts. 'After that we can start putting on their synthesized voices.'

'Sure,' said Robert. 'It shouldn't take too much longer.'

But as he spoke one of Matts' assistants came over to them, 'we have confirmation from Boston, everything went according to plan.'

'Excellent,' Robert replied.

'Perfect,' said Matts looking pleased and standing up. 'In that case let me just break off for a moment, I want to double-check they have all the right number series.'

'Yes, very important,' agreed the Professor.

Matts followed by Robert and the Professor strolled over to another computer. He typed into its terminal and an extensive array of multiple digit alphanumeric combinations began to scroll down the screen. 'All these numbers have been issued by the U.S. Treasury within the last year,' he informed.

'Ideal,' nodded the Professor with another twinkle in his eye. 'It means the bills will be scattered far and wide. We can't go wrong!'

'Let's hope not,' said Matts typing more instructions into the keyboard. 'Anyway I'll be back with you as soon as I've contacted Boston.'

'Okay, see you in a minute,' said the Professor.

Robert with the Professor began to move back to the cartoon, but Matts called after him, 'Oh, Robert?'

'Yah?' he replied turning round.

'It's just come to me that I forgot to mention something – I have that phone number on 89th and Madison you asked for.' He pulled a slip of paper out of his trouser pocket.

'Oh, thanks Matts,' said Robert nonchalantly taking it from him. 'Thanks a lot.'

'Don't mention it,' he replied, already re-engrossed in his computer data. 'See you in a minute.'

'Okay,' said Robert heading off to join Dawn and the Professor.

~

Steve Strauss and a locksmith emerged from the elevator on the sixteenth floor of Rosanne's apartment building. True to William's prediction, once he had seen Steve's ID, Larry had made no attempt to ask them where they were going.

'We need 16A,' said Steve scanning the corridor to locate the right front door. 'Ah, there it is.'

The two of them went over. The locksmith looked at the lock and opened his tool bag.

'You want to first check there's nobody home?' the locksmith suggested.

'Okay,' said Steve ringing the bell.

They waited but there was no reply.

'Okay, here we go,' said the locksmith picking up his tools.

'You see any problem getting in?' Steve asked

'No, not really. Shouldn't take me more than a short while.'

~

In a cavernous warehouse in Boston all twelve container trucks were parked in a row and some of the yellow containers had been unsealed. The unloading process was already well advanced as forklift vehicles ferried crates and cardboard boxes through a wide doorway into an adjacent area.

Zak and Gil stood in this adjacent area. Beside them was a long production track of rapidly assembled machinery manned by several operators.

Yet another fork-lift deposited half a dozen cardboard boxes at the front end of the production line. The chief operator and an assistant broke the cartons open. Their contents were revealed to be fairly sizeable sheets of thick white paper. Gil walked over. 'Are we ready?' he asked.

'Yes,' replied the chief operator. 'We're about to switch on, we're going to start with batches of "ones".'

'Good,' said Gil as he watched them load a pile of thick paper into the machinery.

The chief operator reached over to a power switch. 'Everybody stand by!' he shouted and a moment later the whole production line jerked into action.

Zak and Gil watched closely as "sheets" of dollar bills were printed at a rapid rate, first one side, then the other. Further down the track serial numbers were stamped to the left and right of the first President's head. At the far end as the "sheets" rolled off a guillotine machine cut them neatly into individual bills. Finally operators loaded the output into counting and collation equipment. In no time the air in the warehouse was thick with the distinctive aroma of paper money.

Gil and Zak went over with the chief operator to inspect the results. 'This looks good,' said Zak picking up a sample.

'Yes, very good,' smiled the chief operator. 'Indistinguishable from the real thing! As soon as we've completed the "ones" we'll do the "fives", then the "tens", and so on and so forth.'

'Sounds fine,' nodded Gil.

~

Steve Strauss looked on as the locksmith worked on Rosanne's lock. Then, with an adept turn of the wrist, the smith got it to click. 'Okay, we're in,' he announced.

'Good,' replied Steve.

The two of them entered and Steve was immediately struck by the luxuriance of the decor – deep-piled carpet, silk wallpaper, ornate antique cabinets, beautifully upholstered furniture. Just as noticeable were the choice of colors, everything was done in a mass of sensual pinks, light corals, soft greens and muted mauves. One did not need to be Sherlock Holmes to guess that this was a woman's apartment reflected the Mayor's assistant.

He moved on through to check the dining room, the main bedroom suite, the second bedroom and bathroom and lastly the kitchen. Everywhere was definitely empty. 'All right,' he told the locksmith, 'thanks for your help you can go.'

'Okay sir, you're welcome,' replied the man. He picked up his tools and departed.

Once alone Steve removed his jacket and sat down.

~

A waiter smartly dressed in white jacket and black trousers carried a meal tray along a hotel corridor. Arriving at his destination he stopped and knocked on a door.

'Come in!' called the voice of Rosanne from within the room.

The waiter used his pass key to enter. Rosanne was seated at a writing table apparently doodling with a pen on part of the Room

Service menu. In the corner was an open suitcase packed with clothes.

'Where shall I put it, mam?' asked the waiter about the tray.

Rosanne looked up with a slightly vacant glance. 'The table there's fine.'

'Okay, mam.'

The waiter placed the tray as requested and removed the silver dome covering a club sandwich. He went over to Rosanne and handed her the Room Service check. She stopped doodling and signed it. The top of the check read "The Drake Hotel Park Avenue". 'Thanks,' she said.

'Thank you, mam. Have a nice day.' The waiter left the room shutting the door behind him.

Rosanne slowly got up and took a piece of sandwich from the tray which also had on it a carafe of white wine and a bucket of ice. Eating a small mouthful she drifted back towards the writing table and stared down at her doodle. What it was could only be described incredible – it was an outline sketch of Zyron. The style was not quite the same as Robert's and it was without color, but the likeness was devastating. Every detail was accurate: the big eyes, the pointed teeth, the long fingers, the chubby tummy, the fancy waistcoat and tails, the hat with feather, the cheeky mischievous expression.

And the more she stared at the image the more transfixed she seemed to become. It was as if she was almost in a trance, almost as if someone were mesmerising her.

She took another small bite of her sandwich and picked up the phone on the writing table. She dialed, all the time still unable to take her eyes off her doodle.

The phone rang on Jack Grant's desk at Prestige Publications. He picked it up. 'Hello?'

'Jack,' said Rosanne in a tone which lacked her usual self-confidence.

'Oh hello, Rosanne,' he replied with a slight sneer. 'Where the hell are you?'

'Oh Jack,' she said strain showing in her voice, 'Jack, my head is spinning.'

Jack leaned back in his office chair and raised his eyes to the ceiling. 'Jesus Christ, Rosanne, is that so?' he muttered facetiously.

'I'm serious, Jack, I really mean it,' she went on.

'And what am I supposed to do about it? Act like an unpaid therapist again! I tell you, Rosanne, all this is beginning to wear a bit thin, why don't you just cut out the bullshit!'

'Jack, that's not fair,' she pleaded down the phone.

'Rosanne, I expected you to be at your desk today,' he told her matter-of-fact, 'with the power down we've lost a lot of time over the last few days, time that needs to be made up by you as much as by anyone else! You can't just scoot off like this!'

'Jack, I just need a day or two to myself,' she pleaded again still glancing down at her drawing of Zyron whose big eyes seemed to be looking straight back at her. 'Jack, you don't understand!'

'I don't think I do!' he said exasperated. 'Anyway I have a whole pile of messages here for you, some of them are actually quite interesting ...'

Rosanne's eyes flickered. 'From who?' she frowned.

'Well, let's see,' said Jack fingering through a pile of message slips, 'Mayor Donaldson has called four times, and Robert Cook, he's called twice, leaving a number in Connecticut – what's he calling for, surely he knows his article is scrapped?'

Rosanne froze, her brain in overload, she wondered how she was going to make any of this wash. 'Oh, I haven't told him about the article yet,' she said trying to think on her feet and struggling to order her mind. 'But I guess I ought to, give me the number can you?' She quickly scrawled it down on a piece of hotel stationery. 'And the Mayor? What was that about?' she asked hoping her voice gave nothing away.

'Well, I have to tell you Mayor Donaldson is a lot more forthcoming!' answered Jack smelling blood. 'I would have to say his messages are somewhat less than strictly business!'

'What? What do you mean?' she said, her innocent tone in complete contrast to the concerned look on her face.

At this Jack grew tired of pussyfooting around. 'Shit Rosanne! For Chrissakes, you must think I'm stupid or something! William Donaldson is inviting you to a private dinner at the Mayor's Residence at Gracie Mansion tonight! The whole drift of his messages is absolutely positively not business! So don't ask me "what do I mean", you must know very well! You can stop trying to sell me all this innocent little-girl-lost crap because I ain't going to buy it! Why don't you just come clean!'

Rosanne shook her head slowly, another time another place she might have lost her cool but not now. Her response mirrored her mood, it was subdued. 'Okay, okay I do know him,' she began, 'but I couldn't say anything to anyone until he had announced his divorce.'

'So he's one of the guys you were telling me about, one of the guys you've been sleeping with?' Jack asked point blank.

'Yes,' she murmured.

'And I suppose, putting two and two together, Robert Cook is the other?'

'Yes, yes ...' she conceded taking in a deep breath.

'Well, now the cat's out of the bag,' he said hitting hard, 'why don't get a grip on yourself and get back to work!'

Rosanne was more and more disoriented. 'No, Jack, you're over-simplifying it – you have to give me a day or two, I swear to God I'm disturbed!'

He paused and sighed and dropped his voice. 'Okay Rosanne, you have it your way.'

'Thanks, thanks Jack,' she replied gratefully. 'And Jack?'

'Yes?'

'You won't tell anyone, will you?'

'No. I won't tell anyone. Bye bye.'

Rosanne replaced the phone and shifted uneasily on her feet. She looked down at her doodle one more time, why it held some sort of fascination for her she had no idea, after all it was only a drawing. She returned to her lunch tray and poured herself a glass of white wine adding in plenty of ice cubes. Remaining heavily pre-occupied she took a sip.

Jack Grant sat in his office still churning over his conversation with Rosanne. He was thinking hard. After a few moments he reached a decision and spoke into his intercom, 'Katie, I have a photo-journalism assignment in New York, it's immediate. See who's available can you? I need someone really good, what's Jim Parelli doing?'

'Hold on a moment and I'll check for you,' came back the voice.

Jack casually lightly drummed the fingers of one hand on his desk top as he waited.

The intercom came on again. 'Yes, Jim Parelli is available today. What do I tell him?'

A trace of a smile came over Jack's face. 'Tell him there's a private function at Gracie Mansion tonight and I want everything covered. It's a potentially major story suitable for newspaper syndication. Jim'll need a team.'

'Okay,' responded Katie via the intercom.

~

In her hotel room at the Drake Rosanne finished dialing again. The other party answered promptly, 'The Mayor's Office, New York City Hall, can I help you?'

'Is the Mayor available?' Rosanne said, still sounding rather unsteady. 'It's Rosanne Lindblade.'

'Okay, please hold and I'll find out.'

William Donaldson was in yet another crisis meeting in the conference room at City Hall. Commissioner McMichael was there, as were Oakley Cunningham, Scott Taylor and Bruce Dean, who was Oakley's Presidential running mate. In addition there were the normal contingent of civic officials and specialist advisers.

'Look!' exclaimed Oakley, 'Even I am getting pretty tired of hearing excuses! We simply cannot rest while these people remain at large!'

'No one disagrees with that, Senator,' said the Commissioner, 'but in the absence of leads we have precious little alternative but to play a waiting game.'

'Maybe!' bellowed Oakley looking the Commissioner straight in the eye. 'But only up to a point! And let's remind ourselves that it is not, repeat mostly certainly not, any longer "early days"!'

McMichael looked uncomfortable but said nothing. On occasion he was prepared to take issue with William but Oakley Cunningham was a different matter, Oakley was not the sort of person people argued with.

'There is just one possible plus point worth mentioning though,' volunteered Scott Taylor.

'Yes? What's that?' queried Oakley sternly.

'I think our lack of success in gaining any intelligence on these people, unsatisfactory as it is, may be indicative that they've gone to ground. It's possible that the sheer weight of our investigative effort has frightened them off. They may now be a spent force.'

'Well, I hope you're right,' said Oakley. 'But that doesn't change the fact that I don't understand why we're not making any progress!'

'Make no mistake sir, we will,' said Scott.

'We have to', echoed William who had been perfectly happy to let Oakley do his talking for him. 'We're just going to have to re-double our efforts!'

At this moment a secretary came through the door carrying a note-pad. She went directly over to William and spoke into his ear, 'You asked me to interrupt you on this ...' She showed him the message written on top of the pad which read: "*ROSANNE LINDBLADE ON THE PHONE*".

William reacted instantly. 'I'm sorry, please excuse me,' he said calmly getting up, 'there's something I have to deal with, this won't take a minute.' Accompanied by the secretary he briskly left.

William covered the short distance to his office as quickly as his feet could decently take him. He picked up the phone, 'Rosanne,' he smiled in a friendly tone, 'you seemed to disappear from the face of the Earth – What happened to you?'

'I'm visiting my parents in New Jersey,' she replied. This answer she had already prepared. 'But I got your message from my office.'

'Can you come?' asked William.

'Yes, I'd love to,' she smiled. She seemed more relaxed again. 'Who else is coming?' she asked

'Oh, Oakley Cunningham, Bruce Dean,' he replied.

'Doesn't that make it sort of all politics then?' she questioned just looking slightly doubtful. 'I mean, you sure I'm going to fit in?'

'Of course you are, don't worry their wives are coming too. It's a social evening, you'll enjoy it, I want you to be there.'

'Okay,' she smiled.

'Dinner's at eight but I suggest you come a little early. Look, I'm in the middle of a meeting so I've got to go, but see you later.' He rang off and headed back to the conference room.

~

In the cellar in Connecticut Robert, Matts, Dawn and the Professor stood in a small excited huddle. Matts was about to open an envelope which had arrived that very minute from Boston.

'Okay, this is it,' said Matts withdrawing a wad of money from the envelope. He passed each of them a bill.

'Unbelievably real!' exclaimed the Professor holding his bill up to the light. 'Very, very good.'

'Yes, every detail is correct,' agreed Matts. 'The design, the slightly aged paper and, most of all, the serial numbers, watermark, security thread and fluorescence – they're where most forgers come unstuck!'

'Fluorescence?' asked Robert.

'Yes, a lot of people don't know it but U.S. money has a fluorescence, shows up under ultra-violet,' said Matts.

'Oh well, I've learnt something!' smiled Robert.

The Professor began to circle the room with his cane. 'So,' he said re-capping out loud, 'we have $750 in ones, fives, tens and twenties going to every household in America! That's a total of at least $40 billion! That'll make them sit up!'

'Certainly ought to,' said Robert.

'And,' said the Professor waving his cane, 'we were right not to print bigger bills – they would have been totally out of place in poorer areas.'

'No question,' nodded Robert.

'But, explain to me one thing?' interjected Dawn who by nature preferred to listen than talk. 'Maybe I'm being stupid, but why are we sending this money to everybody? Why not to just to the people who need it?'

'It's only "paper" my dear,' answered the Professor kindly. 'It hasn't exactly cost us very much and it's better that everybody gets to hear from us.'

'Yes, come to think of it, it makes sense,' she smiled. 'I guess I was just being slow a bit slow on the up-take, must still be the after effects of my voyage at sea!'

'No, my dear, it was a perfectly reasonable question,' the Professor chuckled. 'And as for all that fresh air, I'm sure it worked wonders for that sharp mind of yours!' Dawn beamed at him affectionately, just like all the others she adored the old man. 'But anyway,' the Professor went on, reverting to a more serious note, 'when do we think all this will hit the public?'

'Within twenty-four hours in most places,' Matts replied. 'The production line was operational by one o'clock this afternoon and I don't think anyone has ever printed money so fast! By 4 p.m. consignments were already on planes to destinations all the country. From there they should meet local mail service deadlines for next day delivery. As an important detail, we're using a variety of envelope sizes and addressing formats so that the risk of attracting any undue attention from postal clerks and so on is minimized. After all this is one hell of a lot of mail!'

'Sounds like another pretty well-thought out operation!' the Professor smiled approvingly.

'Well, that's the general idea!' smiled Matts.

'It certainly is!' exclaimed the Professor.

'And it's kind of amusing,' grinned Robert, 'that we have U.S. Mail doing this for us without even realizing it!'

'Yes, and I'd love to be a fly on the wall when this turns up on some doorsteps!' quipped the Professor.

'Wouldn't we all!' laughed Robert. And the others laughed too.

~

Steve Strauss remained seated in the apartment on 89th and Madison. Looking bored he glanced at the expensive clock on the mantle shelf it was just after six o'clock. He took out his cell phone and dialed.

William Donaldson was in his office in City Hall and about leave for home as he answered the phone. 'Hello?'

'Hello, Mayor Donaldson, it's Steve,' said the young man. 'I've been here all afternoon, but she hasn't shown. You want me to hang on?'

'Gee, I'm sorry Steve,' replied William transparently genuinely embarrassed. 'I've been in a meeting all afternoon and it completely slipped my mind – The lady has contacted me, everything's okay ... But please accept my apologies, I didn't mean to waste your time.'

'That's all right, sir,' said Steve as ever respectful. 'One of those things. Glad anyway that you have it sorted out.'

'Thanks Steve, and thanks again for your help. Bye, bye.'

William put the phone down, paused and rubbed his eyes. He felt cross with himself for making Steve hang around for so long unnecessarily. Also, after that afternoon's long unproductive meeting, he was aware of a slight headache coming on – nothing much, but enough to be annoying. He opened a drawer in his desk and took out a bottle of aspirins which he kept there. He swallowed a couple pulling a face as their bitter taste passed over his tongue.

Then, putting the aspirin bottle back in the drawer, he got up and went to find his waiting car.

~

Meanwhile at Rosanne's apartment Steve put on his jacket and unlatched her front door. However, as he did so, her phone rang. Since it had not rung once the whole time he had been there this last minute call seemed to him like something of a minor event. He let the answering machine cut in and waited and listened.

Rosanne's outgoing message came first: 'I'm not in right now, but if you wish, please speak after the tone.'

Seconds later the "beep" went: 'Rosanne, Robert Cook again at 6.15, I've called everywhere, where are you? If you're hurt about last night I can understand, but not talking isn't going to solve a thing.'

Something about the message intrigued Steve. It was not so much what Robert had said but the way he had said it. He had heard of Robert Cook but that was far as it went, however the tone of the artist's voice unmistakably suggested a familiarity towards Rosanne much greater than that of just a casual acquaintance.

After a moment's hesitation curiosity got the better of him. He left the doorway and pushed the button on the answering machine to go back to the beginning of all the messages on it. He then pushed playback and again waited and listened.

The first message on the tape was from William Donaldson, his voice sounded a mixture of irritated and fraught: 'Rosanne, I really hate these machines but since you force me to leave a message – Just please call me.'

The next message followed quickly after, it was William again, his voice sounded less irritated but more fraught: 'Rosanne, where are you? I want you to come to dinner tonight at Gracie Mansion, it's just a small party I'm giving. Please call.'

Steve raised his eyebrows, whoever this girl was the Mayor was certainly very keen on her.

The voice of the next message he immediately recognized: 'Rosanne, Robert speaking, first I'm sorry, secondly forgive me, I'll try later.'

And the next message presented no identification problems either: 'Rosanne, William – You hiding or something? For God's sake call.'

Straight-laced as he was Steve had to smile, he was finding this veritable deluge of anxious calls quite fascinating. This really must be some girl he thought.

Finally Robert came on again: 'Rosanne, Robert Cook again at 6.15, I've called everywhere ...'

Realizing this was the same message as he had heard in the first place, Steve flicked off the machine. He scratched his head pondering what to make of it all.

   Then he noticed something else. On Rosanne's writing bureau, a beautiful piece of Oriental furniture with inlays of real pearl, was the small digital voice recorder she used when doing interviews. Indeed earlier on he had admired the bureau and wondered to himself how much it must have cost. In fact it had been something Rosanne had seen in a Christie's Auction Catalogue and William had bought for her as a birthday present – it had gone under the hammer for $385,000. However, whereas before Steve had given the small voice recorder perched on top of this fine example of Chinese craftsmanship only the briefest of glances and seen nothing of interest, now the words faintly visible on its LED display stuck out like a sore thumb. The words read: "ROBERT COOK INTERVIEW".

   This was too much for Steve, even if it was not really any of his business he decided on a course of action. He picked up the voice recorder and put it in his pocket, unplugged Rosanne's answering machine and tucked it under his arm, and then left the apartment.

~

   In her room at the Drake Hotel Rosanne had changed into an evening dress and sat in front of a mirror applying lipstick. She looked absolutely gorgeous.

   Satisfied with her appearance she checked her jewelled wristwatch and went to make another phone call. In contrast to how she had felt earlier in the day she was now feeling serenely calm. Even her sketch of Zyron, grinning at her as before, she dismissed as nothing. The Connecticut number she dialed connected.

   Robert, Matts, Dawn and Professor Stewart were busy still working on their cartoon as an assistant entered the cellar and called over to them, 'Robert, phone call for you.'

   'Okay, thanks,' he replied getting up. He waited until he had got upstairs before asking the assistant who it was, the assistant could only tell him it was a lady who refused to give her name. This brought a flicker of anticipation to his face.

   He went into a small room off the house's main hall and closed the door behind him. On a table a phone lay off the hook. 'Hello,' he said into the receiver.

   'Robert,' came back her voice.

'Rosanne!' he exclaimed with obvious delight. 'If you knew how many times I've tried to reach you! I thought you must be so angry with me that perhaps you'd never ...'

'Well, it was a close call, but here I am!' she smiled. Robert smiled too. 'I mean obviously it was a bit of a comedown, but it was late and unexpected and all she was doing was coming home after a trip away ... Well, sometimes one has to try to be, well, you know what I mean ...'

'That's very understanding of you,' he said with much relief. 'But I just want you to know how badly I felt about it. And more important still, I want you to know that you're the one. Yes, you – totally and completely.'

'I feel the same way too,' she replied her voice dropping to a seductive whisper. 'God I love you, you don't know how much I love you.'

'Yah,' he responded softly. 'So when are we going to meet up again?'

'I hope as soon as possible,' she murmured. 'When are you coming back from Connecticut?'

'I haven't decided, but it's flexible.'

'You with friends out there?'

'Yes, just seeing some friends, that's all,' said Robert quite relaxed. 'But what about you, I mean where are you? I couldn't find you anywhere?'

Rosanne frowned at this inquiry, it was less than welcome. 'Oh, I don't know if I can say,' she uttered after a moment's hesitation. 'You'll think I'm crazy.'

'Crazy?' he repeated.

'Yes, quite crazy,' she said edgily. 'But okay, I'll tell you – I'm staying at the Drake Hotel, Park Avenue.'

Rosanne's prediction was correct, Robert looked quite startled. 'What? Why's that? That's hardly any distance from where you live!'

'Very true,' she said friendly but firm. 'But I think we should call a truce on any more question and answer sessions! I have my reasons, let's just leave it at that!'

'All right, I won't press you!' he said with good humor, baffled though he was. 'Still, when are we going to meet?'

'Well, why don't we meet here?' she proposed. 'Yes, here would be good, it's sort of "neutral ground".'

This baffled Robert all the more, what exactly did she mean by "neutral ground", he wondered? Nevertheless he readily agreed. 'Okay, let's meet there. I wasn't planning to return to town tonight but I will if ...'

'No, Robert,' she broke in, 'I didn't mean tonight, tonight's no good for me. I've got such a backlog of things to do. Tomorrow would be much better. Why don't you come for lunch, we can have room service in the room?'

'Okay, whatever you say,' he shrugged. Try as he might he could still make neither head nor tail of what she was doing at the Drake Hotel. Under the circumstances it was simplest just to go along with the gag. 'So what sort of time do you want to make it?' he asked.

'Say about twelve-thirty?' she replied.

'Perfect. See you then. And Rosanne?'

'Yes?'

'I love you.'

'Likewise,' she smiled. 'Until tomorrow.'

She put the phone down and still smiling reached for her handbag and wrap. She went out into the hotel corridor and called an elevator.

CHAPTER 12

At Gracie Mansion William had changed into his tuxedo and then paid a visit to the kitchen. He was neither domestically knowledgeable nor a gourmet in the true sense of the word but that evening's dinner party was especially important to him and everything had to be right. It was to be the first night his relationship with Rosanne would be placed in the open and, furthermore, his guests in the shape of Oakley Cunningham and Bruce Dean and their wives would certainly be the envy of any other host or hostess in the nation.

Dinner that night was to be Beluga caviar, followed by escalope de saumon in a delicate sauce flavored with wild berries, followed by a soufflé au Grand Marnier. Even so in reality he had no need to have worried about the standard of culinary excellence. For ever since he had been elected Mayor just under three years earlier he had retained the full-time services of not one but two of the best chefs from two of the best French restaurants in New York. The expense of hiring them had been exorbitant, but William was in the privileged position of money being no object. He had been an only child and he had been born with something a great deal more costly than a silver spoon in his mouth. Moreover, both his parents were now dead. Various publications including Forbes magazine calculated his annual income as being in excess of $270 million and his net worth at over fifteen times that amount. And yet the stark truth of the matter was that, instead of feeling rather flattered by his reputed wealth, he was one of those few people who were actually able to quietly smile to themselves how understated these journalistic estimates were.

Having shown his face to the experts working around the stoves, William then checked that ample bottles of Dom Perignon, Corton Charlemagne and Chateau D'Yquem were being well chilled. At the same time he did not forget that there also needed to be plenty of ice cold vodka to go with the caviar.

Once fully contented that everything was under control, he walked back across the lobby towards the main sitting room. However, as he did so, Steve Strauss came in through the front door with Rosanne's answering machine still snugly tucked under his arm. William looked at him in surprise. 'Steve, I didn't expect to see you this evening?'

'I realize, sir, and I hope I'm not disturbing you,' he said politely. 'But after I put the phone down to you at the lady's apartment there's just something I stumbled on that you might want to know.'

'Yes?' he frowned looking puzzled. 'What sort of thing? You know I'm giving a dinner party this evening, I can't get too tied up.'

'It won't take long, sir, if we can just go through into your private office I have something I want you to listen to.'

'Okay then, let's go through,' William nodded still looking distinctly puzzled.

~

In the sunny evening light Rosanne's cab drove along East End Avenue towards the front gates of Gracie Mansion. It was about ten minutes to eight.

In keeping with the imminent arrival of a Presidential candidate security on the gates was heavy. At least a dozen uniformed police officers and secret servicemen stood guard.

'Do you want me to go on in?' asked Rosanne's cab driver.

'Yes, it'll be perfectly okay,' she replied and the driver turned towards the entrance to the Mansion's grounds.

At the gates themselves a police officer signaled to them to stop and came over. 'Who are you for?' he enquired as Rosanne rolled down her cab's rear window on her side.

'Rosanne Lindblade for Mayor William Donaldson,' she smiled confidently.

'Okay, hold on a moment, I'll have to check,' the officer courteously replied much taken by her good looks. He went over to speak with his colleagues beside the gates.

However, while Rosanne's cab waited, from the rear seat of a car parked some distance across the street a photographer aimed his long lens surreptitiously in her direction. His camera clicked away at machine gun speed.

A few moments later the police officer returned. 'That's okay,' he smiled waving the cab through.

'Thanks,' she replied and the cab entered the driveway.

With the Mansion coming into closer view Rosanne felt quite excited. It was an imposing building built as a home by Archibald Gracie, a Scottish importer, in 1799. Though much added to and altered since, the house, with its white colonnades and large veranda, still retained its colonial character. Mayors of New York had used it as their Residence since 1942. This was in fact only her second visit there – the first time having been to a press reception eighteen months earlier. It had been at this that she had met William.

The cab stopped right in front of the Mansion's front entrance and after one final glance in her make-up mirror Rosanne got out. A man servant stood in the doorway and showed her in, and once in the lobby a maid took her wrap. Then, as she looked around getting her bearings, a door opened and William emerged from it. He was clearly not happy, his eyes and overall demeanor were angry.

'William?' she said staring at him sensing something was wrong.

'Do you mind stepping through here!' he replied in a low trembling voice barely able to control himself.

'What?' She paused just a split second taking in his intensity. It was as if he might explode.

'Rosanne,' he repeated in the same tone, 'I said I want you to step through here!'

'Okay,' she said still wondering to herself what could possibly be the matter. She followed him through into his private office.

Steve had already left some minutes before and they were alone.

William very methodically made sure the door was shut and then turned directly towards her. 'Do you know Robert Cook?' he asked bluntly.

She hesitated, somewhat surprised by the question. Yet her face remained blank and gave nothing away.

'Don't lie,' he interjected, 'you obviously do!'

'I wasn't going to lie,' she then calmly announced, 'he's just a friend.'

'I'm not sure I believe you,' he replied narrowing his eyes.

'Look,' she said putting on an air of indignation, 'what's got you into this mood because I'm not finding this exactly pleasant!' She tossed her small evening clasp down on a chair and placed her hands on her hips. Looking him straight in the eye she carried on, 'I know Robert Cook because I've interviewed him, that's all there is to it! Does that satisfy you? Anyway I don't understand why you're so interested, where did you get this from anyhow?'

William shifted uneasily on his feet, an effort though it was, he was doing his utmost to control himself. 'That I can't tell you,' he said frostily.

But this non-commital answer really provoked Rosanne. 'Oh come on!' she responded raising her voice. 'Somebody somewhere's been nosing around! I want to know what's behind this! Why are you picking on him, in fact why are you picking on me!'

William glared at her and she glared back. For a moment or two it was a staring match. But, even though his blood was still on the boil, William was all too aware knew that, with Oakley about to arrive and her in danger of erupting, he had one hand tied behind his back. The net result was that Rosanne won the staring match. He turned his head towards the twilight outside the window and replied, his tone was direct but trying to be at least partially conciliatory, 'Rosanne, at times like these all the law enforcement agencies are flat out, it's not a question of anybody in particular being singled out, "everyone" is under scrutiny. More to the point ...!' he continued.

But Rosanne, unimpressed, interrupted. 'Oh that's bullshit and you know it!' she said. 'You trying to tell me that of all three hundred million or so Americans it's just some sort of random occurrence that makes you interested in Robert Cook! You're not answering my question! *Why* are you singling him out? And *why* you are subjecting me to this grilling!'

At this William's attempt at self-restraint finally disintegrated. 'I'll tell you why!' he shouted. 'I think Robert Cook is a little more than "just" a friend! I also happen to think he's a subversive!'

This threw even Rosanne off balance, she was momentarily tongue-tied.

William carried on, his tone was biting, 'If you really want the "truth" agents went to your apartment and removed your answering machine with its messages, plus your interview with him – I was informed immediately of their contents! So what have you got to say!'

Rosanne's eyes opened wide in angry amazement. 'Shit! I'm really surprised at you!' she said scathingly. 'Is this the "Thought Police" or something! Is this country about to go back to the days of witch hunts! What you've just told me is disgusting, unconstitutional and, worst of all, it's unfair – I know Robert Cook quite well enough to say he'd never be involved in anything bad. He's just an artist.' It was interesting that, incensed as she was, she was not letting her temper run riot, on the contrary she was measuring her words carefully.

'Well, what about his ideas!' he exclaimed.

'What about them?' she said giving William a look of contempt.

'What's in that interview is pretty provocative, how do you know he's not somehow mixed up in this horrific situation?'

'Oh, for God's sake, don't be ridiculous!' she answered.

'What makes you so sure?' he pressed.

'William! I know him! You don't!'

'Well, this guy isn't doing himself any favors talking like this! If he wants to draw attention to himself by making dangerous, ill-considered remarks he's got to expect some flak!'

'What's that supposed to mean?'

'Rosanne, as a result of this recorded interview he gave you, I think one is likely to want to ask him a few questions. In fact, I'd say it's inevitable. It's his own fault, there's nothing I can do about it.'

'Don't give me that!' she objected. 'You have influence!' Her choice of words was becoming less careful. 'Just tell whoever is harboring suspicions to forget all about Robert Cook!'

'So you're trying to protect him now are you!'

'No, I'm not!' she shouted. 'There's nothing to protect!'

'This doesn't seem right to me! It doesn't seem right at all!' he shouted back.

'He's innocent, he's done nothing wrong!' she countered. 'I'm not having him turned into a scapegoat because of something he said to me in an interview!'

William's glare only hardened. 'Well, what's he to you!' he said piercingly. 'I think this brings us back to the beginning of this conversation ... Why should you care about Robert Cook? I can see he means something, and I don't like what I see! So give me a straight answer – What's he to you!'

'Really William,' she said, momentarily making her own attempt to lower the temperature, 'you seem to have all this upside down! Either you love me and trust me or you don't. You're reading all sorts of things into this which simply don't have any foundation. But I do like Robert Cook and I don't want to feel responsible for him getting caught up in a lot of needless aggravation just because of a few remarks he made.' Her tone voice suddenly became more forceful again, 'So tell whoever is interested in the recording of my interview with him to drop it!'

He shook his head. 'Rosanne, I can't do that!'

'Well, I really think you'd better!' she said straight out and more forceful still.

This hint of a threat did not go down well with William. 'Why?' he asked looking straight at her and drawing himself up to his full height.

'William, this is unnecessary ...'

'I asked why!' he interrupted. 'Under no circumstances am I making any intervention concerning this interview!'

'Yes, you are, you have to!' she announced, her tone not just strident but scornful. 'Because Robert Cook and I were lovers, once! So if you want to find a selfish motive in all this just think what it would look like for you to be associated with him through me! He's totally innocent, but once mud starts flying it usually sticks! You have to be careful – Isn't it pretty well known that you want to be President of the United States yourself one day!'

Finished, she waited for his response – it was fairly immediate.

William momentarily blinked, what she had just said seemed to take him a second or two to absorb, but then his whole demeanor crumbled, his head sank, his eyes only stared down at the floor, he looked mortified. Her revelation had knocked the wind out of his sails, his original anger had become an irrelevance and deserted him, he was now pole-axed, befuddled, lost in a semi-incomprehensible blur, almost like a beleaguered prize fighter struggling and wobbling on the ropes wishing that the bell might sound and at least provide enough respite to re-orient. Frowning deeply he paused taking a couple of paces across the room. 'Jesus,' he muttered quietly, hardly able any longer to bring himself to look her in the face.

Rosanne observed him knowing she had the upper hand. 'Don't look so non-plussed William, it's all over with him now,' she said straight out in a rather flat voice which was neither harsh nor gentle, 'but really that's all the more reason to keep him out of it! You must surely see that now?'

But he still could not answer, an overwhelming feeling of numbness was paralysing both his lips and his mind. For what seemed quite a while he kept on the move round the room. Finally he sighed, collected himself, and in an unmistakably crestfallen tone uttered quietly, 'You promise it's over?'

'Yes,' she said quite definitely, 'it's over, you have my word.'

William again sighed and allowed himself a few more moments of reflection. 'All right,' he replied heavily, 'I will ensure this interview is buried.' He paused once more, tears were not far from his eyes. 'But this has hurt me, Rosanne ...'

She went over and hugged him. 'I'm sorry.'

'Okay,' he said slowly, 'okay.'

In silence he held her close for at least a minute. Then there was a knock on the office door.

'Yes?' William called out collecting himself.

'Senator Cunningham's motorcade is passing through the front gates!' came back the voice of the man servant from behind the door.

'Okay, I'll be right with you!' replied William. He drew away from Rosanne and managed a smile, she smiled back. 'Let's go and greet them,' he said.

She nodded and they headed out.

By the time William and Rosanne emerged out on to the Mansion's front porch the long line of police vehicles and limousines which made up Oakley's motorcade were most of the way down the drive.

As soon as Oakley's limo halted the Mayor stepped forward leaving Rosanne on the doorstep. The secret serviceman in the vehicle's front seat was immediately on his feet and opened its nearside rear door. Shirley Cunningham, the Senator's wife, was first out.

'Shirley, how lovely to see you,' said William kissing her on the cheek.

'And you,' she smiled.

Oakley was next. 'Good evening, William.'

'Good evening,' William replied warmly.

Lastly from inside the limo came Vice Presidential Candidate Bruce Dean, Senator for Ohio, and his wife, Eileen. 'Bruce, Eileen, very good to see you both,' said William. 'Come along in, there's someone I want you to meet.'

In the evening light he led his guests towards the Mansion's entrance where Rosanne still stood. His heart beat fast as he prepared to introduce her to them.

Then, initial introductions over with, the party of six went through for cocktails in one of the formal reception rooms looking out across the gardens. Even though his wife was present Oakley had a keen eye for pretty girls and Rosanne was an instant hit. As she laughed and chatted with the Senator, William, despite the bitter blow he had suffered only minutes earlier, felt really proud of her. 'What an enchanting lady she is!' exclaimed Oakley to the Mayor as Rosanne stood between them. 'Not only enchanting but beautiful!'

'Well, thank you,' said William. Rosanne just smiled.

'I tell you something, I wish I was young man again!' he winked making sure his wife was out of earshot.

Rosanne smiled again feeling much flattered. 'I've heard so much about you, Senator Cunningham,' she told him.

'What?' jested Oakley. 'Both the good and the bad!'

'No, only the good!' laughed Rosanne tilting her head on to William's shoulder.

'And anyway,' he said, 'remember that to you my name is Oakley.'

Unquestionably another fresh victim succumbing to the Senator's charm Rosanne smiled all the more.

William averted his eyes through the window, the sun had still not quite sunk. 'I tell you,' he said, 'it's such a lovely evening, shall we step out on the veranda before we eat?'

'Yes,' said Oakley, 'it's always pretty out there.'

'Shirley, Eileen, Bruce,' William called over to where they were standing. 'We're going on to the veranda, you going to join us?'

'Yes, why not,' smiled Shirley Cunningham who was quite an elegant woman in her mid-fifties, though her smile would have been better were it not for perhaps one too many face-lifts.

All six of them holding their cocktail glasses filtered outside. From the veranda they had a panoramic view of the high apartment buildings on one side and the East River on the other.

'This is a great city,' said Oakley waving his hand across the expanse in front of him.

'One of the greatest,' agreed William.

Yet, unbeknown to the Mayor and his guests as they stood there, other eyes were trained on them. From a room high up in an apartment house on East End Avenue another photographer with a longed lensed camera looked down on the Mansion. Through his lens he had a perfect shot of the party. He clandestinely clicked away.

Out on the East River in a small boat which gently swayed, yet another photographer with yet another long lensed camera also had an uninterrupted view of the veranda. He was every bit as busy as his colleague. He knew every good photograph spelt only one thing: money.

'Okay, we've got it, let's go!' the photographer shouted to an associate driving the boat. And as he carefully put away his camera the craft headed back to shore.

~

Dinner in the Mansion's dining room went smoothly, everybody enjoyed themselves. The conversation was light-hearted and convivial punctuated by sparkling anecdotes from Oakley who, as usual, liked to hold the floor.

Only towards the end, and then only briefly after they had finished the dessert, did the subject of the recent problems come up when Oakley said how inept he thought President Charles Guthrie had been in misleading the public about the time it would take to restore electricity supplies. 'Lying becomes a habit,' he went on, 'once you start lying you have to keep lying, that's why Guthrie's such a jerk, that's why he's going to lose this Election – the people have got his number! It's back to Abraham Lincoln, you can't fool the people for long!'

Everyone nodded approvingly, but then it was Rosanne who chose to make the next comment, 'So do you think this terrorist threat is finished?'

'A threat can't finish if it wasn't even a threat in the first place!' quipped Oakley. Rosanne's question had been rather direct and might have been seen by some as out of order, but her looks gave her license to express herself denied lesser mortals. 'No, Rosanne,' Oakley continued, 'these people are just insignificant dregs, they won't even leave so much as the smallest dent!'

'I'm very glad to hear it,' she replied with another ingratiating smile.

'They'll be brought to justice and that will be it,' added Bruce Dean who was politically even more right of center than Oakley.

'So there's nothing more to worry about?' she asked.

'Nothing,' said Oakley, 'even our experts think we're well on top of it. You won't hear any more from these people, they're not even worth wasting one's breath on. Indeed, the news black-out on them is one of the very few things the President has done right – Discussing them in public is an absolute no no! It would bestow on them an artificial importance totally offensive to every decent person in the country.'

'Even so, it still makes one think at least a little bit,' said Rosanne somewhat pensively. 'I mean, don't get me wrong, but there *are* a lot of poor people.'

William looked at her, he was just for an instant slightly worried that she might have said, or might possibly be about to say, something inappropriate. But he need have had no fear, Oakley was much too pleased to have her undivided attention. 'No, no,' the Senator smiled at her, 'for sure there are a lot of poor people. No disagreement about that. But God helps those who help themselves. The Government's job is to make sure this remains the land of opportunity, as long as that is so there is no reason for anyone of sound mind and body to be poor, it's a myth.'

Rosanne just nodded and smiled.

'I second that,' emphasized Bruce Dean. 'There's no financial problem hard work can't cure. My parents taught me plenty about what it was like during the Great Depression. And as for myself I started with nothing and had to make it the hard way, believe you me I know what it's like to have an empty stomach.' This was true, at sixty-eight and the oldest present, the Vice Presidential candidate had indeed come from very humble beginnings. And the fact that he had since become a very wealthy man had in no way altered his perception of the world.

'Indeed, let us have no more talk of terrorists or poverty,' said Oakley as if he were addressing an auditorium not a small dinner party, 'let us instead celebrate the fact that all the indications are that we're well on course for an historic Electoral victory! Actually, if anything, it looks like we're pulling away!'

'Let's drink to that,' said William raising his glass and the others followed suit.

'And thank you for a most delightful evening, William,' said Oakley.

'No, it was a very great pleasure,' he replied.

'Eileen and I thank you too,' said Bruce Dean with a smile.

'Yes, it was a lovely evening,' concurred Eileen Dean who had spoken least of all. Pleasant enough though she was, she was a typical example of a politician's wife being greatly overshadowed by her husband.

'Well, it was just a thrill and an honor having you all here,' said William graciously. 'Now may I offer anyone anything else to drink?' he asked glancing round the table.

'No thanks,' answered Oakley, 'Bruce and I have Network TV tomorrow and need to be fresh.' He turned to focus his gaze on Rosanne and smiled. 'But once again, William, I approve, in fact I am smitten! I look forward to having you both back to dinner at the White House before too long!'

Rosanne smiled back, her appetite for compliments knew no bounds.

Oakley rose to his feet. 'Thank you again, William, we must be going.'

'I'll come and say goodnight to you,' replied William standing up too, as did the others. Everyone filed out in the direction of the lobby and the front door.

In the driveway police and secret service attended their vehicles, the sea of flashing lights looked more like a huge outdoor discotheque than one man's means of getting home to bed. William and Rosanne bid their farewells and waited for the motorcade to move off before returning inside.

'It went well, and what a success you were!' smiled William as he and Rosanne stood in the lobby by the Mansion's staircase. 'Do you want a nightcap?'

'No, William,' she smiled taking his hand, 'let's go straight upstairs!'

Not about to disagree William put his arm around her and they began their ascent.

~

Early the next morning a U.S. Mail truck turned through the Mansion's front gates and made its way up the driveway. Birds sang in the trees and Carl Schurz park was deserted, all the tight security and commotion of the night before had departed along with Oakley.

William and Rosanne sat at a small table in the Mansion's breakfast room finishing their coffee. Dorothy, William's private secretary, entered carrying some mail and newspapers. She was a homely looking slightly quaint woman in her late forties and had been with William for years. 'Good morning, Mayor Donaldson,' she said.

'Good morning, Dorothy,' said William in the warm tone one frequently reserved for trusted and valued employees.

'Here are this morning's papers and your personal mail.'

'Thanks, Dorothy,' he replied taking them from her. Then affording Rosanne a friendly smile, which Rosanne returned, she left again.

William, as was his normal practise, glanced at the various newspaper headlines first. However, almost immediately, and unusually for him, a broad grin came over his face. 'Well, well, look at this!' he said to Rosanne holding up the front page of *The Daily News*. 'The media don't hang around!' On the front page was a photograph of Rosanne on the Mansion's veranda standing between himself and Oakley, plus a close-up picture of her as she sat in the back seat of the cab while she waited on her arrival to be waved through the gates. The headline read "*THE MAYOR'S NEW GIRL*".

In contrast to William's grin she blinked and looked unsettled. 'You're going to have to get used to this!' he added cavalierly after noticing her reaction.

'But Goddamit,' she said struggling to keep her composure, 'talk about snooping!'

Her unease only seemed to make him grin more broadly. 'Well, that's the price we all pay when we enter the public eye!' He handed her the paper, 'take a closer look.'

Looking pained she stared down at it. Maybe she had been slightly naive but this much exposure was a most unwelcome shock. She was angry with herself and, when she saw who had taken the photographs, she was angrier still with someone else – a certain magazine editor called Jack Grant. But, for once, in William's presence she had no choice but to keep her anger bottled up.

'At least they're nice photos of you,' William volunteered in a carefree aside as he flicked through the Stock Listings in "The Wall Street Journal".

Rosanne just gritted her teeth in silence.

Completing his initial quick run through of the papers William moved on to check his personal mail. The first envelope he opened contained an invitation to a charity function and he put it to one side with little interest. However, the second envelope he unsealed was rather thicker, he wondered what it was. When he withdrew from it a wad of "money" his expression was one of surprise to say the least. He took the wad and spread the bills into a "fan" to gauge the amount, he then looked back inside the envelope and noticed there was a typed letter still in it. He removed the letter and began reading it out loud under his breath, his expression was now one of astonishment, it was as if he could not believe his eyes, '"*You have $750, keep the "ones" and spend the rest, as long as you REGISTER TO VOTE the NUMBER on one of the ONE DOLLAR BILLS may be your lucky number to win one of ONE HUNDRED THOUSAND PRIZES of $10,000 each ...*"

'Shit, this is something!' he exclaimed with some alarm.

'What is?' said Rosanne who had not been paying attention.

'The terrorists!' he replied jumping to his feet. 'I can't stop now, you'll have to excuse me.'

Before Rosanne could say any more William was gone, she frowned bemused.

~

In the cellar in Connecticut Matts sat in front of one of his computer screens. He wore a pair of headphones. By now their "money" was already "news", a sudden $750 windfall was for many people far too much to keep to themselves. By monitoring reports from local TV and radio stations and countless Internet chat-rooms, Matts was building up a picture of the extent of their penetration. Robert strolled over and tapped him on the shoulder. 'Everything okay?' he asked.

'Everything,' said Matts with an air of achievement, 'our envelopes are getting through all across the nation. Listening to some of these radio phone-ins you'd think it was the Second Coming, some people have never had so much money in all their lives!'

'Good,' nodded Robert. 'Anyhow I'm going back into town for a while.'

'Okay,' said Matts resuming his survey.

~

After her breakfast at Gracie Mansion Rosanne had wasted no time in stopping off at Prestige Publications en route to her hotel room at the Drake. She had a score to settle with Jack Grant and she was going to let him know what she thought.

As it so happened when she arrived he was in a meeting in Prestige's boardroom, but this made no difference, she stuck her head round the door and insisted on seeing him immediately in his private office. One look at her face in front of the important advertising clients he was addressing convinced him that he had better agree. He excused himself and went with her.

'What are doing busting into a meeting like that, Rosanne?' he asked in obvious annoyance the moment they were behind closed doors.

'This is what!' she shouted unfolding the front page of *The Daily News*.

'Yes?' he frowned pretending to be surprised.

'You bastard Jack, how could you do it?' she screamed.

'What?' he said in all innocence. 'Why are you looking at me?'

'Jesus Christ,' she yelled, 'you know damn well!'

'Rosanne, there's clearly something the matter with you, it's nothing to do with me.'

'You can drop that crap!' she said in cold anger. 'Look who gets the photo credit – Jim Parelli! Who is it you turn to when you have a tricky assignment? Answer: Jim Parelli. If you really want to put it to the test I know Jim Parelli quite well, I can call him up and he'll tell me!'

Jack's expression changed, on reflection it occurred to him that further denials would be useless. 'Well, Rosanne, I guess it's too bad,' he conceded unable to think of a better reply.

Given the chance Rosanne would have liked to have killed him, instead she had settle for one final venomous tirade, 'Jack, you're a rat! I despise you! You stink! From now on you can take our friendship as over!' At that she stormed out slamming the door so hard that even the wall shook.

Jack just sat down at his desk wearing a smirk. He waited a minute before he called through to reception to check that Rosanne had left the offices, he then strolled back to his meeting. He was not going to lose any sleep over this, enough was enough was enough.

~

That morning on the way to meet Rosanne for lunch at the Drake Hotel Robert stopped by at his studio. He was eager to check his mail and sure enough when he got to Greenwich Village he discovered that even he had received a $750 envelope! However, his journey from Connecticut had taken longer than expected and it was now gone noon. Not wishing to be late for her he decided to take the subway up town.

A few minutes later he emerged from the subway exit on 59th and Park Avenue and began to head the short distance down to the Drake. Then, suddenly, passing a newsstand, he noticed something, it was the front page of *The Daily News*. He had to do a double-take, it was as if he could not accept what he saw, for an instant his feet seemed frozen to the sidewalk, he was unable to move. Then, coming to his senses, he went forward and grabbed a copy. For a moment or two he stared at it in disbelief.

'Hey man,' came the irritated voice of the newspaper seller, 'you going to buy that or not! This ain't a lending library!'

'Here you are,' muttered Robert handing over a dollar. Looking fazed he wandered on.

At the next corner the traffic lights were against him and seeing a litter can he threw the paper away. When the lights changed, still in deep thought, he crossed over and entered the hotel.

Whereas the Drake would not have been considered among the top half dozen or so hotels in Manhattan it was not far behind. It was a luxury establishment and aimed to protect the privacy of its guests. Consequently Robert knew that since Rosanne had omitted to give him her room number, he would have to call up first. He walked up to the reception desk, 'Can you tell me where the house phones are please?'

'Just over there, sir,' the receptionist pointed.

'Thanks.'

Robert went over to pick up a house phone. Inside he felt distinctly hollow and churned up but, blessed with an even temperament, he had already made up his mind that he was going to play it low-key. 'Miss Rosanne Lindblade,' he told the hotel switchboard. A moment later he was put through.

Rosanne answered her phone, she was trying to sound relaxed but in fact sounded edgy, 'Hello?'

'Rosanne, it's me,' said Robert in a flat tone.

'Great, come along up, room 1108.' She put the phone down.

Shortly later he knocked on her door, still trying to mask a feeling of unease, she went over to open it. 'Robert!' she exclaimed effusively.

'Good to see you,' he smiled kissing her on the lips. He was remarkably laid-back.

There was a pause as he walked into the center of the room. 'How was Connecticut?' she asked trying to break what remained an atmosphere of underlying tension.

'Oh, Connecticut was fine,' he coolly replied affecting to study the décor of the room. He paused again to tighten the screw for, quite apart from his own feelings, he by now sensed that she knew that he knew that everything was not as it should be.

Another uncomfortable silence ensued. And as Robert gave up on the décor and switched his attention to the view outside the window it was becoming all out psychological warfare.

Finally it was Rosanne who spoke next. 'Robert,' she said awkwardly, 'I've got something to say.'

'What about?' he enquired in a monotone without taking his eyes off the traffic on Park Avenue passing below.

'Robert, I don't know how you're going to take this,' she said hesitantly, 'but ...'

'William Donaldson?' he replied suddenly turning towards her.

'So you know?' It was really only a rhetorical question.

'I should think by now most of the City knows,' he answered dryly. But then his voice became more direct, 'What are you playing at?'

Rosanne rushed up to him, there was no mistaking her earnestness, 'Robert, I love him too, but ...'

'Yes?' he said staring at her.

'But I love you more! I love you so, so, much more!' She paused looking like she were about to cry but instead fought it off. 'Believe me, Robert,' she re-emphasized, 'I love you a lot, lot more.'

'Jesus,' he said under his breath shaking his head. He felt so many conflicting emotions that it was as if his mind were almost grinding to a temporarily halt.

'I know how you must feel,' she went on, 'but try and be reasonable about it.'

'It's hard to be reasonable when you find out you've been cheated on,' he drawled.

'No, you must be able to see there are two sides to this,' she said persuasively, in fact she was becoming less and less emotional and more and more lucid. 'I mean after all I knew him before I knew you, and after all you have Dawn. And anyway,' she paused knowing this was the punch line, 'I think this thing extends beyond personal relationships! It's heavy!'

'What is?' he frowned not understanding.

Rosanne heaved a deep sigh, looked at him full in the face and then let go, 'You're skating on thin ice! They're no more than a whisker away from being on to you! I think only I can save you!'

Robert blinked. 'I don't know what you're talking about,' he said.

'Oh yes, you do!' she insisted. 'You're in with terrorists!' Robert managed not to move a muscle in reaction but this did nothing deflect her, her words gathered speed, 'I heard Dawn the other night at your studio – that careless comment about when "we" put the lights out! That's not the sort of thing normal people say as a joke! And anyway I could tell by her voice that there was no way she was joking! Worse still, I know somehow William Donaldson has got hold of the recording of our interview and the messages on my answering machine with your voice on it!'

Robert just blankly stared at her.

'By the way,' she continued in top gear, 'how the hell did you get my number! But anyway that doesn't matter! What does matter is that the whole thing has made William suspicious! I mean really really suspicious! Can't you see the jeopardy that puts you in!'

Robert still just stared at her.

'Stop trying to look so dumb!' she half-shouted at him. 'You must be in with the terrorists – time and time again your whole attitude has more or less advertised it to me!'

Robert slowly crossed his arms, by now he was actually succeeding in looking bored, there was no taking it away from him – he was good under pressure.

Even so Rosanne was not giving up. 'But can't you see it's kind of a blessing in disguise!' she implored. 'I mean if I stay with William I can help you! I've already told him not to attach any importance to the interview, and I don't mind saying that as far as William Donaldson goes I have *influence*!'

Convinced that she must have got through to him she waited for a reply. None came. Robert remained expressionless, not moving an inch, not so much even looking at her as right through her.

'Come on, Robert!' she pressed. 'Don't just stand there! What do you say!'

He finally responded. 'Well, Rosanne, you've certainly got a vivid imagination!' he smiled.

This simply wound Rosanne up all the more. 'Oh, how can you be so stupid!' she scowled. 'I want to be on your side!'

Robert just shook his head.

'Okay, be like that!' she said irritably. 'But just you think about it!' She went over to the writing table and picked up the Room Service menu. 'And while you're thinking we might as well order some lunch. This is on me by the way, so what are you going to have?'

'I'd better have a look,' he said casually. Rosanne handed him the menu. But as he took it all the composure he had so guardedly preserved seemed to desert him: His eyes opened wide in incredulity, his face went pale, his exquisitely formed hands clutched the menu so tightly that it might have been torn apart at the seams. Definitely something had knocked him sideways with every bit as much force as had the sight of the front page of *The Daily News*. It was bizarre, it was unlike him, it was inexplicable, it was as if he had seen a ghost. In fact all he had actually seen was Rosanne's sketch of Zyron.

'What's the matter?' she said quite puzzled.

He was speechless. It took him several moments to steady himself. 'Where did you get this from?' he suddenly asked.

'What do mean?' she frowned all the more baffled.

'You couldn't have seen this, it's impossible,' he said totally astounded. 'How did you know?'

'Know what?' she asked, she still had no idea what he was referring to.

'This drawing,' he replied holding it up.

'What about it?' she said no less confused. 'It was just an innocent doodle I did yesterday.' And she was being quite honest, indeed she had virtually forgotten all about it. But Robert still looked utterly dumbfounded. 'Really, what's come over you?' she went on. 'I mean I often do sort of little sketches when I'm thinking, it helps me relax, it's nothing unusual, loads of people do it, you know that! Come on now, is this some kind of decoy to change the subject because you don't want to admit you're one of the terrorists!'

A decoy it was not. Robert just kept looking at her in amazement. In his judgment her denial of the drawing having any significance had the ring of truth about it, and yet the lack of any explanation merely added to the awful conundrum he now faced. He felt he was well and truly between the devil and deep blue sea. His choices were either to trust her and confess his terrorist involvement, and he was painfully aware that love and trust did not always go hand in hand, or, alternatively, to try and ride it out.

But riding it out had as many if not more problems as playing it straight. What would happen if and when she saw the cartoon? If she had not been taken into his confidence she could not fail but be as astonished by it as he had been by her doodle. What then might she say to William Donaldson, or whoever else for that matter? And furthermore, seeing his reaction to the drawing and then seeing the cartoon would only count for her as the ultimate cut and dried confirmation of what she already so strongly suspected.

After a few seconds he had narrowed his two options down to one. 'This is uncanny, really uncanny,' he began. 'However, I'm leaving, and I think you'd better come too.'

'What?' she said.

'We forget about lunch, there are more important things to worry about,' he replied with a newfound gravity.

Then she tumbled. 'So you are one of the terrorists?'

'Yes!'

Rosanne's eyes opened wide. Robert picked up the phone and began to dial.

CHAPTER 13

In a small town, which could have been anywhere but was actually on Route 66 about forty miles south of Springfield, Illinois, a hobo walked slowly down Main Street. He was about fifty, dirty, disheveled and unshaven. His clothes were worn-out and he stank of stale sweat, alcohol and tobacco. He was a nobody.

Reaching his intended destination he stumbled into a liquor store. The store owner, a fat middle-aged man, was not pleased to see him. 'What the fuck you doing coming in here,' he barked. 'I told you to stay away!'

The hobo was so used to being abused that insults had lost all meaning. He grinned a toothless smile as if the store owner's greeting were the epitome of politeness. 'I want to buy something,' he announced in a gentle, good-natured slur.

'The usual can of beer I suppose,' replied the store owner sarcastically. 'Well, be sure you don't try and take anything else out with you when you leave!'

'No thanks, no beer today,' said the hobo quite unoffended, 'I think I'll have a whole bottle of whisky and ...' He paused to glance along the shelves. 'And a couple of bottles of that nice looking expensive Chardonnay.'

'I warn you don't fool around with me!' growled the store owner sternly. 'Let's see your money first!'

The hobo reached into his filthy jacket. 'Oh, I've got plenty of money,' he smiled withdrawing a fistful of bills, 'I had some good news.' The store owner looked staggered. 'By the way,' the hobo continued, 'you don't happen to know where you register to vote round here, do you?'

~

'Well, heaven be blessed!' smiled Cornwall in his rasp as he fingered a wad of "money". 'It looks like Christmas has come early this year!' He was sitting with Jam, Tom and Ray in the third floor room of the rundown tenement building on 123rd Street. Ironies of ironies, as luck would have it, not only was the building still standing but none of the four of them had got even so much as a scratch in the night of rioting.

'Right on, man,' smiled back Tom waving his own wad, 'how come we all get these $750 envelopes? You've almost got to think that somebody somewhere's made a mistake!'

'Well, if that's so,' exclaimed Jam counting his wad for the umpteenth time, 'I ain't goin to be about to point it out!'

'No way, man!' laughed Cornwall kissing a $20 bill.

'And I'll tell yer somethin else,' declared Jam in high spirits.

'What's that?' asked Ray smiling from cheek to cheek.

'I registered to vote! Ain't never ever bothered to vote before in my life!'

'Well, me neither,' rasped Cornwall with a wicked grin, 'but you know by some funny kind of coincidence this time around I decided to get registered too!'

'What a coincidence!' yelped Jam. 'It wouldn't be nuthin' to do with having your eye on one of those $10,000 prizes would it!'

All four men collapsed into laughter.

~

But no one was laughing in the conference room at New York City Hall. William and Oakley and their supporting staff sat uncomfortably round the table. They were having to ponder the unpleasant fact that any belief that the last had been heard from the terrorists was now clearly severely mistaken.

'So about the money itself, there's nothing we can do?' asked Oakley just to get everything absolutely straight in his mind.

'No, nothing,' replied Scott Taylor stony-faced. 'It looks one hundred per cent genuine and the serial numbers are current and non-consecutive. There is simply no way you can tell the difference!'

'And every household in the country has received this cash?' asked William.

'As far as we can tell,' Scott answered.

'It's extraordinary,' said Oakley as if he could not fully accept the situation for real. 'How can people print and distribute this much money and get away with it!'

'Well, let's face it, they have,' said William heavily.

'I'm informed that at the White House this morning they discussed the idea of asking people to pay it back,' Steve Strauss interjected. 'It was dismissed in less than five seconds! Some hope!'

'None whatsoever,' said Oakley, uncharacteristically unable to manage a smile.

'But what's most disturbing of all,' Steve continued, 'is the Political side – the money's one thing but the message that went with it is quite another – there's been a stampede to register to vote just about everywhere. You don't need me to tell you what the implications of that might be!'

'You mean every bum who has never voted before we now have to contend with?' said William.

'Yes,' nodded Steve, 'and that's at least twenty per cent of the population! Mostly from the poorest economic groups.'

'Exactly the people who the terrorists with their crazy welfare ideas will be appealing to most,' said Senator Bruce Dean picking up the drift. 'Exactly those same people may now decide to vote.'

'And those people have the capacity to tilt the Political balance,' concurred William with some concern. 'In fact, tilt it quite drastically!'

'That's obviously what the terrorists are aiming to do,' volunteered Scott. 'You get ten or twenty million extra people out there voting because they've been sent $750 and because they think it's going to give them higher social security handouts, well, anything could happen.'

'I think that's rather far-fetched,' retorted Oakley. 'I understand what you're getting at, but I don't see it happening.'

'It's still got to be a worry,' said William rubbing his eyes, he had another of the slight headaches he got from time to time and it was bothering him. In fact he had gone so far as to book himself in for a routine check-up later that day.

'No, not really, William,' disagreed Oakley. 'I mean, what's the worry? Okay, these people register to vote, but then who are they going to vote for? Nobody's told them that! And anyway that's presuming they vote at all – registering and voting are two different things!'

'That's fair comment, Senator,' said Scott Taylor, 'but I think I ought to point that this latest move by the terrorists does seem to represent something of a shift in direction.'

'And so?' Oakley interrupted.

'I think,' Scott went on, his voice assuming the meticulous tone it always did when he was thinking hard, 'that these people probably have some follow-up planned on this, I think they will try and tell the public who to vote for.'

'And how are they going to that?' asked Oakley somewhat impetuously.

'I don't know,' Scott replied. 'But whereas I was wrong in my view that they'd gone to ground I now feel pretty certain that this money thing will not have been done in isolation. I don't like saying it but these people are intelligent, they know that just getting people to register would not be enough. They're going to seek to influence the public for sure.'

'And you think the public's going to take their advice!' said Oakley dismissively.

'Sir, I don't have a crystal ball,' answered the C.I.A man.

'Hmm,' grunted Oakley reflectively, 'I just don't see it.'

'It is true to say that President Guthrie's stance on Welfare is less rigid than ours,' conjectured Steve.

'Yes, but we're not talking apples and oranges,' protested Oakley. 'Nobody's going to sign a check for, what was it they wanted?'

'Four-point-eight trillion dollars over five years,' Steve replied.

'Thank you for reminding me!' boomed Oakley. 'I mean it doesn't bear thinking about! Nobody's going to come up with that sort of money! Not me, not even Charles Guthrie! From us there's no way they'd get another cent! We know that the only sensible thing to do is cut Welfare not increase it!'

'On that we're all agreed!' echoed Bruce Dean.

'Yes, we are,' nodded William his confidence restored.

'So let's not overreact,' continued Oakley, 'this money and so on is a very serious development but let's keep it in perspective! It isn't going to materially affect the Election! Not in a thousand years!'

'Yes, you're right,' said William affably.

'I know I'm right!' exclaimed Oakley finding just one small fleeting smile before resuming at full throttle. 'Is this country going to let itself be governed by the rule of democracy or by a handful of desperados? Could the opinion of individuals who have murdered and plundered and stolen ever command even the slightest respect from the people of America? Both are such stupid questions I won't even attempt to answer them! And Scott!'

'Yes?' he replied slightly cowering under the weight of Oakley's overpowering invective. 'I've heard what you say and I agree these people must have something else planned! But get to them first! If they've switched away from hit-and-run tactics and are trying to fool around with some kind of screwball propaganda campaign then to my mind they've got to heighten their profile! That's got to give all the Agencies a better shot!'

'Yes, sir,' Scott nodded politely. He realized no personal criticism was intended. Moreover, he fully endorsed what the Senator had just said. Indeed, privately he was extremely angry, ashamed and embarrassed at the lack of success to date. Obsessive by nature the whole situation had become an all-consuming crusade for him – no one, absolutely no one, was more determined to see a breakthrough than him.

~

Later that afternoon William's limousine drew up outside Dr. Arthur Oberstein's consulting rooms on 70th Street between Madison and Park. His headache had now gone but having made the check-up appointment he was going to keep it.

On the way there he had given a lot of thought to the meeting earlier. On the one hand he had no doubt Oakley was right, frayed nerves in the run-up to an Election were only natural but there was no justification for them in this instance: all the forecasts put them miles ahead in the Election. Yet, on the other hand, he had to grudgingly admit that what the terrorists had done was inspired: who would have ever imagined that they would aim to exhort the poor to flex their muscles by means of the ballot box? Doomed to failure as he considered it to be, it was still an ingenious idea.

As for the meeting itself he was too overdosed by meetings to have much of a view. It had got to the stage where they were having meetings for the sake of meetings and little else – time and energy were being eaten up to no good effect except perhaps to provide a palliative impression of false comfort. As he left his car and walked into the doctor's offices he resolved he was going to try to cut back on their number – if anything was giving him headaches he was sure it was the endless hours in the conference room.

'Good afternoon, Mayor Donaldson,' smiled the pretty receptionist. 'You can go straight in. Dr. Oberstein's waiting for you.'

'Thanks,' William nodded. One advantage or disadvantage he had in Manhattan, depending on how one looked at it, was that he seldom ever had to introduce himself. He proceeded on into the consulting room, Arthur Oberstein had been his physician for almost as long as he could remember.

'Hello, William,' said the doctor warmly rising to his feet. He was a small man with grey hair and a clever face.

'Nice to see you, Arthur,' smiled William.

'And you,' said the doctor in an avuncular way. There was no doubt that they regarded each other as personal friends. 'Now I realize you're a busy man and your secretary told me you wanted to be in and out as quickly as possible, so I won't delay you with lots of chit-chat!'

'Really Arthur, I'm not that pressed!' smiled the Mayor.

'No, no, no – We'll get on with it, we can talk as we go along. We'll have your case handled in under an hour. You can start by taking your jacket off.'

'Okay, Arthur, you're in charge,' said William doing as he was told.

And the doctor was as good as his word, within less than forty-five minutes they were already finishing up.

'Okay, William, you can get up, your blood pressure's fine,' said Oberstein releasing the band from his arm as he lay on a couch.

'Thanks,' he replied sitting up.

'Now, last of all, I want to have a look into your eyes,' said Oberstein. 'Come over here and sit in that seat.'

William obeyed and took up a position on one side of an ophthalmoscope. Oberstein sat down opposite. 'Place your chin firmly on the rest,' he instructed making adjustments as he peered through the apparatus. 'Good, that's perfect ... Look left ... Look right ... Now straight ahead.' He paused concentrating hard, he was clearly a first rate practitioner. He craned his head to take an even closer look through the instrument's eye-pieces, 'William,' he began again in the slightly stilted croaky voice of someone doing something intricate while talking, 'you came in here requesting a pretty thorough physical, and that's what I've given you! And I can tell you, you seem in good shape to me.'

'Really,' mumbled William his jaw pushing down on the rest rendering speech difficult.

'Now look up ... Now down ... Yes, everything is normal ... Okay, you can sit up and relax.'

'Maybe it's just stress and overwork,' suggested William, 'but I still seem to get headaches, feel tired, have throbbing eyes.'

'Yes, but your eyes are very clear. William, I'd say try and take things a little slower, but otherwise I have to give you a clean bill of health.'

'You sure, Arthur?'

The doctor looked at him benignly. 'How long have I looked after you, William?'

'Twenty years or so,' he smiled.

'Yes, so I ought to know by now! You are perfectly fit!'

'Oh well, that's good to know,' William conceded.

'Just try and slow down a little,' the doctor urged.

'I will,' said William reaching for his jacket. 'And thank you for fitting me in at such short notice.'

'No, no, always a pleasure, my boy,' replied the doctor kindly. 'Let me see you out.'

They both walked towards the door.

'By the way, William,' said the doctor in an affectionate confidential tone as they stood in his reception area, 'I saw the paper this morning.' By which he meant *The Daily News*. 'What a lovely, lovely girl!'

'She is,' the Mayor acknowledged with an appreciative smile. 'Thanks again for everything, Arthur.' He shook hands and left.

~

More or less at the same time William was commencing his medical examination, Rosanne arrived by car at the terrorists' house in Connecticut. As they pulled up in the driveway Zak was at the wheel with Robert in the front beside him. Rosanne, blindfolded and bound by the wrists, lay under a blanket on the back seat. 'Okay, Rosanne, sit up, we'll help you in,' said Robert getting out of the vehicle and opening one of its rear doors

'Okay,' she replied and Robert gently took her by the arm. Then, as soon as she was on her feet, Zak came round to her other side and together they led her across the gravel towards the entrance.

Robert's phone call from the Drake had been to tell Zak to meet them across the Hudson River at the mainland end of the 34th Street temporary pontoon. They would get to that spot by cab. Then, before leaving the hotel, he had told Rosanne three things. First, that she was taking her life into her own hands. Secondly, that the final decision on her recruitment was not his alone. Thirdly, until such time as she were accepted, a blindfold, plus wrist bindings to ensure she could not remove it, would be necessary to preserve the secret of the location of their H.Q. She had raised no objections.

In fact, far from resenting the restrictions imposed upon her, she appeared to rather relish the cloak and dagger aspect of the exercise. During the car journey to Connecticut she had chatted vivaciously virtually non-stop about this, that and the other. She had even given an account of what had happened that morning when William received his mail – this, understandably, made Zak and Robert smile.

Once inside the house they escorted her, still blindfolded, across the hall towards a panelled library. However, attracted by the clatter of footsteps on the marble floor, Dawn emerged from a side door. Just before the trio disappeared from view Robert and Dawn's eyes met, her face had dropped.

In the library Rosanne was guided into a chair, her hands untied and her blindfold at last removed. She blinked disoriented in reaction to the light.

'You all right?' Robert asked.

'Yes.'

'Good. Zak'll stay with you until I'm back.'

'Fine,' she replied calmly.

Robert left to go and find Professor Stewart. But as he re-entered the hall Dawn had lingered there waiting for him. She looked considerably less than happy. 'What is *she* doing here?' she frowned.

Robert hesitated but, despite being in a hurry, knew he had to provide an answer. 'Dawn, I know it looks rather weird but ...'

'Weird!' she questioned narrowing her eyes as if to suggest that jealous thoughts might not have misplaced after all. Perhaps feminine intuition really was a law unto itself.

'Yes, it is weird,' he replied as briskly and as openly as he could. 'You obviously didn't see the newspapers – She is the girlfriend of William Donaldson!'

Dawn was completely thrown. 'No!' she gasped. 'Her? His girlfriend?'

'Yes, it's true,' he said. 'But there's no time to elaborate, I have to go and see the Professor!' He headed off towards the cellars.

In the basement Professor Stewart was with Matts seated in front of a computer screen. Indeed, given the amount of time he spent looking at screens, it was surprising that Matts' eyes were not as square as his spectacle frames. Maybe it was his thick lenses which protected him. 'So with the cartoon ready,' enquired the Professor, 'how long before you have to go and supervise the broadcasting intercept?'

Matts checked his watch. 'Cunningham and Bruce Dean are on at nine, it's nearly five now, so I'll head off shortly. I just want to finish this Credit Card thing.'

'You have it all worked out?'

'Yes, plain sailing,' he replied with a grin. 'They're in for a nasty surprise!'

'The bigger surprise the better,' twinkled the Professor. At this point Robert made it over to them.

'Hello, Robert,' said Matts looking up from the screen. 'All's well – Just the finishing touches.'

'Good,' Robert replied before anxiously turning his attention towards the Professor, 'Paul, I need an urgent word with you, something has cropped up.'

'Something important?' the Professor asked in his usual easy-going manner.

'I would say so,' answered Robert, 'but I think it's better you judge for yourself.'

'Okay,' said Professor Stewart grabbing hold of his cane. 'Matts, we'll leave you to it.'

Matts nodded once again absorbed by his computer data.

~

William had decided that by the time his check-up was over it would be too late in the afternoon to warrant returning to City Hall. Instead he had told Steve Strauss to meet him at Gracie Mansion where they would have their routine weekly session at which they went over his program. The two of them sat alone in his private office.

'Okay, sir,' said Steve with pen poised over a note pad, 'so we cross that out of your schedule.'

'That's right,' William confirmed, 'I'm trying to thin out my commitments, there just don't seem to be enough hours in the day at the moment. Any way I have to give priority to Oakley and Bruce now that they're coming out to stay with me over the weekend.'

'I understand, sir.'

'Good,' said William tidying up the papers on his desk, 'I don't have anything else, so I guess that's that. See you tomorrow, Steve.'

'Okay sir,' he replied rising to his feet. But then suddenly he remembered something he had meant to mention. 'Oh, just one other thing?'

'What's that?' said William.

'What did you decide to do about what was on the answering machine and the Robert Cook interview I brought to you?'

William responded without batting an eyelid, 'Oh, you're right, I should have said something to you about it. The fact is Steve I've looked into it very carefully, spoken with the lady in detail, got Scott to check it out with the Bureau and the other Agencies, and it turns out there's nothing in it. We can forget it, no further action is called for ...'

'Okay, fine,' said Steve fully satisfied. 'See you in the morning.'

'Yes, see you then, and I look forward to hearing your views on how you think Oakley and Bruce's TV broadcast has gone down.'

'Nine o'clock tonight, we'll all be watching,' replied Steve with a smile as he exited.

~

Robert insisted to the Professor that they go somewhere as private as possible to speak and they had ended up in a small room lined with empty wine bins just off the main cellar. The room had once been stacked to the ceiling with all the great vintages of a bygone era, but as it was the Professor had to content himself with the bourbon on the rocks he had carried through with him. He had listened with some amazement as Robert had revealed all. 'It really is quite extraordinary!' he exclaimed with the familiar twinkle in his eye when Robert had finished. 'I have never heard of such a bizarre combination of events all coming together in all my life!'

'You can see I had no choice,' said Robert seeking assurance.

'None at all!' replied Professor putting on his reading glasses and holding up the menu from the Drake. 'But how on Earth did she know about our cheeky goblins – or one of them at any rate?'

Robert could only shake his head. 'How she came to do that drawing has got to come under the heading of one of the great mysteries of the Universe! Sort of psychic ... kind of telepathic?'

'Ha!' chuckled the Professor. 'Well, it was you who were talking about ideas being in the air! Maybe that's the explanation! But if that's so what I'd like to know is who puts them there in the first place! Ha! It really is most mysterious, you'll telling me that you are one thousand per cent certain she had no way of knowing?'

'Ten thousand per cent certain,' he replied.

'Oh well, I guess that proves it, ideas are in the air! *Quod Erat Demonstrandum*! But even so,' the Professor's voice suddenly changed to being stern and businesslike, 'I think in involving her we have to be very careful!'

'I agree,' nodded Robert with equal gravity, 'but it does put us on the "inside"'.

'It does indeed. And you say you love her?'

'Yes.'

'Well, I suppose that's a complication, but you don't need me to tell you to be mindful of your loyalties.'

'No, you don't,' Robert sighed heavily.

'Anyway,' said Professor instantly smiling again, 'I'd better go and speak to her. Ha! To think she was with William Donaldson when he opened his "money" envelope! That's funny!'

'Yes,' smiled Robert, 'I'll lead the way.'

~

Out at sea, over thirty hours after the "Belle Epoque" had left Boston, Eliot and Warren were still on board. Stefan had pestered them incessantly about when they were going leave but now was somewhat quieter as they stood out on deck watching a small vessel approach in the distance. It was the same deep sea fishing boat which they had arrived on. Eliot and Warren had their holdalls slung over their shoulders ready to depart and Warren looked through his binoculars. 'Yes, this is them,' he confirmed.

'Good,' nodded Eliot staccato.

'Only twenty-four hours late,' Stefan complained sarcastically.

'Not really,' said Eliot not bothering even to look at him – ignore them as he did, he was fed up with the Captain's protestations.

However, Stefan, once worked up, had what could only be described as a bad case of verbal diarrhea. 'It was still supposed to be off Boston yesterday! You can't deny it! Why are all Americans such assholes! And liars too!' By now he was really slipping into overdrive. 'You keep me waiting for ten days with that wimp of a woman, now you've kept me waiting again! You can't deny it, you said it would be yesterday! That's exactly what you said!'

'So what? Maybe I did,' said Eliot bored by his rantings. 'Okay, Warren let's go over to where the ladder is.'

'I am not happy,' Stefan went on, 'I expect ...'

Eliot's patience was at breaking point. 'Look!' he glared. 'You can fucking shut your mouth or I'll shut it for you!'

But Stefan ignored this threat and just carried on, 'I said I am not happy! Also I think you have behaved very badly ...!'

'Me? Behaved badly? Why don't you take a look in the mirror!' Eliot jested dismissively.

This merely made Stefan all the more rabid. 'Is that supposed to be an insult? So you think you can insult me? I don't care about insults from you, insults can only come from people you have respect for! Not from you, you're nothing! But anyway now, much more important, I want the rest of my money. Where is my money?'

'That you will get it when this is over,' said Eliot focusing his attention on the approaching fishing boat.

'Over?' he exclaimed. 'It is over!'

'I said shut up!' repeated Eliot, this time with a force which seemed to register, and Stefan appeared to simmer down.

Arriving at the ladder by the ship's railings Eliot, Warren and the Captain waited in silence. Shortly the deep sea fishing boat was alongside. Half a dozen or so men stood on the small vessel's deck including Gil and Conrad, who was another one of the terrorists.

Suddenly Gil and Conrad clung hold of the rope ladder on the ship's side and began to climb.

Stefan reacted instantly. 'You are leaving!' he stated sounding alarmed. 'Why are they coming up!'

'Relax,' said Eliot standing right beside him.

'Answer my question!' he pressed excitedly.

'We're leaving, but they're arriving!' announced Eliot.

Stefan's eyes darted angrily from side to side, he turned to attract the attention of his seamen up on the bridge, at the same time his hand reached for the gun in his shoulder holster.

'I wouldn't try that!' warned Warren grabbing hold of his arm.

Simultaneously Eliot had whipped round his hold-all bag and snatched out a sub-machine gun. He pointed it straight at Stefan. 'No, I wouldn't try anything!'

Stefan froze, his face white with anger.

Gil and Conrad reached the top of the ladder and scaled the ship's railing on to the deck, they had hold-alls concealing sub-machine guns which they took out too. 'Nice to see you, Eliot,' said Gil calmly.

'Yeah,' nodded Eliot with his usual lack of emotion.

Stefan looked as if he were about to lash out, but with a machine gun six inches from his head it was difficult. 'What are you doing!' he blurted.

'I told you to shut up!' said Eliot. 'Gil, get the other men up.'

Gil obeyed and leant over the railings to wave to the men waiting down below, they immediately started to climb.

'I don't understand!' protested Stefan unable to keep quiet.

'No reason for you to either!' Eliot told him scornfully. 'You want to know something, Stefan? I really don't like you!'

'But this isn't what was agreed!' he shouted.

'No? Well, maybe this is what you get for being such a pain in the neck!' Eliot retorted. 'You and your men are confined to quarters, we're taking over this ship!'

'What!' screamed Stefan.

'Don't waste your breath,' said Eliot letting Gil and Conrad take over the job of training machine guns on the Captain.

By now six other well-armed terrorists had made it up on deck from the fishing boat. Eliot swung himself over the railings, 'Gil, we'll stay in touch.'

'Okay, so long for now,' he replied.

'So long.' Eliot disappeared down the rope ladder, Warren followed him and they were gone.

~

The Professor's meeting with Rosanne in the library drew to a close. He had to concede to himself that he was rather taken by her, what a mixture of brains and beauty she was. They had touched on everything, her upbringing, her education – 'You were at Wellesley were you? I once lectured there!' he chuckled – her career as a model, her career as a journalist, her beliefs and aspirations, her hopes and fears.

The Professor kept their exchange very informal, but, given his powers of perception, it might just as well have been an interrogation. He knew better than anyone there was little room for error in the view of her he arrived at. In essence, as he had made very plain to Robert in the small wine cellar beforehand, a straightforward decision had to be faced: either let her 'in' or, at the very least, lock her up – maybe for a very long time!

However, fortunately for her, the Professor was as satisfied as he could be by what he heard. 'Well, my dear,' he declared, he called all women under fifty "my dear", 'it does seem to me that you are very knowledgeable, very bright and care a great deal about the suffering in this country and the world outside. You must respect the fact that we are taking a chance in admitting you into our scheme but, naturally, we must also respect the fact that you are taking a big chance too. But yes, I do indeed feel you could make a unique contribution to our cause.'

'Well, thank you,' she smiled.

'Now, my dear,' said the Professor beginning another of his short circular meanders around the room, cane in hand, his eyes twinkling all the while, 'the only course of action for you now must be to return immediately to Manhattan. You have told us William Donaldson expects to see you this evening, that being the case it is a commitment you must fulfil! In other words, what I am saying is that for your involvement to work to our best advantage normal relations between you and him need to be maintained. It has to be ... well, how should I put it?' he asked himself in search of the right words. 'Yes, I know the expression I was looking for, it has to be "business-as-usual"'. He halted his perambulation and fixed his gaze on her. 'I trust all this is agreeable to you?'

'Yes, of course. I understand completely,' she answered without hesitation, though at the same time not failing to catch out of the corner of her eye the look of unease on Robert's face.

'And finally my dear,' added the Professor, his tone lighter, 'as we have intimated, do not be surprised if you see something unusual on TV!'

'I won't,' she smiled, knowing full well what he meant, for in vague terms they had told her about the cartoon. Furthermore, they had gone so far as to show her one of Robert's own drawings of Zyron and her astonishment at the similarity had surpassed even theirs – not that she, or anyone else, were able to shed any more light on the matter than they had done before. Moreover, this total failure to come up with any rational explanation made the Professor think of an obscure conversation reported to have taken place between two of the finest scientists of long ago. Not that it was all that obscure to the Professor for his knowledge was encyclopaedic. One of the scientists was Sir Edmund Halley, the other Sir Isaac Newton. Halley, who was Newton's friend, had attacked him for his interest in Astrology and Alchemy, both of which he dismissed as Occult nonsense. The drift of Halley's criticism had been 'How can you, Sir Isaac Newton, the most eminent scientist of your generation be interested in things as ridiculous as these?' Newton's reply was simply, 'Because, Sir Edmund, I have studied them and you have not!' And yet whereas, after three centuries, Halley was only mainly remembered for his comet, Newton was now generally regarded to be one of the greatest geniuses of all time – this did not make him right and Halley wrong, but it was food for thought. Maybe there really were many more things in Heaven and Earth than we understand the Professor concluded.

'Okay, Robert,' said the Professor, 'let's get Zak to take her back.'

'Okay,' he replied, 'I'll fetch him.' Robert left the room.

'Most enchanted to make your acquaintance,' the Professor added cordially once they were alone.

'And yours,' she said, 'I won't let you down. I know how important this is to you. And to Robert too'.

'And to many, many people,' mused the Professor.

'I know,' she nodded pensively, 'I know.'

'You see,' he went on trying not to sound quite as serious as he felt, 'when a system fails somehow someone has to fix it! That's all there is to it, I mean if you don't fix it it will get worse and worse. But solutions never come easy.'

'That I appreciate,' she accepted.

'Particularly,' he added, 'when there are so many conflicts of interest – You can end up with most people seeing there's a problem but no one having the power to act.'

'Precisely,' she concurred, 'I think you put it very well.' She paused to reflect, there was no ambiguity that her agreement was genuine enough, she could see what the Professor was getting at, it was only her continuing doubt about their prospects of success which she chose to keep to herself. 'But at any rate,' she said finding a smile after a moment or two, 'please don't think I'm being flippant, but I want to tell you something that's kind of personal.'

'What's that?' he smiled back.

Her gorgeous face looked at him front on. 'I want you to know that I think you're a really sweet guy.'

'Ha! What flattery!' he good-humoredly remarked.

'No, not flattery at all! No way!' she enthused.

'Well okay, if you insist, I won't try and argue!'

'Better not – you get into an argument with me and you'll know it!' she jested, fully aware this was the truth.

'Is that so?' he grinned.

'Very so!' she laughed.

The Professor simply smiled and sipped his bourbon, this really was some girl!

Then the library door opened and Robert returned with Zak. 'We all set?' Zak asked.

'All set,' echoed Rosanne rising to her feet.

'I'm afraid I think we would still like you to wear a blindfold,' said the Professor gently.

'That's all right, no problem,' she smiled only happy to oblige, one thing was for sure she and the Professor had struck up an instant affinity.

With the blindfold applied Rosanne was led out on to the driveway in front of the house.

And yet, even as she was being bundled into the back of a car for the return journey to New York, she still remained by and large oblivious to the real extent of the activity afoot. Matts was already out in the field with the contents of some of the other containers unloaded at Boston. These had not contained printing presses or paper for dollar bills but enough transmission equipment to start a TV station – not that the terrorists had any intention of so doing , it was far more effective to "borrow" somebody else's.

If all went to plan it was going to be quite something.

CHAPTER 14

In a repeat performance of the previous evening, though minus prying photographers, a cab carrying Rosanne drove up to the front gates of Gracie Mansion. Even so she was surprised to see security so tight again.

'Yes?' said the police officer who had halted her cab.

'Hello,' she smiled, as if she expected to be recognized.

She was. 'Oh, carry on Miss Lindblade,' came the officer's immediate friendly reply.

'But officer? Why all this?' she asked. She was referring to the number people on the gate.

'Senator Cunningham.'

'Oh, I see.' Her cab headed on through.

At the Mansion's entrance it was the usual circus created by the motorcade. As Rosanne arrived Oakley and Bruce Dean were just emerging from the front door with William. 'I'm told it's likely to be a TV audience between eighty and a hundred million,' said Oakley striding to his limo.

'Couldn't be better,' said William.

'And you can be sure I'm going to give them their money's worth! Strong government, strong leadership, that's what this country needs!'

'You betcha,' William agreed.

As Oakley sunk into the back seat of his limousine he noticed Rosanne walking over from her cab. 'Howdy!' he called out to her giving her a wink and smile. She smiled back as she headed over to join William. They kissed affectionately before turning to wave farewell to the departing fleet of vehicles. They then strolled indoors.

~

Oakley's motorcade, sirens blaring and lights flashing, snaked its way through the evening traffic towards the TV studios. Oakley and Bruce Dean chatted as, with patrolmen manning every intersection, they shot through one red light after another. 'You know, Oakley, I still think this interview could still have its sticky moments,' said Bruce.

'No, Bruce, we're going to have every bit as smooth a ride as we're having now,' he replied confidently. He turned briefly to raise his hand to some well-wishers who had waved to him from the sidewalk.

'Even so,' his running mate went on, 'in Barcroft we've got a tough interviewer, he can be a wagon load of monkeys.' And he was right, Eugene Barcroft had the reputation of being the most hard-hitting political TV journalist in America.

'Sure, Bruce,' said Oakley, 'but tonight Barcroft'll be a pussycat. If you can attract an eighty million plus audience you call the shots, my people have been toing and froing with the Network all day about what we're prepared to discuss. We won't have any problem. I've made it very clear what's out of bounds.'

Bruce nodded taking the point. 'So no references to "you-know-what"?'

'None at all!' Oakley exclaimed. 'Anything to do with that is taboo! More to the point completely irrelevant! The future of this country will be decided by the law abiding citizens who make a fair contribution to society and no one else!'

'You don't need to convince me,' his running mate nodded again.

A couple of minutes later the motorcade drew up at the studios. Oakley and Bruce, plus entourage, filed in.

~

William and Rosanne sat on a settee having a drink in the Mansion's formal drawing room, these days he preferred it to the more relaxed surroundings of what Mary and he had used to call the 'family living room'. This was partly because he felt that formality impressed Rosanne and partly because, like most people, there were some memories he would sooner forget.

'I didn't expect Oakley and everyone to be here as I arrived,' Rosanne said casually.

'Just a last minute conference before they face the Nation,' he replied.

'I see. But how come you and Oakley are so close?' she asked out of interest.

'Well, to begin with we're old friends,' answered William, 'and, more than that, I have been an enormous contributor to his campaign. Which in turn of course helps my own political goals.' He paused a moment to collect his thoughts. 'I mean if you want to be President you have to think ahead!' He stood up to switch on the TV with the sound down. 'Just making sure we don't miss the broadcast,' he added explaining his action.

'So I was right?' she said.

'About what?'

'The Presidency is your burning ambition?'

'Oh yes, very much so. In fact I intend it to come about.'

'When do you hope that might be?' she asked.

'Eight years time, after Oakley, I'll only be forty-eight.'

'But what about Bruce Dean? Mightn't he have first run?'

'No, Bruce is just a stop-gap, for one he wouldn't be all that interested, and anyway he'd be over seventy-five and that's too old, even Ronald Reagan was only sixty-nine. In fact it's possible that

Bruce might not even want to do two terms as Vice-President, in which case I have this understanding with Oakley that I would be offered the job.'

'I see,' she said with warmth. 'Sounds like you've got it pretty well worked out!'

'Well, that's the plan,' he smiled. 'But just as important to me is that you, yes you, the one and only love of my life, will be my First Lady!'

Rosanne beamed happily, she leant over to kiss him on the lips.

~

In a dressing room at the TV studio a make-up artist finished applying light touches to Oakley and Bruce Dean. 'Senator Cunningham, Senator Dean, we're ready when you are,' announced a Production Assistant entering through the door.

'Okay Bruce, let's go,' said Oakley standing up and buttoning his jacket.

When they reached the main studio they were shown to their seats and miked up. Eugene Barcroft came over, 'Good evening, Senators.'

'Good evening, Eugene,' replied Oakley shaking hands. Bruce Dean nodded and did the same.

'You're happy with the list of questions I trust?' asked Barcroft, his tone polite, precise and matter-of-fact but not in the least obsequious – he had been interviewing major Politicians for over twenty years and as far as he was concerned had seen it all.

'Yes, I'm happy,' replied Oakley dryly.

'Good,' said Barcroft settling down with his notes.

'Stand by two minutes!' shouted a Floor Manager to the entire studio. More overhead lights went on, cameras manoeuvred into position.

~

'This is the hardest thing I've ever put myself through,' said Robert with a deep breath. He was alone with Professor Stewart in the library of the house in Connecticut.

'Yes,' said the Professor wishing to be sympathetic. 'I know it must be tough.'

'Have you ever sent somebody you really love to sleep with another man?' asked Robert. 'I mean, I know of course you haven't, but can you understand how I feel?' Robert was really only using the Professor as a shoulder to lean on.

'Sure I can understand,' smiled the Professor. 'Even at my age one still has memories of one's hotter emotions!' He had been happily married for forty years but his wife had passed away some time ago. 'But what do you want me to say?'

'Yah, I don't know,' sighed Robert accepting the futility of his anguish, 'I realise there's nothing anyone can say. But shit, there's Dawn to consider as well, and that really bothers me too. Just think of it, how can I walk out on her? Or supposing she finds out about Rosanne? Jesus,' he sighed again, 'this has all the makings of turning into a mess.'

'No, it won't Robert, I know you too well, you won't allow it to. Now,' he glanced at the old fashioned watch on a chain he kept in his pocket, 'we had better get to a TV! And you, young man, had better cheer up!'

'I'll try,' he smiled.

By the time they made it to the TV in the cellar Oakley Cunningham and Bruce Dean had already been on air a minute or two – not that the Professor and Robert felt they had missed anything, they had not had much interest in seeing the very start of program anyway. Oakley's face was on camera and filled the screen.

'We have to put our own house in order, if we don't then of course I agree the consequences are bad,' said Oakley in response to a question on the economy from Barcroft.

'But then how did we get into this situation?' pressed the interviewer. 'You seem to talk as if we were pushed into something we didn't want to do! I can't go along with that! After all aren't we a consumer society? Didn't we go into this with open eyes? These deficits didn't creep up on us overnight, they've been building up gradually for years!'

'Only because our policies have been so sadly misguided,' answered Oakley with all the same unshakeable confidence that Henry VIII had found when it came to getting rid of wives. Indeed, had he had a beard, his resemblance to the King would have been almost frightening. 'You see the fundamental problem we have,' he continued, 'is that the United States has let the whole World feed off it like so many leeches. And if you let the bloodsuckers get a hold of you for too long you're a dead man!' Oakley's gift for metaphor was clearly considerable. 'To underline my point, there's no doubt that without the United States there would have been *no* strong Western Europe, *no* wealthy Japan, *no* ever more powerful China, *no* collapse of communism, *no* example set to the rest of humanity on how capitalism should operate! Put all those together and it adds up to one hell of a debt in *our* favor!'

'That's all very well, Senator Cunningham,' responded the interviewer, 'but if you look at the books, you know as well as I do, we're the nation in debt. What would you do about it?'

'I've said what I'd do many times,' Oakley answered without hesitation, 'as a number one priority the trade barriers need to go up again! That gives us a chance to sort out our problems without having to carry everyone else on our back, it also would show the rest of the World *who* really owes *who* – they'd be in for quite a shock!'

'Okay, Senator,' said Barcroft, 'but then I have to ask you this, surely you can't seriously blame all our domestic problems on outside factors alone? That seems to be what you're suggesting?'

'No, Mr Barcroft, I never said anything of the sort,' replied Oakley using a little tactical condescension. 'We certainly have a lot of problems at home of our own making, you know that, I know that – drugs, violent crime, illegal immigration, racial tension, unemployment, welfare, it's a long list. But if conditions had been right in the first place they wouldn't have assumed the dimensions they have. We now have to rebuild a climate which is hostile to these problems! Get the basics right again and you'll be surprised how quickly things'll get back on course! It's going to take some tough measures, perhaps even some pain and hardship, but it'll be worth it! It has to be our priority!'

'But,' said Eugene Barcroft, his mind suddenly working over-time, he prided himself on always controlling the direction of his interviews, 'I'm sure, Senator, that everyone shares your concern about the problems we face, but are you saying the events of the last few weeks have made no difference?'

'What?' said Oakley with a trace of consternation. 'Can you please rephrase that?' All of that instant there was tension in the air. Barcroft knew it; Bruce Dean, who had left center stage to Oakley, knew it; anybody looking in on the TV knew it too. All across the country, sensing there was going to be a confrontation, friends who were watching were calling friends who were not telling them to switch on, the TV ratings were mounting by the minute.

Barcroft permitted himself a strategic pause, 'Of course I'll rephrase the question for you, Senator Cunningham: There is some suggestion, mistaken maybe, that there might be better ways to deal with the problems you are referring to, that instead of cutting social programs they should be increased, I was merely seeking some comment from you?'

Oakley was already red in the face. 'Rephrase that again will you!' he said just suppressing simmering anger.

This time Barcroft did not hesitate, 'I'm talking about some of the pressures that some people, from some quarters, appear to be trying to bring into play?'

'Hold it a minute,' interjected Bruce Dean, 'I feel ...'

But Oakley interrupted, 'Look, you're way out of order, that sort of question wasn't on the list! Now let's get ...'

But Barcroft was having none of it, 'I think it was on the list,' he interrupted back.

'No, it was not!' said Oakley. 'To get into what you're attempting to discuss is not doing anyone any favors!'

'I'm sorry, what do you mean?' said Barcroft as calm as a lily on a mill pond.

Oakley's anger broke the surface, 'Am I stupid or are you! We all know about the Manhattan bridges, about the power sabotage, about this phoney money! But that is criminal activity, it should not have, in fact does not have, anything to do with this Election! Do you understand what I'm saying!'

William and Rosanne watched in the drawing room in Gracie Mansion. William was concerned, 'I hope Oakley doesn't let himself get too wound up, it never looks good ...'

But Barcroft was not going to be deflected from his line of questioning. 'With respect, Senator Cunningham,' he pressed, 'I'm not sure your refusal to touch on what has been a period of national crisis is going to satisfy people in general!'

Oakley exploded. 'This is irresponsible! Totally irresponsible!' he shouted. 'Both I and the President want to deny these people publicity! Now you're asking me to talk about them as if they had a right to be sitting here discussing things too!'

'Just hang on a moment,' said Barcroft now seeing the need to try to calm things.

Oakley had no intention of hanging on. 'Don't you try to bullshit me, Mr Barcroft!' he bellowed. 'This subject is closed! Got it!'

'No Senator, please, just wait a second ...'

'I'm not waiting a second for you or anyone!' yelled Oakley, 'This subject is closed! Totally, absolutely, completely C, L, O, S, E ...' But before he got to the letter D something happened, the TV monitor screen on the table in front of him in the studio "snowed" over into wobbly static and, a split second later, a new clear picture broke out.

It was the cartoon face of Zyron in close-up. He looked resplendent in his green hat with red feather. 'Hello folks!' he grinned, his voice robotic but life-like enough.

Then came a close-up of Axma. 'Yes, hello folks!' he chirped. 'Good evening to you all!' He looked every inch as colorful and cheeky as his friend.

From then on the cartoon showed both of them in their striped knickerbockers standing side by side. 'Now,' announced Zyron his big blue eyes wide open, 'we're only indirectly the people who've caused a certain amount of inconvenience ...'

'For which we apologize,' said Axma.

'But we are their spokesmen!' smiled Zyron suddenly spinning around on one foot performing a pirouette.

'What the hell is going on!' shouted Oakley dumbfounded. 'Is this Alice in Wonderland or something!' Scott Taylor's prediction of a "follow-up" had prepared him for nothing like this.

The atmosphere in the TV studio was electric, confusion was everywhere, nobody knew what to do, technicians struggled to "cure" the problem but without success.

The cartoon gathered pace, there was no hanging about as the two of them took it in turns to speak. 'Now,' said Zyron, 'because of the inconvenience we've caused ...'

'And the deaths,' added Axma, 'of quite a few ordinary people we had no quarrel with ...'

'We felt,' said Zyron, 'we had to explain.'

'Now we realize we can't explain everything,' smiled Axma, 'and we can't please everybody, but we felt a few positive gestures would go a long way to making amends!'

'So we started with our money mail shot!' exclaimed Zyron.

'You know all about that!' said Axma reaching up to remove his purple and yellow Moroccan fez cap.

'Yes, you all know about that!' echoed Zyron flashing his shiny sharp teeth.

'So register to vote,' said Axma whipping out the magical expanding blackboard from inside his fez cap, 'and ...'

'And,' continued Zyron as the blackboard grew into full size on the wall behind him, 'if you've got a lucky number on one of the one dollar bills we sent you then one of 100,000 $10,000 prizes could be yours!' He swaggered over to the board, removed the red quilted feather from his hat and scrawled the figures "$10,000" boldly across it. The figures flashed pulsatingly like a neon sign from red to violet through every color of the rainbow. Then he waved his red feather like a wand and the black board instantly vanished in a cloud of glittering spangling gold and silver stars which drifted off above their heads.

'Hee! Hee! That was a pretty slick trick, wasn't it!' chuckled Axma. 'But, even so, more seriously, we felt that just handing out $10,000 dollars prizes wasn't anything like enough!'

'Nothing like enough!' chirped Zyron replacing his feather and straightening his hat.

'Yes, we've got to do more than that!' said Axma.

'A whole lot more!' declared Zyron.

'I mean we're trying to work at poverty, and who likes poverty?' asked Axma.

'So,' continued Zyron, 'we've come up with something else besides! Which is, as of this point in time ... What's the time now Axma?'

'Oh, just after nine,' Axma replied checking his wrist-watch.

'Well, as of now,' announced Zyron, 'all you with Credit Card debts can forget about paying!'

'That's right,' smiled Axma getting quite excited waving his long fingers in the air. 'Just tear up your bills! No charge! No comeback!'

'We mean it!' emphasized Zyron with a mischievous grin. 'We've wiped out the records, kind of written them off!' He reached into his pocket and lit a small cigar. 'Up in smoke!' he jested as he exhaled.

The eyes were popping out of Oakley Cunningham's head, 'Jesus Christ!' he boomed to his aides standing in the wings of the studio. 'Somebody get on to the Credit Card companies fast! I want the truth of that confirmed or denied!'

William reaction at Gracie Mansion was no less traumatized. 'My God!' he muttered in disbelief. Rosanne looked at him but her face gave nothing away.

'Now,' chirped Axma fiddling with the yellow tassle of his purple Moroccan fez, 'you may ask yourselves: What are we really trying to do? Well, I'll show you!'

'Yeah, Axma, you do that!' egged Zyron.

'Here we go!' exclaimed Axma and he suddenly executed a spectacular acrobatic somersault.

'Yes, that's right, he's shown you!' exclaimed Zyron. 'What we're aiming for is a somersault, a somersault in values!'

'Precisely!' said Axma. 'And for whose benefit?'

'Everyone's!' answered Zyron.

'Yes, everyone's!' Axma resounded. 'All of society! And we're going to move fast!'

'And when we say fast,' enthused Zyron, 'we mean FAST! Just you watch!' They launched into a brief breakneck dance routine. It would have left anyone from Fred Astaire to Michael Jackson standing cold. Their shiny buckled shoes shifted through step after step, their coat-tails swung, their chubby bodies gyrated first one way then the next locked in perfect unison.

In Connecticut the Professor watched with Robert and Dawn arm in arm beside him. They were spellbound by the result of their efforts. Temporarily emotional quandaries were forgotten. One day, the Professor observed, whole movies would be made this way – "real" actors would become superfluous, every physical image, every facial nuance, seen on screen would simply be generated from numbers stored in graphics computers. The careers of stars from Clark Gable to Marilyn Monroe, from Errol Flynn to Rita Hayworth, might not be over yet!

'Phew! Hot work!' exclaimed Zyron stopping and affecting to catch his breath.

'Yes, very hot!' grinned Axma taking a green handkerchief from his pocket to wipe his brow. 'But back to the point ...!'

'Yes, back to the point,' said Zyron. 'Now of course we can't guarantee each and every person will find happiness – that's asking too much.'

'But at least,' Axma carried on, 'we can remove a lot of obstacles in your way!'

'And the issue isn't just Welfare payments,' said Zyron with another cheeky smile, 'we're talking broader than that.'

'Much broader than!' pointed out Axma waving his finger at the audience. 'Much, much broader than that!'

'But sounds a bit pie in the sky, don't it?' suggested Zyron.

'Yeah, probably heard that sort of talk lots of times before!' said Axma.

'Maybe you have!' said Zyron. 'But this time it's for real!'

'So how's it going to come about?' said Axma looking to his friend.

'Good question!' Zyron exclaimed. 'Very simple! First of all vote!'

'Correct!' concurred Axma. 'Vote for the side that's going to help you the most.'

'And who that is will become apparent before too long,' informed Zyron putting on a serious expression.

'Second,' said Axma, 'be sure to hang on to those one dollar bills we sent! They're really even more special than we've admitted so far!'

'Yes,' confirmed Zyron, 'remember that, those one dollar bills are really very, very special!'

'And third!' exclaimed Axma doing another pirouette. 'Watch this space! We'll be back with a progress report!'

Abruptly the studio TV monitor, and screens everywhere, cut out. A moment later the face of Oakley Cunningham, looking totally confused, returned to the picture. 'What? What's happening now?' blinked Oakley trying to gather himself.

'Senator Cunningham, we're back live,' replied Eugene Barcroft equally confused. 'Do you want to continue?'

'How can we continue?' questioned Oakley still dazed.

'It's up to you,' said Barcroft.

'Did everybody see that "Mickey Mouse" thing?' Oakley enquired.

'It seems so,' the interviewer nodded receiving information through his ear-piece.

'Well, I don't think continuing now would be appropriate,' said Oakley beginning to regain his composure.

'Do you have any final comment?' asked Barcroft.

'No,' said Oakley categorically. Then he had a second thought, 'Yes, one thing and one thing only! Whoever is behind this will never get anywhere! Okay, that's it.'

'And Senator Dean?' said the interviewer turning to him.

'No, nothing,' replied Bruce Dean, 'except to underscore what Senator Cunningham has just said.'

'Now if you could kindly switch off these cameras and close out this program,' instructed Oakley transparently disgusted with everything.

~

In a huge computer room outside Manhattan things were far from right. A computer technician unloaded a data tape from a long bank of machines. A senior corporate vice-president stood beside him. Both men looked grim-faced. 'I can't believe it but it's true,' said the technician in despair, 'all the billing information's gone!

'It can't be so,' said the vice-president as white as a sheet. 'There must be a fault with the equipment.'

'No, there's no fault, I've checked everything!' he replied certain that his judgment was correct. 'What's happened is that somebody's got into the systems! All transaction and account histories have been destroyed, and all backup data corrupts on loading! What we have here is a catastrophe!'

'I don't understand!' pressed the senior vice-president.

'They've managed to put a virus into the data structure!'

The senior vice-president was aghast, 'A virus!'

'Yes, and a pretty all pervasive one too! This is a cyber-attack!'

~

Oakley had his aides summon everyone to an emergency meeting and, rather than convene at City Hall, his hotel, The Carlyle, was chosen as the venue.

It was past eleven o'clock at night before William, Commissioner McMichael, Scott Taylor and various specialists and supporting staff sat round a table with the Presidential candidate and his running mate.

Tired as William might have become of unnecessary meetings he had no reservations about attending this one, after what had taken place earlier that evening, it was crucial. 'A massive cyber-attack using a virus? What exactly has this virus done?' he asked addressing a computer expert who had been brought in.

'Oh, it's acted in a classic way like an electronic time bomb,' replied the expert. 'And in this case it appears to have wiped everything.'

'Wipes everything?' Commissioner McMichael frowned. 'Seems almost impossible?'

'Well, I can understand you thinking so, but that's what's happened,' the expert answered. 'Different computer viruses can do different things, but the way this one turns data into gibberish is really something, and they've done it to all the major Credit Card companies through every level of their installations, including their back-ups!

'I see,' nodded Bruce Dean grasping the gist of what he had been told, 'I find it amazing.'

'I find everything amazing!' boomed Oakley who had been listening restlessly. 'This goes from bad to worse. So somebody tell me, how the hell did they interrupt the broadcast!'

'Hijacking the airwaves has been done before,' said Scott Taylor, 'though, admittedly never quite like this. All you need is enough equipment and an understanding of how television signals are transmitted – which they obviously have.'

'So they could do it again?' asked Oakley.

'Possibly,' said Scott, his tone as clinical as ever. 'That's if we don't get to them first.'

'Yes,' muttered the Senator refraining from re-expressing his annoyance that they had not been arrested already.

'But nothing from the White House?' asked William looking to Steve.

'No, not a thing.'

'Not the slightest indication of their attitude?' said William with a hint of concern.

'No, still no reaction at all,' replied Steve emphatically. 'Not even as much as a word, in fact complete silence! Under the circumstances I have to say I find it unusual, I would have expected the President have said something by now.'

William frowned. So, significantly, did Oakley too.

~

Matts had made it back to the cellar of the house in Connecticut. Everyone's mood was ecstatic. 'Went superbly!' the Professor congratulated.

'Just a team effort, that's all,' said Matts modestly.

'No, I have to give credit where credit is due!' the Professor insisted.

'Well, you can bet there's a lot of credit going spare tonight!' quipped Robert. 'And as for Oakley Cunningham, you should have seen his face when he came back on air!'

'Yes, it was priceless!' chuckled the Professor.

They all laughed and Dawn could not resist throwing her arms around Robert. Even so, as they stood cheek to cheek, it was as well she could not see into his eyes, for beneath the smiles and euphoria there was also a look of apprehension. The sort of look that so often accompanies mixed emotions.

~

Rosanne sat alone in bed reading a book in the master bedroom at Gracie Mansion. She hoped William's meeting would not go on too long into the night but felt wide awake. The book was only commanding half her attention, the other half was taken up churning over the TV broadcast and all the ramifications of the position she had now placed herself in.

The cartoon itself she had found hilarious and several times during it she had only just avoided a severe attack of the giggles which, in front of Willliam, would not have gone well at all. Its inventiveness also impressed her, it showed how fabulously gifted Robert really was and made her love him all the more. And this love at last provided her with a possible reason, or at least a possible theory, why their drawings had been so similar. It was a profound manifestation of the harmony which existed between their inner beings, an indication that even their spirits and souls moved in unison, a proof that their minds and not just their bodies, could be as one. True or false, she liked the idea of this explanation anyway.

And as for William? The sooner he walked in the better, she was looking forward to making love with him. No qualms. To her two serious relationships at once were not a problem – they were a bonus.

As she turned the next page of her book she heard the door handle turn. It was William. 'Hi,' he said, friendly but tired.

'Hi,' she smiled looking up.

'Forgive me for being so late it was a long and tough meeting, very tough.'

'What happened? How did it go?' she asked attentively.

'Badly,' said William undoing his tie. 'Nobody knows if they're coming or going. There was a huge audience for the TV, the Credit Card companies are in turmoil – how many billions of dollars they've lost is anybody's guess – and, worst of all, there's a whole new angle opened up on what might happen next.'

'What's that?'

'We can't yet predict what impact what we saw on TV made on the population in general.'

'What does that mean?' she said not quite seeing what he was getting at.

'Public opinion can be very fickle, the fall-out from something like this is damned hard to judge. It's an emotive subject, people's attitudes on welfare can vary almost according to who they last spoke with.'

'You're telling me that a silly cartoon like that could make a difference?' The innocence of her delivery was perfect.

'Not on its own,' he replied, 'but, if you take everything together, it can't be written off completely.'

'What does Oakley think?' she asked.

'Oh, he's going to stick to his guns come hell or high water, no way is he going to alter the policies he believes in! And of course he's right. But what's worrying is that we waited and waited and yet the White House has issued no statement.'

'Should they have?' she frowned.

'Yes,' he replied standing near the end of the bed unbuttoning his shirt.

'Why haven't they then?'

'Politics is a dirty business, and this close to an Election everybody's looking for every ounce of advantage they can get – we don't know for sure but it appears the President's chewing this over very carefully.'

'So you think he's going to try to spring something?'

'Yes, could be,' he said. 'And that's the danger, because if he ...' But then William halted inexplicably in mid-sentence, suddenly his eyes were rolling, he reached panic stricken for his forehead. 'Oh, my head!' he yelled in agony, his face was contorted, his legs were unsteady.

'William!' she called out in alarm as she sat up in bed. 'William, what's the matter!' He was having convulsions, his body swayed more and more violently, he was groaning like a madman, a moment later he lost balance and fell to the floor. 'William!' she again called leaping out of bed. For a second or two he threshed and twitched uncontrollably on the floor. Then he ceased to move, he had blacked out. She lifted his head in her hands, she felt his heart, his pulse seemed feeble, she dashed over to the phone, there was a direct line to the night watchman, 'Hello, this is Rosanne Lindblade,' she said speaking rapidly, 'I need an ambulance very urgently! It's Mayor Donaldson!'

Minutes later an ambulance, sirens blaring, screeched away from Mount Sinai Hospital, which, though a few blocks above 96th Street, had escaped all but superficial damage during the night of mob mayhem.

In the bedroom Rosanne had put on a bathrobe and been joined by the night watchman and a police officer who had been on duty at the front gates. William still lay lifeless on the floor. 'You sure we shouldn't do something more?' she asked.

'No, his airways are open, he's breathing okay, it's better to wait for the paramedics,' said the officer.

'He lost control and then collapsed?' questioned the night watchman.

'Yes, it happened very quickly,' she answered, but as she replied William uttered a low groan and opened his eyes. Rosanne and the others were startled.

William raised his arm up to his brow again, 'Where am I?' he asked fuzzily.

'Please sir, lie still, you passed out,' urged the police officer.

'What?' said William trying to work out what he was doing on the floor. No, I'm all right.' He began to sit himself up without difficulty.

'No, William, really!' pleaded Rosanne. 'Don't try and get up, the paramedics will be here any moment!'

'Paramedics?' said William. He clearly had no idea what had taken place. But already the sound of the ambulance siren could be heard coming up the driveway.

CHAPTER 15

The next morning, another bright sunny hot late August day, the sun streamed in through the windows of William's private hospital room overlooking Central Park. Dr Arthur Oberstein sat beside his bed as the Mayor tried to explain, 'in all honesty Arthur, I can't tell you very much, I got one of my headaches, it got worse and bang! I was out cold! Never ever happened to me before. But now,' he added shrugging his shoulders, 'I feel fine, really absolutely okay. I feel pretty stupid lying here, I ought to be up and about. Even so, I think you'll agree, it's a little scary all the same.'

Oberstein paused a moment thinking hard. 'I don't know, William,' he frowned, his tone was cautious, 'I know I said I thought you were really quite healthy, but something like this wasn't the sort of thing we were looking for.'

'Looking for what?' asked William with a nervous smile. 'You're beginning to make me feel worried!'

'No, William,' the doctor smiled back reassuringly, 'don't get me wrong, it may still prove to be nothing. But I think we should give you a brain scan.'

'Yes? What's that involve?' said William all the more nervous.

'Oh, it's pretty painless, trust me – just think of it as a glorified X-Ray.'

'Okay then, you're the expert,' accepted William. 'But Arthur, I do ask for one thing?'

'What's that?'

'I want you to ensure total confidentiality. I mean since last night the Press have been hanging around here like a bunch of circling vultures, I don't want them hearing about whatever's wrong with me before I do ...'

'No, William, I fully understand,' the doctor broke in, 'I will personally ensure your privacy is protected.'

'Thanks,' he smiled. 'So when do we go?'

'No time like the present! The scanning department are waiting for you right now.'

'Okay,' William managed to grin, 'I'm all yours.'

Minutes later he was wheeled fully conscious into the scanning machine. The equipment was complex but the procedure, for experienced technicians, perfectly straightforward. It was only a short while before he was back watching TV in his room.

~

Rosanne's day had started with a phone call to William at the hospital. She had offered to come by but he had told her that he was expecting Oberstein imminently and, anyway, hoped he would not be detained for more than a couple of hours. Genuinely relieved that he felt okay, for, odd as it in some ways seemed, she did care about him, they left it on the basis that she would call back later.

Freed from her immediate obligation to visit William, her next call was to Robert in Connecticut. Strictly instructed the previous day by him and the Professor to say nothing incriminating on the phone all she said was she needed to come out. It was arranged she would be met by car again at eleven o'clock that morning at the mainland end of the 34th Street pontoon.

Then she called Prestige Publications to leave a message for Jack Grant that she was extending her absence. She intended to couch this message as a statement, not a request – if her Editor did not like it too bad. However, unbeknown to her, Jack had left instructions with the switchboard that any call from her was to be put directly through to him. Nevertheless, what might have been a frosty conversation quickly thawed as he profusely apologized over the photographs and suggested she stayed away on full pay for as long as she wished.

Of course, in reality, Jack was neither sincerely sorry nor feeling generously inclined, his motives were strictly commercial – as the Mayor's new girlfriend and something of an instant celebrity she was now an asset to the magazine probably worth five times her salary even if she never wrote another word. But such considerations, which Rosanne was quite bright enough to be aware of, were neither here nor there. All that mattered to her was that she got what she wanted, which, as usual, she had.

Lastly, she went to the Drake Hotel and checked out. Remaining there no longer made any sense. She dropped her case back at her apartment on 89th Street and headed straight on across the river. Zak was waiting as planned and by noon she was back at the house in Connecticut.

Blindfolded and bound by the wrists she was led into the library, the Professor and Robert were already there. 'Boy, have I got something to tell you!' she said as her blindfold was removed.

'Yes?' smiled Robert.

'Yes,' she replied. And so she began to relate the events of the previous evening. They listened with keen interest. What had happened to William was extraordinary to say the least.

'And it hit him just like that?' questioned Robert quite stunned.

'Yes, literally just like that,' she said flicking her fingers for emphasis. 'It was so strange, it was as if he had a million volts going through him! Then, a short time later, he was okay again.'

Robert paused and looked quizzically at the Professor. 'Well, sue me, I don't know what to make of it, have you any ideas?'

'Epileptic fit maybe?' the Professor ventured.

'Yes, it was definitely some kind of a fit,' she concurred. 'But anyhow, they've kept him in today for tests – I guess we'll know more after that.'

'And the reaction to the broadcast was all sixes and sevens?' asked Robert.

'Yes – William said they don't know what to do, it's really put them on edge, especially since President Guthrie's said nothing ...'

Suddenly one of Matts' assistants burst in. 'White House Press Release coming through!' he announced urgently.

'Well, talk of the Devil!' twinkled the Professor. 'It looks like the President's saying something now! This could be interesting, we'll be right down. Rosanne, you can come too.'

Pleased by this sign of increased trust she followed them down into the cellar.

~

At around the same time as Robert, the Professor and Rosanne reached the basement of the house in Connecticut, the corridor outside William's room at Mount Sinai Hospital overflowed with police and secret service. Oakley was paying the Mayor a visit to see how he was.

'Gee, I'm pleased that you're all right,' said the Senator as he sat alone with William beside his bed.

'Storm in a tea-cup, Oakley,' replied the Mayor. 'They want me to remain here under observation for the rest of the day, but I'll be out tomorrow morning at the latest.'

'Well, that's good,' said Oakley warmly, 'you're an important player on the team, we need you around.'

'It's nice to feel wanted,' he smiled.

At which point one of Oakley's aides entered in an obvious state of panic. 'The White House! They're compromising!' he uttered breathlessly.

Oakley's expression changed to a heavy frown. 'Say that again?'

'They're backing off on Welfare! President Guthrie's announced he's ordering an exhaustive review!'

'It can't be!' boomed Oakley rising to his feet.

'It's what we feared most of all!' exclaimed William just as shocked. 'It's an attempt to seize the Electoral initiative from us!'

Oakley was red in the face again, in fact more red than he had been on TV the night before. 'It won't work, it can't work, it can't be allowed to work!' he bellowed. 'William, excuse me, we'll speak again later.' The Senator hurriedly went towards the door.

'I think I should come too,' said William.

'No, no – you wait until the doctors release you – I can handle this!'

'No, Oakley,' replied William picking up his bedside phone, 'I'll speak with my doctors and then catch you up.'

'All right, up to you!' answered Oakley, he was already halfway out the door.

~

Oakley had had his teams of advisers, analysts and researchers working since the crack of dawn on every conceivable aspect of the situation. The only missing piece in the jigsaw had been how President Charles Guthrie was going to react. Now that this was known the overall picture was rapidly brought into focus. As the Senator chaired the meeting he had called at his New York campaign headquarters, temporarily rented offices on West 56th Street, he was having to hear all sorts of things which were not to his liking.

'Look,' said Oakley in a deafening voice, 'what the President has done is basically a sell-out, it's a cheap trick done out of desperation and nothing else! Maybe not today, maybe not tomorrow, but give it a while and it will backfire on him!'

'Yes, but may I say something, sir,' asked Steve Strauss who had a transcript of the President's press release in front of him.

'Go on,' said Oakley.

'I think it's very relevant, politically speaking, that the President has only said he's prepared to "look" at Welfare – he hasn't actually committed himself to anything specific.'

'You think that makes him clever!' barked Oakley.

'Vague promises are always the hardest to combat,' Steve replied.

'Nonsense!' boomed Oakley. 'I don't think there's anything particularly vague about what the President has said! Specifics or no specifics, I'm not in the business of splitting hairs! As far as I'm concerned the only word to describe what the President is doing is surrender!'

The door of the meeting room opened and William came in, he was dressed in one of his usual dark blue suits. 'I'm sorry about the delay in my arrival, please carry on.' He took a vacant seat.

'William, we're talking about this attempt by the President to gain the upper hand,' informed Oakley in a quick aside.

'I see,' nodded William orienting himself.

But with the interruption over Steve immediately resumed, polite as he was, he felt compelled to take issue with what Oakley had just said. 'Yes, but with respect, sir, speaking matter-of-fact, I'd call what you dismiss as merely an attempt by the President to get the upper hand as rather more than just that! It looks like succeeding! And here there's no hair splitting – listen to the research!' He glanced towards a Political Researcher inviting him to speak.

The researcher, a man in his fifties, obliged. 'Okay, my organization has telephone polled twelve thousand people, that's a pretty good-sized sample. 63% said they had some sympathy with improving Welfare! That figure is a great deal higher than expected. Then when we asked the same people whether Welfare policy might "materially" affect their voting decision over a third said yes. You don't need me to tell you that that's significant!'

Oakley was not impressed. 'What if you'd polled the relatives of those who'd been gunned down in the bullion robbery or ended up in a watery grave under those bridges!'

'Okay,' replied the researcher in a measured tone, 'of course you've every right to give it an emotional slant – but it doesn't change the fact that these people, these terrorists whatever one wants to call them, have made an impact! Public opinion is on the move! Your lead is being eroded! There is a groundswell for some action on Welfare! I hate to be the bearer of bad tidings but I would say ignore this research and you could lose the Election!'

'Hmm,' Oakley grunted disdainfully, 'well thankfully I have a healthy contempt for opinion polls!'

William looked on grave-faced, he said nothing.

~

By late afternoon the Media had been out in force gathering opinions first hand. On the TV set in the Connecticut house's cellar Robert, Dawn, Rosanne, Matts and the Professor watched a news item compiled from interviews conducted by a woman reporter in Time Square.

'Excuse me, sir,' said the reporter to a male office worker on the sidewalk, 'who will you be voting for?'

'I was a Cunningham supporter but now I'm not so sure,' he replied in a serious tone.

'Why's that?'

'I think he's being too inflexible, I thought he didn't come over all that well last night.'

Next to be approached was a female pedestrian of about forty whose uniform showed that she worked for an airline. 'Excuse me,' began the reporter, 'may I ask you who you will be voting for?'

'Maybe President Guthrie,' said the woman slightly dithering, 'I'm kind of thinking about it.'

'But President Guthrie in preference to Senator Cunningham?'

'Well, that's the problem,' she replied, 'I was for Cunningham but now I'm undecided – I think the President is looking better than he did.'

The reporter turned to a cab driver waiting at the traffic lights. 'We're asking people about their voting intentions, are you going for Charles Guthrie or Oakley Cunningham?'

'Yeah, good question,' answered the driver as he chewed gum. 'Well, if you want the truth, I was a Cunningham man, but not anymore.'

'Can you give us your reasoning?'

'Sure, I think this crisis has smoked him out, forced him to show his true colors, and frankly I don't like what I see, in fact don't like it at all – he ain't got no soul! Okay, the lights have changed I've gotta go.' The cab drew away.

A hot dog vendor was next. 'Excuse me, sir,' asked the reporter again, 'who will you be voting for?'

'It all depends don't it?' said the vendor, who clearly considered himself pretty street smart.

'Can you clarify that?' said the reporter.

'Yeah sure, let Cunningham match the President's gesture on Welfare – that's what everybody's talking about!'

'You don't think that would be bowing to the wrong type of pressure?' the reporter enquired.

The hot dog vendor shook his head. 'No,' he said quite adamantly. 'Okay, there's been some heavy stuff going on, but all said and done that ain't the issue! The issue's the millions of poor people! There ain't no disgrace in recognizing that! I'd say the shame and disgrace is in turning a blind eye! To me it's simple, if Cunningham wants to be President let him face the facts! If he ain't prepared to, then give the other guy a second term!'

The screen reverted to the face of the news anchorman seated at his desk in the TV studio newsroom, 'And so,' he continued, 'after a day that seems to have heralded in a remarkable turnaround in campaign fortunes we move on to today's other stories ...'

Delighted with what he had seen the Professor muted the TV. '"Remarkable turnaround" is putting it mildly!' he exclaimed echoing the news anchorman's words. 'Things are surely going our way!'

'Yes,' smiled Robert, 'that last guy on the hot dog stand should have been working for us, he was great!'

'He sure was,' the Professor agreed.

'So,' said Robert, 'we've got the ball rolling, now Cunningham's got to go one better than the President!'

'Absolutely,' confirmed the Professor.

Rosanne looked pensive. 'Else he loses the Election? Is that what you mean?'

'Yes, my dear,' the Professor answered. 'And once Cunningham comes round and offers something more concrete on Welfare, then the President may decide to go one better still. Then Cunningham may find he has to match the President, and so on and so forth!'

'You're saying it becomes a sort of auction for power?' she asked.

He nodded and looked at her benignly. 'Isn't politics always like that?'

She reflected a moment. 'Yes, yes I guess you're right,' she smiled.

'Yes,' he twinkled, 'cynical as it may seem I'm afraid that is the truth. And I've been around long enough to know!' Rosanne smiled again. 'But anyway, my dear,' he went on, 'we need you to get back to the center of things in New York. Zak's waiting for you in the driveway, I think we can dispense with the blindfold.'

'Okay, thanks,' she replied, 'bye bye everybody.' Her tone was bouncy and carefree, living dangerously appeared to suit her.

In contrast Robert's heart remained far from carefree but he could not show it. 'Bye,' he said as best he could.

'See you soon,' she replied. 'And, bye Dawn,' she added with a subtle trace of haughtiness making very sure their eyes met.

'So long, Rosanne,' said Dawn with a telling look which was only half relaxed. She had chatted with Rosanne all afternoon but, ignorant as she was of the facts, the more she saw of her the more she sensed that they were both after the same man. Rivalry between women was a special kind of warfare the workings of which men understood little of.

However, no soon as Rosanne had left the cellar than Eliot and Warren entered unannounced having made it all the way back from the "Belle Epoque". In fact their and Rosanne's paths had crossed as they had passed each other on the stairs.

'You're back!' exclaimed Robert finding a smile.

'Yes,' said Eliot, dry as ever. 'But who was that?' he asked about Rosanne. 'I've seen her somewhere before.'

'Well, Eliot, that's a long story,' the Professor intervened. 'But first things first, good to have you back!'

~

As dusk fell over Manhattan Oakley Cunningham's motorcade swept up Madison Avenue and, like many times before, William hitched a lift back to Gracie Mansion in the Presidential candidate's limousine. Even so on this occasion it had been William, and not Oakley, who had suggested they ride together – this was unusual, it was as if William had something private he wanted to say.

Like many fiery people Oakley had the capacity to calm down almost as quickly as he flared up and, though the meeting at his campaign H.Q. had ended on a sour note with him accusing everyone who disagreed with him of talking "hogwash", he was now in a genial mood. 'So what did they tell you at the hospital, William?' he asked.

'Oh, they told me I'm all right,' he replied somewhat distantly, he was thinking about other things. 'They found it was a trapped nerve in my neck.'

'A trapped nerve? How did you get that?'

'I don't know, I just spoke with the people in the Brain Scan department, I'll speak with Arthur Oberstein, my personal physician, later, he'll fill me in ...'

'They suggest a treatment for it?'

'Maybe some physiotherapy, but they said it'll probably clear up of its own accord.'

'That's good news,' said Oakley. 'I'm much relieved.'

'Thanks,' said William, who then paused to clear his throat. 'But Oakley,' he resumed, his voice taking on a quiet severity, 'right now to me the worry isn't my health, it's our electoral prospects.'

'Oh William, not you too!' exclaimed the Senator quite unperturbed. 'You seemed relaxed enough at the meeting.'

'Only because I didn't want to speak in front of the other people.'

'And?' asked Oakley encouraging the younger man to speak freely.

William sighed. 'Everything is going against us, Oakley, and it needn't do. We have mis-judged public sentiment ...'

Oakley shook his head, 'No, William, I don't think so.'

'Then you can't have been listening,' he said as persuasively as he could, 'to me it couldn't be clearer, we ought to be making Welfare concessions too! Look, suppose we do lose? You're saying we just happily sit back and wait four more years?'

'Yes,' said Oakley. 'If it really came to that. But it won't. We're not going to lose.'

William looked dismayed, 'I wish I shared your confidence.' The motorcade was swinging through the Mansion's front gates.

Oakley smiled at him benignly. 'Well, you're entitled to your opinion, wrong as I believe it to be. Nevertheless, I trust I still have your support?'

'Yes, of course you do,' he assured though his tone was subdued. The limousine halted by the Mansion's front entrance.

'I'm glad of that,' said Oakley shaking hands with him, 'and I look forward to our day together at the weekend, we'll have more time to talk things over then.'

'Okay, Oakley,' he replied getting out of the limo, 'but I beg you to think again.'

The Senator smiled a second time, 'Now it's you who isn't listening, William – That's impossible, my principles are not negotiable!'

William did not reply. With a slight shrug of his shoulders and his head bowed to the ground he slowly turned and strolled into the Mansion. The motorcade headed off.

But then much to his surprise as he entered the Mansion's lobby William found Dr Arthur Oberstein sitting on a chair in the corner with a brief case on his lap. 'Arthur? What are you doing here?'

Oberstein stood up but did not smile. 'William,' he said uneasily, 'can we go through to your office?'

William hesitated frowning, he could not miss the serious expression on the doctor's face. 'Yes. Yes, of course we can. What's wrong?' He led the way into his private office.

Oberstein immediately sat on the leather couch which stood beneath a portrait of William on the wall opposite his desk. 'I'd like you take a seat too,' he said.

'Okay,' said William sitting down beside him, 'now can you tell me what's the matter?'

Oberstein waited a moment, then he began, his tone was painfully deliberate, 'William, this is never an easy moment for any physician.' He paused again, every word seemed a struggle. 'William,' he went on, 'what I have to tell is that you have a brain tumor.'

William's eyes opened wide. 'A brain tumor?' he said edgily. 'The people at the hospital told me I just had a trapped nerve?'

'No,' said the doctor, 'you asked for confidentiality and I took every precaution to make sure you had just that. Consequently, as soon as the scan was complete and about to go off to be processed, I made a switch.' Not taking his eyes off William's face he reached down and opened his brief case. Inside were two large photographic transparencies, he flicked on the table lamp beside the couch and held them up. 'See here,' he said pointing to the first of the transparencies, 'this is a normal brain, this is the brain the scanning department think is yours.' William stared very attentively, he had every reason to be interested. 'However, this other one,' continued the doctor swopping the slides around in his hands, 'is actually you. I assume you can see the difference? This large area of abnormality running inside the lower rear of the skull is the tumor.'

'I don't understand,' said William disbelievingly.

'Well, William, I'm afraid it's the truth.'

William was already pale and grew paler. 'I can tell from the tone of your voice, that this is something really bad.'

'Yes,' nodded the doctor, 'I see no advantage in stringing you along, this is a very serious condition.'

'Go on?' said William trying to collect himself.

'This type of tumor is known as an Astrocytoma, the area of the brain it is in we call the cerebellar hemisphere, which is a very important one. This type of tumor is slow growing.'

William frowned. 'So does that mean you need to cut it out?'

'No,' said Oberstein shaking his head, 'surgery is out of the question – an Astrocytoma in the form you have is what we term highly *infiltrative*, that means it runs too deep into the brain. It is inoperable.'

'So what do we do?' he asked anxiously.

'There are various treatments,' came the reply, 'but I don't think you'd thank me for putting up a smokescreen ...'

'Meaning that these treatments are ineffective?' said William, the strain in his voice close to breaking point.

'In a word, yes,' answered Oberstein heavily, 'William, there is no cure for this – all we can try and do is slow it down.'

'Slow it down?' he muttered devastated. He rose to his feet and gazed out the window. 'You're saying.' He stopped and started again, 'you're saying I'm going to die?' He turned back to look at the doctor again. Oberstein's reaction, or more precisely his lack of one, answered his question. William's lips began to tremble, 'Then how long have I got?'

'At best somewhere between sixty and ninety months,' said Oberstein quietly.

'Five to seven years!' gasped William looking up to the heavens.

'Yes,' was the blank response.

'What happens in the meantime?' he asked.

'No reason William why your life shouldn't be able to carry on normally, at least for a couple of years ...'

'What?' he questioned. 'I can't believe this, you're telling me I'm going to die but I may have an interlude in which I may not even show symptoms?'

'That's right,' said the doctor, 'brain tumors can be strange things.'

William emptied his lungs of air, he could feel profuse streams of sweat running down from inside his armpits. 'And what about these "ineffective treatments", can you tell me about them?'

'Well, there are two weapons in our armory, chemotherapy and radiation but ...'

As William and Dr Oberstein spoke, a cab with Rosanne in it drew up outside the Mansion. She got out and went over to ring the door bell. After a few seconds a maid came to open the door.

'Is Mayor Donaldson back yet?' Rosanne asked. 'I know he's no longer at the hospital.'

'Yes, mam,' said the maid, 'he came in about twenty minutes ago.'

'Oh good,' she replied entering the lobby.

In William's office the fateful conversation drew to a close. 'Well,' he told the doctor despondently, 'I'll have to think about it, but it sounds to me that treatments like that make life not worth living.'

'Yes,' nodded the doctor, 'in this sort of case you could be right. But William ...' It showed in his face what an ordeal it had been for him too, 'I'm so terribly, terribly sorry.'

'Yah, thanks Arthur,' he sighed, 'I'm afraid it still hasn't completely sunk in, I don't know what to say.'

'That's only normal,' he said trying to be comforting.

'But Arthur?'

'Yes?'

William looked at him very much man to man, 'Arthur, this will remain just between you and me?'

'Yes – entirely,' he nodded.

'No matter what?'

'No matter what,' assured Oberstein.

'Thanks.'

William went to the door of the office to show the doctor out, however as he did so, Rosanne, who had been wandering around looking for him, was standing in the middle of the lobby. 'Oh, there you are, William,' she smiled. 'I heard the news report earlier that you'd been discharged with an "all clear". What a relief that was!'

William felt drained but steadied himself. 'Yes,' he said, it turned out to be a trapped nerve. And Rosanne, this is Dr Arthur Oberstein, he just dropped by to confirm everything was all right.'

'Nice to meet you, doctor,' she said with another of her bewitching smiles.

'And you,' he nodded politely. 'But William,' he said immediately turning to him, 'I must be going.' Respecting William's wish for privacy was one thing, but the thought of getting caught in the middle of a bogus discussion about trapped nerves was another, it made him feel uncomfortable, he wanted to hurry away. 'We'll stay in touch.'

'We will,' replied the Mayor trying to put on a brave face as they strolled over to the front door. 'And Arthur, thanks again.'

'Don't mention it, pleased to be of service. Good night to you both.' He headed off across the driveway towards his car.

It was only when they entered the Mansion's living room and William gave Rosanne a belated kiss on the lips that she noticed the extent of his pallor, it was death-like. 'William, are you all right?' she had to ask. 'You look like you've seen a ghost?'

'No, I'm all right,' he said, but he was not really convincing.

'You sure?' she asked again.

'I'm fine,' he frowned insistently, he had now drifted over to the far side of the room, unconsciously distancing himself from her. This was out of character and Rosanne, regardless of any other faults she might have had, was good at picking up vibes.

'Well, you don't seem fine to me,' she said. 'You seem all shaken up, is there something I don't know? What's come over you?'

'Nothing,' was his one word answer.

'I don't believe you.' She went over to where he stood and stared at him closely. 'Come on, what is it?'

For a moment he stared back refusing to respond, then he sighed, 'Okay, you win – there is something worrying me, and worrying me a great deal: I'm beginning to get angry with Oakley, his stubborness is going to cost us this Election!'

This surprised her. 'Why?' she frowned.

'Because,' said William with a conviction which seemed to carry all before it, 'now the President has shifted his ground we need to shift our ground too. In politics the one thing you don't do at Election time is ignore public opinion.'

Rosanne thought quickly, there was much to think about, up until then William had never said a word against Oakley. 'Yes,' she replied, 'but surely he'll come round?'

William shook his head. 'No, he won't. He blankly refuses. He thinks he can pull it off, but he can't.' All of a sudden the Mayor seemed strangely resigned.

'You're positive he won't come around?' she asked.

'Absolutely positive!'

'And you really think you're going to lose?'

'Unless we do something, yes! Oakley has got it all wrong!' He covered his face with his hands. 'Oh God,' he murmured rubbing his eyes, 'everything now seems for nothing.'

'Oh, come on, William,' she said gently, 'it's not as bad as that!' She drew him close to her and rang her fingers through his hair. 'Even if the worst came to the worst it's not as if you were going to be President this time anyway, you'll have plenty of other chances ...'

To this he had no reply, he just held her tight.

CHAPTER 16

'So where did you see her before?' asked Robert puzzled to Eliot in front of Rosanne who had come out to Connecticut again the next morning.

'Outside your studio in Greenwich Village, all those weeks ago,' he responded.

Rosanne looked closely at Eliot attempting to recall the encounter herself. But she shook her head. 'No, I have to say I hardly remember,' she confessed. 'Maybe very, very vaguely, but that's all.'

'Anyway it doesn't matter,' said Eliot in his sterile tone keen to get on with things, 'what does is Cunningham – You say he isn't going to play our game?'

'No,' she answered, as always enjoying every opportunity to be the center of attention, 'Cunningham isn't prepared to budge an inch.'

'Yet William Donaldson's in favor of compromising?' said Robert.

'Yes,' she replied, 'I don't get the feeling that he wants to go all that far, but certainly some sort of gesture on Welfare he sees as essential.'

'Well, as an opening shot, that's all we need,' said Eliot.

'Yes,' accepted Robert. 'But tell me this, do we know if Cunningham's aware of Donaldson's views?'

'Oh yes,' she said, 'I'd say there's just starting to be real tension between them.'

'Hmm,' said the Professor who was listening attentively, 'that's interesting.'

'It is,' concurred Robert. 'In fact I don't get it – why should two men originally so close philosophically start drifting apart?'

'Well, your guess is as good as mine,' said Rosanne, 'but, as of yesterday evening, that's the way it is.'

'And Donaldson's health scare?' enquired the Professor, just wondering if it might be relevant.

'Nothing,' she answered without a glimmer of doubt. 'The doctors tell him he's perfectly okay.'

Robert looked across to the Professor, Rosanne looked at Dawn, and Matts looked through his thick owl-like glasses at everyone. It fell to Eliot to break the brief silence, 'So what do we do?'

Professor Stewart took a sip from his glass of bourbon. 'So you tell us Cunningham is visiting Donaldson this weekend? Where's this, his house near Rye?'

'Yes,' she said. 'Both Oakley and Bruce Dean, just for twenty-four hours. William says he expects Oakley to ask him for massive extra TV advertising monies — I can tell you Oakley's going to be in for a stony response!'

'When do they arrive at Donaldson's house, do you know?' the Professor asked, his voice once more solemn and businesslike.

'Saturday, in time for lunch,' she replied noticing the Professor's intensity, 'William's asked me to be there.'

'Okay, very good,' said the Professor reaching for his cane and standing up, his mood instantly lightening again. 'I think it's time we had some lunch ourselves!'

Eliot peered questioningly at the Professor not quite understanding the reason for the abrupt adjournment, but a brief knowing glance from the the Professor put his mind at ease. Everyone filed out of the cellar.

Lunch was fairly brief and entirely uneventful. Some cold meats, a little cheese, a little white wine for those who wanted any. The Professor set the agenda and it was clear to Eliot, Robert and Matts that, for reasons he had yet to reveal, he wished to confine the conversation to small talk.

Straight after lunch Rosanne once again said her goodbyes to everyone and strolled out to a car in the driveway to be driven back to Manhattan by Zak.

It was only after she had gone that Robert, Eliot, Matts and the Professor reconvened in the cellar with a renewed seriousness.

'Well,' said the Professor patrolling the room as he sometimes did, 'we know what has to be done.'

'Yes?' said Eliot clinically who had already half-guessed.

'Yes,' said the Professor quite definitely.

'So we remove them,' nodded Eliot.

'Indeed,' confirmed the Professor.

'What, both of them?' said Robert who also understood what was being proposed. 'Are you sure?'

'Yes,' said the Professor in a weighty tone. 'Remove Cunningham and Bruce Dean and the way is wide open.'

'Donaldson would succeed?' asked Robert.

'He would,' said the Professor without hesitation. 'There would have to be an emergency ballot to nominate a replacement candidate and no one else would get close to him!'

'Yes, you're right,' agreed Robert.

'As Cunningham's closest ally,' the Professor went on, 'as a major contributor to Party funds, as a man for some time already seen as a possible future President – not forgetting he is already Mayor of New York! All those things add up to an irresistible force!'

'Yes, you're absolutely right,' said Robert undaunted.

'Okay, this weekend,' said Eliot, his eyes steelily looking straight ahead.

'Yes, this weekend,' nodded Matts.

~

Three days later on a sunny Friday morning in early September, for August was now over, a group of Verizon telephone maintenance vehicles were parked along a leafy roadside near Rye, New York State. The telephone company men wore overalls, construction helmets and anti-dust masks which partially obscured their faces. The vehicles they had with them suggested they had quite a big job to do, they included a mechanical digger, an air compressor with drills and a road re-surfacing machine. Temporary traffic lights had been set up and a fifty yard stretch of tarmac cordoned off on the northbound lane.

It was only when one looked closely at the team of men in their anti-dusk masks that one recognized among them Eliot, Warren, Zak and Matts. None of whom, nor any of the others for that matter, would have been found on Verizon's payroll.

'Okay,' said Eliot standing in the middle of the road, 'this is the road they'll have to use, let's get this section up.' And, as if they had been doing this line of work all their lives, his half dozen colleagues commenced drilling and digging.

About one hour later, a few hundred yards down the same road near Rye, a local squad car drove along on routine patrol. 'It's a lovely day,' the police officer at the wheel said to his companion.

'Yeah,' replied the co-driver, 'I've got a week's vacation booked in Vermont next month with the kids to show them the changing of the colors, if this weather holds it oughta be beautiful.'

'Sure should,' said the driver.

A few seconds later the squad car rounded a bend and the telephone maintenance "crew" came into view. Already most of a long thin two feet deep trench had been excavated. The policemen decided to draw up alongside. 'Hi fellas,' called out the co-driver in the direction of Eliot and Warren, 'how long are you going to be?'

'Morning to you,' answered Eliot, loosening but not removing his anti-dust mask as he calmly strolled over to them. 'I'd say it's going to take about another hour or so, we're ahead of schedule as it is, we'll certainly be through in less time than our Company gave your Department notification of.' For Matts to implant a false notification of roadworks in the County police's computer records had been no problem.

'Well, that's good,' smiled the co-driver, 'normally you guys say you're coming for the day and stay a week!'

The squad car drove on.

'Assholes!' Eliot muttered to himself. He turned to the other men, 'All right, we ready to lay the cable in the trench?'

'Yup,' shouted Warren, and with their usual military precision one of the vans painted in Verizon's corporate colors was opened up and a large coil of cable unloaded. At regular intervals along this cable were thick bulges which looked like telephone line power boosters.

Within minutes the task of laying cable was complete. 'Okay, now fill it in!' instructed Eliot, and immediately Zak at the wheel of the mechanical digger began to push the piles of rubble beside the trench back into it. The road re-surfacing machine followed on directly behind, its front tank releasing steaming molten tar on to the road and its hefty rear steel roller smoothing out everything in its path.

Eliot went over to Matts who was standing at one end of the filled in trench. A short length of wire protruded from the still wet tar, Matts carefully pushed the wire into the tar making it invisible. 'It'll work submerged like that?' asked Eliot.

'Sure, won't make any difference,' Matts informed.

'Good,' said Eliot. He turned his eyes to scan the landscape which, on this part of the road, was fairly rural. 'Okay, tomorrow we'll need a place to hide — let's check the clump of trees over there, they look as if they should be suitable for our purposes.'

'Yes, they should be perfect,' said Matts, and the two men headed briskly over to what was essentially a small wood set on slightly higher ground about one hundred yards away from the road.

~

The next morning, Saturday, Rosanne, who had driven out with William the evening before, got fully involved in the last minute preparations before the arrival of their prestigious guests. She oversaw two butlers laying the table with the finest silver and crystal in the palatial dining room of what was, by any standards, a palatial residence. One of the butlers picked up a pile of napkins and began to fold them one by one beside each place setting. 'No, no,' said Rosanne to him friendly, 'do it like this.' She took one of the napkins and demonstrated how she wanted it folded. 'See,' she smiled, 'I think that's much prettier, more chic.'

'Like so?' checked the butler copying her happy to oblige.

'Yes, that's right,' she said, 'otherwise I want you guys to know that I think you've made the table look just beautiful.'

'Thank you, mam,' said the butler.

Satisfied that everything was as she wanted she left to rejoin William in one of the house's several interconnecting living rooms.

William, in contrast to her up-beat mood, had spent the morning dejected and withdrawn. He paced like a lion trapped in a cage between Renoirs, Picassos and Van Goghs which hung on the walls. However, whereas Rosanne accepted his disagreement with Oakley as the reason for his loss of morale, she was not going to let it spoil her day. 'Well, everything's going great,' she announced breezily hoping to lift his spirits as she entered through the doorway. 'If nothing else Oakley and Bruce are going to get a terrific lunch!'

'Yes,' he replied as if he had the world on his shoulders, 'but I still think this weekend is going to signal the end of a friendship.'

'Oh William, come on,' she urged, 'it could turn out better than that, after all Oakley needs your money, you'll get something worked out.'

William was scarcely listening, he only shook his head as he muttered to himself, 'Half an hour, they'll be here in half an hour.'

~

A small convoy, consisting of a limousine and a secret service vehicle in the middle, with police cars at the front and rear, drove along the road in Westchester County which led to William Donaldson's home near Rye. In the limo were Oakley Cunningham, Bruce Dean and their wives.

Oakley as usual was more or less monopolizing the conversation. 'I was in Washington yesterday, spoke with the President, told him personally what I thought.'

'Was he receptive?' asked Bruce Dean.

'Was he receptive!' Oakley guffawed. 'I could have been talking to a brick wall! But Charles Guthrie is a fool, he doesn't seem to realize what a hostage to fortune he's making for himself – Even if he won with these promises on Welfare, Congress wouldn't agree!'

'No way,' agreed Bruce Dean, who, though somewhat Oakley's crony, had a first rate political mind of his own. 'The only thing that would force Congress's hand would be if both Candidates gave way on Welfare!'

'Precisely,' concurred Oakley with a chuckle, 'and some chance of that!'

From their vantage point in the woods Eliot and Matts watched Oakley's convoy approach in the distance. 'This is them,' said Eliot lowering a pair of binoculars.

'Okay,' replied Matts who had a bag with him containing some sort of radio device.

'When I lower my hand,' said Eliot raising his right arm.

Matts nodded.

In the limousine Oakley pressed his point still further, 'In the end I have no doubt, no doubt at all, give it a week or two and Charles Guthrie will be left in the lurch, people will see that he's just taken the line of least resistance, that's not the sort of spineless approach this country wants from its President!'

Eliot saw the convoy reach the point in the road where they had laid the cable. 'Okay!' he said dropping his hand and Matts pushed a button on his radio device. Instantly in a line of at least a dozen simultaneous explosions the road erupted, the entire convoy was blown maybe thirty or forty feet off the ground, thick clouds of smoke fanned out in all directions.

'Let's go!' shouted Eliot to Matts. They scrambled off deeper into the woods.

Seconds later, as the smoke on the road began to clear, there was an eerie silence. Chunks of twisted broken vehicles were strewn everywhere. The rear section of Oakley's limousine rested upside down and one of its back wheels still in place slowly rotated. Below this wheel was Oakley's bloodied head which grotesquely protruded from a side window. His tongue hung out, his eyes stared straight into the sun, he was dead, as were the others, no one had survived.

~

At his house William and Rosanne remained alone in the living room waiting for their guests. 'It seems they're a little late,' said William restlessly.

'What's a few minutes, William,' she replied still trying to snap him out of his mood. 'If need be I'll just go and tell the kitchen to slow the lunch down.'

But then the phone rang. William strode over and irritably snatched it up. 'Didn't I tell you I wanted all calls taken as messages!' he barked down the line – for, for the duration of the weekend, it had been considered necessary to install a temporary switchboard.

However, the voice on the other end was insistent and William's expression quickly faded into shock. 'No!' he suddenly exclaimed. 'How?'

Rosanne just stared at him, looking confused and trying to work out what the matter might be. And, as he was given the details of Oakley's death, all he could do was stare back.

CHAPTER 17

Some weeks went by before any funerals could take place, faced with an assassination which had horrified the World forensic experts refused to release the bodies until every conceivable test had been carried out. And yet, even after Herculean efforts by all concerned, the terrorists still seemed no closer to being arraigned.

In a cemetery outside Philadelphia amidst green lawns set against a back drop of browning autumn leaves, four coffins draped in the United States flag attended by Military pallbearers lay beside freshly dug graves. The coffins belonged to Oakley Cunningham, Bruce Dean and their wives for, as Pennsylvania had also originally been Bruce's home State, a joint funeral had been deemed appropriate. The Military presence was entirely in keeping too: both

Senators had in their early days served with credit in the Armed Forces.

To one side of the coffins was a raised platform in the middle of which stood William Donaldson. Directly beside him, dressed from head to toe in black, was Rosanne, and behind her row after row of Congressmen and foreign VIPs.

In attendance too, in a separate section set aside for those who had worked with Cunningham, were Steve Strauss, Commissioner McMichael and Scott Taylor, the latter's beady ambitious eyes permanently on the move, never resting for long on any one thing.

William spoke into an array of microphones finishing an address, a contingent of Press and TV amounting to nearly a thousand monitored his every word. 'Oakley Cunningham was my friend,' he said looking up to all around him, 'in fact, more than that, he was my mentor, I owe him a great deal. And now,' he paused, 'and now, since I have been chosen to succeed him as candidate for the Presidency of the Unites States, I feel not only the burden of terrible sadness but also a sense of duty and obligation to him to strike out and achieve the same goals and standards of excellence he sought for this great Nation. My deepest wish is that I will be able to do justice to these heavy responsibilities and, in so doing, serve to perpetuate the memory of one of the finest men I ever had the privilege to know.'

William stood aside from the center of the platform and down in front of them a lone bugler, dressed in the full ceremonial uniform of the United States Marine Corps, stepped forward to play "The Last Post".

After the funeral William and Rosanne were escorted away by limo to the airport to board the private jet which would take them back to New York. Security was amongst the tightest ever seen – after Oakley Cunningham the secret service had come under fierce criticism, for them it was now very much a case of once bitten twice shy.

Nevertheless, one thing was beyond dispute, Professor Stewart had got it right – after an emergency convention held only a few days earlier at Madison Square Garden William Donaldson had gained the Presidential nomination. Furthermore he had gained it unopposed.

William and Rosanne disembarked from their jet at Newark airport and climbed into another limo for the last leg of the journey back to Gracie Mansion. For William, as the motorcade screamed up

Madison Avenue, it should have been a dream come true – all the paraphernalia of sirens, police and flashing lights which used to accompany Oakley, now accompanied him. Yet, away from the glare of publicity, he had become increasingly introvert, the whole way back from Philadelphia he had barely said a thing.

'How well do you actually know President Guthrie?' asked Rosanne trying to get some sort of conversation started.

'Well enough,' he replied as if opening his mouth was hard work. 'I've known him for years, everybody in politics knows everybody else.'

'But why wasn't he at the funeral then?'

'Because I told him to stay away,' said William sullenly. 'This tragedy has happened to "our" side, any sympathy that comes from it belongs to us alone, we don't need the President trying to get on the act.'

'Yes, I understand,' she nodded pensively. 'And I suppose Oakley's death has brought you a lot of sympathy. In fact, kind of ironic really – people will never know how frayed your relations with him were about to become.'

'No, they won't,' he replied. 'But what I have to do now,' he added suddenly clenching his fists, 'is win.'

Rosanne just looked at him, when he spoke in private he had become so obsessed with victory that even she was startled. Moments later the motorcade swept into the Mansion grounds.

~

The following afternoon in Greenwich Village just off Washington Square a limousine and another vehicle were illegally parked near a corner. It was drizzling lightly. Two passing patrolmen approached the four men in raincoats and dark glasses who stood beside these vehicles and asked them to move on. One quick flash by the men of their ID cards, however, sent the patrolmen immediately on their way.

Rosanne viewed the scene in the street below from a window in Robert's studio. Robert stood beside her. Because William Donaldson had spent most of the last couple of weeks travelling around the country drumming up support and Rosanne had gone with him it was the first time they had seen each other since Oakley's death. 'Those are my secret servicemen,' she said in a blank tone.

'Yeah,' he replied philosophically.

'Everywhere I go, they go,' she added with heavy emphasis.

'Well, it figures,' he drawled. 'You are William Donaldson's girlfriend, no chances can be taken.'

'But I didn't want it this way,' she suddenly protested. She moved away from the window, emotion was creeping into her voice, tears were welling up in her eyes. 'Do you know what it's like to live in a goldfish bowl, to have no privacy at all?'

'It's only for a while,' Robert tried to assure her.

'Yes? And how long is that?' she asked. 'I did this for you, I want to be with you, but now look what's happened, I have no freedom, no independence, no nothing!' Independence was perhaps the one thing that Rosanne prized most highly of all. By now she was having to choke back her tears.

'Rosanne,' he said all too conscious of how upset she could become, 'you volunteered for this. You volunteered because you believed in what we are trying to do. Have you changed your mind?'

She turned away from him and leant with her arms outstretched above her ahead against one of the studio's plain white walls, tears streamed down her face, the sound of her sobs filled the room. After weeks of tranquillity, weeks without a single argument with William or anyone else, weeks in which day after day she had felt at peace with herself, her mood had now once again radically altered. She felt unhappy, confused and vulnerable. It was as if seeing Robert after this enforced interlude had lifted the lid off a whole set of submerged feelings and sent them rushing to the surface with a vengeance. 'No, I haven't changed my mind,' she answered in a tone which was initially flat and measured. 'I believe passionately in what you are trying to do. But,' she glared turning to him with anger suddenly breaking on to her face, 'now William's the Presidential Candidate I feel trapped! Completely, utterly, trapped! My life isn't any longer my own, it belongs to other people! And I'm hating every minute of it! And I ask myself what's in it for me! Yes, me! Me, me, me! You understand! And I don't mind telling you I'm not about to be used – So tell me one thing!' She paused, her voice was reaching a crescendo.

'Tell you what?' said Robert.

Rosanne had whipped herself up into a fury as only she could. 'Tell me, tell me about Dawn!' she shouted. 'I bet you're snuggling up cosily with her each night just like you've always done, I bet most of the time you don't even think of me for more than half a second!' She drew breath, but not for long, 'I said what about Dawn!'

Robert stared at her intensely. It was a strange stare, not resentful, not aggressive, not sheepish, and yet so penetrating that almost anyone receiving it would have been unnerved.

It definitely had the effect of partially disarming Rosanne. 'Why are looking at me like that?' she frowned.

He heaved a much deeper breath than she had drawn a few moments before. He was in no hurry to answer. Then he did. 'Dawn is dead.'

'Dead?' she said in a stunned, subdued voice.

'Yes.'

Rosanne did not know what had hit her. 'How?' she murmured.

'Eliot shot her.'

'What?' she gasped incredulously.

Robert's reply was sombre. 'The three of us – Dawn, Eliot and myself – had a discussion about you. Dawn was not happy, she couldn't accept your role ...'

'So you killed her?' she said uncertainly.

'No, I've just told you, Eliot did. I knew nothing about it ... Till afterwards.'

Rosanne tried to collect herself, her head was spinning, 'What did you say to Eliot when you found out?'

'What could I say?'

'What does that mean?'

'It was over between her and me, Rosanne. But when she found out about you she started to threaten everything.'

'How did she find out?' Rosanne asked aghast.

'I told her,' he replied measuredly.

'You told her?' Rosanne's eyes were open wide.

'Yes,' he answered, 'I felt I had to, it was more than likely she was going to find out anyway. It was better that she found out from me rather from anybody else.' Robert cleared his throat. 'Rosanne, I really don't want to talk about it anymore, but you can put your mind at rest.'

It was now Rosanne who stared at Robert, her anger had gone, but within an instant fresh tears were cascading down her face. She went over and wrapped her arms around him. 'I'm sorry,' she whispered softly into his ear.

And as they kissed she could feel him getting a hard-on, through his trousers it pressed into her more and more, a surge of uncontrollable passion burst through her veins gripping her from head to toe, almost unable to contain herself she pulled him, in fact virtually dragged him, through towards the bedroom.

Down on the street a car pulled up alongside Rosanne's limousine and its escort vehicle. In the car were Scott Taylor and Steve Strauss – who over the last month or so, working together every day as they did and finding they both enjoyed a game of tennis, had become quite friendly.

Speaking from his car window with Steve alongside him Scott Taylor addressed a secret servicemen standing on the sidewalk. 'Anything?'

'She's been up there about an hour,' the secret servicemen replied glancing up in the direction of the studio windows.

'Anyone else entered the building?' asked Scott in a flat tone.

'No,' said the secret serviceman.

'Okay,' said Scott. He paused and looked up towards a helicopter passing slowly overhead. The helicopter seemed to hold some special interest for him. 'Anyway,' he added, 'let me know what time she comes out.'

'I will,' said the secret servicemen, Scott drove on.

~

Later, in the studio, Robert and Rosanne lay relaxed side by side in bed. She continued to gently stroke and caress him, but it was now the calm after the storm. 'You don't know what it's like to see you again,' he said looking deep into her eyes.

'Yes, and you.'

He drew her close. 'I guess we've been so swept up in the run of events we've had to rather side-step the personal side of things.'

'Yes,' said Rosanne, 'and I'm sorry again about my behavior earlier.'

'That's okay, forget it,' he replied, 'it's been a very tense time for all of us.'

'Yah, it has,' she whispered gazing at him.

'And on William?' he asked looking back at her, watchful that he was risking re-entering emotionally dangerous territory. 'Is there anything more to report?'

'No, nothing,' she responded quite relaxed. 'Nothing that hasn't been in the media – he's matched the President's promise on Welfare and as far as he's concerned he feels that's going to be enough for him to win. Put it this way, he's certainly not going to concede an inch more than he has to. After all, at heart remember he's still a conservative and leopards don't usually change their spots.'

'Hmm,' drawled Robert, 'seems we've still got a slight impasse – but it'll be broken.'

'Will it?' she questioned.

'Oh yes, for sure.'

'How?' she enquired. 'What is it you've got up your sleeve?'

'Oh quite a lot,' he said casually with a faint grin.

'Such as?' she asked sitting up.

'No' he said shaking his head.

'You mean you won't tell me?'

'That's right I won't,' he replied. 'And it's for your own safety. It's for exactly the same reason I didn't tell you anything about Oakley – when he died you were as surprised as everybody else, you didn't have to act, your reactions were natural, it's better that way.'

'But?' she objected.

'No, Rosanne, there are no "buts" about it. There's only one thing you can do to help right now.'

'What's that?'

He paused and climbed out of bed. 'I want you to try to set something up, I'll tell you what it is after I've made a phone call.'

~

Early that evening William was in a TV studio, two interviewers were asking him about his policies. The questions were probing but William's style in public was considerably less combative than Oakley's. 'But it does seem that Oakley Cunningham's assassination has colored your judgment?' suggested one interviewer.

'Not at all,' the Mayor responded coolly. 'It had a profound impact on me, it was the saddest day of my life, but has it affected my judgment? Certainly not. I know what you're getting at, you're saying that I've made a change of course. I don't agree.'

'Even so,' said the same interviewer, 'it does seem the hot issue in this Election has become the issue of Welfare, and that was an issue on which Senator Cunningham's views were very clear-cut.'

'Oakley was against hand-outs to those who could help themselves,' said William fully in control, 'and that's something I'm in complete agreement with – as are most people. If there was any difference between us it was only a matter of where you draw the line – no two men think exactly alike.'

'So where you draw the line is more flexible, more lenient, more liberal than where Senator Cunningham would have drawn it?' interjected the other interviewer.

'Well,' William replied with a smile, 'I don't think anybody would describe me as a liberal! But I do think Welfare should be looked at very closely.'

'So, Mayor Donaldson,' said the same interviewer, 'how far on Welfare are you prepared to go?'

'Just like the President I've ordered a review, until I have the results of it I can't ...'

'So you're not willing to give us a precise figure?' said the first interviewer.

'No, not yet – though obviously expenditure will be significantly upward.'

'But nothing approaching these demands? You know what I mean?' the first interviewer pressed.

'You mean the terrorists' demands?' said William still perfectly poised. 'By the way I think by now we can all feel free to mention them.'

'Thank you, Mayor,' acknowledged the first interviewer with a heavy dose of disingenuous gratitude. 'Yes, I was referring to their four-point-eight trillion figure.'

William frowned, then quickly smiled again. 'Well, that figure's balderdash, isn't it. Nobody's going to go as far as that, neither me nor the President. The only thing connected with the terrorists which occupies my mind is the problem of catching them – and that's just a matter of time. On all other fronts I'd say they're irrelevant – which is all they should be, they have no say in this.'

'Okay,' said the other interviewer, 'but I think what you've said has broadly defined the upper and lower limits – at the bottom end you will do on Welfare what your review indicates needs to be done, but, at the upper end you can safely say that whatever you do it will be nothing like this figure of nearly five trillion dollars over five years?'

'Correct,' answered William.

'But you also claim, do you not, that you will be doing at least as much the President?' the other interviewer asked.

'Yes, absolutely,' he replied.

'So in a way,' said the first interviewer, 'you are putting a minimum on it? Estimates of the President's probable package seem to point towards something like four hundred billion over the period of his next term – so, at any rate, according to what you've said, you're going to at least equal that?'

'I repeat,' answered William, knowing full well that these guys were paid to catch him out, 'that I am not in a position to commit myself on firm numbers. But, as a ball park figure, four hundred billion over four years – which after all is less than ten per cent of this crazy five trillion number – does not sound particularly wide of the mark. But in honest truth it might be a bit more, a bit less, we'll just have to wait and see.

'However,' he continued his expression suddenly becoming more aggressive, 'if you're comparing me and the President on this issue I find it distinctly unflattering. My frank opinion is that President Guthrie just jumped on the bandwagon when these terrorists, these scum, managed to capture some attention through their cheap TV gimmick! Had it not been for that I doubt the President would have done anything on Welfare at all!'

'Whereas you would?' asked the first interviewer, his voice ill-disguising a trace of skepticism.

'Very much so,' said William.

'Nothing to do with the extra twenty million newly registered voters?' the other interviewer goaded.

'Nothing at all,' responded William as if butter would not melt in his mouth.

~

Light drizzle still fell as a small truck slowly moved down a street in Harlem not far from 123rd. It was just after dark. Every few doors the truck stopped and a man got out and pushed a thick brown envelope either into a mail box or under a doorway. Each time this was done the man, who turned out to be Zak, then went back to the vehicle and it continued on a little further.

Shortly the van reached a corner and Zak checked his watch. 'Eight more blocks to go,' he said to the driver, 'shouldn't take us more than another half hour.'

The driver nodded.

~

In the cellar in the Connecticut Professor Stewart stood beside Matts who was looking at a computer screen. On the screen was a list of deprived urban areas across the nation, a colored blip started flashing beside the location "Harlem". 'That's confirmation that Harlem's been covered, all $10,000 prizes for there distributed,' said Matts. 'Obviously we don't actually know exactly who's getting them, in fact we have no way of knowing for sure that the people receiving them have even registered to vote, or if they had any particular serial numbers on the one dollar bills we sent out ...'

'Nor could we ever know any of that,' the Professor replied. 'We had to bluff a little in that respect – but the main thing is that the promise of prizes has been kept. Which it now has, and that to my mind is very, very important – if only the politicians were one tenth as good at keeping their promises as we are! Ha!' he exclaimed slightly changing the subject. 'Did you see William Donaldson on TV earlier? The latest word he's found to describe us is "scum"! I think all the politicians must be beginning to run out of vocabulary!'

'Well,' smiled Matts,'as long as we get a whole lot more money out of them I don't care what they call us.'

'We will,' said the Professor sipping his bourbon.

~

In their rundown tenement room on 123rd Cornwall, Tom and Ray sat around. The room was even filthier than it had been before, garbage and empty bottles littered the floor, only a single dim light bulb burnt, rain water from a roof that had not been repaired in years dripped insistently down into one corner.

The mood of the three men was far from elated, they all looked strung out and washed up.

Cornwall sat half-slumped in a chair, his head in his hands, his eyes blood-shot. 'Oh God,' he muttered in his menacing rasp, 'all that money they handed out, gone.' In sheer mindless frustration his huge fist finishing crushing a long empty beer can into a size no bigger than a baseball.

'Yeah, I suppose so,' sighed Tom no less jaded, 'Jeez man, I feel ssshhhit ...'

'Well, yeah,' said Ray, perhaps a fraction clearer headed than the other two, 'I know what you mean, I don't feel too good either ... but I have to say I've felt worse ... '

'I've *never* felt worse,' responded Cornwall tossing away the crushed beer can sending it clattering across the floor into the corner of the room.

'Well, I guess you shouldn't have got into all that stuff,' said Ray.

'What you fuckin' talkin' about!' said Cornwall looking up, the whites of eyes hardly white at all. What Ray had just said, or the way he had said it, plainly annoying him.

'You know what I'm talkin' about!' said Ray. 'Somethin' that begins with "C" and ends in "K"!'

'Oh, fuck you man!' answered Cornwall. 'You ain't exactly "Mr Clean" either!'

'No, I ain't "Mr Clean",' said Ray unoffended but also unintimidated, 'but that $750 just about took you beyond the limit, screwed you up.'

'Well, fuck you!' replied Cornwall rising to his feet and going over to Ray. He was so out of it he was on a short fuse, anger was boiling up within him. 'I said fuck you man, you hear me! All I need is another hit! Don't you preach to me you fuckin' asshole!'

'I ain't preachin' to you, man,' said Ray staring up into Cornwall's wild red eyes, 'I'm just tellin' you the fuckin' truth!'

'No man, you're fuckin' preachin'!' snarled Cornwall, 'and looking at that little bulge in your shirt pocket I bet you still got some fuckin' money.' He grabbed at Ray's shirt ripping one of its front pockets open and exposing a small wad of dollar bills. 'Yeah, I was right, you still got some fuckin money, hand over that fuckin' cash!'

'Back off man!' shouted Ray snatching the small wad of bills out of his torn pocket and angrily taking a couple of paces back out of Cornwall's reach. But Cornwall followed after him. 'I said back off! I kept those one dollar bills back 'cos we were told they were special and connected to the prizes!'

'What fuckin' prizes?' rasped Cornwall relentlessly closing in as Ray retreated towards the rear of the room.

'You so fuckin' out of your head you ain't remember?' shouted Ray in no mood to give in. 'The $10,000 prizes for registering!'

'Oh sure!' rasped Cornwall toppling aside tables and chairs in his path as he drove Ray more and more into a corner. 'You believe that bullshit! Those prizes were talked about weeks ago! What's happened since? Nuthin'! Come on man, hand over that fuckin' cash!'

Virtually at the very far end of the room Ray was running out of space. 'I said back off man!' he shouted again. Enraged he whipped out a knife and waved it defiantly. The veins on his neck seemed to be standing upright under the pressure of blood pumping through them. 'I said back off!'

But Cornwall, flanked by Tom, kept closing in. 'Take it easy, Ray,' said Cornwall.

'No, Cornwall, you take it easy!' he shouted. 'I tell you if you want this money you're going to have to kill me first!'

'Ray, I warn you,' said Cornwall now less than seven or eight feet away from him, 'you want to die for a few bucks!' The look on his face showed he was not kidding.

But Ray only glared back, he had no thoughts of surrender. To free the hand in which he held his wad of dollar bills he put them into his mouth, holding them between his teeth. He swayed from side to side juggling his razor sharp knife between one hand and another daring them to come any closer.

Cornwall stopped advancing. 'Ray,' he said slowly, 'I think there's just one thing you've forgotten, one thing I've got which you've forgotten about which I think you really oughta have remembered!' He drew a gun from under his jacket and pointed it straight at him. 'Yeah, I think you kinda forgot about this!' Ray's face froze in fear. 'You still goin' to fuckin' argue with me!' he yelled. He began to squeeze the trigger. 'You still fuckin' arguing!' he repeated.

'All right, hold it, hold it!' gasped Ray dropping the knife on the floor, his speech impaired by the dollar bills between his teeth.

'That's sensible,' said Cornwall snatching the bills away from Ray's mouth. 'Now sit down man, no hard feelings.'

Cornwall picked up the knife, put his gun away and strolled back to the front window to count the money. As far as he was concerned the incident was over, in fact it was almost as if nothing had even happened, violence to him had ceased to mean a thing.

However, whereas Tom followed Cornwall back down the room, Ray stayed where he was. Not only did he not say anything more, which, under the circumstances might or might not have been expected, but he remained motionless and impassive. More than that, his aggression had deserted him, he seemed dazed, his eyes were rolling, maybe he was not so much motionless as unable to get his legs to move under him.

'What the fuck's the matter with you, man?' rasped Cornwall noticing Ray's strange behavior. 'I said no hard feelings!'

Ray tried to reply but no words came out, his mind was a blur, he was disoriented, uncomprehending, a figure apparently frozen in an impenetrable state of isolation. Cornwall and Tom looked at him, wondering if he had gone crazy. Then, finally, struggling and with great effort, he managed to say something, 'That money's spiked!' he spluttered. 'You hear me? I said spiked!'

Cornwall and Tom frowned at him now thinking he really must be mad.

'I tell you, man,' Ray continued semi-breathless, 'I must have just touched it with the tip of my tongue while I had it in my mouth, that's all, but it's full of dope!'

'What the fuck? What's up with this dude?' Tom asked Cornwall disbelievingly.

'Jesus, I ain't foolin' with you,' said Ray slumping into a seat.

Cornwall looked plenty confused. 'Well, there's one way to find out,' he announced. He took one of Ray's one dollar bills and licked it. He waited a few seconds. Then his eyes lit up. 'Wow! Yeah man!' he exclaimed. 'What is this!'

'What?' exclaimed Tom unconvinced. He grabbed one of the bills out of Cornwall's hand and licked it too.

Cornwall did not need any more convincing, this man capable of cold-blooded murder had become like a six year old let loose in a candy store. 'Wow!' he grinned taking another lick, 'This ain't real!' He looked towards Tom waiting for his reaction, 'See what I mean?'

'Yeah!' replied Tom astonished. 'Man, this is strong stuff.'

'Yeaaaahhhh,' purred Cornwall, savoring yet another lick.

'But what kind of thing is 'dis?' Tom queried

'I dunno, I really dunno,' smiled Cornwall. 'But whatever it is I like it! This is real, real bad, man! It's gone and fuckin' made my day!'

'Yeah, but really, man,' said Tom in high spirits, 'and I mean *really*, don't it make you think you want to know what the fuck exactly's goin' on? I mean – Huh? – What the fuck's with this money?'

'Well, put a bill in a glass of water!' Ray called over from his chair, his head was beginning to clear just a little.

'What Ray?' said Tom.

'I said soak a dollar bill in a glass of water!'

'You serious?' said Tom.

'Just do it, man!' Ray insisted.

Without any more argument Tom picked up an empty glass and walked over to the water tap.

In the dark street directly outside Jam rounded the corner. Wearing a beige leather jacket he was a snappier dresser than his three friends, this was partly because it appealed to him, partly because as an on and off small time pimp it helped him recruit new girls.

He strolled through the front door of the building on 123th and entered its dim lobby. However, as he let the door swing shut, his foot made contact with a small package on the floor. He stooped to pick it up. It was a brown unaddressed envelope simply marked with the word "PRIZE". He opened it. When he saw it contained a thick wad of cash he let out a small yelp. Feeling on top of the world he headed up the staircase two steps at a time.

In the tenement room Cornwall, Tom and Ray gathered round the glass of water they had placed on a table with a dollar bill inside it. Cornwall dipped a finger into the glass and then rubbed the water droplets on it into his gums. 'What do you think?' asked Ray.

'Wow!' rasped Cornwall his blood-shot eyes nearly popping out of their sockets. 'That water's got a kick to it! Those one dollar bills must be full of the stuff! Man, what's in that one glass'd keep you in business for a week!'

'Jeez,' said Tom licking a finger which he has dipped in too, 'this really is some shit!'

'It's weird,' said Ray.

'Sure is,' rasped Cornwall.

At which point Jam sauntered in full of bounce. 'Hey fellas,' he grinned. 'How you doing?'

The three men looked over to him. 'We just made a discovery,' said Tom dryly.

'Really?' said Jam smiling from cheek to cheek. 'Well, so have I! I just won a ten grand prize!'

'No!' said Cornwall amazed. 'Shit man, you ain't serious!'

'I sure am!' smiled Jam flashing the wad of cash in front of them. 'So tell me what's new with you?'

'Oh, we got something you could say is bigger still!' grinned Tom.

'Yeah, I guess we have,' said Ray.

'Oh yeah?' questioned Jam wondering what could be bigger than a $10,000 prize.

'Oh yeah!' responded Cornwall. 'And when we say big, we mean big! First I'm going to tell you, then I think I might as well start lettin' a few other people into the secret!'

'So what you talking about?' said Jam quite puzzled.

'You'll see,' grinned Cornwall, 'but to get you into the feel of things stick your finger in that glass of water!'

'What?' frowned Jam.

'Just do it, man, then lick it,' pressed Cornwall.

Jam did. The other three watched. A reaction was not long coming. 'Well fuck me, phewww, fuccckkk me!' cooed Jam in stunned delight. 'Where did you get 'dis junk!'

CHAPTER 18

Around eight o'clock that evening, more or less the same time as Jam in Harlem was about to dip his finger into the glass of water and get quite a surprise, William Donaldson led the way into his private office in Gracie Mansion. With him were Steve Strauss and Scott Taylor. The expressions of the three men were serious, the atmosphere was less than relaxed. 'Okay,' said William tensely as he sat down behind his desk, 'why this sudden need to see me?'

'Umm,' Steve hesitated, his manner distinctly awkward. The reason for the meeting was simply that a chance casual comment by Steve to Scott had brought to light that Scott had no knowledge of Rosanne's interview with Robert or been told anything about the messages on her answering machine. That this was so seemed incomprehensible. It not only prompted Scott to take an interest in Rosanne's visit down to the Village that day but also led them to both agree that William ought to be spoken to. Even so, the prospect of challenging his boss seemed to fill Steve with a certain amount of trepidation. 'Well, sir,' he continued rather self-consciously, 'this may mean nothing, but Scott and I felt we had to ask you something ... Frankly, sir, I'm not quite sure how best to put this but ...'

'Can you please get to the point?' William interrupted impatiently.

'Yes, of course we can,' said Scott, altogether much more direct. 'Mayor, as I believe you know, Rosanne Lindblade did an interview with Robert Cook?'

'Yes, that's right,' William nodded.

'Then why,' said Scott, 'did you tell Steve that you had spoken to me about it so I could check it with my Agency when in fact you hadn't?'

'I don't recall that I did,' replied William.

'Yes, you did,' said Steve looking straight at the Mayor.

William frowned, he realized he had to change tactics. 'All right, so what?' he said raising his hands in conciliation. 'The truth of the matter is that I really didn't see anything in it. And I still don't ...'

'Okay,' said Scott, polite but blunt. 'Do you realize that Rosanne Lindblade and Robert Cook still see each other?'

For a split second a look of consternation came over William's face. However, he recovered, 'Yes, of course I do,' he said lying as convincingly as he could. 'And that was what made any fuss over the interview ridiculous – they're old friends.'

'I see,' said Scott, his expression giving no clue as to his thoughts. 'That was all we wanted to know.'

'There's no special reason you attach any importance to this, is there?' queried William doing his best to appear unconcerned.

'None at all, just routine,' said Scott standing up preparing to leave. 'I hope you didn't resent us asking.'

'No, you're welcome,' the Mayor replied, though he did not mean it. 'Good night to you both.'

'Good night,' said Scott.

'Good night, sir,' said Steve, and he and Scott departed.

However, as Scott and Steve crossed the Mansion driveway towards a car, their day was not over yet. Scott wanted to take Steve to a place he had not been before. Furthermore, Scott had not yet even told Steve why he was taking him there.

A few minutes later their car pulled up outside a building between First and Second Avenue not far from the United Nations. They entered. The building belonged to the Intelligence services and housed a variety of secret facilities. 'So what is it you're going to show me?' Steve asked Scott as they walked along a corridor.

'You'll see,' he replied in a blank tone.

'But I still think,' said Steve as they continued down the corridor, 'that with the interview and so on the Mayor was just using his own discretion, I don't think he was deliberately trying to hide anything.'

'That I'm prepared to accept,' said Scott. 'Even so there remains a side to this I don't think we can sweep under the rug.'

'Yes?' questioned Steve.

'Yes,' Scott emphasized, it's something Mayor Donaldson seems blissfully unaware of.'

Steve frowned intrigued. The two men approached a doorway.

'Steve, before we go through,' the CIA man added, 'I have to underscore one thing: nobody but me and you knows the identities of the people we'll be looking at. Therefore I will refer to Robert

Cook as "Banana" and Rosanne Lindblade as "Peach". "Banana" for Robert Cook, "Peach" for Rosanne Lindblade, remember that.' Scott pushed the door open, Steve just looked all the more intrigued.

The walls of the room they walked into were stacked high with hi-tech video equipment. A single technician, Bud, sat at a control console. 'Hi,' said Scott.

'Hi,' Bud replied. He was a somewhat overweight man with a receding hairline, fat cheeks and spoke with a slight wheeze.

'So what do you have for us?' asked Scott.

'Well,' smiled Bud noisily drawing in air, 'you could kind of call it "hot" stuff.'

'Yes?' said Scott not smiling back. 'Let's see it then.'

'Sure,' said the technician, 'here goes. I warn you, don't be surprised if your pulse rate shoots through the roof!' He hit return on a keypad to run a video file that began merely with ten-second countdown display.

By now Steve looked so perplexed that Scott felt he had better explain. 'The video sequence we're about to look at,' he said, 'was taken from a chopper circling over "Banana's" home this afternoon using an infrared heat sensitive camera – the images were then computer enhanced. Remember we know for sure that "Peach" was the only other person in the building.'

'And?' asked Steve still unclear.

'You'll understand in a minute,' Scott replied.

'Okay, this is it,' wheezed Bud as the countdown ended.

Up on the screen came a mixture of reds, purples, greens and blues. The reds and purples unmistakably represented the silhouettes of two bodies writhing one over the other making passionate love. The greens and blues formed the background of the picture. Steve's mouth was already dropping wide open.

'You understand this?' said Scott dryly. 'The heat of the bodies shows up red and purple, the cooler areas such as the rest of the room and the sides of the bed are greens and blues.'

'Jesus!' muttered Steve virtually speechless.

'Looks like "Banana" and "Peach" were having a good time,' said Scott without a trace of humor.

'Yeah, one hell of a time!' chuckled Bud. 'And just look at her! Wish I knew girls who did things like that! What is she, a contortionist or something!'

But Steve saw the funny side no more than Scott did. 'Oh boy,' he sighed slowly shaking his head as he stood and stared at the screen.

~

In a reception room at Gracie Mansion William paced to and fro as he usually did when he had something on his mind. It was gone nine o'clock. The phone rang and he picked it up. 'Rosanne, I expected you over an hour ago,' he said the moment he recognized her voice, he was less than pleased.

Rosanne was seated with her legs curled up on her sofa in her 89th Street apartment. She had gone there directly after leaving Robert.

'Yes, I know, William, I'm sorry' she said calmly, 'but I felt a little off-color and decided I'd go home. I've got a bit of a headache and so on, it's getting close to that time of the month for me ... Also Jack rang today and asked if I'd do a piece about life on the Campaign trail – So all in all I thought I'd stay here this evening, if you don't mind.'

William frowned. 'Yes, I do mind!' he said. What he had learnt at his meeting with Steve and Scott had far from pleased him. 'In fact I mind very much! I'm coming right over! Rosanne, I need to talk to you!'

'Talk to me about what?' she asked coolly.

'I'll tell you when I see you!' he replied. 'I'll be right over!'

'No, really William, I genuinely do feel rather below par this evening, try and be understanding, let's leave it till tomorrow.'

'No, Rosanne, I'm not prepared to wait,' he stated quite bluntly.

'William, don't you think you're being somewhat less than sensitive...?'

'No, I don't think so at all. I'll be over in a couple of minutes!

'Oh God, William, what is this?' she scowled. 'Stop behaving like a child!'

'I said I'm coming right over!' he repeated forcefully.

Rosanne paused and drew a deep breath, she really did feel she wanted a quiet evening to herself. 'Shit, well all right,' she said in a sour, resentful tone, 'if you're going to be like that, I'll come to you!'

~

'So what do we do?' asked Steve Strauss, his face full of concern. He was sitting with Scott at a relatively quiet table in an otherwise crowded bar on 3rd Avenue. Scott did not immediately reply. 'I mean this is mind-boggling!' he added. 'If this got out!'

'Yes, I know,' said Scott, his cold piercing eyes staring straight ahead. 'The only thing in our favor is that fortunately so far it hasn't.'

'But?' said Steve.

'Well, I think we have to look at it this way,' Scott replied, 'we're very close to the Election and we both want Donaldson to win. Okay, he's chosen a girlfriend who, for a Presidential candidate, is somewhat less than suitable, but we don't want to do anything to harm him unnecessarily.'

'I agree,' nodded Steve who had come to respect Scott's judgment.

'Therefore I think for the time being,' Scott went on, 'we just have to keep close tabs on this – Donaldson's personal hot potatoes would be better sorted out AFTER the Election.'

'Yes,' Steve nodded again. 'But should he be told about the girl?'

Scott slowly reached for his drink, knocked what remained of it back and stood up. 'That I don't know,' he replied.

~

Rosanne had arrived at Gracie Mansion and it had not taken long for things to deteriorate into a heated argument. 'You're way out of line!' she screamed at William. 'You don't own me! I'm not a caged animal!'

'For Chrissakes!' he shouted back. 'You must have no sense of responsibility!'

'Fuck that!' she yelled. 'Why shouldn't I see my friends!'

William stared at her, he tried to gather himself, but his feelings were too inflamed. 'Look, Rosanne,' he said his lips quivering in anger, 'seeing your friends is one thing, but we both know damn well that Robert Cook isn't an "ordinary" friend – you were once involved with him! And worse, his political position is ...'

'William,' she interrupted with every ounce of venom she could find, 'I think we've had this conversation before, I'm not about to have it again! I'm tired, and I still have a headache!'

'You've still got a headache!' he retorted in a bitter, sarcastic tone. 'I think of all the problems I have! And you,' he repeated his sarcasm going up a level, 'have just got a headache!'

This pushed Rosanne over the edge, she was beside herself with rage, she grabbed hold of her jacket. 'I don't have to put with this,' she shouted abruptly. 'If this is your attitude, I'm not so sure we haven't made mistake!' She headed straight for the door.

She was already out in the lobby before William called after her, yet in this short space of time his tone had completely altered, it suddenly had a pathetic quality to it, almost like someone about to cry. 'No, Rosanne, please don't go!' he pleaded. 'Rosanne, there's something you don't know, something I've told no one.'

Rosanne ignored him, she merely kept going.

'Rosanne, please ... I have to tell you!' he called again, his tone if anything more piteous still.

Rosanne blinked, she had never heard him quite like this. Caught in two minds she halted and with a scowl turned back to look at him. 'Yes? What? It had better be good,' she said bitchily, she was in no mood to be impressed by a show of emotion.

For a long moment he stood silent and stationary, just staring and staring at her. Then he brought himself to speak. 'Rosanne,' he said in a near whisper, 'I'm a dying man.'

Her first reaction was as if she had misheard him, but another mournful silence began to suggest to her that she had not. She stepped back into the room. 'It's been kept quiet,' he said watching her closely as he went to the door to make sure no one was in earshot, 'but it's the truth, that was the actual diagnosis at the hospital.'

She put her jacket down again and went over to him. His distress was transparent, but her confusion was only just beginning. It was unnerving to see this collapse in his personal dignity, to see someone outwardly so strong, so tough, so forthright, suddenly appear so desperate and frail. 'William,' she said searching in vain for words which seemed suitable, 'I find this hard to ...'

'To believe? To take in?' he suggested quietly. 'Well, it's true.'

'You're dying?' she asked, still unable to come to terms. 'No! Surely not?'

'I'm afraid it's a fact,' said William grimly. 'I have an inoperable brain tumor. I have something like five to six years to live. In the interim I will be okay, I want to make the most of it – There is no reason why I could not still be President.'

Rosanne remained stunned, almost speechless. 'Excuse me,' she said having to clear her throat, 'you'll have to forgive me, this is a bombshell. In fact bombshell isn't even the right word, it's a lot more than that.' She paused a moment staring back at William, all the time trying to digest the awesomeness of the secret he had been carrying around with him. 'But why,' she asked hesitantly as the thought crossed her mind, 'why are you telling me this now when you hid it from me before?'

William swallowed hard. 'Because I thought it was better kept private, buried, out of sight, unseen by anyone ... I thought I could handle the pressure of it all on my own – But I was wrong. I can't.' He rested his hands on her shoulder blades. 'Rosanne, I need you. I need you more than ever.'

He waited for her to speak, but again no words came easily.

'My God,' she murmured almost silently to herself, the full impact of what she had just been told finally sinking in. Coming to Gracie Mansion that evening this stark, bleak, mortifying revelation was the last thing she had ever expected to hear.

'But Rosanne,' he went on, his voice full of emotion, 'it's only now I realize how wrong I was – how could I have expected you to understand if you didn't know? It wasn't fair on either of us, these last few weeks keeping this to myself has been a nightmare for me, I feel a lot better now. But Rosanne,' he paused uneasily, 'now that you know, can you, can you still ...?' he found himself having to pause again to gather himself.

'Say it,' she urged, seeing he needed encouragement.

'Rosanne,' he resumed, 'can you, can you still love me?'

Rosanne raised her hands to his face and kissed him lightly on the lips. 'William,' she said softly, 'you already must know the answer to that – Yes, of course I can! And I do!' She gazed warmly into his eyes, and she could see how much her comforting response meant to him.

'Thank you,' he replied. 'Thank you.'

'No,' she smiled, 'you don't have to thank me, thanks don't come into it. Love, at least true love, isn't ...' She shrugged. 'Well, you know what I mean ... '

'Rosanne, you're wonderful, really wonderful.'

'No, I think it's you who are wonderful,' she said. 'And brave too. Brave to tell me, brave to face up to it like you are, brave to want to carry on ...'

William mustered a wry smile, the release of unburdening himself and the effect of her kind words had worked a kind of magic, he felt uplifted, almost himself again. 'I really do feel so much better,' he declared. 'So much better I just wish I'd told you earlier.'

'Well, you can't turn back the clock,' she smiled.

'No, you can't,' he said reaching out to stroke her hair. 'I have only myself to blame.'

'Never mind, it's behind us now.'

'Yes it is ...' he concurred.

'But I take it that no one else knows?' she asked just to be completely clear.

'No, no one. Absolutely no one,' he replied quite definite and yet with a trace of anxiety. 'Only my personal physician. And no one else must.'

'Don't worry, your secret's safe with me,' she said kissing him lightly again.

'And you won't see Robert Cook anymore?' he asked assuming her reply would be affirmative.

But it was not. 'I didn't say that,' she answered firmly, shifting where she stood just far enough to put a gap between them.

'Rosanne, I implore you,' he said both astonished and dismayed. He realized he had to tread carefully but he made no attempt to hide the strength of his conviction. 'Try and see it as I see it – the guy's a radical, politically speaking for me your knowing him is an embarrassment and a liability, if the newspapers and media got hold of it you know what they can do!'

'No, William,' she said, 'I think I've made my position clear.'

'But Rosanne,' he urged again. 'Honestly. Really. You must be able to see?'

She shook her head, but as she did so another thought occurred to her. 'But I do have an idea,' she began. It was an idea that fitted in perfectly with what Robert had asked her to do that afternoon after he had made his phone call – a phone call that had turned out to be with the Professor. What Robert had requested on his return after the call was that she arrange a meeting between him and William. In response she had said she would do her best but had expressed very real doubts about its feasibility, she simply could not imagine a plausible pretext – Yet now in a flash of inspiration it was as if a pretext had served itself up on a plate. 'The idea's very simple,' she continued in a breezy tone. 'There's only one way to defuse this situation – I want you to meet Robert Cook. Once you've met him the fact that I know him ceases to be news, it all becomes innocent, which it is ... One thing the media doesn't take much interest in is innocence.'

Quite apart from not much liking this suggestion, William found it exasperating. 'Oh, come on Rosanne,' he frowned. 'How can I find time to meet with someone like that? Who do you think I am, you know how busy my schedule is!'

But Rosanne was determined and her expression showed it. 'Half an hour, forty-five minutes, that's all I ask! You're not going to say no to me, are you?'

William sighed. 'All right,' he reluctantly agreed. 'It'll have to be early tomorrow evening, that's the only time I've got.'

Rosanne smiled at him, they embraced. 'Oh William,' she said tenderly after a few moments, 'are you really sure about what you've said? Tell me more about this terrible illness you have?'

But he, head buried on her shoulder, could hardly bring himself to answer, she could sense he was in danger of breaking down completely. 'Oh God, Rosanne,' he struggled to say in a faltering, uneven voice, 'I don't know what I'd do without you.'

She pulled him closer to her.

CHAPTER 19

Early the next morning, as the first wave of commuters were beginning their slow journey to work across Manhattan's temporary bridges, a squad car pulled up outside Police Headquarters on Park Row. In the front of the car were two uniformed officers, but in the back sat Detective Rossi, unshaven and scruffily dressed. He worked undercover.

Detective Rossi got out of the car and walked into the Headquarters building, he carried with him several thick brown envelopes.

Commissioner McMichael, a dedicated cop who had put in at least twelve hours a day most days of his life, had already been in his office for some time as he heard a knock at his door. He was alone. 'Come in,' he called and Detective Rossi entered still holding the envelopes.

'Sit yourself down,' instructed the Commissioner.

'Thanks,' said the detective, his respectful manner belying his trendy, hip appearance. He unzipped his worn-out leather jacket but kept the envelopes on his lap.

'Okay, Detective Rossi,' asked the Commissioner, authoritative and businesslike, 'what is it you've turned up that caused you to ask to see me personally?'

The detective's countenance indicated that he knew he was not wasting McMichael's time. 'Quite a lot,' he replied. 'First of all these envelopes: Members of my team found them in the mail boxes of some empty buildings in Harlem around 4 a.m. this morning. They each contain $10,000 and a note from the terrorists telling their intended recipient that they've won the contents as a prize for registering to vote.' Commissioner McMichael raised his eyebrows as the undercover officer handed him the envelopes. 'My guess is,' the detective continued, 'that hundreds, maybe even thousands, of these envelopes were distributed last night.'

The Commissioner examined one of the envelopes and looked at the thick wad of bills inside. 'It seems the terrorists have done exactly what they said they would,' he commented gravely.

'Yes,' said the detective. 'But there's something else, something even more dramatic.'

'What's that?' frowned the Commissioner.

'Well sir, as you know when the first lot of terrorist money hit the public drugs' dealing increased substantially.'

'With more money in the hands of the users it was inevitable,' responded McMichael.

'Yes,' the detective agreed, 'but last night, as of the small hours, you know what?'

'Go on?' said McMichael disinclined to play guessing games.

'Well, as of the small hours the streets went quiet, narcotics activity plummeted, the pushers weren't doing any business!'

'No business at all?' the Commissioner queried surprised.

'No more than a trickle. Make no mistake, it was dead – Not in all my experience have I ever seen anything like it!'

Commissioner McMichael looked confused. 'It doesn't make sense - a junky's a junky – they can't go without.'

'We all know that, sir,' the detective answered. 'But brace yourself 'cos there's an explanation and you're going to find it hard to believe!' The Commissioner's eyes opened wide in expectation. 'I got this initially on the grapevine from an informant, and I tell you, it really is hard to believe – It's in the money, in the one dollar bills they sent out!'

The Commissioner did not understand. 'What is?' he frowned.

'Drugs,' the detective replied. 'Some kind of narcotic substance which dissolves in water is impregnated in the paper! We don't know exactly what it is but my first stop this morning was at the labs and they tested some dollar bills from the terrorists. The tests were positive, it's definitely true.'

A look of horror came over the Commissioner's face. 'In other words what you're saying is that the terrorists have issued free drugs?'

'That's the way it looks,' he answered. 'It seems to have taken a while for people to latch on. But, if Harlem last night is anything to go by, you can take it from me the news is out now!'

'Jesus Christ!' said the Commissioner in a state of shock. He picked up one of his phones.

~

William and Rosanne were alone in the breakfast room at Gracie Mansion. Finishing his usual morning routine of glancing at the newspapers and checking his personal mail he got up from the table and leant down to kiss her gently. 'I have to get to work,' he said actually sounding quite perky, there could be no question that his telling Rosanne had acted as tonic.

'See you later, William,' she replied with a smile.

'Yes. And you're going to ask Robert Cook for a drink this evening?' he checked, evidently resigned to going through with the encounter.

'Yes, I think I'll pop downtown at lunchtime and see him.'

'Or why don't you just call him up?' William offered as a suggestion.

'No, I think I'd better break it to him in person,' she smiled engagingly, 'I mean even he doesn't get to meet Presidential candidates every day.'

'All right, if you think it's necessary,' he answered, his expression not entirely one of approval but deciding that raising objections would be futile. 'Until later then.'

'Until later then,' she echoed blowing him a farewell kiss as headed out into the Mansion's lobby.

William crossed over the lobby towards his private office to collect some papers for the day ahead and on the way he nodded a good morning to the secret servicemen who guarded the front entrance. However, at this very moment, Commissioner McMichael walked in from the driveway. William was startled. 'Commissioner?' he said.

McMichael went straight over to him, the look on the policemen's face left little doubt that something had happened and it was not good. 'What is it?' William asked.

'Mayor, there's been a very serious development, in fact one of alarming proportions – I felt I had to come and tell you personally, can we speak alone?'

'Yes, of course,' William frowned. They went on into his office.

~

Later that morning in his Greenwich Village studio Robert sat making what appeared to be some small modifications to one of his drawings of Zyron and Axma in their violet and electric blue tailcoats. The TV was on and he was half-watching it. It was a Current Affairs program presented on one of the cable channels by two political commentators, Gus Crenshaw and Lou Jacobs. They were talking about the Election and, as was always the case when they did their midday show, their style of delivery was quick-fire and matter-of-fact yet at the same time chatty – the idea being to hold the attention of casual viewers as well as serious ones.

'So if it's still a close call,' said Gus Crenshaw, 'how do you see this Election going, Lou?'

'Well, it's really difficult to say,' Lou replied. 'The President will be off round the country again this week trying to win extra votes, as indeed will William Donaldson. Both men have moved on Welfare, it's been a really hard fought campaign, I'd say it really is going to be a matter of what happens in these final days.'

'You seem to be suggesting, Lou, that you believe the level of concessions on Welfare may hold the balance?'

'Yes, Gus – perhaps for all the wrong reasons – but it's what's going to count. Not with everyone of course, but with the floating vote.'

'Yes, I have to go along with that,' Gus nodded. 'You know, Lou, it's kind of tough to stomach how much effect these people have had!'

Robert took this comment as a compliment and looked up from his drawing and smiled.

'Absolutely,' agreed Lou, 'a huge effect! The economy, jobs, taxation, international tension, those are the things that almost always come into play in an Election, and it's not as if they're not there not this time. But the terrorists seem to have kind of put their finger on the button and trumped them all, it's like they've opened up a Pandora's Box ...'

'I don't think it's in order to speak well of them, Lou,' said Gus in a disapproving tone.

'I'm not,' he replied firmly, 'they've done some terrible things - I'm just reflecting on what amounts to the reality of all this ...'

'Yes, I know you are,' conceded Gus with a light touch. 'But what about the "reality" once this Election is over? Both candidates have made hefty promises on Welfare ...'

'Neither of which is yet enough!' Robert rapidly interjected to himself.

'But let me ask you this,' Gus continued, 'how is Congress going to take it?'

'Good question,' said the other commentator. 'But again, as has been said before, with both candidates endorsing an anti-Poverty program and large sections of the electorate voting for it, it makes it really very clear-cut! There may well be some hard bargaining but if you want the bottom line – Congress will have to be supportive!'

At this point the door buzzer rang in Robert's studio. He muted the TV and went out into his lobby to answer it. 'Hello?' he said into the entryphone.

'It's me,' came back Rosanne's voice from down in the street.

Robert released the door and waited for Rosanne to come up the stairs. 'So did you have a chance to fix it?' was Robert's first question to her as she reached the top.

'Yes, this evening,' she replied, understanding immediately that he was referring to a meeting with William.

'Good, well done,' he acknowledged.

'But there's more,' she added, her voice tingling with excitement.

'Yes? Important?' he asked in his laidback way as they wandered back into the main studio.

'Very,' she said bursting to break the news, 'it's a twist you could not have foreseen – in its way it's rather shattering.'

'All right, then hold it right there,' responded Robert in an instant sounding a little edgy. He raised his finger to his lips indicating to her to be silent.

'What?' she frowned mystified.

'Let's go out to lunch today,' he said in a firm tone. 'We'll go somewhere uptown.'

This mystified Rosanne all the more. 'What? Don't you want to hear first? What's the matter?'

Robert went right up to her and whispered almost inaudibly in her ear, 'If it's that sensitive, this is not the place – Eavesdropping!'

'You think so?' she uttered quite startled.

'We don't take the chance,' he replied. He did not go so far as to explain that in the night he had thought he had possibly heard silent footsteps on his roof. 'Let me get my jacket.' He strolled off towards the bedroom.

'Okay,' acquiesced Rosanne, she drifted over to the drawing of Zyron and Axma he had been working on earlier and glanced at it. 'I see you've got some more sketches, are going to do "you know what" again?'

'Maybe,' he called out from inside the bedroom, 'but actually with that one I was just fooling around, it's only a copy that's already been used for something else.'

'Yes?' she asked with interest.

'Come along in here and I'll show you.'

Rosanne went on through.

In his bedroom Robert turned on the light, pulled down the window blinds and opened a drawer. Inside the drawer was a white balloon which he took out and blew up. On the balloon was printed exactly the same multi-colored drawing of Zyron and Axma. 'Wow!' exclaimed Rosanne. 'What's it for?'

'I'll tell you later,' he replied, deflating the balloon. 'Let's go. Your bodyguards can drive us!'

~

William Donaldson, Commissioner McMichael, Scott Taylor, Steve Strauss and others including a Narcotics Expert were seated round the table in the conference room at City Hall.

'These dollar bills,' said the Narcotics Expert, 'and let's not forget there are millions of them, contain a mixture of synthetic morphine and a type of synthetic stimulant similar to cocaine ...'

'Synthetic?' interrupted William who was really wound up.

'Yes,' said the Expert. 'Such drugs exist, they are very highly concentrated – You could hide enough of them under a postage stamp to supply an addict for a month! And by the way, as you probably know, heroin is just a derivative of morphine so, all in all, whichever way you look at it, what we have here is a pretty potent cocktail!'

The more he listened the more incensed William became. 'This is going to cause REAL public outrage!' he shouted banging the table in a gesture Oakley Cunningham would have been proud of. 'I think we can be damn certain that the terrorists have made their first big mistake!'

'It's appalling, it's a situation really beyond belief,' said the Commissioner grimly. 'To me the immediate decision that has to be made is do you we warn the public?'

'I understand the White House is against saying anything,' Steve volunteered. 'They hope this "discovery" will be confined to drugs' users.'

'Come on now,' responded William finding this suggestion ridiculous, 'you can't seriously expect to keep this under wraps! And what if nobody's warned and the drugs get into the hands of very young kids or something!'

'I was just indicating the official line, sir,' said Steve defensively. 'But also there's the risk that publicizing it could cause panic – I'd say we're faced with a tough choice.'

'Maybe so,' William retorted, 'but to me trying to hush it up is still fanciful thinking, how do we know the terrorists won't publicize it themselves! They could just put it out on the Internet! And that's as if it's not probably all over the Internet already!'

'True to an extent maybe,' said Scott joining in the discussion. 'But we've now made it very difficult for them to communicate anything at all from here on in. For a start, the President has declared a cyber-emergency and ordered the Internet in the U.S. shut down!'

'The President's shut down the Internet?' exclaimed William. 'Is that doable?'

'Yes, maybe not literally 100%, but very substantially, and that's enough,' answered Scott.

'Indeed, it vastly shrinks their audience,' Steve added. 'Shutting it down's going to have disastrous short-term consequences for business and commerce, but if it denies the terrorists access to the

Internet the President considers it worth the cost. All Internet Service Providers have fully co-operated.'

William merely frowned, his eyes flashing from person to person round the room.

'Then, on top of that,' Scott continued, 'U.S. Mail will definitely intercept any more mail shots long before they hit the streets. And, as for broadcasting, we have the capacity to jam any further attempt made on any TV Network – they would get maybe five seconds on air at most.'

'You quite sure of that?' William pressed.

'As sure as I can be,' replied Scott. 'Furthermore,' he added sternly, 'we have AWACs planes flying to locate any illegal signal, Air Force jets or Marines would then move in and wipe out the terrorists' transmitting equipment – we may not have caught these people, but the counter-measures that have been introduced are pretty tough!'

~

Robert had simply instructed Rosanne's secret service bodyguards to drive uptown without telling them exactly where they were going for lunch. He was not about to give anyone an opportunity to plant surveillance equipment in a restaurant prior to their arrival.

At 6th Avenue and 52nd he asked the limousine driver to turn east and shortly later they approached '21' Club. 'Okay, pull over here,' he said. He and Rosanne got out.

'21' Club, a one-time speakeasy, had a long and celebrated history as a restaurant, but it's particular advantage on this occasion was that it was always very busy, which eliminated the risk of being overheard. Indeed, normally it would have been necessary to make a reservation there in advance, or at least perhaps endure a long wait. However, with Rosanne with him, not only one of the most beautiful women in New York but also the girlfriend of the Presidential candidate, they were immediately shown to the best table in the room.

During lunch Robert listened to what Rosanne had to tell him. He remained relaxed but the significance of the development was not lost on him. It was a development that put a whole new slant on the situation, there was much to think about.

Towards the end of the meal the conversation briefly lulled and Robert took a sip of his coffee. Momentarily his eye caught an elegantly printed card on the table. It read, "*WE RESPECTFULLY APOLOGIZE TO OUR CLIENTELE THAT IN COMMON WITH OTHER BUSINESSES WE ARE UNABLE TO ACCEPT CREDIT CARDS AT THIS TIME*". He looked knowingly at Rosanne and pointed to the card, she smiled. 'And second opinions?' he asked reverting to the main subject.

'He's taken several,' she replied, 'all anonymously of course, in fact I doubt there's a top specialist in the World who hasn't seen that scan. But they all say the same, the tumor is confirmed.'

'I see,' he drawled. 'Well, it's sad for him, but a plus for us.'

'Yes,' she acknowledged quietly. 'For him it's about the cruellest twist of fate imaginable.'

'It is,' he agreed.

'But Robert?' she said, her beautiful face slightly frowning.

'Yes?' he replied with curiosity, he could see she had something important to ask.

'Robert,' she paused to gather her thoughts. 'Robert, do you believe in fate as such, er, I mean do you believe in fate as an actual concept?' Her mood was suddenly deeply reflective.

'Believe in fate as an actual concept?' he answered, he found the question a little odd. 'I suppose it depends exactly what you mean when you use the word.'

'Oh you know, destiny, the idea that in some way our future is mapped out for us by forces we can't control, the idea that there are higher powers at work behind the scenes that we're not aware of.'

He looked at her quizzically. 'I don't know,' he replied in his laid-back tone. 'Do you?'

'I didn't used to, but now I'm not so sure.'

'Really?' he asked her, noticing the somewhat glazed look in her eyes.

'Yes,' she said hesitantly, her voice rather tense, 'perhaps I oughtn't to tell you this, you'll probably think I've had too much to drink or something, but lately I've sort of begun to think of myself as a kind of medium, a kind of channel.'

'Channel to where?' frowned Robert mildly intrigued.

'I don't know, it's hard to describe,' she said cautiously. 'A channel to something or somewhere?' She fought to think of the right word. 'A channel to something or somewhere, something or somewhere, *cosmic*. Yes, cosmic is the best word. Cosmic, and communicating with me.' As if to relieve the tension she felt she tossed her head to get rid of the strands of her long blonde hair that had crept over her eyes.

'You're telling me you hear voices in your head, that sort of thing?' he asked uncertainly.

'No, not voices, impulses. Impulses as if my will were being manipulated, like I were a pawn on a chessboard, like I was a piece just being moved around in somebody else's game, a game so massive that it includes the whole world.' She looked at him to gauge his reaction, his expression was serious. 'I mean,' she went on, 'don't you ever feel impelled, feel you've just got to do something even though you don't know why, even though maybe you might even feel that it's against your own free will?'

'Hmm,' he said pensively, 'I know what you're getting at, but I wouldn't put it as strongly as that.'

But Rosanne had more to say. 'Then there was my drawing of your cheeky goblin that gave you such a shock.' She again checked to see if he were really listening, he was. 'Well, I've done all sorts of doodles before in my life but never one remotely anything like that, in fact I did it without even thinking, almost as if it drew itself! At the time I thought nothing of it, then I came up with the theory that I picked up your idea because I'm so madly in love with you. But now the whole thing makes me wonder, I lie awake at night thinking about it. You know I even dream of that guy?'

'Which guy?' he questioned.

'Oh, your cartoon character, Zyron whatever you call him. He seems to haunt me. And it's all connected with this channel, this psychic thing I'm trying to explain.'

Robert looked at her with interest, everything she said he found inevitably reminded him of his private discussion with the Professor in the wine vault in Connecticut the day he had first taken her out there. He had also not forgotten that the idea of Zyron and Axma had first come to him at precisely the same time as when she had walked into his studio to interview him. How mysterious it all seemed. And yet these recollections did not make an intelligent response any easier to come up with. 'Yes, it is strange,' he frowned. 'But I don't really know what to say to you. It sounds like you find some of this quite disturbing?'

'Oh yes, sometimes. Sometimes very much,' she said. He stared at her for a moment or two. 'But I don't know,' she added breaking into one of her dazzling smiles, 'I don't want you to take it too seriously. Probably I'm just being silly!'

'No, you're not,' he smiled back. 'After all, who knows? Who's to say? But if you want my honest opinion I think the main thing is to try not to let it worry you too much.'

'Yes, you're right,' she smiled, her mood had once again completely altered, she looked unbelievably gorgeous.

'At any rate,' he said, 'we should be going. Credit cards or not, I'll get the bill.' He waved to the head waiter. 'Captain, the check please.'

The Captain hurried over with the utmost diligence. 'Mr Cook, Miss Lindblade, no check. It is our pleasure to have you here.'

'You sure? I'm more than happy to pay,' he replied.

'No, Mr Cook, we insist,' said the Captain obsequiously, 'you are guests of the house.'

'Okay, thanks, we enjoyed our meal,' said Robert and, helped by a bevy of waiters, he and Rosanne got up from the table. And, as they strolled out of the restaurant, it was almost embarrassing as every other head in the room turned to get a final glimpse of William Donaldson's girlfriend. Not that Rosanne minded, she was used to it.

The secret servicemen were waiting in the restaurant lobby. 'I'm just going to wash my hands in the men's room,' announced Robert.

'Okay, I'll hang on here for you,' Rosanne replied.

A short while later they emerged from the restaurant on to the sidewalk and headed over to Rosanne's parked limousine, the secret servicemen flanking them two paces behind. 'Okay, it was great seeing you,' he said giving her a peck on the cheek as the limo driver opened the door for her. He was anxious not to appear too familiar towards her in front of the bodyguards' prying eyes.

'And you,' she smiled back as she lightly squeezed his arm. 'And I love you so, so much,' she mouthed almost silently before releasing her grip.

Robert stared into her eyes but did not reply, he stepped back and watched her sink into the back seat. 'Bye,' she waved, 'and see you again soon.'

'Yes,' he replied. 'See you soon.'

Her limousine pulled out on to the street and Robert immediately hailed a passing cab. 'Greenwich Village, just by Washington Square,' he said climbing in.

The cab driver suggested they take Park Avenue because Fifth was snarled up, Robert replied fine.

However, as they approached the intersection of Park and 34th, Robert peered casually over his shoulder for the third time since they had left '21' Club. What he was looking at was a brown station-wagon, for by now there was little doubt in his mind that it was following them. 'Okay, Driver,' he suddenly said, 'change of plan. Take a left here and carry straight on, I want to go to the East Side heliport at 34th Street.'

'Okay,' said the driver. And, as they did so, Robert glanced over his shoulder again and noticed the brown station-wagon do the same.

Ten minutes later the cab drew up at the heliport. Robert got out and walked briskly into its reception building and straight through on to the landing area beside the East River. A helicopter, with Warren at the controls, was waiting for him. He climbed aboard and it took off.

As the chopper rose into the sky Robert could see the brown station-wagon parked beside the heliport building. Two men in dark glasses stood helplessly beside it. It was final confirmation that his suspicions had been correct. He was pleased that during his visit to the Men's Room at the restaurant he had called Warren and told him to fly in.

~

Some days earlier Gil had stood out on the deck of the "Belle Epoque", beside him had been Conrad, the number two terrorist on board. Stefan and his crew remained confined to their quarters.

The ship was passing through the last section of a narrow waterway and in front of the two men was open sea. It was the completion of yet another leg of what had turned into a marathon voyage. Conrad studied the scene around him. 'So that's goodbye to the Panama Canal.'

'Yeah,' replied Gil taking in a deep breath, 'the Pacific Ocean here we come. We head North again, back into colder waters.'

'Yah,' nodded Conrad gazing out to the distant horizon which lay in front of them.

And, leaving Central America far behind, head North they did.

And now, over one week later, the ship was most certainly approaching colder waters – Sightings of seals and whales and walruses had become an everyday occurrence.

~

The helicopter had whisked Robert directly back to Connecticut. In the cellar the Professor held an inflated white balloon in his hand with the same design of Zyron and Axma on it as Robert had shown Rosanne at his studio before they had gone to lunch. 'See the small white plastic valve attached to where you blow it up?' the Professor said enthusiastically. 'Well, that valve allows for a slow gas release, makes sure that when it goes "up" after a time it will slowly come "down" again!'

'All we have to do is gauge wind direction,' added Matts.

'And, of course, every balloon will be tagged,' said Eliot.

'Yes, it's perfect,' grinned Robert, who, having filled them in on his latest news, which had caused quite a stir, was now getting up-to-date on theirs. 'Anything else?' he enquired.

'Well, somebody's definitely found out about the drugs,' said Matts. 'In fact the news has spread like wildfire, I've gotten into the police computers and since last night crime has dropped heavily across the country – and when I say heavily I mean heavily!'

'Hardly surprising,' commented Eliot dryly. 'Nobody's having to steal to buy drugs, and the Dealers ain't got much action to fight each other over!'

'Yah,' nodded Robert, 'and thank God the news has broken – despite our hints that they were special it was taking so long for people to tumble the dollar bills that I was beginning to think that we'd have to go out and tip off a few junkies personally! However, as it turns out, the discovery coming as near as this to the Election may well wind up being ideal timing.

'Do we have any other angles?'

'No, not yet,' said Matts, 'it's too early to glean any Banking information, but, give it a day or two, and that's going to be interesting.'

'Yes, very,' twinkled the Professor sipping his bourbon.

'Still,' smiled Robert, happy with everything he had heard, 'I guess it's off for my drink with William Donaldson!'

'Yes, and be sure to give him the squeeze!' said the Professor.

'I will,' he replied as he headed for the exit.

'I know you will,' said Eliot with a blank expression.

The meeting broke up.

CHAPTER 20

Robert took a car he kept at the house in Connecticut and drove himself back to Greenwich Village. He was due at Gracie Mansion at seven o'clock sharp and decided it would be easier to have his own means of transport rather than have to worry about cabs to get there and back.

He showered and, unusually for him, even went so far as to put a suit on before setting off. He arrived at the gates of the Mansion at 6.55 and, after identifying himself to the security staff, was waved through. Parking his car in the driveway he walked over to the Mansion's front door. Rosanne, who had made a point of looking out for him from an upstairs window, went down to the porch to greet him. 'Hello, come in,' she smiled warmly.

'Thanks,' he said, 'lovely to see you.'

'And you,' she replied. They kissed each other lightly on both cheeks, this charade once again performed for the benefit of the secret servicemen who hovered in the lobby. 'William's in the formal living room, follow me, we'll go and join him.'

~

At the same time as Robert's arrival at the Mansion Steve Strauss and Scott Taylor were back with Bud, the technician, in the Intelligence building between First and Second Avenue near the United Nations. They were listening to a recording of Robert and Rosanne's conversation at his studio that morning. Scott, in particular, was craning his neck and straining his ears in order to hear every word.

'Did you have a chance to fix it?' asked Robert's voice from the recording accompanied by the sound in the background of Rosanne's footsteps reaching the top of the stairs.

'Yes, this evening,' came back her voice.

'Good, well done,' he replied.

'But there's more,' she said.

'Yes? Important?' he asked.

'Very,' she answered, 'it's a twist you could not have foreseen – in its way it's rather shattering.'

Bud halted the playback. 'Then he seemed to shut her up,' he said frustrated. 'I'm afraid we have no specifics to go on, no way of knowing what these people were referring to – though it sounds as if whatever it was it was pretty significant.'

'Yah,' frowned Scott scratching his head. 'Anyway, thanks Bud. Steve, let's go.'

The two men headed out into the corridor and walked towards the elevators. 'What do you make of it?' asked Steve.

'I think it's very dangerous,' Scott replied tensely.

'On what level?'

'Lots of levels,' he answered. 'We have no indication yet that Robert Cook is breaking the law but he's certainly acting like someone who's got something to hide!'

'What are you going to do?' said Steve seeing how keyed up the CIA man had become.

'We can't let this ride any longer!' he replied. 'Love triangles are one thing but what we have here is a potential major security risk! The first priority must be to give Donaldson the full story – he has to end this relationship!'

Steve nodded. 'And Robert Cook?'

'That will have to wait, our first concern is Donaldson!' An elevator arrived, they entered it.

'But in the morning he's off on a campaign sweep through the South West,' said Steve.

'I realize,' Scott replied. 'We go to Gracie Mansion right now!'

The elevator reached the building's underground car park, the two men went to their car.

~

In the living room at Gracie Mansion William looked a little incredulously at his guest. Robert had not wasted much time steering the conversation in the direction he wanted. 'So you think all these things that have taken place are for the good, do you?' the Mayor asked.

'Yeah, actually rather overdue,' drawled Robert, seated in an armchair.

'Come on now, Mr Cook,' said William, feeling relaxed and fully in command, 'I mean I don't want to get heavy with you, after all we're just having a drink – but don't be ridiculous!'

Robert paused for effect and glanced towards Rosanne who was on the sofa next to his armchair. 'Well,' he said casually, turning back to face the Mayor, 'we can talk about the weather if you like, but I think this is more interesting – it's pretty clear from the tone of your voice that you still think that everything that's happened is really bad?'

'Shit, what do you expect me to think?' exclaimed William, he was beginning to find Robert's nonchalant manner rather irritating. 'Are you telling me that blowing hundreds of people away in the name of poverty is quite okay! That according to your standards saturating the country with counterfeit money and then with dangerous drugs is perfectly all right!'

Robert was unmoved by William's more excited tone. 'It's all interrelated,' he answered quite unrattled, 'you have to see what they're trying to get at.'

'And what's that?' the Mayor frowned.

'Drugs, Poverty. Poverty, Drugs – they're tied in,' said Robert. 'It's all part of the same vicious circle – that's what the terrorists are highlighting, that's their message!'

'So you're now telling me there's a message in all this?' William blinked bewildered. 'What are you trying to do, preach to me or something?'

'No,' replied Robert, 'I'm purely stating the obvious – you ain't going to do anything about Poverty until you sort out Drugs, and you ain't going to do anything about Drugs until you get to grips with Poverty. By the way, Mayor Donaldson,' he added glibly, 'are serious about doing anything about Poverty anyhow?'

William was not used to be being spoken to in this way, 'I think that's a rather impertinent question, Mr Cook, frankly I'd say it's insulting, I didn't invite you here to be subjected to ...'

'No offense intended,' Robert interrupted before the Mayor could finish. 'All I'm trying to point out is that the new measures on Poverty talked about so far just amount to wishful thinking! They simply don't come anywhere near to matching up to the scale of the problem.'

'Is that so?' said William disparagingly, he was still in two minds whether the best way to handle Robert was to be plain rude or simply dismissive. 'So what would you propose?' he asked.

Robert looked straight at him, he paused before going on, when he did his voice was uncompromising, 'I would propose nothing less than exactly what the terrorists recommend. And remember the terrorists are not finished yet!'

'I would surely say they are!' retorted William.

'No, you're wrong,' said Robert shaking his head.

'No, Mr Cook,' replied the Mayor categorically, 'it is you who are wrong! The terrorists may not have been apprehended but they've been fairly well driven into a corner! Most of all, they have no further means of communication with the public – and without that they're impotent!'

Robert's initial reaction was to smile.

~

Even as William spoke several men dressed in black stood on the deck of a tug which towed a large barge. The two vessels were a few miles out at sea off Manhattan and in the darkness the lights of the City glowed on the horizon. A huge canvas tarpaulin covered the barge's cargo. At a given signal the men on the deck of the tug pulled on a series ropes attached to the tarpaulin and hauled it aside. Immediately thousands of white balloons, each emblazoned with a picture of Zyron and Axma and each with a small printed label, drifted up into the night sky.

In New Jersey, at approximately the same moment, two enormous trucks stopped on the crest a deserted ridge surrounded by green fields. Warren, Zak and others climbed down from the cabs of the trucks and untethered the ropes securing their loads. Instantly more large quantities of white balloons ascended into the air.

Indeed, over the course of the next few hours, dozens of similar balloon release operations took place across the United States.

~

'No,' said Robert calmly to William as they continued their discussion at Gracie Mansion, 'there're lots of ways to communicate with the public and I'm sure the terrorists will find a few you haven't thought of! More to the point, you can't stop a message getting through if it's one people want to hear!'

'A message people want to hear!' uttered William exasperated. 'You seriously think people welcome this chaos, this violence, this challenge to the system!'

'Of course people don't like it,' Robert replied, 'but deep down they also realize you can't have a Country with over 40 million poor people and close to 10 million drugs addicts! You just can't!'

Rosanne sipped her white wine. 'Well,' she chipped in, 'I'm staying out of this, but that much I don't think anyone would argue with.'

'Hmm,' said William to Robert after a moment's consideration, 'it's pretty damned easy to say something's wrong – putting it right, that's the hard part! If the solutions to drugs and poverty were that straightforward, don't you think something more positive would have been done by now?'

'No,' answered Robert with conviction. 'Because all the politicians have tunnel vision, they seem totally unable to depart even as much as an inch from all the things that have been tried and failed before!'

'Oh sure,' said William patronizingly. 'You know how I'd describe you, Mr Cook? A misguided idealist!'

Robert just smiled. 'People might have said the same about Napoleon, or Gandhi, or even George Washington!'

'You really think so?' sneered William.

'I know so,' said Robert. 'And I'll tell you something else, if something isn't done pretty damn quickly this Country's finished!'

It was now William who had to smile. 'All right, Mr Cook,' he said, 'let's play "what if". What if almost five trillion dollars were spent on Welfare?'

'That money would help a lot of people, and it wouldn't just be spent on Welfare but on schools, hospitals and all types of infrastructure.'

'But it's other people's money, taxpayers' money!' the Mayor objected. 'Worse, do you really think throwing money around like that would make any lasting difference? It would just get quickly sucked down the tubes and in no time you'd be back to square one!'

'I don't agree at all,' said Robert. 'The money would be re-spent, it would be re-cycled back into the economy, the people who paid the taxes would eventually get it back after it had filtered through the system – and in the process of filtering through that money would have benefited a lot of people, it wouldn't have just sat idle collecting interest in some bank account!'

'So you're an economist too are you?' condescended William.

'No, but I know people who are! But let me make it clear that I'm not claiming that big expenditure on Welfare and public works on its own would be enough.'

'Oh yes? And what else would be needed?' smirked William.

'I've already told you,' he replied. 'You have to combat the drugs crisis, combat it head on and at full tilt!'

William smirked again, he was starting to find listening to Robert mildly entertaining. 'And what bright suggestions have you got on that?'

Robert's expression became deadly serious. Drug distribution must come under Federal control – it must be removed from the hands of gangsters.'

'Addict registration?' William interjected. 'That doesn't work.'

'I'm not talking about addict registration,' said Robert, 'I'm talking about legalization. It's not a new idea, but it's an idea that so far no one's done anything about – now all that's got to change!'

William stared at Robert. 'You really are crazy,' he muttered.

'No, I don't think so,' he responded, 'and I'll tell you why! The situation we're in now is a direct parallel with Prohibition, trying to ban alcohol caused more problems than it solved! It's the same now!'

William's only reaction was of increased amazement, to him any suggestion of drug legalization was unthinkable. 'You know, I can't believe what I'm hearing!' he declared. 'Okay, let's have another round of "what if". What if heroin, cocaine, PCP, etcetera, etcetera were made available over the counter? I tell you what, you'd end up with three times as many addicts!'

'No, you wouldn't,' said Robert shaking his head. 'In fact I think if the problems of the ghettos were alleviated at the same time you'd get a lot fewer! Get rid of the dead-end mentality that plagues the poor and cut out the vast profits that come from dealing and you'll begin to haul things back – haul them back in a way no number of Drug Enforcement Agents could ever do!'

'Yes, well I have to admit your candor's astonishing,' said the Mayor, 'but I'm afraid I think your argument's full of holes.'

'That's only because you're incapable of looking at it with an open mind!'

'Oh bullshit!' retaliated William. 'It's not just drugs, think of all the drug related crime!'

'Crime rates have dropped since yesterday like they've never done before!' Robert was quick to point out.

But William was having none of it. 'Then what about danger to people's health? Don't you take that into account? I thought you're supposed to be a *caring man*!'

'How you can have everything so distorted leaves me speechless!' Robert hit back. 'Do you know how many Americans die each year because of tobacco? Something like four hundred thousand! Do you know how many because of alcohol? Not far short of one hundred thousand! For illegal drugs believe it or not the figure's a fraction of that!

'By the way those statistics are official!'

'Are they?' said William unimpressed.

'Yes!' asserted Robert. 'But it's not so much a matter of death rates or whatever alone — it's essentially just a matter of facing reality in all its ugliness and accepting there isn't a perfect answer! Mayor Donaldson, if you think I'm an idealist then I think I've been quite badly misunderstood!'

William shook his head and looked at his watch. 'I'm afraid nothing you've said can sway me. And, for your information because we're going to have to call a halt to this discussion shortly, the correct approach on drugs, which is the one I'm going to pursue, is stiffer penalties at home and intensive measures to strangulate the sources of supply.'

'Jesus,' protested Robert, 'how much out of touch can you be! We've had stiff penalties for years - what's been the result? Nothing! As for restricting supply, you must be joking! As long as there's a demand all that would achieve would be to push up prices, and if you succeed in that you'll not only send crime through the roof but you'll also end up lining traffickers pockets even more! You ask the Mafia or the Drugs cartels if they want drugs legalized! They'd tell you no way, it would be disastrous for them! That ought to give you a clue which is the right direction to go if nothing else does!'

'Well, Mr Cook,' said William, 'one thing I will give you is that you're articulate, however we're going to have to agree to disagree.' He got up from his seat. 'It's been nice meeting you, but regrettably we've already gone on longer than I planned and I have other commitments.'

Robert got up too. 'Have you listened at all?'

'I've listened,' the Mayor replied leading him towards the door.

'Well then,' said Robert halting in his stride, 'I'd like you to understand one more thing!'

'Okay,' said William restlessly, 'make it as brief as you can.'

'It's very brief,' said Robert, his tone unequivocal. 'The man who comes nearest to the terrorists' demands will become the next President of the United States!'

'Is that a fact?' scoffed William.

'You'd better believe it,' said Robert gazing steelily into William's blue eyes.

The Mayor frowned. 'You want to know what my reaction to that sort of statement is?' he responded breezily. 'You need your head examined!'

Robert just smiled. 'I enjoyed my drink anyway,' he said.

'I'm pleased you did,' answered William walking on again. 'I'll see you out. You going to come and say goodbye, Rosanne?'

'Sure,' she smiled, she had said little but the spectacle of her two lovers meeting face to face had held for her a peculiar fascination all of its own.

Yet, as Rosanne rose to her feet, Scott Taylor and Steve Strauss came into the lobby from the Mansion's dark driveway with an urgent sense of purpose. 'Is the Mayor in his office?' Steve asked one of the secret servicemen on the front door.

'No, he's with a guest in the living room,' the Serviceman replied.

'Do you know who?' pressed Scott.

But before the agent could answer the living room door opened and William, Robert and Rosanne emerged. Scott and Steve froze, at the sight of Robert they were aghast, for a moment the room fell silent.

'Is something wrong?' asked William somewhat bemused.

Scott and Steve still seemed dumbstruck.

'Well, something's obviously bothering you,' he said heading on towards the front entrance, 'let me just say goodbye to my guest.'

'No!' Scott suddenly uttered. 'I insist you do no such thing! This man is not to leave!'

William had to blink, Scott sounded almost frantic. 'Not to leave? Why's that ...?'

But Scott had no time for courtesies. 'You heard me! He is not to leave! Absolutely, absolutely not!'

'What?' William frowned all the more perplexed. He turned to his assistant, 'Steve, what is this?'

'It's something we have to tell you, sir,' answered Steve. 'It concerns this man.'

'Yes?' said Robert coolly. 'What is it I'm supposed to have done?' Outwardly though not inwardly he was completely relaxed.

'I think you know very well!' said Scott uptight.

'I'm afraid you've lost me,' replied Robert unflustered.

'We'll see about that!' responded Scott. He turned to address the Mayor, 'This is something which has got be sorted out! I think we should go through to your office.'

William frowned again, he was finding Scott's manner less than civil. 'All right, let's do that then,' he said in clipped tone after a moment's thought.

'In that case I'll leave you and go upstairs,' said Rosanne hoping to extricate herself.

'No!' barked Scott. 'You're needed too!'

Rosanne looked to William for guidance. 'Okay,' he said slightly raising his voice, 'we'll all go through. But Scott kindly calm down! And, by the way, this intrusion is not appreciated right now, so the reason for it had better be good!'

Scott did not reply but looked undeterred.

However, as William, Robert and Rosanne headed over towards his office, Steve lingered with Scott who went over to talk to the three secret servicemen in the lobby. Scott was very direct, 'Just forget you ever heard this conversation, okay! Also make sure we're not disturbed!' The three agents nodded.

As Robert entered the office with William and Rosanne, and before Scott and Steve had caught up, his heart was pounding. He sensed the precariousness of the position and knew something had to be done. He turned to the Mayor with a piercing glance, he spoke rapidly but quietly, his tone was matter-of-fact, 'There's something I'm going to tell you straight – I've got half an idea what this pair want to talk to us about!' William looked at him edgily but Robert continued without pausing. 'It might be as well for you to know that I know you're not as *well* as you look!'

For a split second William was visibly shaken, the color drained from his face, hearing Scott and Steve's approaching footsteps he fought to collect himself, he turned in half panic, half anger towards to Rosanne. 'Rosanne, did you hear that?' he uttered. 'Did you tell him!'

Rosanne's expression was blank. 'Yes I did,' she replied icily not even bothering to look at him. 'And if you want the truth our affair is still on!'

William covered his mouth with his hand to control what would have been a gasp, but the shock in his eyes said it all.

At that moment Scott and Steve strode in. Scott, unaware of what had just transpired, went over to light switches to turn on some more lamps. 'Okay,' he said officiously, clearly intending to take command, 'this may take a while – Everybody sit down.'

But William was now certainly in no mood to take orders from anyone. He turned on Scott, 'Do you mind!' he glared indignantly. 'This is my house! So stop trying to tell me what to do! I don't have to listen to any of this if I don't want to!'

'You'd be foolish if you didn't,' replied Scott undaunted. 'In fact, if you don't listen now, you're going to have to listen later!'

'Are you making a threat!' exclaimed William. His mind was in turmoil, he felt caught in a sandwich between desperation and despair.

'No, but I mean to see this through,' the CIA man replied.

'I think you are making a threat' responded William, his face now red. 'I think both of you should leave right now! And as of this evening you're both off my staff!'

'No sir, hear us out,' said Steve trying to calm things.

'Hear you out!' shouted William. 'Who do you think you are barging in here anyway!'

'Sir,' Steve responded, 'don't make this any harder than it is already.'

Realizing his back was to wall William seemed to gather himself, 'Okay,' he said.

'That's better,' Scott replied.

'But look,' said William, 'let's try and keep this in perspective.' With whatever political and personal future he had disintegrating by the second he was having to think fast. 'I really don't need you two to tell me what I already know! Do you think I'm unaware that Miss Lindblade and Robert Cook are still involved? Do you think I'd ask him here for any other reason but to try to resolve this!'

Scott and Steve looked slightly thrown by this statement. In contrast Robert and Rosanne showed no expression at all.

Sensing his ploy might have worked, William decided to sit down, the others took the opportunity to do the same. 'I mean,' he went on persuasively, 'unless we're all going to be hypocrites, I don't think pristine, faultless private lives either qualify or disqualify people holding high public office!'

Scott stared closely at William. 'Well, Mayor Donaldson,' he replied in a measured tone, 'all that's as may be. But,' he added looking towards Robert, 'we feel the problem goes a little deeper than that.'

'Do you? Why?' said Robert getting up again and strolling round the room.

'There're other possible connections which I don't like,' said Scott eyeing him very carefully. 'We all know what's happened in this country in the last three months, I'm not so sure you don't have some involvement!'

'You reckon so?' said Robert calmly, standing by a window and casually opening it.

'Leave that window alone!' Scott shouted. 'You can't escape!'

Robert grinned and moved away from the window. 'I'm not trying to escape,' he said, 'but the heat in here is getting a little warm. And I'd like you to know,' he goaded, 'that without proper evidence you're not entitled to make accusations like the ones you're making.'

'But I am entitled to call you in for questioning,' said Scott narrowing his eyes vindictively.

'No, I'm afraid I'm going to lay down the law here,' interrupted William determined that the episode go no further than those four walls. 'This man is to be left alone.'

Scott shook his head. 'I'm sorry, Mayor, that's not in your authority, I'm not about to forgo a lead which I think ought to be pursued. There is every cause for suspicion!'

'That's just your opinion,' said Robert, his manner under the circumstances seemed so carefree it was unbelievable.

And Robert's manner riled Scott. 'Shit,' he said, 'you really are one hell of smartass, and like hell you're going to pay for it!' Behind his beady eyes there was a hint of sadistic relish. 'If you want the real truth, the more I see of you the more I smell something wrong!'

'Well, that's too bad,' said Robert dismissively.

'No,' said Steve butting in, 'I'm privy to the facts too! If it's too bad for anybody, it's too bad for you! Mayor, this man's a ... aarghh!' Suddenly Steve's head slumped lifeless in mid-sentence, a silenced bullet from the direction of the open window had hit him in the back of the head, blood trickled over his collar. Scott reflexively swung round towards the window himself, as he did so another silenced bullet thudded dead center between his eyes.

In an instant Eliot leapt into the room from the outside. 'Silence. Total silence!' he ordered pointing his gun straight at William's head. Disoriented, the Mayor obeyed. Rosanne had nearly screamed but had just stopped herself.

A second later two more terrorists dressed in black balaclavas climbed in from the darkness. They swiftly manhandled first Scott's, then Steve's, bodies over to the window and dumped them out into the garden. The bodies fell into two large garbage containers positioned below the window ledge beside two other similarly dressed terrorists.

Eliot and the men who had entered the Mansion jumped back down into the garden again. 'You already picked up the bodies the two secret servicemen we hit?' Eliot asked the men below.

'Yah,' one of them replied. Eliot nodded approvingly. The group of terrorists moved off pushing the garbage containers along with them.

Robert strolled over and opened the window in William's office wider to get rid of the smell of cordite fumes which hung in the air. Rosanne shifted uneasily in her seat, despite her near scream she had managed to recompose herself, and yet, with all the personal issues now out in the open, she was unsure which way to turn.

As for William, he looked drained. Drained not so much out of fear or cowardice, after all Rosanne had been right when she had praised him for his courage in the face of his affliction, but drained out of sheer mental overload. His face was awash with sweat.

'I didn't quite plan it this way,' announced Robert returning to the center of the room and checking he had the Mayor's full attention, 'but those guys knew too much.' William uncaring at this moment about the niceties of human behavior chose to wipe his brow on the sleeve of his jacket. 'At any rate,' Robert went on, 'now you know everything! What you suspected about me a long time ago was all too accurate!'

William hesitated. 'You can't get away with this!' he said in a slightly trembling voice.

'That's what everybody's been saying,' replied Robert airily. 'I think everybody's wrong.'

William frowned. 'You think you own me because I'm dying? Is that it?'

'No,' said Robert. 'But it's a factor.'

'But you think I'll play ball with you?'

'If you want to be President, yes.'

William paused to consider his options, his eyes drifted towards Rosanne, the look he gave her combined many things, torment, self-pity, sadness, some hatred.

'William,' she said sensing his agony and seeking to soften the blow, 'I sincerely believe these people mean well! That's why I did as I did!'

But her words only backfired on her. 'You!' he scowled in disgust. 'I can't talk to you! I don't care what you believe, all you've done is betray me!'

'William, I haven't, I haven't!' she pleaded. 'I did this because I love you.'

'Love me! Are you mad?' he exclaimed. 'And I suppose next you're going to tell me that you love him too!' His eyes flashed across to the other man in her life and back to Rosanne again.

'It's not the point!' she protested close to tears.

'No, it isn't the point!' Robert forcefully intervened. 'For the time being personal matters have to be put to one side! What has to be decided right now is what you want your fate to be. I'd say you have little choice!'

William's eyes flashed again. 'Don't try and present me with ultimatums! I could have you arrested on the spot!'

But this was only bravado and Robert knew it. 'You could,' he smiled, 'but then I'd make very sure everything blows up in your face – You'd be left with nothing.'

A short silence followed, William finally heaved a deep sigh. 'Yes,' he muttered numbly, 'yes, you're right.'

'Good,' said Robert businesslike. 'So we work together. Rosanne, you stay here. Okay?'

She nodded passively, for once it was as if she preferred to be told what to do.

'And you,' continued Robert diverting his attention back to the Mayor, 'you can now show me out. As for the men who were shot, just tell whoever asks that they had to leave early by the back door – their bodies will not be found.'

'And what then are you going to do?' William enquired with undisguised skepticism.

Robert was about to reply when suddenly his eyes were distracted towards the open window. He smiled. One of the balloons released by the terrorists had drifted into the room.

William looked staggered as Robert grabbed hold of it and took it over to him. 'I think this will answer your question, I told you we hadn't run out of ways to communicate!'

William was baffled. He examined the balloon and read out loud the message on the label attached to it: "'*OUR ADVICE ON WHO TO VOTE FOR WILL APPEAR ON YOUR TV ONE EVENING THIS WEEK AT 10 P.M EASTERN TIME – BE SURE TO TUNE IN ... BY THE WAY WE ARE EVERY BIT AS MUCH ANTI-DRUGS AS WE ARE ANTI-POVERTY BUT WE DO BELIEVE A NEW APPROACH IS NEEDED ON BOTH. FURTHERMORE, UNLESS YOU ARE A HABITUAL DRUG USER, WE SUGGEST YOU DESTROY ALL ONE DOLLAR BILLS RECEIVED FROM US.*'"

All the more flabbergasted William paused and stared long and hard and incredulously at the motif of Zyron and Axma on the balloon. 'Jesus,' he murmured shaking his head.

'So now I'd say you're in the picture,' grinned Robert.

'Yes,' he said quietly. 'But TV, forget it! You haven't got a hope of repeating what you did before!'

'That's our problem!' replied Robert in his breezy tone. 'But in the meantime you cancel your Campaign trip to the South West tomorrow and start revamping your Welfare proposals! For once the poor, the homeless, the needy are going to get a fair deal.'

'But what about the Public and Drugs?' William queried nervously. 'How am I going to make them swallow that?'

'Just explain to the Media what I've explained to you,' answered Robert firmly. 'Now I must be going.' Robert took the balloon from William and pushed it back out the window. 'Good night, Rosanne.'

'Good night,' she replied with a flicker of a smile and William escorted Robert out.

Nonetheless, as the two men entered the lobby, there seemed to be some commotion. A secret servicemen came over and intercepted them before they could reach the front door. 'Mayor Donaldson,' he said polite but edgy, 'we request you stay inside the building – a couple of our guys out in the grounds have gone missing unaccounted.'

'What?' frowned William convincingly looking both surprised and concerned.

'It may be nothing, sir,' the Agent went on, 'but I think caution's called for until we clear it up.'

'Okay,' William replied. He turned cordially to Robert, 'I'll have to say good bye to you here then.'

'Sure,' smiled Robert shaking hands. 'Bye bye, and thanks again for your hospitality.'

'My pleasure,' said William in a surreal gesture of false politeness and Robert headed out alone into the night.

CHAPTER 21

The next morning, as the sun rose over Grand Army Plaza, dozens and dozens of "Zyron and Axma" balloons drifted along the sidewalks outside Bergdorf Goodman and the Plaza Hotel. The few people passing by at this early hour as they picked them up and read their labels seemed almost as confused as William had been the evening before.

All the same, from coast to coast, travelling by word of mouth, it was not long before the contents of the terrorists' latest message was known by all.

~

At Gracie Mansion Rosanne stirred in bed beside William. William was lying on his back staring at the ceiling, he had been awake for hours. 'Hi,' she yawned reaching out to run her hand over his forehead.

'Hi,' he replied subdued and reflective, 'I hardly slept at all.'

'Oh, William,' she sighed softly trying to comfort him, 'you mustn't be like that.'

'Yeah, sure,' he answered, 'you've been sleeping with this guy all along, and you've known what he represents all along.'

'No, William, that's only half true, I loved him first, only afterwards did I realize the rest.'

William drew in a deep breath. 'And you want me to believe you love me too?' he asked turning his eyes towards her. 'You trying to tell me that you can love two people at the same time?'

'Yes, it's possible,' she murmured, 'very possible.'

'And that's your justification, is it?'

'Justification for what?' she frowned.

'Justification for putting me through this,' he replied.

'No,' she said, 'I can't help who I fall in love with, but that's nothing to do with it — as I keep saying, I believe in what these people stand for! They want to change this country for the better.'

'And what if I don't agree?' he asked.

'You have to agree,' she exclaimed drawing herself closer towards him. 'And if you institute what they're asking for you'll be remembered for all time! You'll go down as a hero.'

William slowly shook his head. 'Nice idea but I don't think so,' he said. 'Nobody's ready for this, nobody'll understand it.'

'Then you have to make them understand,' she urged.

'Easy to say,' he sighed still shaking his head, never before had he sounded so dejected. 'And you?' he paused. 'Where do I stand with you? Will you stay with me if I do this?'

Rosanne's expression suddenly hardened, 'I'll leave you if you don't.'

Unable to reply William slowly fixed his eyes back on the ceiling, his jaw tightened, he gritted his teeth, he was a man on a rack. 'So help me God,' he muttered.

~

Later that morning the Press Briefing room at City Hall was jammed to bursting point with reporters and TV News crews. They had been summoned at very short notice and jostled and jarred each other as they jockeyed for prime position.

Shortly a side door opened at one end of the room and William entered. He walked up to a battery of microphones set up in front of a podium. 'Good morning,' he said. He waited a couple of seconds to allow the gathering to settle. Then in a voice which was strong and authoritative he resumed, 'I have cancelled my original plans to visit the South West and called you here today because, with the Election nearly upon us, I see the necessity to make a definitive statement ...'

In the house in Connecticut it was now standard practise to have someone monitoring TV broadcasts round the clock. 'He's giving a Press Conference! "Live" TV coverage!' announced one of Matts' assistants dashing into the library where the Professor, Eliot, Robert and Matts were convened.

'Yes? So soon?' said the Professor with some surprise, for time zone differences usually meant that major East Coast Press Conferences of national importance were only rarely held in the morning. 'We'd better go see!' And in a considerable hurry, and not knowing quite what to expect, the Professor and the others descended into the cellar to catch the transmission.

In the Press Briefing room at City Hall William continued speaking. 'Now,' he said choosing his words carefully, 'there are a lot of things I could say but I think the time has come to talk as plainly as possible. Therefore I will not delay you with any lengthy preamble, I will get straight into the substance. There are two new initiatives which, after much deliberation, I now propose. They are as follows ...' The room fell into a hushed silence. 'Firstly,' he said unwaveringly, 'I have decided to commit myself to a Welfare program not subject to budgetary constraints – in other words I will continue to spend funds up until the point our objective of the ELIMINATION OF POVERTY is achieved and, until such time, we will not flinch!' He halted to glance around him, already a wave of spontaneous surprised whispering was spreading from one side of the room to the other.

'Excuse me, sir?' asked a male journalist standing up.

'Bear with me, will you,' interrupted William. 'I will perhaps have time for a couple of questions later.'

The journalist sat down, William carried on. 'Secondly,' he declared, his voice becoming more emphatic still, 'I will take fresh steps to contain the drugs problem, and I do not hesitate to add that this will involve some painful and controversial choices!' He paused, the room was hushed again. 'My aim will be to take the profit out of drugs trafficking, and, to do that, my Administration will implement a policy permitting illegal substances to become legally available to those who want them!' A gasp rose up from the Media, stunned disbelieving faces looked at one another as if to seek assurance that they had not misheard, the atmosphere was electric. 'I know, I know,' he said raising his hands, 'that this is a really radical step to take – but, terrorists or no terrorists, we are a Nation at war with ourselves and I think we have to find a way to re-unite, otherwise we're only going to keep sliding downhill.' He paused to scan the room again. 'And when I talk about war,' he stated as an afterthought, 'it's not a word I use lightly, but it's the only appropriate word to use! And when you're fighting a war you hopefully fight it to win!

'Okay,' he concluded boldly, 'now I'll take one or two questions.'

'Mayor,' said a woman journalist near the front, her tone was tough, 'forgive me for being so blunt, but is it purely coincidental that this sounds like the terrorists talking?'

William looked unperturbed. 'Well, I don't know quite what you mean by that,' he replied refusing to be seen to take the question too seriously. 'But, on the other hand, I don't think anybody has a monopoly on good ideas.'

But the woman was not going to be so easily deflected. 'Yes,' she pressed, 'but don't you think that it's a little uncanny that these balloons go out and so on, and then ...'

William cut in on her. 'You going to argue with me that there isn't a connection between drugs and poverty?' he said perfectly controlled. 'To me the position couldn't be clearer – we've got to shake this whole thing up because at the moment our efforts to deal with it are going nowhere.' He looked away from her. 'Okay, next question from somebody else ...' He pointed to another woman journalist who had her hand up.

'Mayor,' asked the female journalist, 'may I ask about the rumor that some members of your staff and some of the people protecting you have gone missing?'

'It's not a rumor, it's true,' William replied, 'we're very concerned about it, unfortunately at this point in time I know no more than you.' He turned his attention to one of the Network Correspondents who was signaling to speak. 'Okay, I'm going to make this the final question ... Go ahead ...'

'Mayor Donaldson, what I wanted ask,' said the Correspondent, 'is how do you take the terrorists statement that they're going to re-appear on TV and tell the public who to vote for?'

William managed to put on a faint grin. 'I would hope the public have more sense than to listen to them! In any case the President has taken measures to prevent them getting on air ...'

'What measures?' the Correspondent asked.

'I can't discuss that,' he answered, 'maybe you should ask the President!

'Anyhow,' he continued, 'I've got to run, thank you all for your time,' and, despite a barrage of attempts to detain him, he left the room.

In the cellar in Connecticut a look of delight had spread all across the Professor's face. He switched off the TV. 'We've got him!' he twinkled.

'Yah, we have,' smiled Robert. 'Amazing!'

The rest of the day after his Press Conference, for reasons which were all too obvious, William did the exact opposite to what most Presidential candidates would have been expected to do in the final days before an Election – he laid low. He knew he had to contend with such a sea of doubt, disdain, and even derision, from all quarters, friends and foes alike, that there was really very little alternative – rather than try to dodge a hail of gunfire it was better just not to offer oneself as a target. However, the next morning, as he sat with Rosanne in the breakfast room at Gracie Mansion the headlines of newspapers from coast to coast did not make for encouraging reading: "*DONALDSON THROWS A CURVE BALL, REACTIONS MAINLY OF DISBELIEF*" read *The New York Times*. "*INSANE OR ENLIGHTENED?*" said *The Washington Post*. "THIS MAN IS A FOOL", an exact quote of a jibe against William made the day before by President Guthrie, was how *The Daily News* saw it. And "*DONALDSON ADVOCATES DRUG U-TURN*" plus "*PRESIDENT GUARANTEES TERRORISTS' BROADCAST WILL NOT GO OUT*" formed twin lead stories in *The Los Angeles Times*.

William tossed the pile of papers on the floor, he was angry. 'All I've done is make myself look an idiot!' he exclaimed.

'Not so,' Rosanne replied seeing the mood he was in. 'What you've done is throw down a gauntlet!

'You could say the same of a Kamikaze pilot!' he retorted.

'No William, it's nothing like as bad as you think. It's going to work out. Anyway, there's no turning back now.'

But William rejected this notion outright. 'There is turning back, and plenty of it, if I wanted to!'

'I don't think so,' she said.

'Well, I do!' he said bitterly. 'I think you may have pushed me far enough! Remember before too long I'm going to be dead! And I'm not about to be prepared to die in disgrace!'

'You won't,' she responded, 'really you won't!' She was acutely aware of the fragility of his frame of mind. 'Look, if you don't believe me then speak to Robert!'

William pondered, frowning heavily he tried to collect his thoughts, 'Okay,' he said fitfully, 'I'll see that little ...!' He restrained himself from using the next word which came to him, it would have been a great deal less than flattering. 'He'd better come out to Rye

– it's a better place to have a private discussion, and it will have to be today, I don't really have the time but I guess I'll just have to make it! Jesus, you realise the Election's the day after tomorrow!'

~

Rosanne contacted Robert immediately and a few hours later he drove himself towards William's home at Rye along the same road on which Oakley Cunningham and Bruce Dean had been assassinated. As he passed the exact spot no trace remained of the momentous incident of a few weeks earlier.

Rosanne's phone call to him, as usual, had conveyed little except he could tell from her tone that all was not well. In truth he would rather have avoided seeing William again so soon, but after a chat with the Professor they had decided it would be too dangerous to refuse – as the Professor had pointed out, men who had just been coerced into something were often at their most volatile. Even so, Robert resolved that the encounter would be as short and sharp as possible.

At the gates of William's house he was let in by the secret servicemen on duty. A butler showed him from the front door through the suite of interconnecting reception rooms to the main living room where William and Rosanne sat. On the way, had it been another time, Robert would have been tempted to pause and look at the fabulous collection of Art which hung on every wall, but as it was he kept his mind firmly on the job in hand. 'Hi,' he said dryly as William stood up to greet him.

'Hi,' the Mayor replied tensely.

Robert gave Rosanne an affectionate glance which she returned. 'So,' he said to William, 'you asked me out here, what's the problem?'

'The problem can be phrased as a simple question,' he responded with considerable consternation. 'How are you going to get me elected?'

Robert raised his eyebrows as if the question were absurd. 'What's the matter, lost your nerve?' he asked casually.

William clenched his fists in frustration. 'I see absolutely no prospect of being elected!'

Robert smiled. 'Are you saying we can't deliver?'

Yet again William was finding Robert's laid-back attitude difficult to cope with. 'For God's sake,' he uttered, 'stop answering every question with another question!'

'All right,' said Robert, 'I'll answer with a statement – You're in!'

'What do you mean "I'm in"? Have you seen the newspapers? They're tearing me to shreds!'

'It doesn't matter,' he answered, '10 p.m. tonight.'

William's eyes opened wide. 'That's when the TV is?'

'Yeah. And don't tell me it ain't going to happen because it is. I'll see you after the Election, "Mr President"!' Robert headed towards the door.

'But!' William protested.

'But what?' said Robert.

'I think it's only reasonable I should be given more details than that! You can't walk out on me after just two minutes!'

'I can,' replied Robert nonchalantly, 'I have nothing more to say.' And without waiting for any further response he left. Short and sharp the meeting had been, he had kept to plan.

CHAPTER 22

The Aleutian Islands, United States territory, formed a vast arc over one thousand miles long across the Northern Pacific. At their Eastern end was Alaska and at their Western extremity the International Date Line which also formed the border between American and what once would have been referred to as Soviet but remained Russian waters.

It was early afternoon local time and Gil and Conrad were up on the bridge of the "Belle Epoque". 'That's Attu the furthest West major island of the Aleutians,' commented Conrad pointing to a small area of land on the edge of the ship's radar screen.

'Right ,' said Gil, 'so that makes us nearly where we want to be.'

'Yup,' Conrad replied.

'Okay, we carry on a few more miles and then hold position. I'll tell the others to get the boats ready.'

'Okay.'

Down on the deck of the "Belle Epoque" four of the terrorists had broken open the seven yellow containers which Eliot had told Stefan not to unload at Boston. Eliot's statement that they were not going to be needed had been far from true. Inside the containers were about a dozen powerful satellite dishes and the four men were in the process of finishing erecting them.

Gil emerged from the ship's superstructure out on to the deck. He shouted over to the men, 'As soon as you've got those dishes aimed start lowering the lifeboats!' They nodded, he went back inside.

~

After leaving William and Rosanne at Rye Robert had returned directly to Connecticut. In the cellar of the house, with the United States Eastern seaboard six hours ahead of the Aleutians, it was now evening. There was much activity. Robert, the Professor and Eliot stood beside Matts as he and his technicians operated communications equipment. 'Okay,' said Matts, 'we're commencing transmission through to the ship of all the material for re-transmission.'

'Excellent,' said the Professor.

On board the "Belle Epoque" Conrad and Gil had moved into a cabin where video and satellite equipment, also part of the contents of the seven yellow containers, had been set up. 'We're linked up with Connecticut, it's coming over,' announced Conrad monitoring the equipment in front of him.

'Good,' replied Gil. 'As soon as you've got it, see you out on deck – we're already evacuating.'

'Okay, won't be more than a couple of minutes,' said Conrad.

Gil headed out the door.

On deck with the satellite dishes all in position the two lifeboats were being lowered and Stefan and his crew were being herded into them at gun point. Stefan, looking disoriented and dejected, glanced at the scene around him wondering what was going on but said nothing. 'Everyone hurry up!' shouted Gil and the terrorists began to get into the lifeboats themselves.

A minute later Conrad came running out from the super-structure. 'Everything's done,' he informed.

'Good,' said Gil and as the last of the remaining terrorists left the ship he lingered briefly on deck. Raising a pair of binoculars he could see a trawler some way in the distance. Satisfied, he too swung himself over the railings.

Once the lifeboats hit the water, their winch cables were disconnected and they headed off under the power of their small motors in the direction of the trawler. The "Belle Epoque" was left deserted, its engines still running but making only two to three knots at most.

Half an hour later the lifeboats came alongside the trawler and other terrorists on its deck helped everyone from them up on board. Gil turned to take one last glance at the "Belle Epoque" in the distance. 'Okay,' he shouted to his colleagues, 'let's get as far away from here as we can!'

~

In the reception room at Gracie Mansion William paced around listlessly while Rosanne, altogether more composed, sat quietly in a chair. The TV was on without sound and the clock on the mantelpiece showed the time approaching 10 p.m. Every few seconds William used the remote control to flick through the TV channels. 'I'll believe this when I see it,' he said uneasily. 'Don't even you have some clue what they're going to say?'

'No idea,' she replied, 'honestly, they've told me nothing.'

William frowned and tried changing channels again. 'And we don't even know which station it's going to be on either,' he muttered in irritation.

'No, we don't,' she said, her tone becoming somewhat distant.

~

A United States "E-3 Sentry" AWACS plane, a flying radar station, patrolled high in the evening sky over Colorado fulfilling its role in President Charles Guthrie's plan to frustrate and interdict any attempt by the terrorists to take over the airwaves again. The plane's massive circular toadstool-like "radome" set above the wings of its Boeing 707 fuselage was monitoring radio traffic in all directions. The seventeen man crew on board were on maximum alert.

On the plane's flight deck the mood was one of expectation. 'If it's going to happen, it's either now or tomorrow,' commented the pilot observing that 10 p.m. Eastern time was only ten seconds away.

'We'll know pretty soon,' said his co-pilot.

~

In the cabin of the "Belle Epoque", where the video and satellite equipment had been set up, a digital display which was counting down hit zero. Automatically the light on a computer hard-drive that contained the video file that had been transmitted through from Connecticut began to flash. On the deck of the ship the satellite dishes looked up to the sky.

~

At Gracie Mansion William flicked through the TV channels yet again, this time with the sound up. All they got were regular news programs, chat shows, soaps, sports, etcetera, etcetera. 'I told you – nothing!' he exclaimed.

But then, at that very instant, the picture altered. 'Welcome folks!' announced the familiar face and smile of the cartoon character of Zyron. 'Here we are!'

'Yes folks! Here we are!' echoed Axma, momentarily doffing his purple Moroccan fez in a welcoming gesture. 'Now, first of all, we think you ought to know that they may try and jam us out! But don't worry – that'll be difficult!'

'Yes, it will be!' exclaimed Zyron, the picture now showing both of them. 'You see they reckoned we'd only use one station! Well, hee, hee, hee,' he chuckled, 'they reckoned wrong! We're on ALL of them!'

'That's right,' grinned Axma, 'so if your picture goes and you want to stay with us just switch channels and we'll be there!'

William, astonished, changed station to test if what there were saying was true – sure enough Zyron and Axma were still there.

'You see,' said Zyron, his big blue eyes blinking cheekily, 'we're a lot smarter than they are!'

~

In the main cabin of the AWACS plane the atmosphere was frenetic. Messages were being bounced back and forth between the Air Force technicians on board and the personnel at ground stations below. 'We can't block this out – they're on every frequency!' said a voice over the radio from one of the ground installations responsible for jamming.

'Okay, understood,' acknowledged a technician into his headset aboard the AWACS, 'we're still trying to get a fix on signal location.'

'We have Attack aircraft waiting at fifty bases,' said the radio voice. 'Move it up, can you?'

'It's coming from somewhere West,' announced a second technician inside the AWACS studying his instruments. 'Yes, somewhere West, but not from the mainland! Must be out in the Pacific!'

'Wherever it's coming from, it's beaming through several different satellites!' stated the first technician.

'Yeah, I've got it now,' the second technician said. 'It's from way, way North West! It's practically coming from Russian waters!'

'Yeah, you're right,' confirmed his colleague. 'Russian waters!'

'Jesus!' responded the ground-based radio voice. 'Need to take advice. Out.'

~

William and Rosanne stared at the cartoon on their TV at Gracie Mansion. 'Now we know time is precious,' Axma went on, 'and we don't want to take up too much of yours ...'

'And we hope you'll all be voting the day after tomorrow!' Zyron interjected.

'And by the way,' said Axma conjuring a bright pink cartoon telephone out of thin air, 'even if the TV were blacked out – You can always hear what we have to say on the phone!'

Incredulous, William grabbed the phone – as good as their word the voices of Zyron and Axma were there. 'Jesus Christ,' he exclaimed, 'it's true – they've got into the phone system!' Rosanne simply shrugged, it was as if nothing surprised her anymore.

'So we come to the "question",' said Zyron rubbing his long-fingered hands together. 'The big, big question: Who are you going to vote for?'

'Well, there's the President,' grinned Axma. 'Now, what's he got in his favor?'

'Well, he seems solid enough,' said Zyron.

'And he's made concessions,' added Axma.

'Yes, quite big concessions,' agreed Zyron. 'But is he,' he asked, suddenly taking Axma's pink telephone and effortlessly compressing it like putty into a basket ball which he then let bounce away, 'is he "really" all that solid?' He paused, smiled, and gave the audience a questioning look. 'We'll come back to that later.'

'Yes, we will,' said Axma. 'Then there's the other choice – William Donaldson – who's made even bigger concessions!'

'Yes, he has. And we quite like him,' chirped Zyron. 'The problem is can he deliver?'

'I mean,' said Axma continuing the thread, 'William Donaldson has gone the whole way, he's promised EVERYTHING – but has anyone who has promised everything ever succeeded?'

'Though maybe the higher you set your sights the better your chances?' Zyron suggested.

'Or is it the higher you fly the harder you fall?' his friend retorted with a grin. 'It's a tricky thing to weigh up you know ...'

'Yes, it sure is,' said Zyron, 'extremely tricky, it really ain't so easy – even we're having to think ...'

'For a start just think of the things there are to think about,' continued Axma. 'We've got to think about poverty!'

'Then we've got to think about drugs!' said Zyron.

'Then we've got to think about the environment,' said Axma.

'Yeah, sure are a lot of things to consider!' concluded Zyron.

At the very least having expected the cartoon to be brief and to the point, William was by now finding Zyron and Axma's drawn-out pitter-patter infuriating. 'Jesus Christ,' he shouted, 'what are these people playing at! Why don't they just come out with it!'

Rosanne did not respond, she was miles away, in fact so transfixed by what she was seeing on the screen that she might not even have heard William speak.

~

Regardless of the problems connected with the broadcast's unforeseen and sensitive geographical origin, war planes had been scrambled anyway. Four F-15E Strike Eagles had taken off from a U.S. base on Adak Island in the Aleutians. Their flight time to the "Belle Epoque" would be no more than a few minutes.

'Weapons fully armed, still awaiting orders,' said the flight commander of the F-15Es into his helmet mike.

'We're still waiting too,' replied a ground-based radio voice. 'Confirmation will come direct from the White House.'

On the TV set at Gracie Mansion Zyron and Axma merrily carried on. 'So,' chirped Zyron pulling up his striped knickerbockers which had slipped down a little over his chubby girth, 'with so much to think about it's really a matter of us giving you the facts first ...'

'Yes,' Axma concurred, 'we provide the facts and then you'll be able to decide for yourselves whether our recommendation makes sense!'

'What the hell is with these people!' yelled William nearly out of his mind with frustration. 'I wasn't expecting a debate!'

But Rosanne was ever increasingly in a world of her own, only listening to the TV.

Suddenly an aide knocked and hurried in carrying a special mobile phone. 'Sorry to interrupt, Mayor, but with regular communications disrupted I have the President for you on this line ...'

William grabbed the phone. 'Turn the TV down a moment,' he told Rosanne, he had left the TV's remote control on the coffee table directly in front of her.

But she did not react.

'Rosanne! I said turn it down!' he repeated more loudly, but to no effect. William, phone to one ear, frowned wondering what was wrong with her.

'It's okay, sir, I'll do it,' said the aide.

'Thanks,' said William, and the aide went over and pressed the mute button on the remote control, Rosanne still seeming oblivious. William then spoke into the special phone, 'Charles?'

'No doubt you're watching this?' said the dry voice of President Charles Guthrie.

'Yes,' William replied.

'Well, there's really no time to talk but I want you to know something,' said the President.

'What is it?' William frowned.

'This broadcast is coming from a ship that's drifting, or at any rate slowly moving, into Russian waters – I've tried to talk to Moscow to get their permission to intervene but they're refusing a quick answer. But I think you'll agree that this has to be stopped ...'

'And?' asked William.

'I have ordered the ship to be destroyed anyway. Despite our rivalry, I wanted you to know ...'

'Okay, thanks,' replied William edgily. He hung up. 'Something's going to happen,' he announced. 'Put the sound up again, can you?'

The aide reached down to press the remote control again, but this time Rosanne, more receptive, leant forward and grabbed it first. She put the sound up.

Affording Rosanne a rather puzzled glance the aide headed out again leaving the special phone behind.

And William was puzzled by her erratic behavior too. 'Are you all right?' he asked.

'Sure,' she said dreamily, not looking at him, only looking at the picture on the TV.

~

In afternoon sunshine the group of F-15E Strike Eagles continued towards their target. The weather remained calm, the visibility good. 'I have the ship on radar,' announced the flight commander in his cockpit.

'Okay,' replied a radio voice.

~

In the cellar in Connecticut Robert, Eliot, the Professor, Matts and others were gathered round the TV. Zyron and Axma continued pontificating. 'Yes,' said Zyron doing another one of his somersaults, 'everywhere you look everything needs changing!'

'And there really aren't any sides to this!' exclaimed Axma.

'No, because we should all really be on the same side!' said Zyron straightening his red and black polka dot bow-tie.

'But what about Middle America?' asked Axma suddenly looking more serious. 'What about the "Silent Majority"?'

'Yeah,' nodded Zyron looking straight out towards the TV audience, 'you probably hate us!'

'But we don't hate you,' said Axma shaking his head, 'all this is as much for your benefit as anybody's!'

'Of course it is!' said Zyron. 'But naturally you won't see it that way right now – that's an understandable reaction.'

'Sure it is,' emphasised Axma. 'Spend trillions on the poor? Distribute drugs? No, no, must be wrong, mustn't it?'

'And that,' continued Zyron, 'brings us to another catch in all this, which is, whoever we recommend to vote for, a lot of you will inevitably feel bound to vote for the opposite!'

'Yeah,' said Axma, 'stop and think about that for a moment!'

~

In Connecticut the Professor was smiling as he watched. 'I bet you by now the whole nation is looking in!' he declared.

Eliot nodded but looked anxious. Too tied up in other things he had had no involvement in the second cartoon's preparation and he was now seeing it for the first time. 'But are you sure,' he questioned, 'we're not making a mistake in going on as long as this?'

'No,' answered the Professor, 'you must remember that when it comes to crunch decisions people can't be told, they have to be persuaded!'

'But supposing the signal source is found and destroyed before we've finished?' said Eliot.

'In Russian waters?' twinkled the Professor. 'They wouldn't dare! Don't forget Russian friendship only extends so far. Moreover, they've got so many problems of their own that they've been watching what's been going on in this country and loving every minute of seeing our politicians squirm!'

~

At Gracie Mansion William and Rosanne kept watching too. 'Now of course,' chirped Zyron, 'if someone holds the office of President one of the main things you have to think carefully about is his character!'

'And,' said Axma, 'a man's character includes all sorts of things.'

'His friends, his motivation, his habits, his interests,' said Zyron.

'And not everything is as PURE as it seems,' said Axma.

'Unfortunately not!' quipped Zyron. 'And so, we've got some revelations to make!'

'And I tell you,' Axma continued, 'we've been pretty probing!'

Rosanne looked more and more in some kind of strange daze, her head was moving ever so slightly rhythmically to fro on her shoulders almost as if it were an object attached to a steel spring, beads of sweat were forming on her brow. 'You say they're about to wipe this out?' she muttered.

'Yes!' answered William fretfully. 'And, the way things are going, not a moment too soon! And,' he added staring scathingly into her face, 'I don't mind saying if anybody's responsible for putting everybody in the shit it's you!'

'No, William,' she said finding his criticism upsetting, 'please don't say that, William.' Her speech was becoming slurred, her manner bordering on delirium.

'From now on I'm going to say what the hell I like!' he replied.

'No, no, William,' she responded emotionally, 'please don't be cruel, you don't understand, it's my mind, I feel as if my mind is going!' Suddenly she reached up to her head and held it in her hands, she was shaking. William, far more worried about what was going to happen with the broadcast, had no time for this. He turned his eyes back to the TV screen.

~

In the Northern Pacific the "Belle Epoque" crept forward like a ghost ship, its communication dishes locked on to satellites in the sky. But then, flying in at low level, a Russian Air Force "Bear" reconnaissance plane plus Russian fighter aircraft came into view. The planes began to circle the ship.

Simultaneously the U.S. F-15Es arrived on the scene. 'Jesus, we've got company!' said the F-15E flight commander into his headset. 'Heavily outnumbered, about a dozen "bogeys" surrounding the target!'

'Identify, can you?' said a ground-based radio voice in shocked surprise.

'Either "Fulcrums" or "Foxbats", hard to tell,' replied the flight commander. The "Fulcrum" was the MiG-29, the "Foxbat" the MiG-25. Both were high performance interceptors which, from a distance, looked similar. As the flight commander spoke one of the Russian fighters zoomed right past him, 'Just got a closer view – "Fulcrums"'.

'Okay, have to re-verify instructions,' said the radio voice with urgency. Given the numerical superiority of the MiG-29s the situation had all the makings of an uneven contest.

~

'Why haven't they taken the ship out yet!' yelled William staring at the cartoon. Rosanne, still with her head in her hands and still trembling, paid no attention to him, nor he to her.

'Now,' said Zyron, 'if you're getting a little restless, we're now coming to the meat of it!'

'Yes, we are!' said Axma. 'For a start there's something about William Donaldson that nobody knows!' William looked alarmed.

'Yeah,' said Zyron, 'but there's something about the President and Drugs which is kind of juicy too!'

'Yeah,' grinned Axma, 'all kinds of secrets in all kinds of directions!'

'I think we'll hit the President first!' exclaimed Zyron.

'Yes, this is what we have on Charles Guthrie,' said Axma, 'we can tell you that he has advisers who might have no interest in solving ...'

~

As the U.S. and Russian fighters vied with each other the F-15E flight commander suddenly received a radio message in his cockpit, 'Go in low, hit the ship and run! Do it now!'

'Okay,' he responded professionally, 'we'll give it all we got!' The F-15Es immediately peeled away dropping to less than a thousand feet. They released their 2000 pound bombs and instantly the "Belle Epoque" became a mass of explosions and flames. The U.S. planes banked steeply and rushed away.

~

'It's gone blank!' said Eliot looking at the TV screen in the cellar. 'I told you this might happen!'

For the first time the Professor was almost lost for words, 'No, I don't believe it!'

'They've done what you said wasn't possible!' Eliot uttered aghast.

~

William and Rosanne also now looked at a blank TV screen. 'See, gone!' said William. Tense and confused he went over to pick up the regular phone and then slammed it down again. 'And the phone's silent too! They made the mistake of making a meal of it! But now nobody's been done any good!'

But Rosanne was only becoming more disturbed. 'No! No, wait!' she said in a loud feverish voice.

William frowned. 'Come on!' he said unsympathetically. 'For Chrissakes what is the matter with you? Stop acting like some kind of lunatic!'

Rosanne again did not seem to hear him, she just trembled and shivered all the more, her hands clasped tight against the sides of her sweat drenched face, her lips quivering seemingly bracing themselves to make their next utterance. William was about to make another attempt to try to get at least some sort of semi-lucid reply out of her when suddenly the special high security phone rang again. He picked it up. 'Hello?' he barked.

'William,' said the voice of the President, 'I did it – I stopped it right under the Russians' noses!'

'Did you, Mr President?' said William dryly, still looking perplexed at Rosanne. 'And how did you do that?'

'Diplomacy,' the President replied, 'at the last minute Moscow agreed to our intervention.'

'Well, I'm sure they didn't agree out of the kindness of their hearts,' said William cannily. 'You must have made a deal with them. What deal?'

'That's my business,' the President responded. 'The main thing is at long last these people, these terrorists, have been headed off ...'

'But things won't ever be the same, Charles, nor can they ever be ...'

'That's as may be,' said the President, 'but whichever way you look at it I don't rate your electoral chances at all!'

'Nor me yours,' answered William with a wry smile. At this very moment his attention was attracted away from Rosanne towards the TV screen. It was blank but flickering again. Slowly but surely some sort of image was beginning to take shape. What it might be was initially very unclear, but it was something. 'By the way, Charles,' William added more out of jest than seriousness, 'are you really sure you got rid of that ship! Have another look at your TV!'

William put down the special phone, the TV screen kept spluttering.

And like everywhere else in the United States, the TV screen in the cellar in Connecticut was flickering too. 'What's happening now? What is it, Matts!' asked Eliot with obvious concern.

But Matts had no answer. 'I don't know! It's nothing to do with us!'

Robert and the Professor were equally confused. Robert turned to glance at a person standing just to his right behind him, it was Dawn. Her death had been a lie, nobody had shot her, she had been kept out of sight in the house these last few weeks, it had been Robert's one concession to dishonesty in order to appease Rosanne.

~

At Gracie Mansion the TV set flickered faster and faster, it was like a stroboscope – flash, flash, flash, flash. Rosanne started to groan, her trembling turning into a swaying of her entire body, her arms becoming outstretched, her eyes staying fixed solely and exclusively on the screen. She was spellbound, possessed, like some Mambo, some Voodoo High Priestess about to drift on to a higher plane. 'I can feel it! I can feel it!' she called out.

'Feel what!' asked William beginning to feel worried for her.

'I can't explain!' she shouted loudly. 'I can't explain!' Her response wasn't addressed to William, it wasn't addressed to anyone. 'Something's coming! Something's coming through the air!'

'What's coming through the air?' he frowned in exasperation.

'They are!' she cried.

'Who's they?' he questioned.

'Look!' she screamed. She suddenly sat bolt upright and froze, motionless, ossified, her arms still outstretched, catatonic.

Turning to the TV screen William's eyes nearly popped out of his head. A new picture had appeared. It was a picture of Zyron and Axma. But, although their angular cheeky faces and colorful clothing were exactly as in Robert's cartoon drawings, what was on the screen now was not a drawing at all. It was the *real* Zyron sitting beside the *real* Axma in their spaceship. Their big blue luminescent eyes glowed brightly, their sharp pointed teeth sparkled brilliant white and their brocade waistcoats shimmered in the starlight. Behind them, through one of the spaceship's windows, was a magnificent view all across the Universe.

'Hello folks!' chirped Zyron. 'Thought we'd quit before we'd finished? Absolutely not!'

'No way!' chirped Axma.

'And, unlike our "earthly" cartoon counterparts,' said Zyron, 'we're going to be real quick!'

'Yes,' said Axma, 'but first we would just like to offer a word of thanks to that very fine artist who did such a good job on our cartoon!'

'Yes, thank you very much,' smiled Zyron raising his green hat with red feather, 'you made us both look nearly as handsome as we really are! But now down to business! This is the situation ...'

William was so utterly and completely stunned all he could do was to sit down in a chair. He glanced at Rosanne, her eyes wide open, her body like a statue, her mind in a trance, he almost felt he must be hallucinating.

'Well, you'd better know to start with,' continued Axma, 'that as far as this Election goes you're in fix!'

'And that's putting it mildly!' quipped Zyron. 'You sure have a difficult choice for President!'

'For openers,' said Axma, 'the Incumbent, President Charles Guthrie, has at least four Cabinet members and about ten key Congressmen who are directly or indirectly receiving funds from people involved in Drugs trafficking – so, not putting too fine a point on it, some of the guys running your country are "owned" by the Underworld!'

'Surprised?' blinked Zyron licking his lips. 'Axma, I think they all look surprised!'

'Well, don't be,' said Axma, 'after all money is money, and money talks ...'

'Yeah, you bet it does!' Zyron agreed. '*That* was what our "cartoon" friends were about to say when they were so rudely interrupted. And, if you want to know how we found this out, I'll explain!'

'Yes, Zyron, you explain!' said Axma.

'Well, quite simple really,' grinned Zyron. 'We simply monitored all banking receipts after free drugs were put out! And I don't minding saying that quite a few INTERESTING people's cash flows dropped like lead balloons!'

'Yes, they did,' said Axma, 'and, worse still, the President must have felt on shaky ground himself because we happen to know that he was so desperate to get our broadcast discontinued that he made a promise to the Russians ...'

'You see the broadcast was coming from their waters,' Zyron clarified.

'And,' said Axma, 'I don't mind telling you it was some promise!'

'It certainly was!' grinned Zyron. 'You're going to find this pretty hard to believe!'

'You know what he promised!' Axma exclaimed. 'He promised he would negotiate to hand back to Russia the entire State of Alaska!'

'You see,' volunteered Zyron, 'you may not know it but Alaska was originally part of Russia!'

'But that was a long time ago,' Axma pointed out.

'A very long time ago!' echoed Zyron. 'But that's your President for you – Open to blackmail and all sorts of sinister pressures on Drugs, and prepared to sign away U.S. territory!'

'Not exactly impressive, is it!' exclaimed Axma. 'But we have to hand it to those Russians – they sure still know how to drive a hard bargain!'

'And so,' said Zyron moving on, 'what of your other choice – William Donaldson?'

'Yes, what of William Donaldson?' asked Axma breezily. 'Well, if the truth be known, he's in the pockets of these people who've been making such a nuisance of themselves! You know who we mean! We mean the terrorists!'

William cringed, there was nothing else left for him to do. From the look on his face someone might just as well driven a nail straight between his eyes. He turned towards Rosanne. She still sat in her seat, her eyes staring, her arms outstretched, frozen, motionless.

'But there's more to it than that,' said Zyron.

'Yes, there is,' grinned Axma. 'You see the other thing about William Donaldson is he's incurably sick – he has a brain tumor. So perhaps his judgment really isn't all it should be!'

William buried his head in his hands.

'And then, hee, hee,' Zyron chuckled, his voice getting louder, 'there are *WOMEN* mixed up in all this too!'

'Aren't there always!' grinned Axma.

'Yeah, but this time around it's better than usual!' exclaimed Zyron.

'I guess it is!' agreed Axma. 'But wake her first, don't you think?'

'Okay,' declared Zyron with a laugh, 'wake up, baby, your face is about to be on TV!' And sure enough, astonishingly, Rosanne snapped out of her trance, dropped her outstretched arms and blinked. 'That's better, now here we go!' chirped Zyron taking a photograph of Rosanne out of his tail-coat and showing it. 'First of all we've got this one, pretty isn't she? Public knowledge I know! But I can tell you she made a difference!'

'She sure did!' concurred Axma. 'But then there's this other girl also,' he added, 'who's most certainly worth a mention too!' He reached into his own tail-coat and pulled out a photo – it was of Dawn. 'And whilst this lady won't be so familiar to you, there's something you should know about her ...!'

'What's that?' asked Zyron, knowing they both knew the answer perfectly well.

'You listening, Miss Lindblade?' Axma goaded. Rosanne certainly was listening.

'Yes, I reckon she's listening,' chirped Zyron.

'Okay then,' grinned Axma, 'just wanted everyone to know that this lady's still ALIVE!'

'No!' gasped Rosanne.

'Yes!' countered Axma with considerable glee. 'What's that old saying, all's fair in "something" and "something"?'

'Can't remember!' winked Zyron with a mischievous grin. 'But anyhow, is that it?'

'Yup,' smiled Axma, 'time to go, the clock's running out – it's the end of the fourth quarter, the end of the ninth innings, or however you want to put it! Bye!'

'Hee! Hee! Hee! Hee!' laughed Zyron.

'Ha! Ha! Ha! Ha!' laughed Axma.

'Good luck America!' waved Zyron.

'And Good luck the World!' grinned Axma waving his green handkerchief.

And abruptly the TV screen went blank.

EPILOGUE

In their spaceship Zyron and Axma were laughing so uncontrollably they nearly fell off their seats. Indeed, had it not been for their eagerness to know the result of the game, they would certainly have ended up rolling on the floor. 'You took the *GIRL*, but did it do you *any* good?' roared Axma.

'I don't know!' giggled Zyron just about coming to his senses. 'Okay, no "knock-out", but maybe a "points" victory!'

'So you think you won?' Axma smiled.

'I'm not counting chickens,' Zyron chuckled, 'but I think I've got the edge!'

'Even with my 10 point start for you taking the *girl*?' said Axma.

'Yes,' said Zyron, 'even with your 10 point start!'

'Well, we'll see. Do the score,' chirped Axma.

'Okay,' said Zyron. He leant forward and pushed a button on a computer whose screen was laid out like a score sheet. Zyron's name was on one side and Axma's on the other, and each had spaces below their names where their running totals, initially set at zero, were displayed. Immediately the scores began to mount thick and fast.

First Zyron had more points, then Axma, then Zyron, then Axma, then Zyron, then Axma – the see-sawing was relentless. And as the totals climbed each event where points had been scored was listed on the screen. And the list read like a lifetime flashing in front of one: the Gold Robbery, the Bridge Destruction, the Power Sabotage, the Love Affairs, the Riots, the Phoney Money, the Ship Seizure, the Cartoon, the Fit, the Brain Tumor, the Assassination, the Drugs, the Gracie Mansion Murders, the Balloons, William's Capitulation, the Final Cartoon, the Aleutian Showdown, the Final Intervention.

And then, finally, the numbers came to rest. Axma's column read 8878, Zyron's 8889. 'Told you so!' yelped Zyron in triumph, 'even taking the 10 points off and I still win by 1 point! Real tight, but *my* game!'

'Yeah, well done,' chirped Axma. 'Couldn't have been much closer could it?'

'No, it couldn't!' grinned Zyron. 'But what a game! I like this Planet – What a great place to play! '

'Sure is!' concurred Axma. 'Excitement guaranteed!'

'Yes, thrills and spills all the way!' said Zyron. 'Just as well those humans never ever get more than an inkling!'

'Absolutely! That would spoil the fun!'

'Yes, very true,' agreed Zyron. 'Far, far better to keep it to ourselves! But, in any case, shall we have a look at what happened afterwards?'

'Sure, always interesting,' chuckled Axma, 'I'll shift forward in Time.' He stretched his long fingers out to adjust his bank of controls. Then, as Time moved ahead, he looked down at a smaller TV monitor positioned in front of him between his knees. He began to report what he saw on it. 'They had to postpone the Election,' he announced.

'And then?' asked Zyron.

'William Donaldson won ... He got major reforms through Congress ...'

'Including ones on Drugs and Poverty?'

'Yes, he turned everything around,' Axma replied still studying the screen. 'Then, after his first term, he stepped down because of his health.'

'Who took over?' enquired Zyron with interest.

'You'll never guess,' Axma suddenly smiled.

'Robert Cook?'

'Not bad – but wrong,' smirked Axma. 'Have another try.'

'Rosanne Lindblade?'

'You got it!' said Axma with an enormous smile. 'She stayed with Donaldson, Robert married Dawn, the terrorists never suffered any comeback ... Lastly, though nobody claimed responsibility, our "personal" TV appearance was just dismissed as another terrorist gimmick! So, all said and done, I think that more or less brings us up to date!'

'Oh well,' reflected Zyron, 'it shows you ANYTHING can happen!' He rubbed his hands and smiled. 'So, one game to you, one game to me! What next?'

'You hinting you want a decider?' chuckled Axma.

'You bet!' grinned Zyron.

'Okay,' said Axma, 'I'll set it up again – Clear the decks as they say!' He adjusted his console and on the big TV monitor in front of them the Earth was seen to frizzle like a super over-barbecued steak finally turning into a bleak black sphere. 'Hee, hee,' Axma giggled much amused, 'that picture, for your information, is the Earth only a couple of thousand years further on! I guess the place must have just got too hot! What a shame!

'Okay, now re-constituting ...'

And as Axma turned another knob the big monitor screen once again slipped into a kaleidoscopic blur of backward running images too quick for the eye to see. Then, in almost no time at all, the picture halted and present day New York, as before, stared them in the face.

'We going to have the same "Time" and the same "Location"?' asked Zyron.

'Why not?' chirped Axma. 'No point in changing.'

'Fine,' said Zyron. 'But who gets the *girl* this time? Shall we toss for her?'

'No,' said Axma with a smile so big it stretched half-way round his face, 'I've got a better idea!'

'What's that?' grinned Zyron.

'Why don't we share her? *AFTER ALL SHE IS THE PRESIDENT!*'

At this they both burst out into fresh hoots of hysterical laughter. In fact soon they were laughing so much that it was quite a while before the next game was able to start.

Printed in Great Britain
by Amazon